ALICE IN
PORNOLAND

ALICE IN PORNOLAND

Hardcore Encounters
with the Victorian Gothic

LAURA HELEN MARKS

For Ella — because you tweeted that you would read it. :)
Laura Helen Marks

UNIVERSITY OF ILLINOIS PRESS
Urbana, Chicago, and Springfield

Library of Congress Cataloging-in-Publication Data
Names: Marks, Laura Helen, 1981– author.
Title: Alice in pornoland : hardcore encounters with the Victorian
    gothic / Laura Helen Marks.
Description: Urbana : University of Illinois Press, [2018] | Series:
    Feminist media studies | Includes bibliographical references
    and index.
Identifiers: LCCN 2018034000 | ISBN 9780252042140 (hardcover :
    alk. paper) | ISBN 9780252083853 (paperback : alk. paper)
Subjects: LCSH: Pornographic films—History and criticism. | Film
    adaptations—History and criticism. | English fiction—19th
    century—Film adaptations.
Classification: LCC PN1995.9.S45 M27 2018 | DDC 791.43/6538—dc23
LC record available at https://lccn.loc.gov/2018034000

Portions of chapter 1 were previously published in "Behind
Closed Doors: Pornographic Uses of the Victorian," *Sexualities*
17.1–2, 159-175. Copyright (c) 2014 SAGE Publications. Reprinted
by permission of SAGE Publications.

Portions of chapter 4 were previously published in "A Strangely
Mingled Monster: Gender and Spatial Transgression in the
Hardcore Metropolis of Paul Thomas's Jekyll & Hyde," *Neo-
Victorian Cities: Reassessing Urban Politics and Poetics*, ed. Marie-
Luise Kohlke and Christian Gutleben (Boston: Brill-Rodopi,
2015), 247–282. Reprinted by permission of Koninklijke Brill NV.

ISBN 9780252050886 (e-book)

CONTENTS

ILLUSTRATIONS

PREFACE

One of the beneficial side effects of the Victorian prohibitions
of sex is that a residue of sexual fantasy found its way into
many "mainstream" outlets. Repression necessarily forced
the writers and artists of the time to find metaphors—terrestrial or supernatural—that gave voice to their unexpressed
desires.

—Wash West, adult filmmaker

Pornography's favorite terrain is the tender spots where the
individual psyche collides with the historical process of
molding social subjects.

—Laura Kipnis, *Bound and Gagged*

This project came about in circuitous, unintentional fashion. A graduate student at Louisiana State University, I was interested in pornographic parody
and appropriation. Then, I was required to take a nineteenth-century course.
I had come to the end of my coursework, but my failure to pay attention to
grad school guidelines meant that in order to move forward, only one course
offered at that time would satisfy requirements: Dickens. I was reluctant, to
say the least. This course had absolutely nothing to do with my area of research, and I wasn't particularly interested in Dickens. With a roll of my eyes,
I signed up. Looking back on this moment, I thank the powers that be that I
was forced to take the class. In an effort to render the course more useful to
me, I casually investigated the existence of Dickens porn. I quickly discovered
Shaun Costello's *The Passions of Carol* (1975), an adaptation of *A Christmas
Carol*. At that time, I was at the lower point of an incredibly steep learning
curve and simplistically imagined (or hoped) that pornography routinely
offered subversive renditions of gender. I was excited to watch a film that, by
virtue of its unsimulated sex, would offer some kind of defiant response to

traditional, Victorian gender norms. Instead, I discovered something much more unusual and contradictory. Yes, the film does in some way subvert treasured notions of femininity, sexual activity, maternity, and childhood. Yet it is also shot through with a strangely conservative condemnation of autonomous sexual women seizing control of their sexuality as a commodity. The mere presence of sex, I realized, does not necessarily equate to a revolutionary or sociopolitically subversive text. In fact, the film is remarkably faithful to Dickens, conservative in its condemnation of sexual capital, particularly when controlled by women, while the sexual representations are by turns sweet, perverse, exciting, and depressing.

The Passions of Carol shook up my understanding of pornography. Prior to this point, I uncritically accepted what I had been told: pornographic depictions are designed to be arousing; porn is a series of sex scenes with, if you're lucky, some plot in between. I had never stopped to question what this actually meant—what constituted arousal and what constituted plot. Moreover, a former anti-porn feminist, I approached pornographic films in these early years with caution, reading their gender politics quite literally and ignoring my own complicated responses.

The contradictions and oscillating gender dynamics I found operating in porn are the inspiration for this project. Here, I seek to explore the contradictions foregrounded by the neo-Victorian Gothic and to interrogate how and why pornographers persist in drawing pornographic substance and meaning from the Victorian Gothic. Thus, while I do not consider myself a Victorianist, Victorianist ventures such as historical and cultural contextualization and literary analysis are nevertheless imperative to an understanding of the films I address. Likewise, understanding the pornographies and sexual attitudes of the Victorian era informs much of my investigation of the films I explore. I feel this project has much to offer in terms of Victorian studies. Shifting our frame of reference for "Victorian studies" to include the pornographic afterlives of its cultural projects can illuminate understandings of the Victorian, understandings of pornography, and the legacies of the Victorians in terms of sexual representation. In turn, bringing Victorian studies into the fold of porn studies, and drawing film and literature together, can illuminate the important connections between the legitimate and illegitimate—media and cultural spaces that we are told are entirely separate but in fact work in tandem with one another.

While the films I discuss shed new light on Victorian culture and art, my interest here is in the *culture text* of the Victorian; the particular Victorianness that pornography prefers, and the particular mythologies of the Victorian era that fuel pornographic fantasies. I explore what these persistent uses and subsequent conflicts suggest about pornography as a genre. Pornography seeks to speak the unspoken, to lay it all out there sexually, in a culture that demonizes sex. Many pornographers such as Wash West understand the Victorians as having to resort to metaphor in order to speak their repressed sexual desires, and yet what of the wealth of Victorian pornography? Are the Victorians all that different from us in their supposed struggles with sexuality and representation? If we use porn as a lens, the answer is a resounding and simultaneous yes/no, for pornography constructs quite contradictory, flexible, and playful notions of the Victorian for pornographic transgression. The particular construct or novel of choice in a given pornographic film depends on what forms of sex, what types of bodies, and what materializations of gender the film seeks to explore. At the same time, the chosen context and novel will inflect the film with particular formulations of race, gender, and class.

On the most basic level, my discovery of a veritable subgenre of neo-Victorian porn spanning several decades prompted me to ask, if pornography is a genre that merely aims to depict sex, that only includes enough plot and characterization to generate excuses for sex, why do pornographers persist in utilizing the Victorian? What idea of the Victorian do pornographers like to use? What does the Victorian offer pornography in the way of grist? Why this novel in this particular way, over and over, even in an era where pornographers are purported to have dispensed with narrative and fiction?

The contradictory and incoherent nature of the neo-Victorian films discussed in this project tells us something about pornography that differs from what anti-porn, or even pro-porn, people would have us believe: pornography is diverse, not inherently misogynistic, and not essentially transgressive. The array of films and scenes I discuss in this project might seem esoteric, but they are also representative of a broader pornographic impulse: that of transgression, duality, crossing lines, and opening up, not to mention the special pleasures of "doing dirt," to borrow D. H. Lawrence's phrase, to the mainstream, the legitimate, the lofty, and the sacred. These are the treasured goals of the pornographer. In addition, while some may dismiss films in this project as unusual and therefore invalid, or as "exceptions that prove the rule," I have encountered so many so-called "exceptions" over the years—couched within the mundane, included (or left in) by accident, or carefully and purposefully developed in a complex audiovisual treat—that exceptional pornographies often feel like the rule. The notion that interesting pornographies must be exceptions amounts to a dismissal of the genre rooted in confirmation bias, as is the assumption that unsimulated sex on film is empty of meaning or that a film must include character development, traditional Hollywood narrative, and spoken words in order to be a text worth investigating. These are attitudes this book attempts to redress.

The films discussed in the following pages nominated themselves for selection by virtue of their toying with the Victorian in one way or another. I subsequently chose a hefty handful that spoke to an assortment of concerns and that I could fit into these pages. All of the neo-Victorian hardcore texts I have encountered, in one way or another, touch on these concerns. At the same time, each specific Victorian novel, setting, or theme tends to generate particular concerns and tropes. Still, all of these films, videos, and scenes collectively attempt to speak the unspoken of the original texts—Victorian Gothic novels and nineteenth-century spaces that are perceived to suggest *something* sexual yet are found to displace that sexuality onto something else.

Pornography attempts to speak that absence through unsimulated sex acts. But what does this *speak*? What is liberated from or, conversely, restrained from the source text; what is spoken, and what is left unsaid? In addition, and more central to this project, what is liberated or deployed in the pornographic film when it draws on the Victorian? the Gothic? What is constrained or revealed? The neo-Victorian Gothic impulse in porn has resulted in a mass of films that are problematic, contradictory, and above all revealing of the complex discursive threads running through this diverse medium—threads that tie back to the Victorians themselves.

Porn is not a monolith, nor is it inherently transgressive or degrading. It is, however, hyperaware of its own construction, its legacy, its place in (un)popular culture, and the way it intersects with and is regarded by "mainstream" culture. "Pornography seems to live on perpetual standby to represent the nadir of culture," Laura Kipnis observes, "on call to provide the necessary opposition to culture's apex, which is, of course, the canon. It's indicative of just how much the canon needs pornography as the thing to mark its own elevation against" (182). In turn, so too does pornography need the canon to mark its own abjection against and to stage its careful and deeply unstable transgressive moves.

ACKNOWLEDGMENTS

Over the course of my journey with this project, I enjoyed the contributions, support, and generosity of knowledge and wisdom from a wide range of people in several different spheres: filmmakers, performers, academics, mentors, friends, archivists, fans, and family. Many of these people occupied several of these roles at once. Without these wonderful individuals, this book would never have been initiated, let alone completed.

Working with the University of Illinois Press, in particular with my editor Dawn Durante, has been dreamlike. Attempting to secure a book publication is intimidating, to say the least, but Dawn quickly established a relationship characterized by support and encouragement. Dawn's promise that her role would be that of collaborator held true, and many decisions I made concerning the manuscript originated with her bright ideas and helpful suggestions. The anonymous reviewers were also incredibly helpful, providing concrete, careful, sensitive, and warm critiques that I was able to understand and put into practice. These reviewers reflect the ethos of UIP as a whole in their generous spirit, and a desire for dynamic scholarship developed in a cooperative context. Still, this journey may never have begun if it were not for the guidance and help of Amanda Wicks, who, through her familiarity with the world of academic publishing, gave me useful tips for moving forward and ultimately connected me with UIP. Thank you, Amanda, and everyone else at UIP for your unwavering belief in this project.

My professors and mentors at University of Wales, Swansea, and Louisiana State University provided me the tools, confidence, and support needed to put my research into action and complete a successful doctoral project. It was at xiv · ACKNOWLEDGMENTS

Swansea, my undergraduate institution, that I had the pleasure of studying under Dr. Marie-Luise Kohlke. Her work on trauma studies inspired me to pursue a graduate degree in that field. After I decided to pursue porn studies, I assumed she and I had academically parted, only to find some years later that we had serendipitously dovetailed back to one another through the dynamic field of neo-Victorian studies. At LSU, Nicole Guillory was the first person to suggest that my side project might be the stuff of a PhD, and Zetta Elliott, during her visiting professorship, went out of her way to engage with that side project and offer useful advice during a time when I had never considered researching pornography as my primary area of study. While never formally mentoring me on any committee, both Dr. Guillory and Dr. Elliott mentored me on their own time and had a profound influence on my studies. I am very grateful to them and have not forgotten their generosity and wisdom in the earliest stages of my entry into porn studies. Having decided that this field was indeed something I found rich enough and fascinating enough to devote my time to, it was my fortuitous placement in Sharon Aronofsky Weltman's graduate Dickens class that moved my nebulous porn research into the uncharted territory it now inhabits. It is no exaggeration that Dr. Weltman's input had a life-changing effect. Without her spirited encouragement, this book would never have been conceived.

I am also fortunate to have had a wonderful group of colleagues and scholars who have been unfailingly supportive and incredibly generous with their time, energy, and wisdom. Many thanks to Michelle Massé and Patrick McGee, as well as Rachel Hall and Rosemary Peters. Their cautious, detailed, and enthusiastic guidance ensured a thorough and challenging research process that, miraculously, did not destroy my soul. I emerged from my doctoral program excited and eager to continue with the project, and I credit these individuals, and the LSU English Department more broadly, with this achievement.

A good deal of my knowledge concerning porn has come from online fan communities, in particular Adult DVD Talk (ADT). Thank you to R. Gelling, Ken Johnson, Redish, Savoy, Pringles, Gregory Armstrong, Jason, Draxxx, Mister Fahrenheit, Daniel Metcalf, and many others I engaged with over the years. ADT provided a space to discuss porn with incredibly knowledgeable and intelligent fans, as well as performers, directors, writers, and producers across the globe. These same fans also wrote detailed reviews, conducted useful interviews with performers and directors, shared articles concerning porn, sex work, and sexual politics, chatted about books, and discussed scholarly articles. Through this avenue, I was able to hash out ideas and think through my positions more clearly. Many thanks to Drew and Steph for creating this stimulating community and for providing me access to so much information.

At LSU and Tulane, several colleagues read drafts, discussed ideas, and provided support. Michele White provided much needed solidarity, wisdom, and cocktails. Isa Murdock-Hinrichs was a dedicated partner in our Saturday morning writing rituals, helpful with suggestions and also motivating me to write. Vikki Forsyth became my closest friend and colleague at Tulane, commiserating and congratulating, jigsaw puzzling and eating pizza when told to do so, and accompanying me in many fun and stress-reducing escapades across the city and state. Vikki is also a talented writer, educator, and editor. She helped to transform bloated and confusing chapters into something publishable. I remain sad at her departure for the homeland and miss her very much, but I am so thankful I was able to enjoy her presence in my life for those regrettably short years. During my graduate studies at LSU, a number of faculty members and graduate students assisted in the form of writing groups and other avenues of academic support; chief among them were Dan Novak, Elsie Michie, John Edgar Browning, Casey Kayser, Cara Jones, Wendy Braun, Conor Picken, Susan Kirby-Smith, Laura J. Faulk, and Kristopher Mecholsky. Special thanks to Emily Beasley, my accountability buddy, who kept me motivated and positive and became my friend in the process.

I owe a debt to the porn studies community, the most supportive, funny, energetic, enthusiastic, and generous group of scholars I have had the luck of falling in with. Somehow, most of us know each other, and if one of us does not know another, we are quickly introduced. In fact, scholars in other fields have told me they are envious of our special society, while others have grown so inspired that they shifted their research in our direction. For me this sense of community began with Amy E. Forrest who, in 2013, created the now-defunct porn scholar network X-Circle. Through this network I connected with several scholars I now call colleagues and friends: Alessandra Mondin, Tiffany Sostar, Florian Voros, Evangelos Tziallas, Anne-Frances Watson, Carol Ribeiro, Heather Berg, Diana Pozo, Katherine Ross, Sarah Bull, Sarah-Taylor Harman, Sarah Stevens, and Peter Alilunas. It is hard to imagine what my scholarly life would be like had I not been introduced to this network, and I am eternally grateful for Amy's persistence in linking us all up. I reconnected with my X-Circlers thanks to Facebook; online groups and academic conferences broadened this circle thanks to the incredible generosity of spirit and openness to collaboration that can be found among porn studies scholars. For their friendship, collaboration, camaraderie, and support, I thank Lynn Comella, Susanna Paasonen, Jackie-Tran Newton, Rebecca Sullivan, Martin Brooks, Mariah Larsson, Brandon Arroyo-Vasquez, Madita Oeming, Paul Iannone, Johnny Walker, Neil Jackson, Clarissa Smith, Feona Attwood, Kevin Heffernan, Federico Zecca, Giovanna Maina, Enrico Biasin, Lucas Hilderbrand, Elena Gorfinkel, Finli Freibert, John Stadler, Nicholas De Villieres, Kevin Bozelka, Diana Pozo, Heather Berg, Dan Erdman, and Oliver Carter. Special mention must go to the Facebook group, Porn Scholars and Historians Unite, created by Casey Scott. This group has provided a much-needed safe space to ask questions, share resources, crack jokes, vent frustrations, offer support, and initiate collaboration. Researching pornography can be an isolating experience, and I am grateful to Amy and Casey for transforming this aspect of the work.

Several of those I connected with in the above capacity read multiple incarnations of multiple chapters and responded to troublesome paragraphs in a matter of hours. Thanks especially to Dan Erdman and Heather Berg, who were always available to read scrappy drafts and tangled sentences. Thanks also to Peter Alilunas and Whitney Strub, who have become my go-to people for academic questions big and small, for writing anxieties in the dead of night, and as an extra set of eyes to tell me whether I am on the right track. Humble, honest, funny, reassuring, and, most of all, brilliant, Peter and Whit read several incarnations of book chapters and passed down invaluable wisdom to me gathered from their own book-writing process. I hope I can someday be as talented a writer and researcher, and as compassionate and helpful a mentor, to budding porn scholars as they have been and continue to be to me. Lucy Neville, my buddy across the pond, has proved to be an important source of inspiration, support, and collaboration. I thank her for her continued sharing of wisdom, intellect, and reassurance.

Two individuals in particular have made my academic life easier and my personal life richer. Both Desirae Embree and Amandine Faucheux initially reached out to me as emerging scholars seeking my mentorship, yet they quickly became my mentors as well. They have both counseled me in times of crisis, reassured me when the writing and research felt insurmountably difficult, read my work, offered advice, celebrated my achievements, shared their achievements, made me laugh, understood my gripes, and provided a vital emotional support system without which I would have been a complete wreck. Amandine was seemingly always on call to read outrageously long chapters and promptly used her editorial skills to whip many a clunky passage into shape. Academia is a cruel mistress, rife with insecurity and rejection. Whenever I feel anxious, in need of a boost, have something to brag about, want to share a crazy story, or talk about a book or film, Des and Amandine are my go-to gals. I hope I have provided some of this in return. I thank them for being there for me every step of the way.

I feel very lucky to have Annie as my close friend, confidante, and sharer of stories. I have learned so much about the world, thanks to her, and I have relied on her wise outlook and sound ethical stance on the world many times. Her insights on education, sexual politics and law, and a host of other important social concerns have profoundly influenced my scholarship and teaching. I thank her for being so awesome.

I am also lucky to have Fish and Linz in my life. Y'all are a grounding presence. Finding y'all in my house when I come home is an immediate calming influence, and I find myself leaving the stresses of university life at the door. More important, you were both loud and insistent champions of the work I was doing long before it became cool. Having you both there to remind me that my research was important got me through some difficult periods of my life. As for Harper, my little buddy and rascal in crime, you rock. Few people make me feel so magical and fantastic. Hanging out with Harper is a true escape from the pressures of adulthood—an exhausting escape, but an important one nonetheless. We share a dizzying array of interests and she understands the importance and fun of diligent organization, filing, color coordination, repetition, and play. I have never had my neuroses so warmly validated. Solidarity with you, my little friend.

I am lucky to be able to call many of my former students my friends: Naomi Detre, Pritika Sharma, Kameron Kane, Julia Marks, Reid Bowman, and Lara Muster to name just a few. I thank each and every one of them for the interest they took in my research, the baffling questions they posed, and the enthusiasm they expressed at being able to talk about a topic they typically kept to themselves. I particularly want to thank the incredible Tulane students who embarked on my independent study, Intro to Porn Studies: Orion Valentin, Maggie Kobelski, Sophia Witheiler, Lexi Arnold, Amit Ben-Baruch, Rachel Tarbox, and Allie "Mad Dog" Schneider. I thank them all for the laughter, the insight, the enthusiasm, and the shared curiosity and confusion we enjoyed. They are all amazing people and I will treasure those semesters for the rest of my life.

Porn studies would be nothing without its fan-scholars. We academics benefit tremendously from the hard work and dedication of these historians, collectors, and writers who operate outside of the ivory tower and yet freely offer up their rare collections, valuable knowledge, and indispensable connections. Martin Brooks provided me with all manner of old advertisements, posters, film reviews, and other adult film ephemera that simply do not exist

xviii · ACKNOWLEDGMENTS

in any formal archive. He continues to send along any and all neo-Victorian references he happens across in his pursuits. Steven Morowitz of Distribpix allowed me access to the Distribpix archive, handing me bags full of vintage materials and a wealth of knowledge besides. Ashley West and April Hall gave me the incredible opportunity to interview several adult film performers and directors on their indispensable podcast, *The Rialto Report*, and gave me my first high-profile platform for exploring my academic research in a nonacademic setting. In addition to writing his vital history of all-male adult film, *Bigger than Life*, Jeffrey Escoffier proved to be a generous mentor and contact. Robin Bougie of *Cinema Sewer* and the *Graphic Thrills* series of adult film poster art has been a consistent champion of my writing and is someone I consider a friend even if we have never met in person. To all of these wonderful people, thank you.

I reserve an especially huge thank you to Joe Rubin, archivist, porn oracle, and co-creator of Vinegar Syndrome who, over the past several years, has been my primary source of firsthand knowledge, an encyclopedia of all things golden-age porn, and a contact to connect with performers, directors, and writers. I discovered many of the titles through Joe. If I had an obscure question concerning release dates, alternate titles, alternate cuts, or any other seemingly impossible inquiry, Joe either had the answer or found the answer in a matter of hours or minutes. His knowledge is frankly intimidating. He functions as a key motivator for me to be as accurate and thorough in my research as possible. Joe is also incredibly supportive of my written work. He has championed my scholarly endeavors, connected me with important interview subjects, archivists, and historians, read drafts of essays and chapters, and enthusiastically engaged with me on the topic of adult film on a consistent basis for many years. On a larger scale, without Joe we porn scholars and fans would not have access to the fabulous adult films he has collected and restored over his (absurdly short) life thus far. His respect for adult film and porn studies has enriched the field, and we all owe him a debt. I thank him for his dedication, generosity, and motivation.

During the course of this research, I have been lucky enough to interact with the generous and enthusiastic talent behind the films I analyze. I am inspired by the persistence, sincerity, and punk-rock attitude of these creative minds. Utmost thanks to the energy, optimism, and support I have received from Nica Noelle, Eric Edwards, Shaun Costello, Penny Antine, Wash West, Charles Webb, Mistress Alice, Freaky T, and Pandora/Blake. Thanks also to the many more industry workers I have chatted with and/

or befriended over the years and who, via their wisdom and knowledge, strengthened my work.

Without Frank Zachariah, I don't know what my life would look like. He and the Wild Flower nursery transformed my life in a way that is hard to wrap my head around. It is through him and the Wild Flower institution that I found financial security and emotional peace (the latter being tenuous, depending on Frank's level of annoying), qualities that are in notoriously short supply in academia. Furthermore, Frank is the only person I know who has read all of my publications and has impressed on me the value of my research. I also developed a separate set of skills completely removed from academic ones that I can utilize until the day I retire. Most important, as an expat with no blood relatives nearby, I am forever grateful to Frank for providing a sense of family. Then there are the Wild Flowers—Dom, Josh (E. Kins), Erik, Gabe, Stu, Ryan, and so many more over the years—who made work fun and let me ramble on about whatever was on my mind for seven hours a day, in one-hundred-degree heat and stifling humidity, while we dug around in the mud. Toddy (RIP), Chance (RIP), and Maya (still lumbering around at the time of writing), I love you all. You are the closest things to my own pups I ever had. Your gracelessness, sagging bellies, wiry coats, arthritic tails, refusal to play fetch, persistent escapes, and general disinterest in performing the duties of a dog continue to inspire me.

Also performing the role of a family away from home are my in-laws and stepson. Marie Therese and Sherman have proved to be the most generous, thoughtful, and welcoming parents-by-marriage anyone could hope to have. Cameron is the smartest, funniest, and kindest stepson I could have imagined taking on. When I first met him, he was eight years old. I assumed his sweet nature would change once he became a teen. It did not. Now, a full-grown adult, he is still the good-natured, genuinely decent human being he's always promised to be. I still can't believe how easy it has been for us, and I truly enjoy his friendship (particularly his impressive willingness to indulge my obsession with Stallone).

I am so grateful to the members of my family who, for the past decade or so, have been far away in my homeland of England while I am here in my adopted home of Louisiana. I miss them all terribly and yet I know they are all there for me if I need them and hope they know the same is true in reverse. My stepmum, Patsy, made many sacrifices in order to join our family and provided all kinds of support through childhood and adulthood. I thank her for helping me get to where I am today. To Helen (never Auntie Helen!), many thanks for being the big sister I never had. I thank my brother

Adam and sister-in-law Denice for being such great friends and shoulders to cry on when needed. To my mum and dad, this project would never have materialized had they not supported my education, free thinking, and independent spirit from birth through to adulthood. Even when they don't really understand what I'm talking about (or would prefer not to know), they are both unfailingly proud and encouraging. I am lucky to have them as parents, and they both continue to inspire me.

Finally, I sincerely do not think I would have been able to finish this project without the unwavering support, friendship, loyalty, and love of my husband, Jeremie. My partner of fifteen years and counting, he has truly endured this process with me, staying by my side during times of intense stress. There have been extended portions of our life together where everything seemed to revolve around me and my research, yet he handled these periods with grace and patience. More than this, he meaningfully and sincerely engaged with my research to the extent that I was able to discuss ideas with him and untangle complicated thinking in a way I was not able to in other spheres. There are not enough words to properly articulate how wonderful he is and how lucky I feel on a daily basis. Sometimes I stand back and am mystified by his presence. He is my best friend, confidante, partner in crime, and intellectual sparring partner. This is for Jeremie.

ALICE IN PORNOLAND

INTRODUCTION
Skin Flicks

Sexually repressed Victorian England
is the fertile crescent of sexual deviance.
—Shaun Costello, adult filmmaker

Although our society today is relatively liberated, Victorian
ideas about sex are still there lurking underneath—like a
seam of coal tar that can be mined and used to fuel the
lamps of today's sexual imagination.
—Wash West, adult filmmaker

The word "Victorian" is used in everyday life to connote a variety of ideologies, attitudes, sensibilities, and styles. "Victorian" might conjure images of white ladies in hoop skirts, covered piano legs, storefronts displaying obscene books and postcards, impoverished children begging on urban sidewalks, white men slaughtering natives in a foreign land, prostitutes walking the city streets or being murdered and dissembled, the spectacle of the Hottentot Venus being exhibited by white men as a sexual curiosity, or chivalrous white men helping ladies into carriages. These seemingly conflicting images reflect the troubling and fascinating matrix of race, gender, class, and sexuality that is "the Victorian." Indeed, the Victorian is at the heart of myriad competing narratives on these intersecting themes. The Victorian is so infused with issues of gender, sexuality, race, and class that to examine the Victorian, the Neo-Victorian, or the Gothic Victorian is in fact to examine all of these narratives together and simultaneously, even as we may attempt to parse them.

Hardcore—that is, unsimulated—pornographic film has been engaged in the project of examining the Victorian for several decades. Pornographic filmmakers use the Victorian as an erotic vocabulary with which to articulate the culturally fraught pleasures and outrages of gender, sexuality, race, and class. Fascinated as it is with gender, sexuality, class, and race, and attracted as it is to dominant cultural texts with which to play, pornographic film boasts a rich and heretofore largely ignored legacy of neo-Victorian analysis. Pornography's preoccupation with gender, sexuality, race, and class has been well documented by both mainstream and scholarly writers and should come as no great surprise. Perhaps less well known is pornography's preoccupation with nostalgia, legacy, and Gothic transformation. In this book, I explore how these areas of interest intersect in the neo-Victorian pornographic project and what these intersections reveal about pornographic media and our erotic investment in the past.

Pornography repeatedly stages and violates private, secret, and forbidden sexualities as a way of generating erotic excitement. Thanks to our perception of the Victorians as simultaneously repressed and perverse, they are the ideal canvas upon which to stage this process. They are the symbolic set of people, places, and discourses most ripe for pornographic exploitation. In our cultural mind, the Victorian period connotes the repressed, the backward, and the elite, steeped in sexism, colonial racism, and a (white, male) stiff upper lip. It is also a period characterized by sexual secrecy, with a middle class that viewed sex as "forbidden, confused, and diffused into the most unlikely areas" (Pearsall xiii). Meanwhile, the upper classes are having a debaucherous old time and the working-class poor are unashamed and flagrant in their vulgarity. This "contrast between the furtive gloom of the agonized and repressed, and the gay life so evidently there for all to see" constitutes our clashing yet strangely harmonious ideas about the Victorians (Pearsall xvii). Our notion of the Victorian circles pleasurably around our knowledge that the Victorians were obsessed with, but also deeply concerned about and afraid of, sex. Social transgression, the breach of secrecy, and the exposure of hypocrisy, I will argue, are core pleasures of the pornographic text regardless of genre or source text. As I will show, the neo-Victorian provides a space in which to explore these erotic themes.

In addition to being our embarrassing ancestors with woefully backward politics and practices, the Victorians are a radical, revolutionary influence. In addition to evoking a sense of sexual repression and hypocrisy, the Victorian period—particularly the fin de siècle—connotes forward thinking, radical politics, and progression. The Victorians are our foremothers and forefathers in industrial revolution, scientific innovation, sexology, art, literature, photography, and, yes, pornography. These legacies are taken up by pornographers in the twentieth and twenty-first centuries. Neo-Victorian pornographies exploit both understandings of "the Victorian" simultaneously, constructing a pleasurably conflicted and constantly shifting site of eroticism.

A significant portion of my argument here revolves around the way pornographic media represents "the Victorian" as what Ann Heilmann and Mark Llewellyn call "a homogenized identity" (2). Indeed, the term "neo-Victorian" has become homogenized to mean any range of texts that engage with, revisit, or rewrite the Victorian period and its texts. Heilmann and Llewellyn believe this blurring of the term to be dangerous, insisting that "neo-Victorian" be used to describe texts that are in some way "*self-consciously engaged with the act of (re)interpretation, (re)discovery and (re)vision concerning the Victorians*" (4, italics in original). To claim that the pornographic films discussed in this book are self-consciously engaging Victorian literature and culture with historical specificity is far too lofty. Indeed, while certainly some of the films I address are engaged in these forms of re-visitation, many might think they "lack imaginative re-engagement with the period, and instead recycle and deliver a stereotypical and unnuanced reading of the Victorians and their literature and culture" (Heilmann and Llewellyn 6), marking them as undoubtedly outside of this conception of neo-Victorianism and well within the realm of garden-variety historical fiction or mere pastiche. However, I believe this would be an unfair dismissal of a body of work that has much to offer neo-Victorian studies.

Pornographers *use* the Victorians as a structuring device and as a vocabulary of precarious, oscillating fears and desires concerning gender, class, race, sexual orientation, and technology. Yoking these fears and desires together is a sustained inward and outward gaze: a sense of separatism from the above board as well as a gesture toward a fluid and transmedia sexual and artistic legacy. I argue that these conflicted and dynamic interactions with legitimate and illegitimate media (phantasmatic realms that are nevertheless all too real and remain steadfast in their structuring principle even as genres, artists, texts, and mediums travel between them) and with the intersecting moments in the history of sexual representation, social mores, cultural change, and technology compose an integral part of pornography across the decades and centuries.

Thus, while this book is not primarily invested in defining or redefining the neo-Victorian, or invested in the historical accuracies of these pornographic appropriations, I hope to advance the idea that porn is indeed analytical, self-conscious, and engaged in a neo-Victorian project. For this reason, I use the term neo-Victorian but not strictly in the sense of Heilmann and Llewellyn's definition. Instead, my understanding and use of the term is more closely aligned with Louisa Hadley's broad definition: "contemporary fiction that engages with the Victorian era, at either the level of plot, structure, or both" (4). Still, in pornography there might not be a plot or traditional narrative structure. This means that in order to discuss pornography that engages with the Victorian, an even looser definition of neo-Victorian is necessary, one that also allows that this engagement with the Victorian era simply be at the level of character, costume, or setting. This definition provides space for discussion of pornography within discussions of the neo-Victorian. My usage of neo-Victorian is not intended to be fixed, static, or definitive, but rather a way to initiate a discourse on the surprising, dynamic, moving, intellectual, witty, conservative, boring, repetitive, and unimaginative ways that the Victorians have been porned.

Porn and/as Gothic

It is no coincidence that the most popular texts for neo-Victorian pornographic re-vision are explicitly Gothic. Pornographers have drawn on and engaged with almost every cinematic and literary genre imaginable, with robust legacies of hardcore science fiction, comedy, romantic comedy, noir, musicals, Westerns, and thrillers.[1] However, it is Gothic horror that pornography seems most fascinated with and which we might regard as pornography's cousin. Gothic, that slippery and inherently nebulous term, is, like pornography, preoccupied with duality and doubling, excess, boundary transgression, and (sublimated in porn) mortality. More specifically, the Gothic text is associated with "erotic excess, transgender seduction and rape, secret desires and perversity bordering on and including monstrosity" (Jones 3). These themes could easily be listed as qualities of pornography whether that pornography is explicitly neo-Victorian Gothic or not.

If, as neo-Victorian scholars Marie-Luise Kohlke and Christian Gutleben assert, "*neo-Victorianism is by nature quintessentially Gothic*" (4, italics in original), then pornography, I argue, is both quintessentially neo-Victorian and quintessentially Gothic. Just as neo-Victorian fiction is both "product" and "purveyor" of the Gothic, so too is pornography; just as neo-Victorian fiction "enacts Gothic principles and, as such, takes part in the constant re-activation of the Gothic" (3), so too does pornography. Porn is the hidden but pervasive bastard sibling of the mainstream and canon, the Hyde to Dr. Jekyll, exhibiting those hyperbolic manifestations of our culture's unacceptable anxieties and interests. The Victorian Gothic gives pornographers a language with which to stage its transgressions, perversions, and erotic pleasures. The pornographic text provides a space in which to stage Victorian Gothic anxieties, fears, and, again, erotic pleasures. In other words, the Victorian Gothic provides porn with an erotic vocabulary.

Porn performers resemble Gothic icons. Performer Lorelei Lee describes how porn has offered her lessons in "transformations made possible by costuming, [...] the ways that I could make a play out of my gender presentation" ("Cum Guzzling" 207) and the pleasures of dissembled femininity: "women whose makeup became smeared, whose hair was sweat-gnarled, who were contorted and bent in decidedly un-pretty shapes, covered in spit and sweat and lube, laughing or shouting in a full-throated testament to the human capability for joy" ("Cum Guzzling" 209). The indulgent, flagrantly sexual woman or man beside himself or herself with orgasm, physical convulsions, fleshy transformation, and fluid expulsion/consumption is similar to that of the abhuman.[2] Kelley Hurley explains, "The abhuman subject is a not-quite-human subject, characterized by its morphic variability, continually in danger of becoming not-itself, becoming other" (4). The fin de siècle Gothic is ambivalent concerning monsters and the abhuman: "convulsed by nostalgia for the 'fully human' subject whose undoing it accomplishes so resolutely, and yet aroused by the prospect of a monstrous becoming" (Hurley 4). Pornography is a genre concerned with sexual doings and undoings, often blurring the lines between these acts and experiences.

Pornotopia is a Gothic space. The place constructed by pornography, what Steven Marcus famously calls "pornotopia," is timeless and placeless: a remote, removed, liminal space that rests on a threshold. Indeed, for Marcus, pornotopia is analogous to some mighty Gothic-sounding locations: "the isolated castle on an inaccessible mountain top, the secluded country estate, set in the middle of a large park and surrounded by insurmountable walls, the mysterious town house in London or Paris," and so on (268). Pornography, like the Gothic, is indifferent to place and time: "in the kind of boundless, featureless freedom that most pornographic fantasies require for their action, such details are regarded as restrictions, limitations, distractions, or encumbrances" (Marcus 269). Yet Marcus's pornotopia fails to account for the ways in which porn carefully regards time and place even as it obscures it. By no means is pornographic space unintruded upon by anxieties, melancholy, and mortality.

Contrary to Marcus's rather parochial view, pornography is not a hermetically sealed male utopia. Much like the Gothic, it spills out of its confines and refuses to remain neatly in its specially designated category. It is

disseminated across borders of technology, media, and time; it is displayed
for women and children to see in shop windows of the nineteenth century,
it shows up in browser sidebars, sneaks into Disney movies, and interrupts
Super Bowl broadcasts.[3] Porn persistently disobeys Marcus's rule that the only
form of measurement in porn is "the time it takes either for a sexual act to
be represented or for an autoerotic act to be completed" (270). This notion
of a solitary masturbator immersed in a timeless space that caters solely to
uncomplicated sexual desires is a vast oversimplification of how consumers
interact with pornography and how pornographers construct the worlds in
which hardcore narratives take place.

Consumers are not passive objects absorbed into this pornotopic, sealed
space. Porn spills out of these confines, just as fantasies do. The surface level
of the text does not have sovereignty over the reader's/viewer's experience or
engagement with the sexual acts on screen (Ross 195). Pornography "reso-
nates," it does not simply "arouse" (Paasonen, *Carnal Resonance* 16–17). Its
pleasures, displeasures, and meanings alter according to context, company,
and platform in a way that I believe is unique from any other genre of media.
Nevertheless, Marcus's concept is useful in considering the way pornography
constructs a Gothic pornotopia to mobilize contradictions and possibilities that extend beyond the surface of the text. I cannot claim to know how
consumers receive the films under examination. I can, however, interrogate
the methods pornographers use to craft sexual fantasy spaces that might
mobilize the diverse and constantly shifting fantasies and pleasures of their
audience. In addition to this, I assess the rhetoric of various paratexts and fan
discourses surrounding the films in an effort to understand the fluctuating
and mercurial pleasures of neo-Victorian porn.

Porn offers a world where one can lose oneself, reimagine sexual possibilities, embody alternating positions, and explore subjectivities. Men and
women are "undone," orgasmically transported, removed and displaced.
The monster, the abhuman subject, and the complex sensations such creatures arouse are spaces for exploration and re-visioning of sexual identity
in pornography. As Jack Halberstam argues, Gothic fiction is less a static
genre and more "a technology of subjectivity, one which produces the deviant subjectivities opposite which the normal, the healthy, and the pure can
be known. Gothic [. . .] may be loosely defined as the rhetorical style and
narrative structure designed to produce fear and desire within the reader"
(2). Porn, too, is a technology of subjectivity. The monsters in this project
are symbolic, fantastic avatars of a broader pornographic desire for sexual
dematerialization.

In this book, I argue that porn relies on a particular "Victorianness" in generating eroticism—a Gothic Victorianness that is monstrous, violent, repressive, and perverse, steeped in class divisions and preoccupied with gender, sexuality, and race. Pornographic films regularly expose the perceived hypocrisy of this Victorianness, rhetorically equating it with mainstream, legitimate culture as a way of staging pornography's alleged sexual authenticity and transgressive nature. An important component of this staging is an implicit nod to pornographic legacy. The Victorian era, these films seem to say, is tethered to porn in its media, its technology, its sexual concerns and obsessions, its hierarchies, and—of course—its pornographies.

Beyond this, my argument is twofold: that the neo-Victorian Gothic functions for pornographers as a space for the reclaiming and reimagining of women, non-normative orientations, deviant sexualities, and racialized histories of trauma; and that the neo-Victorian Gothic mobilizes unstable genders and queer desires in ostensibly "straight, male" hardcore. The films under discussion are, quite literally, *transformative* spaces for gender and sexuality. Of course, to make such a claim—that the Victoria Gothic derails, upends, or otherwise ruptures "Porn"—would suggest there is a "pure Porn" to upend, one that is airtight, secure, and static. This is not the case, and not what I mean to argue. In fact, my focus on neo-Victorian Gothic offers a lens through which we might question all porn and all porn consumption. The intention of such interrogation is to foreground the genre's diversity, the diverse pleasures it elicits, and the ways in which pornographers consciously and unconsciously trace a lineage of sexual discourse and representation from the nineteenth century to the present.

I approach porn in a way that recognizes the neo-Victorian as a constitutive element of the genre, as well as the cyclical nature of this diverse body of film. Indeed, neo-Victorian pornographies reveal a surprisingly uninterrupted legacy of visual pornographies. Repetition is a fundamental characteristic of pornography. The never-ending sequels, remakes, and series, together with the repetition of sexual acts within and across films, constitute what Sarah Schaschek calls "seriality," something that she considers "a source of pleasure" and key to "the fascination and frustration of pornography" (25). Schaschek's focus on seriality and repetition in porn means that she discusses old and new forms of pornographic media. Because of the genre's repetitious nature, Schaschek argues, "digital and analog forms of pornography cannot easily be decoupled; each old medium is forced to coexist with new media" (4). Thus, while she focuses primarily on online porn (much of which was formerly on DVD or released online but with an accompanying DVD release), she observes, "I will continuously make note to 'older' forms, literary and filmic, thus criticizing notions of an 'all new' community-based Porn 2.0" (4).

I make a similar gesture in this project. While I believe sociopolitical context, technology, and exhibition platform affect pornographic content and its reception, I am also engaged with a project that asserts a legacy of repeated iterations made and consumed in a variety of new and changing contexts. I discuss old and new, gay and straight, film and video, theatrical features and online scenes, often together in the same analysis. I do this in an effort to problematize a simple linear movement through time and media; to question the idea that pornographic appeal, preferred tropes, and framing devices are necessarily distinct in each neatly sectioned-off decade. This approach comes in part due to pornography's engagement with history, taking "the Victorian" to mean a variety of homogenized traits shaped to serve that particular erotic text. Certainly, form, style, message, and trends change according to the historical moment from which they derive. At the same time, there is an interest in the Victorian that challenges such conceptions and can be scrutinized across eras without descending into ahistoricity.

Moreover, I find that a neo-Victorian approach mobilizes a more complex understanding of the genre's articulations of desire, gender, and power and avoids the simplistic binary treatments that tend to dominate these discussions, treatments that are reductive and unhelpful. I explore how porn attempts to re-insert an illusory "truth" into mainstream texts, exposing a perceived hypocrisy inherent in mainstream, non-pornographic texts that either simulate, avoid, or dismiss sex acts—what Constance Penley refers to as the "trashing" of the mainstream: an indulgence in what is "always already" trash by its very nature, thereby satirizing and often subverting the "mainstream."[4] It is my aim to move beyond simplistic, dichotomous, and moralistic critiques of pornographic texts in an effort to examine pornography as a significant and signifying genre. I am interested in what this diverse and contradictory genre has to say about the mainstream and canonical culture it is assumed to be so different from, as well as what it has to say about itself.

In this vein, I make little effort to explore "the representative"—that nebulous mass of content supposedly indicative of a broad, generic pornographic substance usually constituted by the worst of the genre. The only gesture of this sort is an attempt to provide material representative of neo-Victorian pornography. In turn, I explore the nature of pornographic appeal through this representative body of work. I make claims about "pornography" that should not be taken to apply to all pornographies everywhere. Rather, this project is an attempt to isolate some of the key pleasures and interests of the genre of pornography understood through the lens of the neo-Victorian. In essence, I explore pornography as a whole by looking at an interesting and, some might say, esoteric subgenre that has nonetheless appeared in a wide range of eras, locations, and levels of the industry.

Porn studies would richly benefit from the same selective and esoteric approach that so many other literary and media studies projects take. This book is an attempt to move away from generic study of the representative, away from attempts to assess what we imagine the lowly porn consumer must be uncritically absorbing, and toward a study of the specific, the strange, the marginal, the subgeneric, and the mainstream. In the process, I interrogate something just as "representative" of pornography as textual choices designed to maintain the notion that porn is violent, racist, and misogynistic, and just as worthwhile as work based on random selections from Pornhub.

This project explores the terrain of pornography and its habit of prodding what Laura Kipnis calls the "tender spots" of the cultural psyche. More specifically, in the proceeding pages I interrogate the ways in which the Victorian era serves as a primary tender spot for modern pornography. "Pornography's ultimate desire," Kipnis argues, "is exactly to engage our deepest embarrassments, to mock us for the anxious psychic balancing acts we daily perform, straddling between the anarchy of sexual desires and the straitjacket of social responsibilities" (167). When Kipnis speaks of pornography's delight in transgressing and violating social mores, however, she resists turning the same lens of interrogation back on to pornography itself. In this project, I ask: What of pornography's own delicate balancing acts? In speaking the unspoken, what does pornography itself leave unsaid or reveal about itself? What does the neo-Victorian mobilize in regard to a discourse on porn? What, in its careful construction of sex and sexuality, does pornography (and its consumers) anxiously straddle?

Through an analysis of hardcore film texts set during the nineteenth century and/or based on Victorian novels—the canonical and the pornographic—I argue that neo-Victorian porn is a useful lens through which to understand the construction of pornographic desire and how the genre situates itself historically and in relation to the mainstream. If porn is a hyperbolic reflection of our collective cultural memory and fantasy, then this investigation unearths a broader cultural engagement with our Victorian doppelgangers and suggests how we use it to construct our sexual selves. Pornographic articulations of the Victorian Gothic can point us toward a more complicated and nuanced understanding of how hardcore works to achieve its aims and, indeed, what those aims might be.

Feminism and Pornography: A Gothic Binary

As a scholar of pornography I attempt to avoid the anti-/pro-porn binary. Yet I find myself repeatedly drawn back into it due to a societal push to classify the work I do according to strict lines drawn up by feminism. The feminist study of porn has moved on from the sex wars of the 1980s, producing a diverse and complex body of work now known as porn studies. This highly interdisciplinary field interrogates a wide variety of intersecting issues as they relate to pornographic media. Recent interventions include Mireille Miller-Young's groundbreaking ethnographic analysis, *A Taste for Brown Sugar: Black Women in Pornography* (2014), Peter Alilunas's 2016 study of the cruelly undervalued 1980s adult video era, *Smutty Little Movies*, and John Mercer's 2016 book, *Gay Pornography: Representations of Sexuality and Masculinity*, in which Mercer reveals the plural masculinities on offer in internet pornographies. An academic journal devoted to the field, *Porn Studies*, was also introduced in 2014, a move that legitimized the field and caused quite a bit of outcry and a lot of sensational headlines. This emerging scholarship reflects the intersectional, critical approaches porn studies scholars have been adopting over the past couple of decades in order to grasp a more nuanced and informed understanding of the wildly diverse and slippery genre of pornography.

Yet, anti-porn feminism is currently enjoying something of a renaissance. This brand of scholarship and activism rejects the standard academic approaches in favor of "a kind of knowledge that discards the scholarly apparatus of analysis" and "appeals to common sense and emotional intelligence, precisely because this is the ground on which their arguments find most fertile purchase" (Smith and Attwood, "Emotional Truths" 46–47). This has often resulted in quite hostile conflict between anti-porn feminists and porn scholars, the latter of whom are engaged in academic interrogation rather than blanket condemnation. Thus, these porn scholars are often erroneously labeled "pro-porn" and accused of being in cahoots with the sex industry.[5] In 2013, just months before the inaugural issue of *Porn Studies* journal, Gail Dines, figurehead of the anti-porn movement, lashed out at the editorial board. Dines felt the board was overwhelmingly "pro-porn" and thus biased, stating, "These editors come from a pro-porn background where they deny the tons and tons of research that has been done into the negative effects of porn. [. . .] They are akin to climate-change deniers. They're taking a bit of junk science and leaping to all sorts of unfounded conclusions" (Cadwalladr). Without having read a single essay from the journal, Dines's organization

Stop Porn Culture (now retitled Culture Reframed) started a petition. The stated goals were as follows:

> In the interest of academic integrity and thorough critical inquiry, it is imperative that a journal titled *Porn Studies* creates space for critical analyses of porn from diverse and divergent perspectives. Our hope is that you will change the composition of the editorial board, confirm the journal's commitment to a heterogeneous interrogation of the issues embedded in porn and porn culture, and ensure that diverse perspectives are represented—on the board and also in the essays published in the journal. Failing that, we ask that you change the name to reflect and make evident the bias of its editors (Pro-Porn Studies) and create another journal which will represent the position of anti-porn scholars and activists and the voices of mental health professionals, porn industry survivors, and feminist scholars whose analyses examine the replication and reification of misogyny, child abuse, and sexual exploitation in mainstream pornography (for instance, Critical Porn Studies). (Routledge Pro Porn Studies Bias)

These goals assume that the journal, and by extension the field, does *not* analyze porn from "diverse and divergent perspectives" and that the journal will resist work that criticizes porn.

Rather than address the more complex and difficult roots of racism, misogyny, poverty, and violence, or interrogate pornography in a way that acknowledges genre, audience, era, and the complexities of agency, anti-porn activists (be they religious, conservative, or feminist) scapegoat the handy category of pornography for a bewildering array of social ills. These scholars and activists "cast pornography as a monolithic medium and industry and make sweeping generalizations about its production, its workers, its consumers, and its effects on society" (Taormino et al. 9). They offer little to no critical thought about the way society frames porn or the way consumers interact with porn, let alone the specific content of specific scenes and films.

I remain sex radical and porn critical in that I "attempt to contextualize pornographies in relation to other media genres, forms, and aesthetics, in relation to a variety of producer and consumer groups and communities, and in relation to the broader frameworks of cultural regulation and value" (Smith and Attwood, "Anti/Pro/Critical Porn Studies" 11). No doubt, some will interpret this to mean I am "pro-porn." I am not, and I don't know what that would entail, considering the breadth and diversity of pornography. Regardless, in this book, my interest does not lie in whether a film is "good" or "bad" for society, nor in concluding definitively that a film is feminist or misogynistic. I do not believe that any text or genre fits neatly into these superficial categories. I do not think ascertaining porn's position on this narrow spectrum is a useful objective if we are concerned with the complexities of sexual representation. Rather, I am interested in the contradictions and navigations offered up in neo-Victorian pornographies, the contexts from which they emerge, and what the rhetorical choices made by pornographers suggest about pornographic genre, modern consumers, and pleasure. Gender, race, sexuality, and class are foremost in these analyses.

Porning as Adaptation

The very notion of a "pornographic adaptation" is rife with conflict. I. Q. Hunter observes the tension between the parodic text and the pornographic text, noting that the sex scenes that drive porn are distinct from traditional narrative. This creates a dual text sometimes at odds with itself (Hunter 21–22). For this reason, I use the term "porning" alongside adaptation. I approach pornographic adaptation in a way that incorporates appropriation, adaptation, re-vision, and reproduction. While many of these films do indeed faithfully adapt the original text, offering "a more sustained engagement with a single text or source than the more glancing act of allusion or quotation," many of the films appropriate the source text in that they "carr[y] out the same sustained engagement as adaptation but frequently [adopt] a posture of critique, even assault" (Sanders 4). Sanders's definition of appropriation is very similar to my understanding of "porning."[6]

I deploy "porning" to describe the combined act of lampooning, reproducing, and re-visioning "legitimate" culture through a pornographic lens as a way to self-Other porn as rebellious, truth telling, and authentic in the face of a hypocritical mainstream. Porn insistently goes to places mainstream would never dare, tastelessly sexualizing stories, people, and places that the mainstream handles with sanctimonious sobriety. Porning also recreates areas of culture to recenter women, the sexually marginalized, the gender nonconforming, and the sexually deviant and perverse. Gay male porn, for example, performs what John R. Burger calls "one-handed histories." Marginalized and historically silenced communities, such as LGBTQ communities, women, and people of color, must do the work of rewriting themselves into history. This action is often performed through fictional and fantastical narrative. Burger observes, "Pornography (specifically video pornography) is a most underestimated and misunderstood manifestation of gay popular memory" (3). It is also a site of forbidden, silenced, and perverse pleasures rooted in our tortured histories of misogyny, colonial rule, and slavery. For example, as Ariane Cruz observes, interracial pornography set during the nineteenth century "brings into relief the vexed question of the enslaved black female's unspeakable pleasure and its messy entanglement with issues of consent, will, and agency" (98). Pornography is constantly reaching into the traumatic past to conjure an ecstatic and conflicted version of this past in the present.

The novels that pornography tends to adapt are examples of what Paul Davis calls "culture texts," collectively remembered texts disconnected from the words of the text's author, repeatedly retold, reimagined, and dispersed, and constantly in the state of creation. Culture texts change "as the reasons for its retelling change" (Davis 4), generating a wealth of diverse appropriations that reflect and respond to a particular cultural moment. Neo-Victorian porn adaptations "porn" and, to borrow Constance Penley's term, "trash" canonical texts that have become culture texts via Hollywood, television, and other forms of mass media. In turn, these moving image texts both draw on and contribute to the creation of the culture text, leaving traces of the pornographic in the margins of the novels. In this way, the act of porning is an act of political and cultural antagonism.

I don't want to overstate the case by suggesting that pornography is solely or even primarily a politically antagonistic genre seeking to overturn hegemonic power. Now more than ever before, it is a capitalist venture, and many porn films appear to have been made with the goal of doing the absolute bare minimum necessary to move product with no thought for art, politics, or even the customer.[7] Still, pornography has always been, and remains, populated by cultural and political outlaws. Furthermore, for better or worse, many of the representations found in porn cannot be found elsewhere in culture. Burger's simple point that "pornography makes gay men visible" can also be applied to sexually deviant women. Many have entered the industry as cultural radicals and rabble-rousers intent on defying stereotypes and cultural demands on their sexual and gender expression. These outlaws seek to make money, certainly, but capitalist venture does not preclude a political agenda. Pornography as a product of mass consumer culture is a core component of what McNair calls "sex-political progress" (6). And, in many cases, especially now that financial returns on porn are so dismal, political agenda (or pleasure) precludes capitalist venture.[8]

Nevertheless, just as performers and producers are not inherently sexual radicals, porn parodies, remakes, and adaptations are not inherently subversive. As Foucault observes, "If sex is repressed, that is, condemned to prohibition, nonexistence, and silence, then the mere fact that one is speaking about it has the appearance of a deliberate transgression" (*History of Sexuality*, 6). Indeed, this is the modus operandi of pornography. Likewise, I agree with David Andrews that hardcore should not be regarded as "*intrinsically* subversive" simply because it is "aligned with free speech ideals or sexual depravity" (56, italics in original). Nevertheless, hardcore does enact a violating force simply by flagrantly depicting unsimulated, indulgent sex. In a supposedly "pornified" culture, these depictions remain ghettoized on special websites, filtered from imdb.com results, and displaced by titillating metonymic mainstream references that merely hint at the actual content. At best, unsimulated sex acts are wrapped up in art film trappings complete with a cautionary tale and the sense that sex must be miserable or dangerous in order to be consumed.[9] To understand the extent to which unsimulated sex is not part of public speech, all one has to do is accidentally leave a porn movie playing on his or her laptop and open it in public.

Even in the laziest efforts, porning does *something* in a rhetorical sense. Porning occurs in "one-joke remakes," as Peter Lehman observes, where the resemblance to the original text is primarily in a punning title. Pleasure in such gestures lies in "selling trash in relationship to respectability" (Lehman, "Twin Cheeks" 49). Pornographic puns and the porning of the mainstream enact a thrill of transgression, of bringing the supposedly legitimate down a rung or two. Former head of publishing at the British Film Institute, and expert on the Western, Edward Buscombe calls this pornographic gesture "stealing." In his short essay "Generic Overspill," Buscombe disdainfully observes, "One way of supplying at least a modicum of narrative structure is to steal it from elsewhere, and so porn films have habitually been parasitic on other genres, giving us pornographic thrillers, horror, science fiction, even musicals, and, of course, the western" (27). Buscombe assumes that pornography is merely a parasitic genre, feeding off the mainstream and exploiting familiar genres for profit. He is in good company.

Yet he and others ignore how these mainstream genres hypocritically feed off of pornography, enjoying the spectacle of pornographic tropes and references even while keeping porn at an arm's length. Attitudes such as Buscombe's also ignore how pornography builds upon and speaks back to these genres for this very hypocrisy. Ariane Cruz is careful to highlight this when she describes the *Django Unchained*–inspired nineteenth-century set, *Get My Belt* (2013), as "plantation porn—an important extension of the plantation genre and not just indebted to it" in that it "reveals the already pornographic place of slavery in the filmic imaginary" (94–95). Porning is a much more complicated and self-conscious affair than fucking in costumes. Pornographic adaptations and appropriations of sacrosanct texts, spaces, people, and places are a textual assault on the mainstream, an assault that I argue is a key pleasure of pornography and an important way to invoke, exploit, and destabilize canonical manifestations of gender, sex, class, sexual orientation, and race.

Pornography: A Victorian Invention

While sexually explicit, "lewd" materials existed prior to the nineteenth century, the Victorians honed the sexually explicit art form into what we now regard as "pornography" proper. The term "pornography" has since been applied to visual and written materials as far back as Aretino's postures in the 1500s, yet the word itself only entered English lexicon in 1857. The critical distinction between the sexually explicit literature and art of the nineteenth century and that of the decades and centuries before it lies in the nature, intention, distribution, and regulation of the genre. Pornography has historically been tied to political antagonism and was often prosecuted alongside sex-education and reproductive-rights pamphlets, but between 1880 and the early twentieth century, "pornographers stripped away characterization, plot, and setting, and opened up room for an intense formulaic focus on specific sex acts" (Sigel, *Governing Pleasures* 82). Penetration became a core theme, fetishes were developed as a focus of the narrative, and sex was offered up as something to consume and enjoy for its own sake. To be sure, the material retained some political antagonism, but detailed (and often laborious) descriptions of the mechanics of sex took priority.

The nineteenth century is also notable for the sheer volume of pornographic material it produced. In addition to political and cultural change, technology had much to do with this explosion of smut. Not only were printing presses capable of churning out volume after volume of magazines such as *The Pearl* and novels of every possible persuasion, but also visual technologies were no sooner invented than they were put to work representing carnal lust. The magic lantern, daguerreotype, and most crucially the photograph were all conveyors of the pornographic image during this time. Finally, at the very end of the 1800s, Thomas Edison's motion picture camera brought porn into the twentieth century and continued pornography's march toward the twenty-first in remarkably uninterrupted fashion.

The abrupt division between "then" (the Victorians) and "now" (the moderns and postmoderns) we tend to craft when discussing pornography has more to do with how we use the Victorians than it does with the legacy of technology and pornographic content. The continued pornographic fascination with the Victorians that occupies the focus of this book acknowledges but also obscures the fact that the Victorians starred in our very first visual pornographies. While some of the films discussed here recognize an uninterrupted technological progression from nineteenth to twentieth to twenty-first century, the majority prefers an analogue Victorian era so as to more clearly stage a technological distance while also eroticizing the simplicities of Victorian private eroticism.

Visual pornographies abounded in the nineteenth century. The Victorians enjoyed all manner of still images through devices such as the stereoscope (invented 1838), which created the illusion of viewing in three dimensions by presenting two copies of the image in question and showing them to the viewer's eyes through two separate lenses. The View-Master, a toy many of us over thirty will remember from childhood, is the mid-twentieth-century version of the stereoscope. Victorians also enjoyed the daguerreotype (invented 1839), the first publicly available photographic process and one that remained popular for the ensuing two decades. The photographic process went through various evolutions, shifting to the collodion process in the late 1850s and the gelatin process in the 1870s (the primary method for black-and-white photographs today). Predictably, all of these developments in technology were used to host, document, and exhibit pornographic imagery.

The Victorians also enjoyed moving images very early in the century thanks to the manipulation of existing still-image technology. It should come as no surprise at all that these moving-image technologies were also instantaneously used for illicit pornographic materials. The magic lantern is the most significant origin point for the development of moving images and is no exception when it comes to disseminating smut (Heard). The device involved a concave mirror in the back, a light source that would be disseminated by that concave mirror, a glass slide featuring painted scenarios slipped into place before the light source, and a lens at the front through which the light would shine, projecting the details of the small glass slide onto the wall or screen (Pfragner 9–21). While the lantern technology was invented and developed in the early eighteenth century, the nineteenth century became so enamored of it that the magic lantern is most often associated with the Victorians.

The magic lantern could also be manipulated to create a sense of motion and is the foundation for future moving-image media such as the praxinoscope, introduced in the 1880s. In addition, the zoopraxiscope (invented 1879 by Eadweard Muybridge) and the kinetoscope (1889) were precursors of the modern motion-picture camera and in fact can themselves be considered the first motion-picture cameras.[10] At each step of the way, logic, rumors, and meager documentation suggest that pornography played a role in each and every technological development of the nineteenth century.

In spite of so much technological change, Victorian pornographic tropes, positions, framing, and structure remained relatively unchanged. Even today, pornographic imagery is not significantly different from that of the nineteenth century. In his book *Black and White and Blue: Adult Cinema from the Victorian Age to the VCR*, Dave Thompson remarks, "In the world of erotic film, after all, it's not the content that has changed, but the presentation of that content. The human body remains the same as it ever was, and those souls who advocate an end to all forms of explicit sexuality would be as offended by the contents of the sex films of their great-grandfather's generation, as they are by the hottest new release" (xvi). Thompson's contention that the presentation rather than the content has changed has a lot of truth to it, but he overlooks the power of nostalgia, antiquity, and ironic distance in diluting the shock value of sex on film. David Church argues that further ironic distance may be mobilized by "the bewildering effect of seeing documentary evidence of sexual acts performed in past time periods not often associated with sexual explicitness" (*Disposable Passions* 15). The antiquated look of the media, the old-fashioned styles, and the diverse and perverse sex acts these Victorians and Edwardians enact might variously make for a quaint, shocking, amusing, or sexually arousing experience. Indeed, while there are many representational cues that erotically distance vintage pornographies from present-day consumers, as Susanna Paasonen asks, "Why should they be seen without lust?" (142). If aesthetic camp creates detached viewers, neo-Victorian porn signals that aesthetics of a bygone era also generate erotic intimacy and attachment.

Circularity in Pornographic Form

The "golden age" of 1972–1984 that saw the rise of the fully realized narrative feature, so privileged as the focus of porn studies, is rightfully considered by Peter Lehman to be a "bizarre aberration that quickly passed" ("Revelations" 88); a fifteen-year-or-so blip on the radar of pornography as a whole. Even the lengthy novels of the nineteenth century were typically sex heavy and in stark contrast to the Hollywood-esque, glossy, narrative feature films of the porno chic era. Prior to the 1970s, pornography tended toward sex-heavy short films—stags and loops—and after the 1980s quickly circled back to this formula. The material produced today resembles the stag films of the early twentieth century more so than "cinema." The introduction and rapid expansion of the internet sped up this process, enabling pornographers to produce scenes, rather than full-length features, for studios and individuals to upload decontextualized and truncated portions of scenes to tubesites, and for fans to gather mere snippets of those scenes and turn them into gifs. Thus, here we are in the internet age with the feature film practically dead and Tumblr pages rich with "microporn."

Even Victorian literary porn bears similarities to the moving-image hardcore of today. Victorian literature in general reflects a new visuality, one born of developments in visual technology, specifically the stereoscope. With the introduction of this device, the Victorians grew to recognize that "what the eye begins to 'see' is that vision occurs from within a body and is therefore also of and in the body" (Williams, "Corporealized Observers" 11). The new technology differed from the camera obscura in that it revealed the role of subjective perception in the process of seeing. This shift in the experience of seeing, together with a culture interested in spectacle and the alleged authenticity of the photograph, is reflected in the literature of the time (Flint 27). Thus, Victorian- and Edwardian-era pornographic literature offers a vast array of visual evidence of sex and climax, describing in great detail "the gushes which now came slopping, jet after jet, into her mouth and ran in streams down her throat" whereupon "gorged with the slimy discharge, and half-choked by its abundance, she was compelled to let go of this human syringe, which continued to spout out its gushes in her face" (Anonymous, *Ways of a Man* 29). Facial cum shots, meat shots (close ups of genitalia), and other generic conventions exist in nineteenth-century literary and photographic porn, just as it exists in twentieth- and twenty-first-century moving-image porn.

With all this technological progression and structural circularity in content, together with the thematic consistency in pornographic uses of the Victorian, it makes sense that much of my analysis appears to flatten context. However, it is important to observe the shifts in content and style over time in order to fully untangle the different ways in which pornographers have utilized the Victorian over the years. For while my goal here is in part to present a neo-Victorian impulse that has altered very little, there are undoubtedly cultural, technological, and political forces at work that contribute to the way the Victorians are porned. This is something I take up sporadically throughout this book as I attend to each text, discussing alongside one another films that are sometimes made decades apart.

Neo-Victorian Pornographies

Naturally, pornography has tapped centuries other than the nineteenth. The nineteenth century is simply a particularly fertile site of exposure, thanks to stereotypes of the Victorians as sexually repressed. Mainstream culture is situated as the hypocrite, but one that provides the fuel for pornography's continued erotic transgressions. Pornography, like the Gothic, has a conservative streak. Gothic horror, again much like pornography, "has a power closely related to its pleasure-producing function and the twin mechanism of pleasure-power perhaps explains how it is that Gothic may empower some readers even as it disables others" (Halberstam 17). Even while porn transgresses and destabilizes, it seals up many of these fissures in its wake, reinforcing social and sexual norms at the same time. Like Halberstam's understanding of readers of the Gothic, some viewers of porn will find pleasure and empowerment, while others will only find degradation (and some will find both in conjunction with one another). Pornography and the Victorian Gothic, then, enjoy a symbiotic relationship. Hardcore re-imagings of the Victorian Gothic are couched in the deliciousness of repressed Victoriana, the perversions of slavery and empire, and the tantalizingly subversive (and often quite sexy) monsters of the Gothic—monsters that materialize from these nineteenth-century repressions, perversion, and horrors. Pornography as we know it is one of these monsters.

In investigating the relationship between pornography and the Victorian Gothic, I seek to historicize hardcore in a way that reaches across centuries (a gesture curiously lacking in porn studies) in an effort to tease out the genealogy of modern porn's engagement with mainstream culture and its own past. Even as I trace this genealogy and highlight consistencies over time, I want to avoid flattening the complexities of each passing decade. Pornographic content is shaped in large part by technologies, sexual politics, legal shifts, and distribution and consumption methods. However, one of my goals is to reveal a legacy of porn characterized by a surprising nonlinearity and remarkably consistent tropes. In tandem with this, I trace a line from the Victorian to the present, distant cousins united by a clear legacy characterized by technologies of representation. "We" (Edwardians? Modernists? Postmodernists?) picked up where the Victorians left off and have been reproducing and revisiting that space ever since.

Adult film adaptations and appropriations of the Victorian straddle revision (subversive) and reproduction (nostalgic), never solely subverting or nostalgically reproducing, but always engaged in both at once (Gutleben). The mere act of porning, of inserting sex into a well-known narrative deemed too coy to include the dirty bits, asserts a critical intervention by highlighting the perceived gaps and silences in the original text. Whether this act of porning serves as a sustained deconstruction and challenge to hegemonic norms varies according to text, but I don't particularly find useful or want to argue whether or not a given hardcore text (let alone the genre as a whole) categorically challenges social norms or somehow permanently alters understandings of gender, race, and sexuality. Rather, I seek to outline the ways in which pornography, pornographers, and the rhetoric surrounding these texts invoke particular notions of the Victorian and particular Victorian novels (the monstrous, the Gothic, and the fin de siècle) as a way of pleasurably situating pornography as an heir to the Victorians and as a subversive antagonist to their puritanical ways. According to Louisa Yates, neo-Victorian fiction is on a "consistent quest to reconcile subversion with nostalgia, parody with pastiche," and I contend that hardcore as a genre is engaged in this quest.

There are practical reasons why a low-budget genre such as pornography might draw on these icons and culture texts. As hardcore director Charles Webb reflects, pornographers are always on the lookout for a hook—a concept on which to hang the sexual action and attract the viewer with minimal financial toll (Webb). Characters such as Dracula and Alice are easily recognizable, thanks to their many visual representations in book illustrations and film adaptations. Useful for low-budget genres, the texts are also public domain and the characters' costumes are readily available for low cost at any Halloween outlet. In the case of Alice, for example, the costumes used in the various adaptations I discuss can easily be purchased online. Dracula capes, fangs, and other accessories are similarly cheap and accessible. Yet there must be more to this than simple economic ease. For one thing, many of the Alice adaptations do away with the traditional pinafore dress and Alice band, opting instead for a modern alt twist or a simple white dress. Dracula, too, appears in various guises, his identity signaled only by his name, as with Vladdy (Deep Threat) in *The Accidental Hooker* (2008) or Vlad (Rocco Siffredi) and Dracu (Omar Galanti) in *Voracious* (2009). Meanwhile, characters such as Dorian Gray and Dr. Henry Jekyll/Mr. Hyde are not known so much for their appearance as for their behaviors, activities, and props. Furthermore, even in films where the characters signal their identity through iconic costuming, plots can be elaborate not only in terms of sets, reproduction of narrative, and script detail, but also in terms of deviations from and subversion of the cultural baggage and content of the original novels. The sheer effort that some of these productions evince suggests that an interest in the Victorian is more than just a lazy and affordable way to spice up the sex.

While this project centers on hardcore's special interest in the Victorian Gothic, other eras, literary periods, genres, and authors have also enjoyed pornographic treatment. It is a cultural truism that no text, genre, or concept is safe from pornographers ready to exploit a trend for a buck. For example, in his book *Unspeakable Shaxxxspeares: Queer Theory and American Kiddie Culture*, Richard Burt discusses the popularity of hardcore William Shakespeare adaptations of the late 1980s and 1990s. Softcore film of the 1970s also tapped literature such as *Pinocchio* and *Cinderella* in an effort to challenge hardcore's seeming monopoly through bigger budgets and sophisticated narratives. This sophistication was enabled by a mainstream-friendly level of explicitness that, the producers hoped, would attract mixed gender audiences and revitalize revenues that were dwindling in the face of porno chic (Schaefer, "Sexploitation after Hardcore"). Adaptations of literature, and the use of costumes, also infuse the low-class genre of pornography with the high-class legitimacy of tasteful culture even while it flouts this legitimacy.

Like neo-Victorian porn, Shakespeare adaptations, Burt argues, attempt to "undo the romantic couple and the institution of marriage. They give reign to a sexual pornotopia, including gay and lesbian sex and even incest, rather than uphold heteronormative sexuality" (82). Yet Shakespeare adaptations—along with adaptations of *Candide* and Chaucer (*The Ribald Tales of Canterbury*), porn versions of Cleopatra and Casanova, and other period films—draw on a cultural object already associated with bawdy humor, sexual excess, lack of restraint, and the carnivalesque. The Victorian era, much more popular with pornographers than any of the above eras and culture texts, carries a special and tantalizing association with sexual repression and hidden perversion, making it particularly ripe for violation by the act of unsimulated sex. This depiction—actual penetration, actual genital contact and arousal, actual ejaculation—is critical here. As scholar of adaptation I. Q. Hunter asserts, "The status of pornographic adaptation is unique" (425). Hardcore pornography "denotes a separate and wholly toxic sphere so far as visual material is concerned. Its specific dislocation (top shelf, sex shops, sex cinemas, NSFW porn sites) is crucial to its identification as tolerated but ethically fraught material" (Hunter 425). Hardcore exists in its own carefully demarcated and ghettoized space—a leaky Gothicized space that is both on and off scene—no matter how "pornified" our culture has arguably become.

Without unsimulated sex, and the accompanying rhetorical declaration that the *point* is unsimulated sex, no true cinematic violation of propriety or cultural boundaries is executed. As Hunter rhetorically asks, "What could be more degrading than a porn version?" (426). To paraphrase Angela Carter, in order to porn, one must have a canvas to poke a hole through. The Victorian Gothic is that ideal canvas. To porn is to disrupt, to violate, to reveal, and to subvert. The fact that hardcore is so very taken with the nineteenth century speaks volumes about the function of hardcore porn as a cultural irritant. Hardcore prefers a canvas of precarious modesty on which to execute its political gestures. That hardcore prefers that version of the nineteenth century to be sexually ambiguous and populated by monsters speaks to the sexual tensions and pleasurable instabilities inherent to the genre.

Neo-Victorian Erotics of Race

Pornography is as preoccupied with racial identity as it is with class, gender, and sexual identity. Race and colonial history haunt the margins of nineteenth-century British literature, particularly around the fin de siècle. Dorian Gray witnesses the "half-caste in a ragged turban and shabby ulster" (Wilde 157) during his slumming expedition to the east-end opium dens; Carmilla is accompanied by "a hideous black woman, with a sort of colored turban on her head" (LeFanu 22). Sensual and terrifying, the traces of colonialism and slavery permeate the literature of the nineteenth century. For the Victorians, Asia, Africa, India, and the Americas constituted what Anne McClintock terms "a porno-tropics for the European imagination—a fantastic magic lantern of the mind onto which Europe projected its forbidden sexual desires and fears" (*Imperial Leather* 22). These "uncertain continents"—dark, foreign, Gothic, Other—promised strange and lascivious sexualities and served as repositories of racialized sexual fantasy. Present-day pornographies drink from the same well, returning to these sites of trauma and fantastical sexual excess for reflective and often neurotic erotic appeal.

During the nineteenth century, pornographic novels such as *Venus in India* (1889) and *A Night in a Moorish Harem* (1900) revealed the intersection of colonial rule, racism, and pornography most explicitly. The famed Cannibal Club, too, reveals the intersection of science, racism, and pornography, as its members were mutually interested in both pornography and the different sexuality of colonized peoples, resulting in a body of highly racialized pornographic literature (Wallen; Sigel, *Governing Pleasures*). These histories of racism and violence have been taken up in neo-Victorian novels such as Jean Rhys's *Wide Sargasso Sea*, Belinda Starling's *The Journal of Dora Damage*, and Barbara Chase Riboud's *Hottentot Venus: A Novel*.

However, in spite of the postcolonial tradition in neo-Victorian fiction and the fact that Victorian England had a substantial population of people of color, neo-Victorian pornographies are for the most part blindingly white. Europe and Victoriana, for all their complex and well-documented colonial histories, are "culturally bleached" in the collective memory (Gilroy xii). Pornographic representations of Europe and Victoriana are no different. This is due in large part to the way mainstream media selectively represents the Victorian period. If pornography primarily draws on existing, easily recognizable mainstream media, then they are primarily drawing on *white* media. This is particularly so when adapting canonical Victorian novels and characters or setting the action in the nineteenth century. The Victorian period through a BBC lens is almost universally white. Novels from the period deal with white people no matter what class. This white washing of nineteenth-century England obscures the fact that people of color could be seen all over the country. By 1851, there were an estimated 2.6 million black people living in London (Killingray 51).

Pandora/Blake addresses this conundrum as a British pornographer trading in the Victorian. For Blake, who runs the spanking site *Dreams of Spanking*, the Victorian era provides a distant play space in which to stage their sexual fantasies of punishment and discipline. Blake enjoys fantasies of submission, loss of control, and objectification, particularly as an object in a larger context, such as serving as a prop in a demonstration. They are cognizant of the gender and class oppressions of the nineteenth century as well as the persistence of these oppressions in the present day; the Victorian period merely renders these inequalities more visible. Distance also allows for a comfortable play space as a white, British woman.[11] As Blake explains, "The fact that it's in the past and in my own heritage makes it more accessible to me, rather than being too close to the bone and too close to genuine atrocities" (Blake). The site offers "arty, fairtrade spanking porn for men and women. Hard spanking, traditional English punishment, severe caning, historical scenarios, edgy fantasies, romance, drama, dominance and submission." Blake says the attraction to the Victorian era is rooted in an attraction to "regimes that are quite oppressive, quite strict, and quite disciplined," but also the interior design, the costumes, the language, all of which symbolize a rigid structure and clear social roles that Blake finds deeply erotic (Blake).

Blake uses people of color on their spanking site as much as possible yet admits that putting people of color in their historical scenes "was quite tricky to navigate" (Blake). On a logistical level, Blake found it difficult to find people of color who were in the BDSM scene and also willing to go on camera. As Blake observes, "You need a certain amount of privilege to be able to intentionally expose yourself to the stigma of being in porn . . . you might not feel you have the privilege to spare" (Blake). Having recruited performers of color David Weston and Lola Marie, Blake was uncertain as to how to go about writing a historical scene for them: "I wanted to do some Victorian stuff because my Victorian stuff had been exclusively white and that had been on my mind. I was trying to decide, should I try to come up with some kind of historical story based around the fact that they're a person of color, and then decided just to not make it an aspect of the story. I just don't really think this is my story to tell" (Blake). Instead, Blake cast Weston in "David's Strict Governess" as a young, upper-class son punished by his governess, and Lola Marie in "The Scholarship Girl" as a schoolgirl in an academy punished by her schoolmistress.

Following release of Marie's scene, Blake discovered fan comments suggesting it would be "hot" if Marie were to play a slave, demonstrating the

1. Pandora/Blake whipping Lola Marie in "The Scholarship Girl" (2014). Courtesy of DreamsofSpanking.com.

entrenched understandings of the historical role of people of color. Blake notes that, "The Past" was a bit more chromatic than we realize [. . .] and a lot of the traditional narratives of what Victorian, regency England looked like are really, really white" (Blake). Part of this is due to BBC representations, but part of it also has to do with Britain's efforts to erase slavery from their history and from the privileges elite officials enjoy, something Blake finds "disgusting." In visualizing a historical space where people of color enjoy submissive positions structured by class and status, and yet are not tethered to stereotypical racial roles, Blake crafts transgressive pleasures for racially diverse performers and audiences while also refraining from telling a story that, as Blake sees it, is "not [their] story to tell."

Neo-Victorian Erotics of Class

While Blake feels discomfort regarding narratives of race, they take great pleasure in exploiting class difference for erotic appeal. Indeed, some of the most prominent tropes of neo-Victorian pornographies are social class, authority, and station. The nineteenth century boasts blatant symbols of class difference that, while inextricably tied to race, can be erotically mined in connection to gender in a less politically fraught way. As Blake puts it, "I'm comfortable fantasizing about class inequality in the Victorian era where I'm an urchin at the workhouse and getting beaten, or a maidservant in a great house and getting mistreated or sexually abused. That doesn't feel gross to me" (Blake). Perhaps for these reasons, neo-Victorian pornographies tend to avoid addressing race directly, instead trading in social hierarchies of gender, age, and class as a way of staging social transgression.

Class and status difference, and sexual transgression of this difference, are among the most popular foci in porn of any era dating back to the sixteenth century (Hunt). Still, the nineteenth century, with its crystallized social structure and rise of the middle class, yields the most pronounced pornographic exploitation of social class and status. Pornography, perceived to be a low-class genre itself, thrives on class antagonism complicated and intensified by age and gender. Couplings of governess and charge, gentleman and maidservant, mistress and stable boy, and so on are common themes in nineteenth-century pornography. Perhaps the most celebrated example of this theme is the anonymously written *My Secret Life*, an eleven-volume memoir written in the late nineteenth century that documents a wealthy gentleman's sexual indulgences, many of them with women and girls of lower social standing. However, almost every pornographic novel of that time eroticizes class transgression whether it be the gentleman paying the working-class male prostitute for his tales of sexual adventure in *Sins of the Cities of the Plain* (1881), the exposure of elite upper-class abuses and Catholic exploitation of young girls in *Autobiography of a Flea* (1888), or the many novels, short stories, and poems that depict governesses whipping their young male charges or gentlemen caning and spanking disobedient children.

Twenty-first-century examples of eroticized class difference are more difficult to frame than those of Victorian pornographies. The Victorian period appears more visibly shaped by and reliant on differences in class and status and thus provides pornographers with clearer-cut social roles and socioeconomic classes. Consequently, moving-image porn has seized upon these clear-cut roles, resulting in a vast body of neo-Victorian material preoccupied with socioeconomic class, age difference, and social status. Part and parcel of such a neo-Victorian erotic preoccupation is the deviant behavior that such strict social structures generate (and are perhaps designed to foster), the inevitable defiance of such structures, and the discipline and punishment one might enjoy from such defiance.

In neo-Victorian pornographies, deviant behavior and defiance of law goes both ways—porn enjoys restaging the sexual exploitations of the working classes and the young, but it also dwells on the exploitation and exposure of the upper classes and the authority figures. Sometimes these groups are shown to enjoy each other sexually in the same scene. Neo-Victorian pornographies are gothic play spaces in which those on both sides of a divide might taste the pleasures available in transgression, deviancy, and rule breaking. These play spaces are necessarily conflicted.

Neo-Victorian pornographies enjoy the pleasures and outrages of social hierarchy and class, capitalizing on uncritical nostalgia at the same time as it exploits the very real injustices of the Victorian era. For example, while Pandora/Blake enjoys "the courtesy and the elegance" of the nineteenth century they have no illusions concerning the injustice and oppression upon which this courtesy and elegance rested, nor the ways in which this legacy persists in the present day. For Blake this conflict is at the heart of the erotic appeal of the past: "I don't imagine it as this utopia. I know that there was so much that was fucked up about it and that's part of what I'm interested in—it kind of explodes a lot of our social problems that are still present. But class is so much more visible in the Victorian era, you can really get your teeth stuck into it and really think about it" (Blake). This visibility—the aesthetics of class—drive much of the pornographic engagement with the Victorian, while other visible differences, such as race, are often avoided or effaced. Even when effaced, however, these traces of violence haunt the margins of the porno-graphic text. The Victorian era yields caricatures and social roles that, while distant and repacked in neo-Victorian trappings, also signal a discomfiting legacy. Pornographers mine this legacy for its potential to arouse, provoke, disturb, and move. The past becomes a play space for erotic creativity and transformation.

*   *   *

In the remaining chapters, I analyze pornographic film adaptations of the Victorian—novels, ideologies, cultural practices—in an effort to understand not only how pornographic film operates as a genre, but also to see what pornographic film has to say about itself, the genres with which it intersects, and the particular idea of Victorian culture it is appropriating. In turn, just as pornography reflects the sexual imaginary of its consumers, so these films illuminate the complex ways in which porn consumers make use of "the Victorian" for erotic affect.

In chapter 1, "Behind Closed Doors: Neo-Victorian Pornographies," I ana-lyze hardcore films that set the sexual action in the nineteenth century. These films appropriate Victorian costume, customs, imagery, ideology, and other symbolism, revealing the rhetoric of transgression and sexual progressive-ness employed by pornography in staging the Victorian for erotic appeal. They illuminate the complex ways in which pornography and its consum-ers make use of "the Victorian" as a repressed yet perverse space populated by rigid class and gender distinctions, tantalizing thresholds and doorways ready to be crossed, secret domestic spaces ripe for sexualization, uptight but secretly sexual women, proper but perverse families, and other nineteenth-century sexual goings-on that pornography claims it has the guts to reveal. At the same time, these films situate themselves as heirs to a violent, racist, misogynistic, and pornographic legacy.

Chapters 2 and 3 address defiant pornographic engagements with two very different Victorian texts. In appropriations of both Bram Stoker's 1889 novel *Dracula* and Lewis Carroll's 1870–71 *Alice* stories, pornographers carve out Gothic spaces for transgressive consumption, oscillating power dynamics, and deviant sexualities. In chapter 2, "'I Want to Suck Your . . .': Fluids and Fluidity in Dracula Porn," I interrogate the status, meaning, use, and con-flation of gendered orifices and bodily fluids in pornographic adaptations of Bram Stoker's *Dracula*. I argue that in speaking the supposed silences of *Dracula*, porn adaptations of the novel must carefully navigate gender and sexuality. These adaptations reveal how hardcore film as a whole operates on anxious ground similar to that of Stoker's novel, simultaneously invoking and resisting sexual anxieties concerning gendered penetration, gendered fluids, and consumption. *Dracula*, as a culture text, mobilizes queered, gendered, and raced reformulations of consumer and consumed, queering ostensibly straight pornographies, destabilizing supposedly rigid gender dynamics, and resituating the colonial Other. Dracula adaptations invoke and redeploy the racialized implications of nineteenth-century vampirism, channeling racial and sexual subjectivity through vampirism. Dracula penetrates a supposedly sanctified pornotopia, enabling diverse and perverse sexual representations that I contend are instructive in understanding pornography as erotically engaged with fluidity, instability, and oscillating power dynamics.

In chapter 3, "'I'm Grown Up Now': Female Sexual Authorship and Coming of Age in Pornographic Adaptations of Lewis Carroll's *Alice* Books," I explore pornographic constructions of female sexual agency through the character of Alice. These films, I argue, use the Alice narrative to play out fantasies of womanly sexual authority through humor and sadomasochism. These films constitute recuperative projects that rescue Alice from her pawn status and position her as object, subject, and author within the pornographic text. I demonstrate the ways in which cultural understandings of the *Alice* stories are used by pornographic filmmakers to depict Wonderlands as joyful fantasy spaces for re-visionings of the normative and for developing and directing a particular pornographic female sexual subjectivity.

Chapters 4 and 5 concern sexual subjectivity and a pornographic legacy that can be traced back to the nineteenth century. Adaptations of *Jekyll & Hyde* and *Dorian Gray* play with duality and doppelgangers in conjunction with technologies of transformation and representation. These adaptations offer a sensory understanding of pornography's vital place in history and the erotic effects of tracing this history. In chapter 4, "Radically Both: Transformation and Crisis in Jekyll and Hyde Porn," transformation and duality take center stage. I argue that hardcore adaptations of Robert Louis Stevenson's *Strange Case of Dr. Jekyll and Mr. Hyde* utilize the concept of dual selves to explore crises in queer sexual subjectivity and female sexual desire. Through an analysis of the gay comedies *Heavy Equipment* (1977) and *Dr. Jerkoff and Mr. Hard* (1997), and the Vivid Video hetero drama *Jekyll and Hyde* (1999), I demonstrate the different ways gay and straight pornographers draw on the erotic pleasures of transformation as a way of exploring sexual crisis and a desire to break free from rigid and illusory formulations of identity and desire.

Meanwhile, adaptations of Oscar Wilde's queer classic *The Picture of Dorian Gray* extend and elaborate on explorations of the double by explicitly invoking histories of sexual representation in connection to the sensual qualities of technology and nostalgia. In chapter 5, "'Strange Legacies of Thought and Passion': Technologies of the Flesh and the Queering Effect of Dorian Gray," I continue my analysis of the relationship between pornography, legacy, doubles, and technology through a close analysis of two films based on Wilde's novel: *Take Off* (1978) and *Gluttony* (2001). More than any other text, *Dorian Gray* engenders pornographic engagement with erotic legacy and the role of technology in the erotics of representation. Like Wilde's novel, these films interrogate beauty and mortality, haunted at the margins by Wilde's tragic fate and the HIV/AIDS pandemic. Drawing on Wilde's magic portrait as a predecessor, *Take Off* and *Gluttony* ruminate on mortality and relate it to the sensual, tactile qualities of evolving, mobile visual technologies and the role these technologies play in sexual subjectivity. Pornographic film, Weston and West suggest, is the inheritor to Wilde's portrait. Both films draw on Wilde's tale in order to address the media on which the self is captured, the shifting technologies used to exhibit this self, and the relationship of technology and media to the corporeal body. Through their reimagining of histories of Hollywood and pornographic film respectively, *Take Off* and *Gluttony* signal the affective relationship between technology, pornography, decay, and popular culture, tracing a hardcore sexual history of the self that constitutes a sexual lineage.

In the conclusion, "Fueling the Lamps of Sexual Imagination," I discuss the recent discourse surrounding sex work and pornography that uncannily recalls the rhetoric of the Victorian age. Current bad-faith efforts to combat "sex trafficking" and regulate pornographic access and content signals a return to the sex panic of the nineteenth century. I argue that porn studies as a pedagogical movement is vital in turning the tide toward a more informed and helpful understanding of sex work and unsimulated sexual representation. Ironically, much of what pornography has to say about the Victorian era applies to the present day, an echo that pornographers are all too aware of. I advocate for further developments in porn studies, greater attention to meaningful engagement with porn as a media product and sphere of labor, and porn literacy as a standard component of education.

The films gathered here range from big-budget, big-studio efforts (*Jekyll and Hyde*) to the underground and frankly bemusing (*The Bride's Initiation*) to the everyday disposable (take your pick). The films cover a range of eras, budgets, genres, and significance within hardcore. I feel this is testament to the degree to which I am not speaking only of a niche subgenre of neo-Victorian porn. There are too many neo-Victorian films, spread across too many genres and periods, to describe this body of work as a niche. Indeed, I am using these films to explore the genre of pornography as a whole. While analyzing pornographic film by era is undoubtedly useful inasmuch as technology and cultural context impact pornographic content to various degrees, there are nevertheless important consistencies and tropes running through these eras that merit cohesive discussion. At the same time, I selected the films I explore in detail based on what interesting things they have to say about pornography and the Victorian Gothic. The fact that porn scholars are expected to explore a genre as a monolithic, "representative" whole, and then only through its most generic and uninspiring efforts, is not only unfair, it also inevitably fails to understand the genre or pornography *through* this very myopic exclusion.

Through my analysis of neo-Victorian hardcore, I contend that adult film responds to the allegedly "high art" nature of mainstream film/art by emphasizing porn's "low class" status, joyously perverting classic literature as a way of emphasizing pornography's alleged authenticity and transgressive nature. Indeed, pornographic adaptations can arguably tell us more about sexuality (or the perceived absence of it) in literature, canonical works, and mainstream culture than any other genre, yet still the pornographic representation does not "show all." We are able to ask questions about the original text being adapted simply by asking of the pornographic work, "Why this text?" and "Why this way?" As Kipnis asserts, pornography's opponents "seem universally overcome by a leaden, stultifying literalness, apparently never having heard of metaphor, irony, a symbol—even fantasy seems too challenging a concept" (163). Kipnis goes on to argue that pornography, so often claimed to have a contaminating, "pornifying" effect on mainstream culture, in fact has a much more complex "dialectical relation . . . to mainstream culture [that] makes it nothing less than a form of cultural critique. It refuses to let us off the hook for our hypocrisies" (166). This dialectical relationship is what I find most intriguing about pornography and is the focus of this project: porn's adaptation, appropriation, and critical reflection on mainstream culture and representation, as well as pornographic culture and representation itself.

BEHIND CLOSED DOORS
Neo-Victorian Pornographies

For the transgression to work, it must be played out
against a background of normality.
—Umberto Eco, "How to Recognize a Porn Movie"

Humans seem to find contrasts and juxtapositions very appealing when it comes to sex. The idea of a gentleman whose
impeccable manners and finely tuned social etiquette mask a
depraved sexual mind—that's a turn on. The refined, upper-
class lady who behind closed doors is a ravenous, insatiable
slut—what man doesn't want that woman? Everything was
so forbidden back then, and of course we know anything
forbidden is an instant turn on.
—Nica Noelle, adult filmmaker

In his review of the notorious German video *Extra Terrestrian: Die Ausserirdische* (dir. Lidko and Sigi Entinger, 1995), popularly known as *E.T.: The
Porno*, online B-movie reviewer The Cinema Snob exclaims, "This movie
takes place in the Victorian era? Why? What the hell is the point of that?"
("E.T. the Porno"). His question is central to my discussion: What is the
point of setting a pornographic film (let alone a pornographic sci-fi film) in
the Victorian era? In the film, E.T. is sent to Earth on a mission to examine
the population's "strange customs." An omnipresent voice informs E.T. on
departure, "This Earth is a place inhabited by strange beings with strange
customs that will perhaps leave you scared." These "strange customs" are sex
acts, which intrigue E.T. enough to gradually get involved. What is interesting about this relatively plotless and amateurish production is that the filmmakers wholeheartedly committed to setting it during the Victorian period,
complete with costumes, period furniture, and stilted dialect. This suggests

that the premise of alien beings learning about sexual customs would do best to visit the Victorian era, where, according to this film, human sexuality and its strangeness are most emphasized. E.T. explains to the humans, "On my planet we do not have this custom, therefore I was invited to come to this planet to learn more of the earthlings. To learn of your ways to act, to think, and to get pleasure." The Victorians, the film suggests, are the best version of "earthlings" from which to learn these things.

The Cinema Snob's baffled query suggests a certain level of incompetence on the part of the filmmakers, as if the setting were a random choice, demonstrative of the hasty and slapdash process of pornography filmmaking. Porn, we are told, is simply unsimulated sexual media designed to inspire arousal, masturbation, and climax, so once the legal parameters are removed, why would a lowly pornographer bother with anything more than two naked humans going at it in a sparsely furnished apartment? Certainly, many pornographers have done just that.

With *E.T.*, however, produced during the 1990s when video had taken over, budgets were typically scant, and quantity often took precedence over quality, it is clear that writer/directors Lidko and Siggi Entinger had something more novel in mind. The costumes and sheer gusto of the endeavor are impressive in spite of the obviously tiny budget suggesting the nineteenth-century

2. E.T. receives oral sex from a Victorian lady in *Extra Terrestrian: Die Ausserirdische*, a.k.a. *E.T.: The Porno* (1995).

setting was no more a random choice than that of crafting a disturbingly sophisticated E.T. costume.[1] The sheer number of pornographic films from various decades and genres that employ the Victorian period suggest that there is indeed a point to setting hardcore films in the Victorian period, even those that feature alien beings. Pornography has consistently drawn on the Victorians as part of a sexual and pornographic legacy, as a way of staging the transgressions of the present and establishing and eroticizing different subject positions in connection to gender, class, sexuality, and race.

Neo-Victorian fictions—"contemporary fiction that engages with the Victorian era, at either the level of plot, structure or both" (Hadley 4)—have increased in quantity and popularity over the past five decades, demonstrating an interest in and need for "the Victorians" as a way of shaping and understanding modern culture. As Louisa Hadley asserts, "Rather than merely being another manifestation of that [wider] cultural fascination [. . .] neo-Victorian fictions seek to both reinsert the Victorians into their particular historical context and engage with contemporary uses of the Victorians which efface that historical context" (6). Moreover, the Victorians serve as a useful cultural touchstone with which to understand and grapple with present-day discourses over sex, identity, technology, and politics. The Victorians are perceived to be the originators of the bulk of our understanding of these areas and are therefore our privileged "historical 'other'" (Kucich and Sadoff xi). With this in mind, it is unsurprising that as soon as the hardcore feature became prolific in the 1970s, pornographic film took to appropriating the Victorian as part of its erotic appeal. In fact, early hardcore films such as *An English Tragedy* (1921), an adaptation of the 1908 erotic novel *The Way of a Man with a Maid*, intimate an uncanny legacy of pornographic representations of the Victorians. This legacy ties together the history of pornography, linking actual pornographic imagery of the Victorian and Edwardian eras to the neo-Victorian recreations of the twentieth and twenty-first centuries. Pornographic uses of the Victorian expose broader uses of the Victorian era as a way of working through gender and sexual politics. In the process, porn exposes "a surprising (and perhaps frightening) closeness to our past" (Joyce 3) that is, nonetheless, pleasurable.

In the present chapter, I will explore and analyze a collection of pornographic films that set the action in the nineteenth century. They appropriate costume, customs, imagery, and other symbolism that twentieth- and twenty-first-century culture associates with the Victorian era, revealing the rhetoric employed by pornography in staging the Victorian for erotic appeal. I have chosen to include films that are representative in their use of the Victorian era and notable in the degree to which certain themes and impulses are present. The chosen texts also offer some of the conflict present in how hardcore utilizes Victorian tropes and ephemera to explore and eroticize gendered, classed, and raced subject positions.

Behind Closed Doors: Porning the Victorians

The phrase "behind closed doors" occurs in pornographic marketing materials with amusing regularity. A representative example of this rhetoric can be found in the blurb for Nica Noelle's all-male movie, *Tales of Victorian Lust: Power and Struggle* (2014), which promises a narrative set when "lust between men could only be expressed behind closed doors." Even when, as with *Can't Be Roots XXX* (2011), the story is set on a United States plantation, the nineteenth-century setting nevertheless mobilizes the rhetoric of Victorian English secrecy: "Evasive [Angles] has brought you a wild journey into the minds of white women back in the day and what really went on behind closed doors!!" The fact that all of the sexual action takes place *out* of doors (or in stables that don't even have any doors) did not dissuade the filmmakers from employing this tantalizing post-Victorianist catchphrase.

The existence of a vast body of nineteenth-century pornography conflicts with our understanding of the repressed Victorian, generating a dual vision of the Victorians as both perverse and repressed. The mid-nineteenth century saw an explosion in pornographic works, both literary and visual, of varying price, collected and traded among the elites, and also sold in public to people of any sex, age, or class. Historian Linda Nead describes Holywell Street of London as the center of the trade in pornography in England, a trade that grew increasingly prolific as the century progressed (161). Literature and pornography are regarded as oppositional, existing in different spheres, occupied with different interests, the latter consumed by "other" Victorians. Indeed, Steven Marcus goes so far as to say pornography is "profoundly, and by nature, anti-literature and anti-art" (195). In reality, canonical works of Victorian literature were adjacent to, not separate from, pornography and obscene works not only in terms of physical proximity but also in terms of style and thematic content. As Tanya Pikula argues, the tropes and language of pornographic literature can be traced in the rhetoric of Bram Stoker's *Dracula*. Pikula asserts that Stoker's "descriptions of vampire-otherness are in fact thoroughly structured by the language and plot codes of the Victorian pornographic industry" (284). It stands to reason that other novelists of the mid- to late nineteenth century were similarly exposed to and influenced by the language and visuals of pornography. Neo-Victorian pornographies seem highly aware of the tensions and affinities experienced with their Victorian ancestors—the originators of the modern pornographic genre and the revolutionaries of sexual discourse.

Pornography, always the distasteful, underground, social-climbing cousin, participates in a complex symbiotic relationship to the mainstream (McNair 15). Pornographic renderings of "legitimate" culture reunite these siblings, revealing the creative influence of pornography on mainstream writers, and not merely the reverse. Neo-Victorian pornographies distance themselves from the Victorian in that they must speak the sexual silences of the nineteenth-century text too coy to speak for itself. Yet at the same time, pornography is performing a recovery project, reconnecting the strands that constitute a discursive and representational legacy stemming from the Victorian period.

Culturally, we recognize and enjoy the competing images of the Victorians. Victorianist Peter N. Stearns argues that scholars of the early twentieth century constructed a stereotype of "the repressed Victorian" (47), which led to the cultural truism that the Victorians were "responsible for creating the sex-negative culture that twentieth century 'moderns' have rebelled against" (47). In an attempt to revise this stereotype, more recent scholars have unwittingly established a new stereotype of Victorian sexuality that is, in Stearns's view, "overly sanguine" (47). The truth, Stearns asserts, is a combination of the two stereotypes: Victorians regarded sex as a powerful force that could lead to good or ill, depending on whether the sex act was "sensual" or "spiritual" in nature. Likewise, in her book *Unauthorized Pleasures: Accounts of Victorian Erotic Experience*, Ellen Bayuk Rosenman explores Victorian sexual dissidence and uncategorized sexual pleasures, arguing that Victorian erotic pleasure was characterized by "fluidity and multiplicity" (4). Rosenman cautions that "the meanings and ideological valences of Victorian sexual behaviors are seldom simple and cannot be understood in terms of our own modern politics of sexual transgression" (4). Nevertheless, we persist in forcing the Victorians into this model for our own erotic gratification. This persistence is particularly visible in neo-Victorian pornography.

Pornographic articulations of the Victorian draw specifically on both the repressed and the sanguine stereotypes of Victorian sexuality to initiate this sense of transgression: while the pornographic adaptation utilizes the repressed stereotype as a way of "exposing" or "opening up" some kind of off-limits group of people, the appropriation would not work without an accompanying sense that what was really going on was much more dirty and perverse. Wash West, writer/director of the neo-Victorian all-male porn films *Dr. Jerkoff and Mr. Hard* (1997) and *Gluttony* (2001) observes, "Repression necessarily forced the writers and artists of the [Victorian period] to find metaphors—terrestrial or supernatural—that gave voice to their unexpressed desires" (West). The act of porning seeks to demystify the metaphor and express those desires.

However, porning upholds other repressed ideas in the process. Pornography needs repression in order to speak transgressively. As Carmine Sarracino and Kevin M. Scott ambivalently observe in their book, *The Porning of America*, "The main difference, then, between Puritanism and porn is that instead of fleeing from sex, porn, proceeding from the same premises, indulges in it transgressively and promiscuously" (200). Pornographic appropriations of the Victorian bring to bear the public/private, sensual/spiritual split that Stearns delineates, both upholding these divides and deconstructing them. This tension is at the heart of pornographic pleasure.

Pornography utilizes "the Victorian" rather loosely as a generic rhetorical lure connoting secrecy, hypocrisy, and strict divisions between public and private. In the majority of these films and the blurbs they utilize, any era marked as antique or more generally "old" will be categorized as Victorian or Edwardian without much concern for the distinctions between periods. The only concern is that antiquity equates to repression and hypocrisy, and repression and hypocrisy equate to the Victorians. The Victorians are sexy in their uptight clothing and attitude insofar as the pornographic film might expose naughty goings-on behind closed doors. A handy example of this tendency in action is the press release for *My Mother's Best Friend Vol. 4: Lost in Time* (2011) posted on the adult film site Adult DVD Talk. The film is part of an older woman/younger man series that flirts with incest, and is a period piece. The publicist states, "It's set in the Edwardian Era and has a Jane Austen look to it." When a porn consumer remarks, "My first thought is that Jane Austin [*sic*] wasn't an Edwardian. She was a Georgian and died 80 years before the start of the Edwardian period." The writer of the press release responds, "I was describing more the style of the porn as Jane Austen not the time period—as in period piece with forbidden love and great costumes" ("Jane Austen Porn"). Likewise, the specific 1915 setting of *Bedtime Tales* is simultaneously referred to as "Victorian" in the film's dialogue. The blurb states that it is an era "when even a hint of ankle could be considered scandalous," but on the other hand, "of course, behind closed doors they were showing off a lot more than just ankles!" In this way, porn flattens the past even as it exploits it for erotic affect.

3. Newspaper advertisement for *The Naughty Victorians* (1975).

The Naughty Victorians (1975) is based on an Edwardian pornographic novel, *The Way of a Man with a Maid* (1908). However, probably due to the novel's consistency with Victorian pornographic style (and the accompanying tendency on the part of publishers to include it in Victorian erotica anthologies), the filmmakers either assumed the novel was indeed Victorian or felt audiences would be more intrigued by a Victorian-set film. No matter the reason, the marketing rhetoric confirms a trading in the Victorian that emphasizes an exposure of sordid behaviors going on behind a screen of propriety: "Queen Victoria would be appalled . . . publicly, at least!" Films such as this demonstrate a pornographic rhetoric that capitalizes on the eroticism of the sexual practices of the supposedly repressed Victorians, but viewed from the vantage point of the supposedly sexually enlightened.

Reclaiming the Feminine in Neo-Victorian Pornography

In a recent interview with oral history podcast *The Rialto Report*, adult-film legend Nina Hartley describes her one and only visit to an X-rated film theater to see the Sharon McNight–directed 1976 film, *Autobiography of a Flea*: "I didn't think at the time, 'Wow, I'm being so bold and feminist by going in by myself.' It was like, I want to go and see the movie and I didn't have any friends who I could say, 'Hey, let's go and sneak into a dirty movie!' I didn't think to ask anybody to go with me. I just *went*. . . . that was the only one— the only time I did it. . . . I just never thought to do it again." The film Hartley snuck into is an early example of a female-directed film as well as one of the first feature-length hardcore adaptations of a Victorian pornographic novel. Marketed using a feminine appeal to high production values and class, the film was what McNight describes as "pretty porn": "It did very well, as it was a great deal more femininely oriented than most of the movies of the time had been. It was pretty porn; it looked like *Barry Lyndon*" (Frank).

The anonymously written 1888 novel upon which the film is based, however, is far from what we might call "pretty." Incest, rape, and graphic descriptions of violent, physically damaging sex abound. Yet McNight's adaptation is indeed pretty and lushly mounted. Moreover, the film transforms the passive victimhood of the novel's female protagonists into a Gothic sisterhood characterized by agency and lust. Hartley is not the only porn veteran to have noted her interest in nineteenth-century pornography. When I interviewed writer/director Nica Noelle in 2012, she told me of her love of nineteenth-century pornography: "There was [. . .] some great, albeit arguably disturbing, erotic literature produced during Victorian times, such as my favorite novel *A Man with a Maid*. [. . .] It's my favorite book. I waited all my life to watch those fantasies unfold in front of me. I imagined them so many hundreds, if not thousands of times over the years since I first read *A Man with a Maid*" (Noelle). Noelle adapted the novel herself in 2009. Furthermore, when I asked what her dream project would be, she stated that she would adapt the novel again in the hopes that her evolution as a filmmaker over the past three years would do the book justice (Noelle). Evidently, these novels carry great weight with women, in spite of—or perhaps because of—the disturbing content.

Pornography is typically seen as a masculine genre, made by men for men. As evidenced by the testimony above, this is not exclusively the case. Neo-Victorian pornographies in particular privilege and glorify the feminine, domestic, private sphere maintained by middle-class Victorian culture, merging the "feminine" heritage film and the "masculine" hardcore porn film. This has resulted in a collection of hybrid texts that typically envision erotic domestic spaces occupied and controlled by women while also signaling violence and danger, if only at the edges of the text. These films Gothicize these spaces through their emphasis on thresholds and secrecy and cast them as rich with potential for feminine exploration, transgression, and pleasure. The repressed, private Victorian canvas offers these pleasures up in tantalizing fashion, promising to reveal the private feminine sexual pleasures going on within. These neo-Victorian pornographies work in the thrilling intersection between the safe, contained, and domestic and the perverse domestic transgression, sexual mobility, and sexual danger afforded by period-bound containment.

Such aesthetic, nostalgic productions might understandably be dismissed as sexist for their promotion of a stifling feminine domestic space and effacement of the race and gender oppression that often shore up these representations. Susan Faludi regards lingerie, a symbol favored by pornographers in exploring the tensions of neo-Victorian erotics, as something that "celebrate[s] the repression, not the flowering, of female sexuality. The ideal Victorian lady it had originally been designed for, after all, wasn't supposed to have any libido" (189). However, as Jane Juffer points out in her analysis of lingerie giant Victoria's Secret, "the nostalgia for a more contained body and a more 'secret' sexuality within the trappings of Victorian, imperialist England" is not simple "backlash" (146). Rather, "the sale and consumption of lingerie . . . illustrate the contradictions and gaps in the attempts to reassert a bounded private sphere; for [Victoria's Secret], the emphasis on privacy is undercut by the appeal to women as consumers in pursuit of their own pleasures—versions of the New Woman" (Juffer 147). Just as Victoria's Secret "wants to claim *both* a tradition and a rearticulation of femininity" (Juffer 161), so neo-Victorian pornographies actively pursue and attempt to inhabit, if only fleetingly, the space opened up by this duality. While Laura Kipnis points out that "pornography would be nowhere without its most flagrant border transgression, this complete disregard for the public/private divide" (171), it would be more accurate to say that pornography is constantly regarding the public/private divide. This divide is constantly being observed and renegotiated for pornographic appeal.

The classy, palatable, and clean female bodies associated with white, middle-class, Victorian femininity distinguish them from the "material, defiantly vulgar, corporeal" bodies of pornography (Kipnis 132). Nineteenth-century set pornographies bring these bodies together in a pornographic recovery of white feminine domestic space that is sexually transgressive, disobedient, and conducted in private. A primary signifying tool in this recovery is the ample use of Victorian clothing and technologies of private communication used to establish and deconstruct boundaries of class and gender represented by public and private space. Clothing (layers to remove, interiors to discover and uncover), architecture (labyrinthine old houses, corridors, keyholes, and doorways), and technology (writing, recording, photography, film) are major components of this transgressive gesture. As Jennifer Green-Lewis notes, the Victorian "designates an aesthetic, rather than a precisely historical, concept" (31). In this way the nineteenth century is sometimes porned through nothing more than a stately home and some petticoats. This engagement with the Victorian may appear one-dimensional and crude, but it is nonetheless meaningful. In the visual vocabulary of porn, these seemingly minor details carry weight. The choices made in these neo-Victorian porn films, whether they be the product of extravagant productions rooted in knowledge of the Victorian era or the residue of accidents, afterthoughts, and haphazard filmmaking, are a method of expressing erotic engagement with and erotic upending of nostalgic feminine Victorian domesticity.

The nostalgic eroticism and feminization of porn enacted by Victorian-set porn films is a more literary form of what David Church calls "cinecrophilia," an eroticized "pastness" to the point of becoming a sexual fetish ("Stag Films" 48). A key aspect of cinecrophilia is the way this pastness legitimizes pornographic texts, transforming them into "erotica" ("Stag Films" 49). For Church, conflicted gender and sexual politics are mapped onto these vintage pornographic films, the good old days seeming less complicated, "more authentic and natural than the world of hardcore today" ("Stag Films" 54). This is where the nostalgia for Victorian "erotica" (for that is what it has become) slightly differs. Certainly, this nostalgia is in part a yearning for the quaint social mores of that time (and, lest we forget, the lavish costumes). But another, not unrelated, aspect of this nostalgia is the appeal of a fantasy play space removed from our own, characterized by sexual repression, oppressive gender and race politics, private perversion and public hypocrisy, and an obsession with sex masked by science.

The Perverse Pleasures of Science and Medicine

In the opening scene of the 1985 porn video *Bedtime Tales*, we are treated to a view of chief maid Miss Cummings (Colleen Brennan), whom we can see through a keyhole. She is undressing in her room. We occupy the viewing position of Walter (Tom Byron), the young master of the house who is crouched down and masturbating. "In another three years he'll be in the trenches in France," the narrator explains, "but now he's a virgin about to experience his ultimate dream." At this point, Miss Cummings notices she is being watched, gathers up her clothes, and bursts through the door. Her initial horror quickly transforms into agitated opportunity as she hastily makes excuses for Walter's misconduct and failure to follow the rules of "[respecting] a woman's privacy."

The well-worn conceit of the male voyeur intruding on the privacy of a woman is complicated in this scene, as Miss Cummings proceeds to bring Walter into the bedroom for a talking to about male sexual needs and the dangers of masturbation. "The common word for it is 'frigging,'" Miss Cummings rambles on in a flustered state, "to—frig oneself. I—I've heard that a young man may permanently exhaust himself by overdoing it. It can do permanent damage. . . . I would suspect that the reason for that would be that the young man, in the heat of his passion, may perhaps grab his, uh—penis, I believe it's called—so hard that he might cause some certain strain or damages. I wouldn't want you to injure yourself, Walter." Miss Cummings proceeds to educate and carefully attend to Walter's penis.

4. Miss Cummings instructs Walter in *Bedtime Tales* (1985).

Bedtime Tales, a low-budget series of vaguely connected vignettes set in different time periods, offers a sophisticated and delightfully perverse understanding of nineteenth-century science. Sexologists such as Richard von Krafft-Ebing (1840–1902) and Havelock Ellis (1859–1939) established a *scientia sexualis* that in the more malignant cases Foucault refers to as a "pornography of the morbid . . . characteristic of the *fin de siècle* society" (*History of Sexuality* 54). Foucault continues,

> What needs to be situated, therefore, is not the threshold of a new rationality whose discovery was marked by Freud—or someone else—but the progressive formation (and also the transformations) of that "interplay of truth and sex" which was bequeathed to us by the nineteenth century [. . .] Misunderstandings, avoidances, and evasions were only possible, and only had their effects, against the background of this strange endeavor: to tell the truth of sex. (56–57)

Pornography, as Linda Williams (*Hard Core*) and others have argued, takes up the same mantle, and more recently has been blamed for its failures in providing sex education to a nation of individuals denied open discourse on issues of sexuality. Lisa Z. Sigel's contention that "pornography and sexology influenced each other at the margins of their disciplines" ("The Rise" 116) is a heritage present in pornographic film of the late twentieth century. The characters and films use feigned innocence and medical objectivity as a way to initiate sex, suggesting that the Victorian era used serious medical inquiry as an alibi for salacious and perverse exploration.

The character of Miss Cummings embodies this alibi, nervously appropriating discourses surrounding masturbation as a way to initiate sex with the young son of her mistress and reverse the power dynamics of their relationship. Spermatorrhea was a quintessentially Victorian disease with no scientific foundation. During the mid-nineteenth century it was believed that "the excessive discharge of sperm caused by illicit or excessive sexual activity, especially masturbation, [would] cause anxiety, nervousness, lassitude, impotence, and, in its advanced stages, insanity and death" (Rosenman 16). Spermatorrhea panic resulted in truly horrific "treatment," including physically and emotionally traumatic nighttime devices such as "penile rings for little boys—spiked on the inside, to insure pain, even bloodshed, if the penis swelled during sleep" (Kendrick 90).

Bedtime Tales takes this painful historical remnant and transforms it into an opportunity for pleasure. Not only that, Miss Cummings uses class and gender distinctions to procure pleasures for herself and also for the bourgeois young man in her stead vulnerable to the horrors of modern medicine. Echoing the Victorian panic over masturbation, Miss Cummings utilizes such sexual "science" as a way of accomplishing results quite in the opposite direction than that intended. She also plays on perceptions of gender and age by situating her sexual advances within her role as governess, educator, and caregiver to the elite young men of the house. Suggesting that "maybe just this once I can assist you in your needs and stroke it in a safe and proper way," but insisting she must not watch, Miss Cummings' actions employ repressive Victorian sexual knowledge in an ironic fashion as a means of initiating forbidden sex. She exploits the medical sphere, as well as her age and gender, in order to indulge her pleasures. In its mockery of the belief in the dangers of masturbation, the scene also demonstrates the paradoxical nature of such taboos: that they are perversely apt to be used in attaining goals contrary to their intention.

Sexology and its perverse pleasures apparently still resonate with contemporary, internet-based pornographers. "Hysteria" (2013), directed by and starring Ned Mayhem, offers a similarly satirical treatment of Victorian medicine through the lens of queer porn. The scene is hosted on the queer porn website, *Pink and White Productions*, a company owned by queer woman of color, Shine Louise Houston. The site is committed to curating queer and feminist pornographies. That is, they produce "sexy and exciting images that reflect today's blurred gender lines and fluid sexualities" ("About Pink and White Productions").

According to the site, the scene in question is a "historically inaccurate tale of medical progress." A Victorian maiden is suffering from hysteria. She seeks medical help, yet the doctor's advanced instruments cannot do the job. No matter which advanced or experimental instrument the doctor uses, the maiden only appears to grow more agitated. Ultimately, the doctor feels he must sacrifice his body in the name of medicine; the only way to cure the maiden's hysteria is to tap into her masculinity. Thus, following doctor's orders, she buggers the doctor using a strap on.

Just as *Bedtime Tales* utilizes Victorian sexology and medical developments to exploit the privileged male, so "Hysteria" turns the tables on the doctor, once his tools prove insufficient. The short film lampoons Victorian sexual concerns, specifically addressing the remarkable medical solutions to "hysteria"—namely, vibrators and other instruments deployed by doctors and midwives designed to elicit orgasm in women. As Rachel Maines explains in her history of the vibrator, "hysteria" was a disease that afflicted women, "thought to be a consequence of lack of sufficient sexual intercourse,

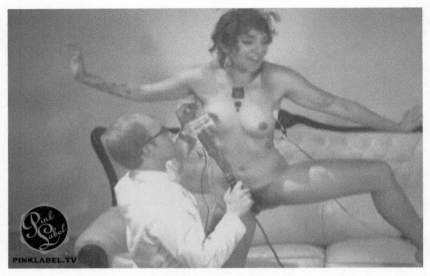

5. The doctor tries to cure his patient in "Hysteria" (PinkLabel.tv, 2012).

deficiency of sexual gratification, or both" (23) and reached epidemic levels in the nineteenth century. Maines argues that the medicalization of the
condition and the manner of treatment at the hands of medical professionals indicates and perpetuates an androcentric standard of sex (coitus) that
has persisted to this day (114–15). According to this androcentric model, if
a woman cannot climax from vaginal penetration she must be faulty.

"Hysteria" satirizes the sexist medicalization of female experience associated with the nineteenth century, transforming medicalization into a means
of sexual pleasure for women (and men). The maiden in the short is clearly
making up her symptoms, agreeing whenever necessary with a wicked grin,
barely able to contain her sexual excitement. Likewise, when the doctor performs the "procedure" (fingering her vagina with his gloved fingers while
she stimulates her clitoris with a Hitachi magic wand), instead of crying out
the standard "fuck me" of pornographic rhetoric, the patient cries, "Oh, yes!
Cure my hysteria! Cure me! Cure me!" The eventual anal penetration of the
doctor, and his evident pleasure embodying the female patient, is suggestive
of the erotics of the doctor-patient relationship (particularly the pleasures
of administering medicine) but it also inverts the power dynamic of this relationship. The medical procedure is performed upon the body of the male
practitioner in order to cure the female patient. In this film, it is the man
who is penetrated for the woman's sexual satisfaction.

Just as with *Bedtime Tales*, the characters of "Hysteria" are shown to be fully in on the joke of exploiting medicine—specifically its absurd and misguided forms—as a means of achieving forbidden sexual pleasure. Both films demonstrate a pleasurable, tongue-in-cheek awareness of the absurdity of Victorian hypocrisy, the paradoxes of antiquated sexology, and the transgressive joys of exposing and reclaiming Victorian medical rhetoric. The rhetoric is seized from the hands of patriarchal doctors and (pleasurably for all) practiced on the male body.

Neo-Victorian Technologies of the Pornographic

It is a popular truism that advances in technology have almost all been spurred by pornography. VHS beat out Betamax because of porn (untrue); the internet is *for* porn (possibly true). Technologies are in this way infused with sexual meaning due to the proximity of their prurient uses and the illicit ends to which these technologies might be put. Technologies also accrue powerful nostalgic force and have been incorporated into neo-Victorian pornographic content as a site for transgression and a method of deviant sexual exploration. The DVD blurb for Nica Noelle's 2009 vignette film, *Lesbian Adventures: Victorian Love Letters*, reads, "In a magical time before email and cell phones, there were only letters. Sweetheart Video rewinds to simpler and more erotic times in this beautiful film about Victorian passions, repression, and undeniable lust." The rhetoric of Noelle's film reflects pornography's characterization of Victorian technology as analog, quaint, and conducive to romance . . . as well as tantalizing punishment. Additionally, the blurb yokes analog technology to the release of repressed pleasure. Victorian technology is reframed as less complicated than the digital communication technologies of today, yet in reality the Victorian period invented and enjoyed many of the same technologies that we claim as modern and that facilitate democratic pornography consumption.

The printing press made copying en masse and distribution of written pornography easier and cheaper, while the expansion of consumer culture in the developing city meant diverse crowds had access to pornography and other media in unprecedented ways. It was (and still is) technologies of the visual and of mass distribution that most worried authorities and prompted legal intervention such as the Obscene Publications Act of 1857, for consumers need not be literate, need not even purchase the product, in order to consume it when it is laid out in storefronts or disseminated cheaply on street corners. Much like the internet today, Victorian mass media was feared in terms of its creation of "an over-stimulated and uncontrollable public" (Nead 154). Nevertheless, we tend to think of the Victorians as a literary crowd. Pornographers do, also, perhaps in ways that mirror our own projected nostalgic desires.

Pornography is a particularly revealing genre when tracing the development of technology from the Victorians to the present. While the only surviving stag films date back to around 1907, the first pornographic films were made at the end of the nineteenth century (Thompson 17). Prior to this, the Victorians enjoyed a multitude of different visual technologies, all of which were used in one way or another for erotic imagery (Williams, "Corporealized Observers" 4). The fact that so much vintage pornography actually depicts Victorians surely bears on the pornographic interest in and erotic associations of Victorianism in the twentieth and twenty-first centuries. What's more, the imagery and narrative structure of these older pornographies bear a striking resemblance to the porn that followed, right up to the present moment. AVN reporter Steve Austin noted in 1991, "What's the difference between the old silent 8 millimeter loops and the video features of today? [. . .] The guys take their sox [sic] off now" (Jennings 226). More recently, Peter Alilunas remarks that the "decontextualized clips" viewed on tube sites are "absolutely the offspring of the [. . .] trajectory from stag films to loops to [Jamie] Gillis's excursion into the San Francisco night [in *On the Prowl*]" (280n3). To this I would add the trajectory from the literary to the visual pornographies of the nineteenth century and on into the moving images of the twentieth.

So, while the Victorians clearly had quite modern technologies, and present-day erotic media is reflected in that of the nineteenth century, pornographers tend to prefer a less advanced vision of the Victorian, one that is private and contained. The Victorians of twentieth-and twenty-first-century pornographic film are typically not perusing pornographic etchings in the windows of shops or trading pornographic photographs with groups of friends. Instead, they are writing letters and diaries from within the eroticized private domestic space. By resexualizing this feminine domain of propriety, pornography resituates the erotic pleasures of technology from the masculine, the public, and the male homosocial to the feminine, the private, and the female homosocial.

Noelle's *Victorian Love Letters* and Eric Edwards's SOV narrative feature *Memoirs of a Chambermaid* (1987) engage with writing and secret erotic communication through an audiovisual format. These films, marketed to a diverse audience during two quite distinct periods in porn history, nostalgically eroticize the aesthetics of Victoriana (architecture, clothing, décor) and premodern communication technologies. They are infused with themes of class difference, forbidden love, disobedience, and punishment, all of which are tied to the written word. These inward, domestic, private, feminine spaces are porned to reveal transformative, deviant, and queer desires circulating in these same spaces and initiated by writing.[2]

The written confessional has been a staple of pornography since Aretino's *Ragionamenti* (1534–1536). Aretino created what would become the prototype for the pornographic tradition: "the explicit representation of sexual activity, the form of the dialogue between women, the discussion of the behavior of prostitutes and the challenge to moral conventions of the day" (Hunt 26). Furthermore, the act of writing itself has been connected to sexuality through authors such as the Marquis de Sade (1740–1814), with his spools of obsessive sadistic pornographic novels, and "Walter," the anonymous author of *My Secret Life* (ca. 1888), a massive eleven-volume confessional detailing the various sexual exploits of a Victorian gentleman. Then there is Henry Spencer Ashbee, "the archetypal Victorian gentleman with a secret" (Gibson xi), a bibliophile who devoted his life to collecting and documenting obscene works, producing three immense bibliographies between 1877 and 1885. The work of these men carries notions of illicit work and secrecy. Walter and Ashbee were elite gentlemen, the former anonymous and the latter working diligently to demonstrate his utter libidinal distance from his subject matter. To wit, "The passions are not excited. [. . .] I give only so much as is necessary to form a correct estimate of the style of the writer, of the nature of the book, or the course of the tale, not sufficient to enflame the passions" (qtd. in Gibson 52). The necessary anonymity of so many pornographic writers and collectors working outside the law, coupled with the now rather amusing denial of any prurient interest, has created a neo-Victorian pornographic indulgence in the illicit thrills of salacious writing and the punishments that might ensue if caught.

Edwards's *Memoirs of a Chambermaid* and Noelle's *Victorian Love Letters* both represent their respective production years. Edwards's film is easily the most narratively complex. Produced toward the end of the 1980s, *Memoirs* is more richly developed than some of its contemporaries because it was made to appeal to the emerging couples market. Noelle's series of vignettes is also slightly more narratively developed than its contemporaries yet demonstrates the extent to which pornography—even that bound by narrative—had by the 2000s become more focused on extensive sex scenes.

Using a vignette format, Noelle presents four scenes in which a sexual encounter is instigated by a love letter. The scenes do not utilize the written word, or verbalization of the written word, beyond the initial premise. The erotics of each scene are in fact grounded firmly in Victorian aesthetics, particularly costuming, with an emphasis on excess material, bodies spilling out of tightly bound undergarments, and sexual contact made through the gaps and holes in the extra-material bloomers each woman wears. As the DVD promises, it "featur[es] authentic Victorian dresses and undergarments, shot and filmed in an [*sic*] real Victorian mansion."

Memoirs of a Chambermaid also utilizes period costuming as well as a Gothic Victorian house, yet it foregrounds oration and the written word as primary sites of eroticism. Noelle's sex scenes are long, relatively unmediated, and aurally punctuated only by the sounds of sexual activity and pleasure. These choices are in line with modern pornographies as well as Noelle's broader concern to construct a sense of authenticity and real female orgasms as opposed to scripted lines during the sex. In contrast, the late-1980s *Memoirs* features sex scenes that are soft-focus and less attentive to the mechanics of sex; they frequently end without the typical money shot and are often disrupted by narrative interruptions and editing. Edwards, aided by his girlfriend (who also co-wrote the script), intentionally created this film for the newly emerging "couples" market of the 1980s. Edwards explains that aside from plot and buildup to the sex scenes, a couples film should not have many "clinical shots. . . . In fact, in a couple's movie, I may not even want to see the obligatory Pop Shot unless it's done tastefully" (Edwards). Indeed, in Edwards's film, there are few "pop shots," very little visual emphasis on penetration—the "meat shot"—and great emphasis on reading, writing, fantasizing, and articulating of desires. As the male love object, Jason repeatedly states to his lover, in place of traditionally pornographic articulations of physical lust, "I love it when you write."

In their own distinct way, *Victorian Love Letters* and *Memoirs of a Chambermaid* eroticize the written word in a manner that frames literature as feminine and private, yet at the same time disrupt this boundary by visualizing it as part of deviant sexual practices playing out behind closed doors for our visual pleasure. Again, by articulating fetishized components of private Victorian culture in film pornography, the cultural boundaries that establish gender and class norms are reinforced in order to be "trashed" by the pornographic impulse. Neo-Victorian conceptions of public and private spheres framed by class and gender open up a thrilling space for women characterized by trespass. Any ensuing punishments, threatened or realized, are framed as part of a pleasurable fantasy encounter.

Hierarchy and discipline are established as erotic components of neo-Victorian porn in two of Noelle's vignettes ("Petulant Little Girls" and "Secret

Muse"). In these scenes, the older woman verbally and physically chastises the younger partner for her secret writings, recalling and eroticizing a bygone era where the categories of "adult" and "child" were distinct and reinforced by society (Sarracino and Scott 32–33). In "Petulant Little Girls," Magdalene discovers Nicole writing love letters and punishes her with an open-hand spanking that eventually becomes a caress. Likewise, in "Secret Muse," Julia Ann jealously demands to see the letter Zoe is writing, leading to a physical struggle for the letter that swiftly turns into a passionate kiss. Noelle eroticizes exposure, shame, and discipline while the private scene of writing serves as the contained, feminine arena that will be pleasurably transgressed.

The aesthetics of Victorian femininity become the focus of contained sexuality and its imminent release. The erotics of each scene rely less on the premise of the written word and more on the concept of the bound, private body and its imminent exposure. This containment and release is framed by disciplinary action and the power dynamics of age and status. Unlike Juffer's clean, "orifice-less" bodies of the Victoria's Secret catalogue, the female bodies in *Victorian Love Letters*, while not grotesque, are certainly uncontained both visually and aurally. The use of corsets, with breasts spilling from the top, sights and sounds of sexual fluids, and the loud and often messy female orgasms emphasize the way pornography relies on the concept of feminine, private, contained space for pornographic pleasure just as much as its deconstruction composes the scene. Graphic, noisy depictions of cunnilingus, then, are emphasized by the framing of a tightly laced Victorian boot in shot.

6. A secret tryst in *Lesbian Adventures: Victorian Love Letters* (Mile High Media, 2009).

In this sense, Noelle nostalgically plays with "the private-public division that has worked, as many feminists have documented, to contain female sexuality within a traditional definition of home" (Juffer 148). For example, the women engage in tea, before nervously suggesting that they go upstairs so that no one will see them. At the same time, these divisions are deconstructed by their unmediated documentation on film and the presentation of the divisions as fantasy constructions offered up for erotic indulgence. The "sense of propriety" and "appeals to privacy, British sophistication" that Juffer locates in the Victoria's Secret catalog (153) are in contrast to the graphic representations of sex and the diversity of female bodies on display. The female performers used in the film vary in age and body type (though not in race) and each scene trades in the erotic power dynamics of age and class and, by extension, social position. While writing serves as the canvas for a feminine privacy soon to be pleasurably violated, or a contrast in social status soon to be exploited, costuming is privileged as the material indicator of these boundaries and social positions.

Gothic romance *Memoirs of a Chambermaid*, set in the 1980s, also utilizes the written word, again employing gender and class hierarchy within domestic spaces as a platform from which to deconstruct gender and class expectations and eroticize this deconstruction. *Memoirs of a Chambermaid* is softer and less graphic than Noelle's vignettes but is narratively more ambitious in breaking down the gender and class hierarchies that operate within the domestic Victorian home. In the film, romance novelist Amy Rogers (Krista Lane) rents an old Victorian house for the summer in the hopes of finding inspiration for her next book. Experiencing writer's block, Amy looks around the house one evening and discovers a diary in the attic written in 1887 by a maid, Molly Mae (Shanna McCullough). The diary details Molly's secret sexual relationship with Jason (Brandon), the youngest son of the family. Amy starts to plagiarize Molly's diary, recording her readings of the diary on her tape recorder. She subsequently has several increasingly sexual experiences with apparitions of the characters involved, and falls in love with Jason. After considering that she may be going crazy, Amy also ponders that perhaps she *is* Molly. At the diary's and the film's conclusion, Jason disappears, leaving Amy alone and heartsick. She picks up a pen and begins to write, at which point we see Amy in Molly's clothes living in the Victorian era with Jason. Meanwhile, the present-day narrative returns to its opening scene, where Molly is arriving at the same house, herself now the novelist, hoping to rent the place for the summer for inspiration. Both women are smiling knowingly, with evident pleasure and satisfaction.

The film functions from within a gendered sphere of romance, writing, and reading, and is consistently attentive to the erotics of reading and writing. Amy is an erotica writer in the 1980s privately (and illicitly) reading the erotica of another woman from a hundred years ago. Furthermore, the film is co-written by a woman (the director's girlfriend) and uses representational cues associated with "women's porn" of the time: lack of emphasis on money and meat shots, soft focus, and a visual emphasis on male bodies and female self-pleasure.

Williams argues in *Hard Core* that the privileging of the money shot and meat shot are characteristic of a presumed heterosexual, male gaze, while the pornography produced for women typically avoids such phallocentric representations of sex. Candida Royalle's company *Femme*, for example, uses medium shots of full bodies and puts less emphasis on always already erect penises that ejaculate to signal the end of the scene. For Williams, the significance of *Femme* is "its serious attempt to visualize women's desire in a genre that has consistently continued to see sex . . . from the viewpoint of the phallus" (*Hard Core* 247). Yet, Williams is also careful to note that "the problem does not lie in the show of the penis itself; the elimination of the money shot does not address the root problems of power and pleasure that only *appear* to reside in this display" (*Hard Core* 247). In this way, *Memoirs* is not subversive simply in its lack of emphasis on money and meat shots. In fact, it could be argued that the lack of explicitness renders the male and female bodies more contained, smooth, and tidy, retaining a certain Victorian sensibility. Meanwhile, the bodies on display in Noelle's films, and in the vast majority of neo-Victorian adult films, are bawdy, out of control, and vulgar, embodying a more serious transgression of corporeal propriety and social boundaries. These are the sweaty, contorted, laughing, and shouting women of Lorelei Lee's describing ("Cum Guzzling" 209) while the women of *Memoirs* are elegant, poised, flawless, and rarely touched by bodily fluids.

Nevertheless, *Memoirs* transgresses these boundaries, but through narrative and discourse rather than physical spectacle and bodily fluids. *Victorian Love Letters* simply utilizes the love letter as a brief means of transitioning into lengthy and relatively wordless sexual activity. As a feature film, *Memoirs* commits to its narrative focus on the written and spoken word, integrating these erotic elements into the story and the sex. Edwards utilizes a supernatural, time-shifting format to engage and eroticize technologies of communication as well as female bonds. Through Amy's efforts, Molly's words weave their way through various devices and ultimately manifest in Amy's

7. Amy dictates the diary in *Memoirs of a Chambermaid* (Arrow Films, 1987).

fantasy life. Indeed, through Amy's fantasies the two women share the same man a century apart. The heart of the film is their long-distance relationship.

Even though Jason is the object of lust, Molly and Amy share an intimacy through the diverse forms of communication and recording technology at their disposal. On discovering Molly's diary, Amy reads it to herself and then adapts it from its private, written form into a cassette recording. These recordings, taped while lounging naked in the bath, will then be transcribed using Amy's electric typewriter and eventually published and marketed to a mass audience of female erotica readers. This journey suggests the erotic appeal of the very acts of writing and reading and in particular as the basis for a homosocial network of women across centuries. Edwards also makes explicit the erotics of the devices themselves. Most striking is Amy's use of the 1980s-era cylindrical microphone. While dictating Molly's diaries, Amy starts to visualize the scenarios. She licks and fellates the microphone before moving it downward, presumably to stimulate herself.

Furthermore, Amy subverts the traditional notion, present in both classical cinema and Gothic literature, that the actively inquisitive, desiring woman must either be a masochistic victim or be punished. Williams, discussing the

8. Amy fellates her microphone while dictating in *Memoirs of a Chambermaid* (Arrow Films, 1987).

female look in classical cinema, observes that those heroines who appear to have a "powerful female look" are eventually punished, "undermin[ing] the legitimacy and authentic subjectivity of this look. . . . The woman's gaze is punished," Williams adds, "by narrative processes that transform curiosity and desire into masochistic fantasy" ("When the Woman Looks" 17). The manner in which Amy becomes consumed by Jason may appear to replicate masochistic trends in Gothic literature and the romance novels that Amy herself writes. But Amy is not simply sexually consumed with Jason; Amy is sexually consumed with Molly's written descriptions and testimonials of Jason. Molly's words are the shaping force behind Amy's fantasies just as Amy's words conjure fantasies for a mass-market romance audience.

Similarly, Amy's willing return to the Victorian period, replacing Molly and relinquishing her modern independent subjectivity for the sake of a man, is presented as part of an ongoing and indefinite cycle, a play space for female erotic fantasy. Modern, middle-class, independent Amy and working-class, confined, Victorian Molly may well switch places again. Just as the Victoria's Secret models enjoy an "erotic mobility" that allows them to "freely cross boundaries of public and private" (Juffer 160), so Molly and Amy trade places in a way that transgresses the class privileges that are typically necessary to such mobility. The implication of a Twilight Zone-esque continual cycle suggests that Molly and Amy may enjoy the pleasures of multiple constructions of gender and class indefinitely and in relation to each other. While Noelle visually and aurally transgresses the boundaries of proper femininity and public/private divides, Edwards transgresses these divides narratively while putting less emphasis on the physical transgressions of a contained feminine body. Both films, however, adopt a liminal, Gothic Victorian space within which women enjoy sexual exploration, rendered all the more pleasurable by the prohibitive backdrop that neo-Victorian porn rhetorically constructs.

Returning the Gaze of Pornography

An unusual example of the pornographic film uses of Victorian technologies is Robert Sickinger's *The Naughty Victorians: A Maiden's Revenge* (1975). Filmed during the porno chic moment, a time when pornographers sought to capitalize on an emerging audience of couples and women through high production values and sophisticated screenplays, this adaptation of the anonymously written 1908 Edwardian pornographic novel, *The Way of a Man with a Maid*, similarly ruptures the masculine control of erotic technologies but with a focus on visual media. It also addresses hierarchies of race, gender, and class channeled through the ruse of education.

An adaptation of a novel that documents the sexual education of a series of girls and women via the pedagogical tool of rape, *The Naughty Victorians* functions as a critique of pornographic legacy, with a particular eye on the technologies used to document what the film seems to suggest is a violent male pornographic desire. Sickinger crafts a complex dual narrative—that of the original novel and that of the film. The novel prioritizes a male narrator (Jack) who offers his "teachings" to his initially resistant but quickly grateful female victims (Alice, Molly, Lady Bunt, and Cicely). The film dethrones this male vantage point, foregrounding a knowing female victim via a frame narrative pleasurably infused with dramatic irony. This sense of dramatic irony positions Jack as the butt of the joke. Indeed, the film plays out as if Jack is the only character still unaware that his (and the novel's) version of events is a fiction. There is a Gothic sense of Alice removed from the narrative, stepping outside of the novel, looking back, and exacting revenge on the pornographic narratives of that era.

The film exacts a form of self-critique channeled toward its forefathers but implicating all of pornography, including, paradoxically, that of the contemporary 1970s. Technologies of pornography come under close scrutiny as instruments of violence against women. In the novel, Jack uses pornographic photographs to assist in the process of "convert[ing]" Alice: "I selected from my collection of indecent photographs several that told their tale better than could be expressed by words" (70). In the film, photography takes on an ominous, exploitative connotation, creating something of a paradox. After having raped Alice and awakened her to womanhood, a process borrowed from the novel, Jack takes pornographic photos of Alice. Alice's expressions of trauma contradict her sprightly narration. As she grimaces on screen, she assures the viewer in voice over, "As reluctant as I may have been that first encounter, how willing I was in our next." This again creates a sense of irony, of Alice stepping out of the novel, her actions and expressions contradicting the artificial pornographic descriptions borrowed from the book.

When Alice exacts her "justice"—the sodomizing of Jack—she and her fellow victims utilize visual technologies, the same ones used to violate these women, as part of the process. First, the ladies gather to witness the revenge, gazing through opera glasses to get a closer look at proceedings. Second, the women project Jack's collection of pornographic photographs onto his body while he is raped. Third, Alice captures the taking of Jack's maidenhood on camera just as he did for hers, rendering the white Englishman, for once, as exploited pornographic object of violent lust.

Neo-Victorian Racial Anxieties

Sickinger's *The Naughty Victorians* is also an unusual example of the use of race as subtle and subversive intervention. While the primary revenge is that of the maiden, it is important to acknowledge the revenge of Jack's students who, like Alice, have suffered violent indignities rebranded as "lessons," similar to the colonial project rebranded as education and civilization. It is Jack's students—those he has been formally teaching—who are brought in to rape him and enact their own revenge. The African student is selected to carry out the rape: "Forget your position, sir. . . . I haven't forgotten all the caning, flogging you gave us boys in class." As with the film's efforts to challenge misogynistic sexual scripts, this attempt to comment on colonial racism is rife with the difficulties of a pornographic film that simultaneously attempts to function as critique. The student arguably occupies a racist stereotype of black rapist, compounded by the way the camera lingers on his released penis. However, the appearance of the African student is not the only reference to the intersections of the British Empire, pornography, and sexual exploitation. Earlier in the film, Sickinger is careful to focus on items that populate the snuggery, such as a stuffed leopard, Moroccan-style rugs, and an Oriental figurine that appears to be gazing at a rape in progress with a judgmental expression.

Furthermore, the pornographic photographs that Jack and Alice look at immediately before Alice's revenge, and that Alice projects onto his body, include exotic images and Japanese art. In this way, Sickinger draws parallels between pornography, the regulation of female sexuality, sexual assault, corporal punishment of schoolboys, and the "teachings" offered by the colonial project. Beerbohn Tree, who plays Jack, remembers that he insisted an African actor play the role of avenging rapist, noting that African pupils were present in London at the time ("The Naughty Victorians"). This appears to be an effort to expose the systems of privilege that govern the narrative strands of the novel, and Victorian pornography more generally, but are never articulated directly.

Thus, while in most cases pornography adheres to the dominant, white, middle-class Victorian project, the symbols of an ugly colonial rule and slave trade erased to make way for nostalgic and erotic visions of class and gender transgression, when pornographers do address race as a historically oppressive system, results are complex and contradictory. Pornographers might be understandably nervous about crafting a nineteenth-century setting that features people of color for, they may believe, this would require racialized characterizations and an acknowledgment of a violent history that many producers and consumers would rather not address in a pornographic context. However, in the rare instances that pornographers do incorporate racial difference as part of a neo-Victorian vision, people of color can constitute important interventions in a sanitized nineteenth century.

The vast majority of neo-Victorian pornographies that deal in racial difference set the narrative in the United States. Indeed, the whitewashing of nineteenth-century England seems to have prompted pornographers to set racialized narratives in nineteenth-century America. In tune with the tendency to view the Victorians as white, this tendency frames slavery and racial inequality as an American problem. The popularity of interracial porn suggests there may be some truth to this in that sexual activity between black men and white women continues to hold erotic cultural currency in the United States. The very fact that "interracial" (IR) as a porn category almost exclusively indicates black male with white female is evidence of a traumatic history of racial oppression still very much part of the cultural consciousness. This legacy is particularly explicit in the rhetoric of the more hyperbolic IR pornographic films of the twenty-first century such as *Little White Slave Girls*

(2002), *Inseminated by 2 Black Men* (2004), and *Oh No! There is a Negro in My Mom!* (2008).

While in the 1970s there were scant performers of color and no coherent category of racialized porn (benchmark titles such as *Behind the Green Door* [1972] are considered unique trailblazers that caused quite a stir at the time), by the twenty-first century, racialized pornographies had become a distinct subgenre often marketed using highly racialized, some would say racist, rhetoric. In response to this rhetoric, Nica Noelle created *Family Secrets: Tales of Victorian Lust* (2010). Set in nineteenth-century America, *Family Secrets* utilizes the repressed, hypocritical, private sexualities of imagined British Victoriana infused with the taboo of interracial sex. *Family Secrets* is an unusual addition to the interracial subgenre in its fetishization of race and interracial sex and concomitant refusal to verbalize racial difference.

Although the film refuses to explicitly acknowledge racial difference, it nonetheless exploits race and class through a neo-Victorian lens. As Noelle acknowledges, "I find interracial relationships and their depictions incredibly erotic. And obviously, the more forbidden the relationship due to society, family, age, whatever the case may be, the more interested I am in telling that story" (Noelle). However, Noelle was not interested in utilizing racially charged language or stereotypes: "I'm very put off by the blatant racism and stereotypical depictions of African Americans and interracial relationships in most porn films, even today. [. . .] [A]s a result of my refusal to depict racial stereotypes, the film got very little promotion and publicity" (Noelle). Racial difference is never verbally acknowledged in the film, in spite of the erotically charged interracial unions that exclusively make up the action. Rather, racial difference augments the power dynamics of nineteenth-century class and gender. This gesture—an American, (de)racialized neo-Victorianism—caused some confusion among fans. "Race," this film and the discussion surrounding it suggests, is an American history, and a deeply complicated one at that. Utilizing the transgressive erotics yielded by Victorian England but situating the narrative in the United States suggests that racial difference and the concomitant taboo therein has greater notoriety (and therefore greater pornographic appeal) as an American saga.

With popular understandings of period and race in mind, it is no wonder that Noelle's *Family Secrets* had some fans puzzling over the historical and regional context of the narrative. Whereas in his imdb.com review, former *Variety Magazine* film reviewer "lor_" remarks with confidence that *Family Secrets* is set during the Reconstruction era, reviewer "picman" on adult dvdtalk.com is bewildered by the inconsistencies in rhetoric and lack of

9. DVD cover art for *Family Secrets: Tales of Victorian Lust* (Mile High Media, 2012).

explanation for the apparent harmony of the races depicted in Noelle's feature: "Using Victorian in the title is a mite misleading, as it's an era attached to the UK. The narrative that sets the stage for this little story is a wee short on exposition. Is it Antebellum or Reconstruction? I'm assuming Rayveness is from the South, but what of Sean Michaels and his brood? Is most of this activity taking place in the North? To what do we attribute this remarkable relationship considering the times they were set in?" While timeless fantasy can mobilize a variety of outrageous pornographic scenarios without much complication, fantasy set in a specific period appears to demand some explanation for inconsistencies. The presence of people of color appears to compound this feeling, making a far-off time feel rooted in reality. This grounding of history ruptures a neo-Victorian fantasy space that, outside of slave narratives, has been whitewashed.

The film stands out as a worthy effort to unsettle or avoid the stereotypical depictions that can often be found in IR porn. In fact, Noelle risked alienating her parent company and distributors by not informing them that the film was "interracial." Upon turning in the finished product, she was "given a talking to" by her studio's sales department, and told that in the future she should ask permission before shooting "niche" genre films such as interracial (Noelle). She was further advised that interracial films were most "sellable" when they featured black performers as racial stereotypes such as slaves, servants, and "thugs," rather than writers or professors (Noelle). Rather than attempt to cast black performers in these stereotypical roles, Noelle instead decided to avoid casting black performers in her subsequent productions; she "did not want to contribute to those stereotypes in adult film" and "did not feel comfortable asking black performers to fill such roles" (Noelle). To Noelle's mind, *Family Secrets* was not of the IR genre in that it did not trade in the racist language and stereotypes of standard "IR" fare. In a way similar to Blake's work, the film reimagines history in a way that glosses over and effaces violence yet at the same time crafts an important fantasy space for historical racialized eroticism outside of the persistent and imaginatively limiting grip of slavery.

In stark contrast to Noelle's film is the intentionally tasteless parody, *Can't Be Roots XXX: The Untold Story* (Dir. TT Boy, 2011). The film—ridiculously over the top, poking fun at slavery, narratives using interracial sex to mock the plantation system—contrasts in tone and yet operates in a space just as, if not more, removed from reality as Noelle's *Family Secrets*. The hyperbole creates an ahistorical playground and functions as an invitation to be shocked and titillated. Adult film reviewer fu_q conveys feelings of intrigue and discomfort in his review, noting that when he watched it he "wasn't fully sure whether reviewing it would be such a great idea. It appears, as well," he said, "that I'm not the only reviewer who felt this way, as no one has written anything up (at least in terms of the reviews logged at www.iafd.com) in the ensuing five years since its release." The reason for this, he believes, is that "this production deals with a touchy subject—slavery in the American south—and it likewise parodies a revered movie on the topic that most people of my generation (say late-30's, early-40's) have likely viewed." Describing this context as "tricky territory, to say the least," fu_q is careful to mention, "I've largely detached myself from the societal gravity of its subject matter...for better or for worse...and I'm looking at it as a fictional porno, not to be taken overly seriously" ("Can't Be Roots: XXX Parody"). This reviewer approaches the film delicately and in a hands-off manner, sure to clarify his mindset in praising the film (he states, rather hesitantly, that the film is actually "fairly decent," "the sex is generally fairly hot," and "the set-ups—although clearly non-PC—frame [the sex] well") so as to stave off accusations of sexually indulging in slavery.

fu_q's rather reluctant praise for *Can't Be Roots* indicates a discomfort with playful and hyperbolic renditions of nineteenth-century racial difference tethered to the horrors of slavery. But this style of neo-Victorian race play should not necessarily be regarded as the racist companion to the progressive likes of Noelle and Blake. In appropriating a treasured book and television series, in embodying the slave so as to mock the plantation system, and in offering visions of interracial lust behind the white master's back, the performers in *Can't Be Roots* enact Mireille Miller-Young's theory of counterfetishization and contestation of the sexualized black male (and female) body. Playful dialogue invokes absurd, stereotypical references to the South, such as slave Toby (TP) telling one of the white daughters, mid–blow job, that her "mouth's warmer than a hot buttermilk biscuit," and asserting that fellatio "makes it all worth it, bein' a slave." Furthermore, the very title expresses the filmmaker's awareness of how tasteless this parody will seem. This *can't be Roots*, the title states, as if to echo our feeling that even a pornographer wouldn't touch *that* classic. Yet they did, and they are flaunting this poor taste right there in the title. The same attitude is expressed in the disclaimer common to parody porn. The disclaimer states bluntly, "This is not Roots," then offers the standard explanation of First Amendment law surrounding satire, and concludes with, "This is a fantasy for the viewers [sic] imagination. Enjoy it for what it is." This last remark essentially tells the viewer to get over it and have fun.

In addition to the in-your-face title and exaggerated Southern accents, the sexual interactions between the slaves and the white women are so brash and out loud that they generate a pleasurably shocking humor.[3] For example, the white daughters talk to their mother about wanting to fuck the slaves in a way that upends the notion of a chaste Southern belle. When Mother warns them not to, one of the daughters replies that they have seen their mother with "the big one" and want to know what it was like. "Don't worry, we won't tell pops," the daughter says smiling. "How was he?" Likewise, when the youngest daughter flirts with the slaves in front of her father, she lifts her skirts in front of them and displays her naked vulva. These kinds of incredible sexual spectacles have an unreality about them that situate the action squarely in the realm of subversive fantasy. *Can't Be Roots* confronts the violent reality of slavery through location and rhetoric that Noelle silences, and yet *Can't Be Roots* simultaneously effaces the violent consequences that would have attended such outrageous defiance of plantation rules. This tension underpins the sexual action and mobilizes fantastical erotic pleasure free of the concerns of sincerity or historical accuracy.

The end credits compound the sense of playful interactions with nineteenth-century race history by making clear that these performers are agents of their own representation. The credits roll next to footage of an orgy involving all of the slaves and white women. Off to the side, the white father and brother are forced to watch from a cage as the slaves and white women hurl insults at them. They laugh and joke around in a way that, familiar in hardcore, blurs the line between script and improvisation, between performance and genuine articulations of emotion. Following the orgy, and to close out the film, the performers (no longer in character) walk up to the camera and introduce themselves with a silly gesture or a smile, while the rest of the cast sit on the carriage in the background cheering and hollering. One of the female performers, Da Puma, who played the part of a slave, grins and says, "I'm just an extra, but that's ok! And I enjoyed myself for this movie!" while one of the men (Black Knight) notes that this is his first production and expresses his thanks to Evasive Angles. Stars of the movie TP and Lucas Stone introduce themselves in character while also acknowledging the artifice of the production. TP states in his affected Southern drawl, "How all y'all doing out there in movie land—I'm Toby," while Lucas Stone, in the booming, affected voice he uses for his character, notes, "I've done fuck everything on this set."

Closing out the film in this manner has the effect of presenting the sexual players as subjects and participants in the joke. They break the fourth wall but remain in character in a way that expresses a knowingness of the playful artifice they are working within. Discussing online porn that engages with colonial histories, Susanna Paasonen, drawing on Jose B. Capino, observes, "Exaggeration and hyperbole produce a sense of 'heightened artificiality,' and the [racialized] films themselves involve tongue-in-cheek acting—stylized performances of race and gender in which roles are taken up with glee and an attitude" (129). In pornographic parodies, this hyperbole also functions to mock mainstream media's representation (and exploitation) of these histories and subsequent effacement of systemic violence. The entire production is so self-consciously silly it borders on a parody of interracial porn (commentary on giant penises are myriad, prompting one recently arrived daughter to ask her mother and sisters, "Are y'all talkin' about penises?"). As a parody, it also functions as a mockery of opportunistically earnest mainstream treatments of slavery, the plantation, and nineteenth-century American and European atrocities. In fact, this aspect of the film—poking fun at media that audiences feel noble consuming—may be as much the source of discomfort as the use of slavery in a porn film.

The fourth installment of PornFidelity's *Get My Belt* (dir. Ryan and Kelly Madison, 2013), also set in nineteenth-century America, is intended to mimic Quentin Tarantino's *Django Unchained*. However, the tone and sex style of this scene is very different from that of either *Family Secrets* or *Can't Be Roots*. The concluding chapter in a series of rough fetish scenes in which women are dominated by a male character as part of an intense power dynamic, this scene is instructive toward understanding the tensions of neo-Victorian pornographic deployments of race in a BDSM context. Contemporary pornographic manifestations of the miscegenation taboo and other tropes rooted in "the erotic storehouse of slavery" (Cruz 77) are not only palatable but incredibly popular. Deployments that actually situate these erotics in their nineteenth-century setting are rare and, evidently, unnerving to some; the compounding features of BDSM—whipping, choking, bondage, and domination/discipline—that resemble the actual treatment of slaves in the nineteenth century are understandably shocking to some.[4] Porn superstar Skin Diamond, playing "Slave," is dragged through the desert on foot by her master on horseback (played by co-director Ryan Madison, credited as playing "Curator of Evil"). He takes her to a shack where he brutally fucks her—he ties her to the wall and then to a chair, physically and verbally intimidates her, and moves her around in a way that expresses complete physical control on the part of the master. The slave appears to indulge in this rough treatment sometimes, though her interactions are by turns ambiguous and ambivalent. In the opening scene, where she is being led through the desert with her wrists bound, she tells us in voice-over that she probably should have attempted escape, "but I've become a bit fond of Master. At first it hurt a little, the lashes, but now I've grown to liking it." Likewise, during the sex scene, it is difficult to tell whether she is enjoying the master's punishments or not. The scene concludes with an internal cumshot (a standard and specialty of this particular website). The slave then strangles the master to death, pushes his semen out of her vagina and onto his face, and rides off on his horse with a smile. In Ariane Cruz's words, "Skin uses the master's tools to kill her master" (102). It is a surprising and triumphant conclusion that, as Cruz notes, inverts the money shot and articulates a sense of liberation, while the scene as a whole—conflicted, ambivalent—complicates notions of pleasure and consent at the intersection of pornography and nineteenth-century slavery.

PornFidelity marketed the scene using hyperbolic language typical of porn in that the rhetoric does not accurately reflect the tone or content of the scene, aiming instead for in-your-face sexual promise—and in fact doesn't tell us much of anything: "Skin Diamond is a slave in the old west, who's tormented

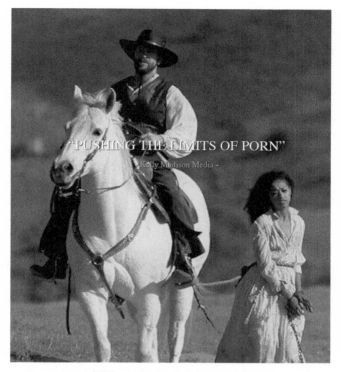

"PUSHING THE LIMITS OF PORN"

- Kelly Madison Media -

10. Promotional still from *Get My Belt* (PornFidelity.com, 2013).

by the conflict of wanting to escape her abusive owner but loving the feel of his hard cock at the same time. Ryan, a hammer wielding black smith, has a problem mixing discipline with pleasure. He owns her tight ass in more ways than one in the highly anticipated fourth and final installment of the *Get My Belt* series." The scene prompted some outcry from fans and reviewers used to the derivative forms of slavery's legacy such as the IR category but less familiar with direct, overtly violent, and unflinching eroticizations of this legacy in the form of BDSM. On an adultdvdtalk.com thread titled "New PornFidelity scene a bit racist? bad taste?" fans describe the scene as "a bit much," "over the line," and an example of "white supremacy." Some fans commend PornFidelity, praising the artistic ambition but clarifying that this is not in line with the fan-in-question's sexual proclivities: "At least they're doing something interesting, although it's not really my thing"; "At least they are trying to do some actual scenario porn. Mind you I don't know if I would have picked a slavery themed one" ("New PornFidelity Scene").

Draxxx, a black male porn fan, poses a useful question that gets to the heart of my argument here: "How [does] showing a recreation of [America's] racist past make the [directors] automatically a 'bit racist'? They chose to set their vignette in a time where that sort of thing actually happened on a regular basis. 'Bad taste'? Why? Because it's a black woman and the era of slavery is shown?" Draxxx illuminates a key point: that racial difference and the violence shoring up understandings and eroticizations of racial difference are standard fodder for pornography, but to address and eroticize the legacy behind the appeal of such pornography is suddenly "bad taste." As Cruz observes, "Reenacting this antebellum 'scene of subjection' in the twenty-first-century context of pornography brings into relief the vexed question of the enslaved black female's unspeakable pleasure and its messy entanglement of consent, will, and agency" (98). Period settings are, for the vast majority of the films discussed in this book, at least in part a distancing method. Racialized manifestations of these settings also provide a distancing method in exploring the power dynamics of race and gender. The discomfort (and erotic thrill) some may feel in witnessing these dynamics played out upon the canvas of slavery speaks to the simultaneous erasure and engagement with this history that shores up the sexual excitement and taboo of genres such as IR. Ironically, the nineteenth-century setting makes gendered racial violence feel more immediate through its unflinching identification of slavery as an origin point for much of the present day's pornographic rhetoric and erotic investments. This identification is what shapes the rhetoric and content of the nineteenth-century IR porn discussed here.

With *Family Secrets*, Noelle attempts to distance the violent legacy of slavery that both *Can't Be Roots* and *Get My Belt* confront. Noelle's feature is a noble effort to disrupt the pornographic categorization and marketing strategies behind the IR brand. The result is perplexing in that Noelle refuses to indicate the social context behind the relationships on screen. Instead of generating pleasure through explicit racialization or tackling the racial dynamics of nineteenth-century America, let alone that of nineteenth-century England, Noelle avoids explicitly evoking racial difference. Instead, she emphasizes a Victorian-period setting, which lends racial difference a taboo eroticism without ever having to name or label race or the violent systems that shore up racial difference, while the "Victorian" reference distances the narrative from a country stained by the legacy of slavery. As with most texts under examination, Victoriana of the United Kingdom and Europe is presented as unproblematic in terms of colonial history while its occupants are almost universally white. Pornography either "exploits *or* effaces difference" (Nash

133), yet Noelle attempts to have it both ways. Ultimately, Noelle produces a text that rewrites race in the nineteenth century, retaining the taboo of miscegenation but doing away with the explicit violence of this period in order to imagine an erotic play space of the past that generates pleasure in difference without the direct trauma of the origin of that difference. Taken together, these three very different neo-Victorian race porn movies demonstrate how fraught neo-Victorian engagements with race can be. They also show the sophisticated and mindful artistic choices pornographers make in crafting fantasy spaces in which excitement and discomfort coalesce; where consumers and performers can engage with the ambivalent erotics of racial difference.

The cultural work done by pornography is integral to individual and collective working out of crises relating to gender, class, race, and desire. The Victorian proves a useful source for such work. Neo-Victorian pornography can point us toward anxieties over gendered, raced, and classed mobility in an age of heightened technology and a perceived decline in individuality and intimacy. As Green-Lewis suggests, "Desire for authenticity may be understood in part as a desire for that which we have first altered and then fetishized, a desire, perhaps, for a past in which we will find ourselves" (43). In this sense, the enduring pornographic use of the Victorian can illuminate not only cultural perceptions of the past but also cultural attitudes toward our own sexual identities as well as the pornographic medium itself. Exposure, revelation, and drawing back the curtain on those areas we are meant to ignore, keep in private, or push to the edge of society are the bread and butter of pornography. Thus, the Victorian period—its texts, mythologies, and monstrous legacies—is the richest space in which to stage such illicit and sometimes unnerving thrills. Which aspects are lingered upon, and which feel too close, reveal the forms of nostalgia and notions of the past we most enjoy envisioning, altering, and fetishizing.

I WANT TO SUCK YOUR . . .
Fluids and Fluidity in Dracula Porn

> The fair girl went on her knees, and bent over me, fairly
> gloating. There was a deliberate voluptuousness which was
> both thrilling and repulsive, and as she arched her neck she
> actually licked her lips like an animal, till I could see in the
> moonlight the moisture shining on the scarlet lips and on
> the red tongue as it lapped the white sharp teeth. Lower and
> lower went her head as the lips went below the range of my
> mouth and chin and seemed to fasten on my . . .
>
> —Bram Stoker, *Dracula*

The next word is "throat," naturally, as this is a passage from *Dracula*, the late-Victorian novel by Bram Stoker, and not a sordid pornographic novel purchased on Holywell Street. You would, however, be forgiven for imagining that this passage is speaking of more than mere blood lust. It is easy to see why vampire tales, particularly *Dracula*, have so enamored pornographers. Indeed, more than sixty hardcore and softcore appropriations of the novel or character have appeared in the twentieth and twenty-first centuries, making *Dracula* the most utilized mainstream text in pornography. Then there are the more generic Dracula- or Carmilla-indebted hardcore films, sites, and scenes of which there seem to be an unending supply. The vampire is the pornographic monster par excellence. More to the point, this passage ably demonstrates two important but often ignored truths about porn: that the appeal of pornography lies in its being both "thrilling and repulsive," and that the men and women of pornography are both active and passive at different moments and sometimes at the same time. These truths emerge most clearly in vampiric porn.

Pornographic adaptations of *Dracula* and other Victorian vampire scripts claim to reveal the dirty bits sublimated by repressed Victorian writers. Understandably, pornographers typically home in on the copious bodily fluids in vampiric narratives, taking particular pleasure in articulating the fluids that Victorian novelists displaced in favor of blood. Adult-film historian and reviewer Robert Rimmer notes that the 1979 film *Dracula Sucks* reveals "what all Dracula movies insinuate—that blood and semen are part of the count's repertoire" (207). Rimmer's observation verifies two important notions about pornography and *Dracula*: the perception of porn as exposing the truth that mainstream fare "insinuates" but doesn't show, and the general cultural knowledge that *Dracula* is a novel *about* sex and sexuality, whether one has read Bram Stoker's original text or not. Indeed, during my own conversations on the subject of Dracula porn, one professor rolled his eyes and remarked, "It just seems so redundant!" while a fellow graduate student scoffed, "*Dracula is* porn!" Sadly, for those with such disillusioned feelings toward porn's originality, no character or text has been adapted by pornography more than the Count.[1] Evidently, pornographers and (presumably) consumers do not find the *Dracula* narrative to be any more redundant than the hundreds of mainstream film producers, comic book artists, and video game designers who have utilized Stoker's character so regularly over the years.

Dracula the culture text holds the promise of deviant, dark, and tantalizingly inverted sexual dynamics. Through an indulgence in this deviancy, pornographic vampires reveal the delicate footwork of the hardcore genre, negotiating the sexual and gender fluidity in, and overtly homoerotic connotations of, the *Dracula* story. These pornings also displace white normative femininities and masculinities in favor of the thrilling, deviant, and monstrous sexualities historically implanted in/written on bodies of color—the substance of the colonial "porno-tropics" (McClintock 22)—sexualities that in pornography are monstrous and thus enticing. Indeed, Dracula adaptations stand out as the most ethnically diverse of the "pornings" in this project, suggesting that vampire narratives are the neo-Victorian pornographic space where race and race history are most comfortably explored. The perilous fluidity and oscillating fears/desires of the *Dracula* narrative have generated a body of hardcore Dracula texts that trade in the erotics of sexual fluidity and transgressive racialized monsters.

Written in 1897, Bram Stoker's *Dracula* was by no means the first vampire tale. Vampires are, however, primarily a nineteenth-century imagining, and while Polidori's *The Vampyre* (1819), Prest's *Varney the Vampire* (1847), and Le Fanu's *Carmilla* (1872) came before it, *Dracula* is by far the most influential and best-known manifestation of the myth. For this reason, I focus on pornographic adaptations of the Dracula narrative and character as a way of exploring more broadly the ways in which the nineteenth-century vampire has been porned. *Dracula* serves as a convenient entry point in this regard.

Due to Count Dracula's peculiar sexual symbolism and (thanks to Hollywood) immediate visual distinguishability, the mere appearance of a man or woman in a black and red cape has sexual signifying power. In his analysis of the Count in Hollywood productions, film scholar Robin Wood addresses the enduring popularity of Count Dracula in film and culture, suggesting a series of sexual qualities that "give the figure of the vampire Count such comprehensive potency" (370). These qualities are instructive in understanding the amalgamation of erotic applications the Count brings to hardcore: "irresistible power, physical strength; supernatural magnetic force," "nonprocreative sexuality," "promiscuity or sexual freedom," "'abnormal' sexuality," "bisexuality," "incest," and "child sexuality" (370–71). In some ways, these qualities conjure up a hardcore pornotopia; still in other ways, a hardcore nightmare.

Pornings of *Dracula* reveal the much-contested meaning and function of different gendered and sexed bodily fluids and orifices in pornographic film—who discharges and who consumes; who penetrates and who is penetrated—in turn exposing the figurative fluidity of gender, sexuality, bodily fluids, and orifices in Stoker's *Dracula*. While *Dracula* appears to pose problems for pornography in that the text is so queer it threatens to destabilize the ostensibly strict and generic gendered arrangements of porn, there are also rich pornographic pleasures in these oscillating positions. In other words, the sense of literalizing the metaphors of the original novel, together with the threat of fluid gender and deviant sexualities, generate risky and paradoxical pleasures that are emphasized in vampire porn yet are also common to pornography as a whole.

The vampire is the quintessential pornographic monster: immortal, beautiful, forever young, and insatiable. The vampire is also predatory, sensual, and seductive. But what makes the vampire ideal for pornography is the tension between active and passive. The vampire is certainly aggressive and feeds on its victims/lovers, but at the same time the vampire *needs* its victim/lover. She is, as Linda Williams describes, the favored woman of both pornography and the Gothic in that she is "*moved* and *moving*" ("Film Bodies" 271). Sarah Sceats describes the vampire as in "mutual bondage" with his or her victim: "the vampire is entirely dependent: s/he can only exist in relation to the victim/host; the overwhelming desire is for oneness, figured in the fleeting act of incorporation of the other" (108). In the context of pornography, this rapacious vampiric hunger crystallizes a broader pornographic desire for the aggressively passive, the receptively active, the masculine/feminine/queer/deviant erotic subject.

Vampirism also offers rich potential for dynamic gendered power play, a favored discourse in hardcore pornography. Vampiric narratives allow for a literal, sexual translation of what is displaced in *Dracula*. At the same time, these narratives literalize the more subversive anxieties that Christopher Craft highlights when he notes that *Dracula* evades and avoids homoerotic contact between man and Dracula: "The vampire mouth fuses and confuses what Dracula's civilized nemesis, Van Helsing and his Crew of Light, works so hard to separate—the gender-based categories of the penetrating and the receptive" (109). Porn, too, works hard to render male and female bodies distinct in terms of who penetrates and who is penetrated. This does not mean men are never penetrated, but in heteroporn it is rare when not specially marked and categorized.[2] In this way, hardcore offers a panoply of different arrangements that are simultaneously segregated, marked out, and carefully gendered. The vampiric porn film subtly mobilizes other arrangements: women penetrate men with their fangs. They are also staked, creating a more complex picture in which female sexual aggression, gender fluidity, and queerness are invoked, indulged, marked as Other, and feared, just as in Victorian vampire narratives. Blood and semen are conflated—and at the same time rigorously segregated. Ultimately, the hardcore realization of *Dracula* creates an unstable product. The instability and fin de siècle anxiety of the original novel translates into the already anxious and unstable genre of hardcore. Hardcore seeks to expose the "truths" of the original Victorian novel and in turn exposes some "truths" of its own.

The Homoerotics of Dracula Porn

Pornographic spectatorship is traditionally homosocial. During the stag era of the early twentieth century, this homosociality is most obvious, as men gathered together in brothels or frat houses to watch pornography; later, during the theatrical golden age (ca. 1972–1984), men once again gathered to watch porn, though this time in a darker room and with the luxury of spaced out seating. Audiences during the theatrical era remained overwhelmingly male, yet even in the hetero theaters patrons sexually interacted with one another. Still, special couples' rates and testimony from the time suggests women were also more frequently in attendance than before, puncturing the homosocial sanctuary (Schaefer, "Gauging a Revolution"; Delaney 25–31). With the inception of home video, spectators are generally characterized as solitary masturbators, yet Emily Shelton argues that in reality these men tacitly understand themselves to be part of a larger homosocial community. While this is persuasive, it is also important to note that while these men may be aware of their brothers in arms, they also must be aware of the rapidly expanding audience which, since the 1980s, has exponentially grown in numbers of women, LGBT consumers, and people of color. Thus, the invisible and anonymous mass of porn spectators are no longer safely housed in the man cave and cannot be relied on to share viewing proclivities or offer virtual high fives. With that said, the sense one gets when hanging out in online forums and comment threads, visiting the video store (if you're lucky enough to have one), or attending porn conventions is that men are the majority and the presence of a few women or queer folks does not cause the safety and sanctity of their brotherhood to crumble.

Hardcore *Dracula* narratives invest their stories with homosocial, homoerotic communication through female bodies inasmuch as pornography does in general; the *Dracula* culture text merely mobilizes more explicit articulations of this generic trope. Shaun Costello's 35mm feature, *Dracula Exotica* (1980), contains a subtle example of this homosociality in the form of vampiric cross-gender mind control that in some way mirrors the late-twentieth- and twenty-first-century homosocial porn audience: one that enjoys a psychological connection to a homosocial mass through a female sexual body yet without the difficulties of having the male bodies in the same room. Of course, in 1980, *Dracula Exotica* would have been screened in theaters where male bodies were in the room—an inconvenience to some, but a sexually titillating opportunity to others.

In either context—the mass of faceless viewing companions of internet porn or the visible, physically proximate viewing companions of the porn theater—the mesmerism scene in *Dracula Exotica* speaks to universal viewing patterns in porn. Vita Valdez (Vanessa Del Rio), recently deceased at the teeth of Leopold (Jamie Gillis), lies naked on the morgue slab. The morgue attendant, Rudy (Herschel Savage), takes advantage of what he believes to be a dead body. As Rudy begins groping Valdez's breasts, the scene cuts periodically to images of Leopold's face as he emerges from his coffin, eyes intently staring. The viewer is to understand that he is mentally connecting with his soon-to-be vampiric minion. Significantly, Valdez's body on the morgue slab and Leopold's body in his coffin depict similar poses. Leopold, like Valdez, also has his eyes closed, while Rudy penetrates Valdez's mouth with his penis. The editing, which juxtaposes Valdez's face with Leopold's, creates the queer understanding that Leopold is mentally experiencing Valdez's violation; that through a mental connection with Valdez, Leopold is also receiving Rudy's penis in his own mouth.

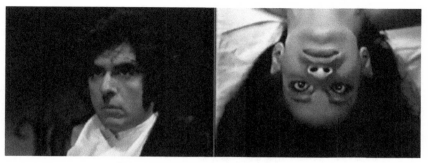

11. Leopold mesmerizes Vita in *Dracula Exotica* (1981).

The ensuing sequence continues to evoke this idea. If we are to understand that Leopold is in Valdez's mind, then Leopold himself embodies
the stationary woman. Thus, Leopold's control of the passive female body
ironically implicates his own body in the woman's physical violation. Rudy
performs cunnilingus on Valdez; Leopold rises from the coffin, and as he
stares intently, the film cuts to Rudy vaginally penetrating Valdez. The
scene steadily builds in this manner, Leopold's physical comportment altering slightly as the panoply of positions varies in the necrophilia scene,
and finally as Rudy approaches orgasm the cutting back and forth between
Leopold, Rudy, and Valdez speeds up until Valdez's eyes suddenly open.
Her moment of consciousness—of Leopold's successful mesmeric intervention—occurs just as Rudy ejaculates onto her stomach, seen from her/
Leopold's point of view. Appropriately, Valdez/Leopold meet Rudy's uninvited penetration and ejaculation with the penetration and evacuation
of Rudy's artery. The homoerotics and gender fluidity of this scene are entirely played out through Valdez's body, mitigating the more discomfiting
insinuations of who is penetrated and ejaculated on, but also indulging in
these very same transgressions. The scene also speaks to the nature of porn
spectatorship: who or what heterospectators look at, desire, or find exciting.
Spectatorial identification with the queer couple, Valdez and Leopold, is
encouraged, even while the completion of the necrophilic rape constitutes
wish fulfillment on the part of the porn consumer for both the passive and
active woman.

Dracula Sucks (a.k.a. *Lust at First Bite* [dir. Philip Marshak, 1979]) is a
curious entry, in that it exists in multiple forms that carefully segregate sex
and violence in response to fears of censorship or persecution. In the process, this editing sifts the explicitly homoerotic content from the explicitly
hardcore. Critics hated the original director's cut due to the lack of explicit

12. *Dracula Sucks* poster (1979).

sex, which screened briefly in 1978 or 1979 (Rubin). As a result, this cut was not screened at all after 1979 or 1980; instead, it was recut in two different versions. The R-rated *Dracula Sucks* released around 1980 includes the violence but removes all traces of the hardcore sex, while the hardcore *Lust at First Bite* released about six months later includes all the hardcore sex but removes the violence, as well as key aspects of the plot, rendering it at times incomprehensible (Rubin). Why the plot details and, significantly, the overtly queer interaction between Harker and Dracula were removed from the hard edit is open to speculation and worth ruminating about.

   Missing from the hardcore version is a climactic scene between Jonathan Harker (Paul Thomas), Mina (Annette Haven), and Dracula (once again, Jamie Gillis). Harker is coded as queer from the outset. In the commentary, recorded in 2014, co-writer, co-star, and assistant director Bill Margold remarks on an early scene in which Harker glances at Dracula engrossingly: "This is where you start to worry about Paul [Thomas]'s sexuality. This is how you know I didn't write this [part]. I never would have intimated that Thomas was homosexual" (Margold). Indeed, Margold is generally conflicted about the homoerotics of the film. His awareness of the queer nature of Stoker's novel vis-à-vis the film's content does not sit well with him as an ostensibly straight pornographer. In the climactic scene of the film, Mina and Harker appear to be embarking on a sexual interaction outside the castle, but the action quickly shifts toward something between Harker and Dracula. Mina is revealed to be a vampire, working with Dracula to secure Harker. Rather than simply offer an implicitly homoerotic vamping of Harker, however, Dracula instead pulls Harker under his cape and pushes his face into his crotch where, we are left to assume, Harker is forced to perform oral sex on the Count. Dracula then offers Harker's neck up to Mina, and she sucks him dry.

   As this scene approaches with the commentary track, Margold asserts, "I knew this movie may be where Stoker wanted to go [. . .] this unlocks all the zippers of *real* Dracula fans" (Margold). Here, Margold understands the inherent but sublimated and repressed queerness of Stoker's novel. Moreover, he recognizes the queer understanding of the novel and culture text that "*real* Dracula fans" hold among them, their zippers unlocked by a pornographic queerness so true to Stoker's ultimate vision. However, when the scene actually unfolds, Margold backtracks and grows less confident about Stoker's intentions: "Yeah, this is *very* strange. I was standing off to the side thinking, 'What the fuck?' [. . .] that's certainly not—maybe that's not what Bram Stoker had in mind" (Margold). No one really knows what Stoker had in mind, but Margold's oscillating, contradictory analysis of the film together with his discomfort ironically indicate the mileage pornography has eked out of Stoker's novel. In some ways, Stoker's *Dracula* offers what pornography claims to offer: something for everyone. The difference is that while *Dracula* offered these pleasures in sublimated and metaphorical fashion, hardcore offers these pleasures explicitly. Or so it claims. Hardcore adaptations of Dracula in fact demonstrate the complexities of representing perversion and sexual deviance in a genre so shaped by categories and spectatorial expectation.

Gender Fluidity and Queer Fluid Exchanges

One of the most obvious promises of vampire lore is the abundance of orifices and bodily fluids, an abundance that pornographic filmmakers have exploited with gusto. And at the same time, vampires, and particularly *Dracula*, pose what Craft calls a series of "disturbing questions": "Are we male or female? Do we have penetrators or orifices? And if both, what does that mean? And what about our bodily fluids, the red and the white? What are the relations between blood and semen, milk and blood?" ("Kiss Me" 109). Hardcore adaptations of Dracula iconography reveal the efforts pornography makes to provide irrefutable answers to these questions, even as it ultimately further complicates them. In this sense, hardcore films that appropriate Victorian culture and literary tropes of that era are "a cultural form of problem solving" (Williams, "Film Bodies" 276) at the same time as they invest and indulge in keeping the problem unsolved. Hardcore revels in a perpetual state of destabilization. It attempts to center the sex that *Dracula* displaces, exposing the "gaps." In the process, it adheres to certain hardcore conventions and contemporary demands, setting up further displacements in a persistent and compelling erotic spiral.

Semen, Craft has pointed out, is a displaced but prominent bodily fluid in Stoker's *Dracula*. This is most clear in the scene where Mina is forced to drink blood from Dracula's chest. The horror of the scene is closely bound up with its palpable sexuality juxtaposed to a desexualized mother-child relation, as the blood Mina drinks is closely linked through Stoker's language to both milk and semen. Van Helsing recalls, "[Dracula's] right hand gripped her by the back of the neck, forcing her face down on his bosom. Her white nightdress was smeared with blood, and a thin stream trickled down the man's bare breast that was shown by his torn-open dress. The attitude of the two had a terrible resemblance to a child forcing a kitten's nose into a saucer of milk" (247). Somewhat excessively—we might say pornographically—Van Helsing adds that blood "smeared her lips and cheeks and chin; from her throat trickled a thin stream of blood" (247). The virtuous Mina feels the pornographic nature of this imagery profoundly. Recalling what has occurred, she regards herself as "'Unclean, unclean!'" and understands her soiled femininity is now a threat to her fiancé, Jonathan.

Mina cannot utter what fluids she has consumed following her forced suckling from Dracula's breast: "I must either suffocate or swallow some of the—Oh my God! what have I done?" (252). Craft notes that the scene leaves "the fluid unnamed" and results in "encouraging us to voice the sub-

WANT TO SUCK YOUR . . .   ·   75

stitution that the text implies—this blood is semen too" (125). Furthermore, as Craft adds, "the confluence of blood, milk, and semen forcefully erase the demarcation separating the masculine and the feminine" (125). Such an erasing or blurring of gender within sexed bodies arguably occurs in much horror fiction, as Carol J. Clover argues in her classic book, *Men, Women, and Chain Saws: Gender in the Modern Horror Film*, yet heteropornography also obsessively reinscribes gender onto these bodies. The frequent vaginal and anal penetration of women, fellatio, and ejaculation on women's bodies perform this reinscribing, and yet at the same time the *Dracula* text, with its penetrating women and conflated bodily fluids, unsettles some of the supposedly clear categories of gender and sexuality.

Just as the flow of bodily fluids composes the narrative core of *Dracula*, so hardcore explicitly trades in representations of abject fluids, specifically the "money shot." Indeed, even the name "Dracula" has sexual connotations related to bodily fluids and orality as evidenced in blowjob compilations such as *Count Suckula* (Wicked Pictures, 2008). It is well established in porn scholarship that the "money shot"—ejaculation onto the man's or woman's body—is one of the most compulsively prerequisite and generically consistent features of hardcore involving penises. Furthermore, the money shot typically signals the conclusion of the sex act for both male and female participants. In 1989, following the pornographic "golden age," Williams observed that "there is something almost *too* phallic about this money shot" (108), noting the extent to which the ejaculating penis has taken the place of the female body as the site of signifying pleasure. The money shot, Williams contends, is hardcore's striving for "maximum visibility" (94) and "visual evidence of the mechanical 'truth' of bodily pleasure" (101).

At the same time, few scholars have acknowledged that this trope was alive and well prior to film pornographies, and that female ejaculation is also of pornographic interest in literature of the nineteenth century and in the squirt subgenres of today. Fluids in connection to gender are obsessively invoked, depicted, and worried over in hardcore. Keeping in mind a robust lineage of ejaculatory depictions spanning centuries of pornographic media, it is no surprise that Williams's prediction that there would be a decline in the money shot (*Hard Core* 117) did not come to pass. Instead, the regularity of the money shot became even more stringently observed, fetishized, and genrefied, incorporating female ejaculation and squirt genres that enable women to shower their female and male partners with liquids. Male ejaculation quickly became so common in hardcore film as to be considered not a fetish but a mere convention prompting the development of more specialized types of ejaculatory finale such as "massive facials" where, usually following a blowbang, the male participants "glaze" the female performer's face until it is almost unrecognizable (sometimes accompanied by laughter and amazement from all involved), and *bukkake* and *gokkun* that focus on coating the entire body or extreme ingestion, respectively (Moore 81).

If, as Isabel Cristina Pinedo puts it, horror is the genre of the wet death (of blood) and pornography the genre of the wet dream (of semen) (51) then the horror-porn, particularly the vampiric porn film, promises to bring these moist strangers together. However, in vampiric porn they do not come together. Indeed, the films promise a union of blood and semen but displace and separate these discomfiting, abject fluids, quite literally in many places. Hardcore routinely equates blood and semen in the rhetoric of the films, yet while Rimmer observes that blood and semen are both part of the Count's repertoire, he never actually ingests both in heteroporn. The performers "dripping with blood, sweat, and cum," as the box cover for *Voracious* (2012) promises, are all female. The rhetoric of season 2 (2014), subtitled *Blood and Cum*, also appears to promise the mixing of these fluids, but the imagery separates them into two streams, once again emanating from a female mouth.

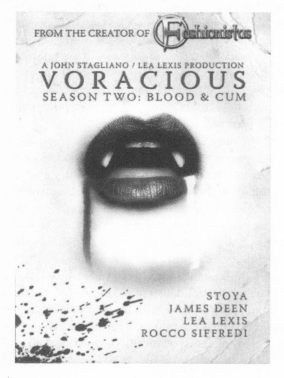

13. *Voracious Season 2: Blood and Cum* DVD cover (Evil Angel, 2014).

In this way, *Dracula* and vampire mythology promise much—the confluence of blood and semen, the queer pleasures of vampirism—that hetero-hardcore struggles to deliver.

The money shot as a signifier in hardcore Dracula films has changed over time. Earlier films produced during a time when there was no coherent "industry" involved more mischievous approaches to convention, utilizing the money shot in ways that disrupt hardcore heterosexual conventions, while later films tend to anxiously hide any conflation of blood and semen in vampire mythology. In addition, older films tend to position women in more traditional gender roles while at the same time more freely playing with the homoerotic implications of the blood-semen connection. Meanwhile, more recent hardcore film emphasizes and praises ritualized active female sexuality and autonomy, but simultaneously reasserts anxieties over gender fluidity and homoeroticism through its invoking of the blood-semen connection even while it treads carefully around it. Paradoxically, these more recent films implicate their own homoerotic subtext through such anxious tap dancing.

The Bride's Initiation (dir. Duncan Stewart, ca. 1973), shot as *The Vampire* and first released as *Demon's Brew*, is an example of the more explicitly homoerotic "straight" content produced in the 1970s, an era that had no coherent "porn industry." During this time, adult filmmakers were guerrilla filmmakers, shooting illegally for an undetermined audience of theatergoers. Without a commercial template, a lot of genuinely bizarre content made its way into porn of the 1970s. In this film (unconventional even by 1970s standards), Count Dracula (Marc Brock) kidnaps a newlywed couple with the intention of using them as part of a ritual to prolong his undead life. It is a ritual he has performed many times before with the aid of his chauffeur, James, and a witch. It involves mixing a "brew" composed of semen, which Dracula drinks and then feeds to a woman he subsequently has sex with. The plot is often incoherent, but it is undeniably homoerotic: captured, bound men are manually masturbated (by women) until they ejaculate into a goblet; Dracula then consumes the ejaculate. Furthermore, when Dracula discovers an appropriately heterosexual love object in Miss Richmond (Carol Connors), the woman he believes "will end my daily tortures and bring me eternal life," things do not go according to plan. James kidnaps the detective who has been searching for the newlyweds, in order to harvest his semen for the ritual, and Dracula drinks the brew in preparation for penetrating Miss Richmond. However, immediately after drinking the "brew" Dracula falls to his knees before the detective, exclaiming, "I love you, I love you, you wonderful one! I must make love to you now!" The detective retorts, "Are you

SHE TASTED THE EROTIC DELIGHTS
...OF FORBIDDEN PLEASURE RITUALS!

THE BRIDE'S
INITIATION

FEATURING SPECIAL
GUEST APPEARANCE BY SUPERSTAR...
CAROL CONNORS

Starring MARK BROCK · CONSTANCE MURRAY · DONNA CORD
AMBROSIA · CANDIDA ROBBINS ·TONY MARSHALL· STEVE MORGAN
Produced and Directed by DUNCAN STEWART· Screenplay by JERRY SHELDON
Music by GREGORY PEEL · COLOR BY PFI · RATED X

14. *The Bride's Initiation* poster (1973). Courtesy of Vinegar Syndrome.

kidding? My husband would kill me!" and the film ends. Multiple different "brews" of semen constitute the Count's lifeblood in *The Bride's Initiation*. It is unclear what is so captivating about the detective's semen that Dracula would instantly fall in love.

The Bride's Initiation is the only straight film that acknowledges the Count's consumption of semen as his life force, yet the Count does not physically engage with any man. Women perform the sexual duties, producing the semen through their sexual machinations in much the same way as one might milk a cow. In this way, the film boldly portrays male consumption of semen without actually depicting the act that leads to such consumption. At the same time, the film haphazardly suggests that semen is so powerful that it could prompt a shift in sexual orientation much in the same way as drinking blood might transform one into a vampire. The moment is so brief, such a seemingly throwaway joke, that a casual viewer might miss the implications. Is the detective's semen the first gay semen Dracula has consumed? Is this why the detective's semen turns Dracula gay? It would seem so. In that case, this is an intriguing analogy. Vampirism and homosexuality are compared as mutually compelling and desirable traits. Moreover, Dracula has been drinking semen for years, perhaps centuries, so it doesn't seem that big of a leap for him to do away with the women and collect that semen from the source. Indeed, to do so would not necessarily alter his identity in any profound way. The sex acts remain the same while the mediating feminine salve is simply no longer required. In this way, *The Bride's Initiation* explores vampirism, fluids, and sexuality in a manner more sophisticated and complex than the stilted dialogue and low production values might suggest.

Dark Angels 2: Bloodline (dir. Nic Andrews, 2005) is an example of the more anxious navigation of the homoerotic implications of bodily fluids in *Dracula* that have become more evident in the twenty-first century as adult film has moved increasingly toward a corporate commodity. *Dark Angels 2* retains the queer blurring of fluids and orifices but sublimates homoeroticism with violence. A sequel to *Dark Angels* (dir. Nic Andrews, 2000) (which in a distinctly *Carmilla*-esque narrative focuses on a female vampire and her female human prey), *Dark Angels 2* riffs on *Dracula*. This sequel is much more ambitious and gory, and it centers on multiple male protagonists and their relationships to other men. The head vampire in this film is Draken (Barrett Blade) who, with the help of his Igorish assistant, Quinn (Evan Stone), is creating a race of zombie vampires called slags in order to procure a woman of pure blood. These slags are created via traditional biting of the neck. Draken possesses "the elixir of life"—a large glass tube of blood that, once empty, will result in his race's extinction. When the blood runs out, his bloodline ends. The slags have impure blood; it is "diseased, like a virus," and they do not have enough of the elixir to fully transform humans into Draken's race. Draken's goal is to capture "the one," whom he finds embodied in a waitress named Jesse (Sunny Lane), drain her pure blood into the tube, and perpetuate his bloodline. With the help of a Van Helsing–type named Jack Cross (Dillon Day), Jesse defeats Draken.

In Stoker's novel, the Count expresses his desire for Jonathan Harker when he chastises the greedy vampire sisters: "How dare you touch him, any of you? [. . .] This man belongs to me!" (43). Still, Stoker stops short of depicting man-on-man vamping. *Dark Angels 2*, meanwhile, has it in spades. Both Draken and Quinn vamp dozens of homeless men and a policeman in order to create more slags, yet these scenes are carefully choreographed violent action sequences so as to mediate the potential homoerotics of vamping. The opening sex scene articulates the sexuality of vampirism and the homoerotic hurdles that must be navigated in both diegetic and nondiegetic ways. The scene involves Draken and an anonymous woman, who have sex concluding with a money shot: Draken ejaculates and the semen, probably unintentionally but certainly serendipitously, lands on her neck. This scene calls for a post-cum vamping finale, which occurs in spite of the singular direction of the money shot. However, when Draken bites the woman's neck immediately following ejaculation, the semen has miraculously disappeared. Male consumption of semen, even of one's own semen, is too queer to allow in this particular feature.[3] It is rare in heterosexual pornography in general. When it does happen, it has either been labeled appropriately, is an expectation of the genre (cuckolding or strap scenes, for example), or is a surprise (pleasurable or not). It is seen as too queer, too feminine, or both. Even *The Bride's Initiation* does not depict the Count drinking straight from the faucet. Within the context of an adaptation of *Dracula* that dares to depict man-on-man vamping, perhaps an opening scene involving the vamping of a semen-coated female neck is simply so queer that the filmmakers (or perhaps the performer) would rather break the fourth wall than have it occur. Even in a vampire porn movie, or perhaps *especially* in a vampire porn movie, bodily fluids are kept distinctly separate, and the gendered consumers of specific bodily fluids are kept rigidly defined. Blood may be consumed man-on-man, yet one may not consume one's own semen. So while *Dark Angels 2* is surprisingly frank in its juxtaposition of sex and violence, it is paradoxically more conservative than Stoker's novel in its refusal to conflate bodily fluids between men.

The complications of the blood/semen dynamic are probably the most narratively realized in Shaun Costello's 1980 film, *Dracula Exotica*. In this 35mm feature, Costello offers an unusual and complex treatment of bodily fluids. Indeed, the film epitomizes many of the contradictory and compelling consequences of the mixing of horror, the Victorian, and pornography. Set predominantly during then-present-day 1980, *Dracula Exotica* does what a lot of Hollywood adaptations have done:[4] it recasts Count Dracula as a tragic figure and recasts the narrative as one of gothic romance rather than horror. Yet Costello retains the sexual sadism and deviancy suggested by the source text, porning it in a diversity of ways and producing a bewildering array of perverse and sometimes disturbing sex acts as well as queer gender formulations. In particular, Costello uses the Dracula narrative and culture text to challenge pornographic expectations of the money shot and mobilize deviant sexual desires.

Dracula Exotica concerns Leopold Michal George Count Dracula (Jamie Gillis) who, at the film's eighteenth-century opening,[5] is in love with Surka (Samantha Fox), daughter of the gamekeeper. However, Leopold's father denies their union due to their differing class status. Heartbroken and frustrated, Leopold gets drunk and rapes Surka; she in turn commits suicide. Stricken with guilt, Leopold curses himself with an eternity of undead bloodlust combined with the inability to ejaculate, and kills himself. The remaining film takes place in the modern day: Leopold's Transylvanian home is now a tourist attraction. Leopold sees an American woman named Sally (also played by Fox), who bears an uncanny resemblance to Surka, and follows her back to the United States. After a rekindling of the couple's romance, the film climaxes with Leopold's climax and his vamping of Sally. This breaks the curse: the two of them transform into doves and fly away.

From the outset *Dracula Exotica* subverts the typical pornographic economies of bodily fluids, particularly the money shot. The first sex scene troubles the strict direction of hardcore hetero semen consumption. Leopold, drunk and depressed, sits at the margins as his bawdy friends partake in some sex workers, all of whom are enthusiastic except one, whom they rape. After having intercourse with an enthusiastic sex worker, one of the men (Ron Jeremy) ejaculates over the reclining woman in a would-be classic money shot. However, the woman delightedly catches the semen on the apple she holds in her hand, takes a bite, and then thrusts it into Leopold's mouth, laughing. Flinching angrily, Leopold pushes the apple away. Leopold's resistance maintains the line between male and female consumption of semen (and thus of hetero- and homoerotic fluid exchange). Still, the delight this woman takes in moving the semen-coated apple to Leopold's mouth is evidence of the pleasures of such queer boundary crossings as well as a hint at the homoerotics of blood consumption metaphorically present in the novel.

Following this curious opening, the film establishes semen, ejaculation, and blood as central components of the plot. The curse uttered by Leopold that shapes the narrative conflates sexual climax with the satisfaction of blood lust. Through this conflation, the film rhetorically claims to speak the silences of the novel, to literalize the metaphorical sexual content of Stoker's text. However, Costello separates blood and semen even as he seems to conflate them: Leopold can consume blood and indeed does bite the necks of women. He cannot, however, ejaculate. Later in the night of the orgy, Leopold rapes Surka in a fit of drunken fury, and she commits suicide. Taking full responsibility for Surka's suicide, Leopold prepares to take his own life, explaining in a voiceover, "With the bloody blade that stilled that pure and loving heart, I swore an oath, taunting God to deny me no sanctuary in heaven . . . or in hell. To forever taint my guilty soul with a need for blood. To fan the burning fire of lust within me, but never be satisfied." Having pierced his heart with the same bloody dagger that Surka used on herself, Leopold plunges himself into an eternity of frustrated limbo centered around desire for two bodily fluids: the consumption of blood and the ejaculation of semen. The former is attainable through the seduction of others; the latter is forever unattainable and rendered more desirable by the former. In porn, this is the ultimate punishment: no sexual fulfillment. For the spectator, this is also the ultimate punishment: no cum shot. Instead, Leopold can only consume the "other" fluid—the red one, rather than delivering the white.

Leopold's curse creates a hardcore narrative focused on the denial of what many have observed to be the primary prerequisite of the hardcore pornographic film. This demonstrates the curiously destabilizing effect of the Victorian Gothic. On the one hand, *Dracula Exotica* exploits the rich sexual metaphors and silences of the coy Victorian novel. On the other hand, pornographic genre is shaken up and diverted by the perversions and Gothic technologies of Stoker's tale. Leopold/Dracula is unable to climax, resulting in three unconventional hardcore scenes that creatively displace the money shot. First, Dracula's vampire brides perform cunnilingus on each other and fellatio on him for what might be expected to be for his pleasure, but in reality is to his perpetual boredom. Indeed, he has his servant Renfroo douse them with holy water before setting off to the United States. Renfroo's act of violence is the scene's conclusion. Second, he hypnotizes cocaine smuggler Vita Valdez (Vanessa Del Rio) during his boat journey to America. He performs cunnilingus on her, biting her in the process, and turning her into his vampire secretary. Third, Leopold appears as an apparition in Sally's mirror while she masturbates to his image, and they appear to connect psychologically, both painfully longing for the other. Significantly, the first two scenes culminate in death or violence (Valdez is vamped), which would seem to corroborate Pinedo's contention that the "wet dream" of the porn film is comparable, even parallel, to the "wet death" of the slasher film (6). In addition, Leopold's inability to produce the ejaculate necessary for a traditional hardcore climax leads to two different climaxes: one, a displaced "money shot" (a scalding dose of holy water to the face); the other, the draining of fluids from the woman's body, an equally violent climax that is nonetheless subversive in its inversion of traditional pornographic fluid consumption. These explicitly violent manifestations of the money shot should not merely be understood as simplistic demonstrations of the violence of pornographic sex. The scenes are indeed violent, though not as violent as hardcore's mainstream cousins. These films function as both demonstrations of and commentaries on what Victorian authors hint at but never fulfill—that is, violent, fearful, and desirous reactions to active female sexuality.

As its finale, *Dracula Exotica* attempts to restore a generic imperative thus far denied: the money shot. After Leopold tells Sally of "the horror of my obscene craving for blood, the agony of my raging passion, which for these 400 years had remained unfulfilled," Sally hopes to fulfill this lack. In this way, the film renders explicit the metaphor of vampirism and the desire to become the vampire's victim. Leopold knows this would result in her death: "I would not pay such coin for my salvation." Sally insists, and a slow and sensual sex scene ensues. Sally offers up not only her neck for Leopold's consumption but also her other body parts for Leopold's sexual gratification and ejaculation. He will draw her fluids at the same moment as she draws his.

The moment of vaginal penetration—sexual consummation, in traditional androcentric terms—is aurally and visually conflated with the penetration of Sally's neck by Leopold. She urges, "Do it now, Leo," and he bites her neck while also entering her vaginally. The money shot that follows is intended as the culmination of 400 years without climax: masturbating over Sally's face, Leopold cries, "Surka!" repeatedly as crashing waves are spliced into the scene. When Leopold finally ejaculates, the magnitude of such a long-awaited money shot is displaced onto stopped clocks starting up again, Vita reduced to a skeleton, and Leopold and Sally's disappearing. This money shot has the power to start and stop life. While the scene presents as traditionally heterosexual, androcentric, and romantic, this is also a moment of mutual fluid exchange and consumption that complicates the traditional gendering of such an exchange. When the couple departs as two doves, it is as partners who have shared not only in blood but also in semen.

Dracula as Racial Other

In his late-Victorian manifestation, the Count is understood by many scholars to represent the greedy, rapacious Jew. Fittingly, he is played in multiple hardcore films by Jewish performers. The character is often rendered romantic and rescued from his monstrous colonial Otherness. While Jack Halberstam warns against stabilizing monstrosity and perversity, he also observes that when Count Dracula appears in the flesh, he "embodies a particular ethnicity and a peculiar sexuality" (91). Dracula's "racial markings are difficult to distinguish from his sexual markings" (100), yet his physical features are undeniably similar to stereotypical anti-Semitic portraits of the Jew: "His face was strong—a very strong—aquiline, with a high bridge of the thin nose and peculiarly arched nostrils; with lofty domed forehead, and hair growing scantily round the temples, but profusely elsewhere" (Stoker 23). In London, Dracula is again described as "a tall, thin man, with a beaky nose and black moustache and pointed beard" (155). On discovering Dracula forcing Mina to drink blood from the wound in his chest, Dr. Seward describes "the great nostrils of the white aquiline nose" (247). Two of the three vampire sisters are "dark, and had high aquiline noses, like the Count, and great dark, piercing eyes" (42). These descriptions, coupled with their Transylvanian residence that, it is emphasized, "is not England" (26), the Eastern European associations of the racial Other become quite clear.

Race, Vampirism, and Sex Work

Popular culture boasts a legacy of black vampires, ranging from Blacula to Blade. Sarah Broderick argues that the black vampire embodies "racial stereotypes and dominant fears about black men and black women," and that black vampire narratives provide "a somewhat covert outlet for the racism and sexism of ages past." At the same time, self-determined representation and a seizing of the vampire myth can be a form of resistance to such stereotyping even while playing up to these fears. The merging of black masculinity and vampirism resembles Mireille Miller-Young's characterization of black performances of the pimp in porn movies hosted by rappers. These performances constitute a "self-articulation that makes use of black men's outsider status and reframes it as an oppositional and autonomous masculinity that is defined by a consciously chosen and managed hypersexuality" (157). Count Dracula embodies a pimp-like character, overseeing his female progeny, managing and directing them. Mickey Royal, in his 1998 guide to pimping, *The Pimp Game: An Instructional Guide*, observes, "The Lord gave us pimps, and ho's [sic] for pimps to feed off of, the same as the Lord provides the world with predators and prey" (7). He instructs the reader, "When you think of a pimp, think of a vampire, Count Dracula" (21). Likewise, in his 2013 memoir, *PIMP: Reflections on My Life*, Noble Dee recalls a pimp who "reminded me of that cat called Dracula, the vampire. Just like Dracula, this pimp could and would suck the life out of a *hoe* with his *pimpin*'" (14, italics in the original).

Royal's and Dee's observations are helpful in terms of understanding the ways in which race, sex work, masculinity, and vampirism intersect, yet they underestimate the agency and complexities involved not only in sex work but also in vampirism. Dracula may well be a predator, but let us not forget that so are his "hos." Moreover, submission to the bite is often coded as deeply pleasurable and something the "victim" is complicit in. Also, Dracula is perpetually hunted. The bravado that accompanies the pimp persona covers over a great deal of vulnerability and codependency when it comes to victims. With all this in mind, an understanding of the vampire/progeny relationship can illuminate overlooked dynamics of the pimp/sex-worker relationship and vice versa. Certainly, several manifestations of the Count in porn portray him as an actual pimp and reveal some of these complexities in ways that pimp anthropologists such as Royal and Dee are apparently hesitant to confess. A major distinction in this regard is that unlike the pimp or the rapper host, the black vampires of porn expose their bodies in ways that engender vulnerability through becoming not just the pimp but also the sex worker and object of the gaze (Miller-Young 160).

The 2008 Wicked Pictures release *The Accidental Hooker* reflects the ways in which pornography provides a space where the pimp/sex-worker relationship is complicated via vampirism, offering what amounts to an analysis of the dynamics of sex work. The black pimp vampire is also a sex worker, in that the performer is a sex worker playing a pimp. In *The Accidental Hooker*, performer Deep Threat plays Vladdy, a vampire who, based on his name and his red satin shirt, is intended to be Dracula. He arrives in his limo to pick up protagonist Silvia; he offers her cash, and she proceeds to provide the sexual services she has been hired for. The explicit transaction complicates Vladdy's characterization as pimp, and yet the film casts him in this light through his "boss vampire" ethos, his accessories (cane, throne), and his physical disposition in an orgy scene where he is overlord of the cavorting vampire clan, watching and enjoying from afar. In this way, Dracula reads as pimp and pimp reads as Dracula.

Likewise, the film explicitly conflates sex worker and vampire, further complicating race and sex work through the technology of vampirism. Wicked contract girl Kaylani Lei plays the role of Sylvia, the titular "accidental hooker," a sex worker who, in the style of *Interview with the Vampire*, is telling her story to a documentary film crew interviewing her for a piece on escorts. The narrative is made up of her various interactions with clients, and it concludes with a twist ending: Silvia is a vampire, and each of those scenes we just enjoyed actually ended not simply with a money shot but with Silvia's enjoyment of the client's other fluid—blood.

The limo scene between Vladdy and Silvia is her turning—she is both "turned out" as a sex worker and turned into a vampire. At the moment of Vladdy's ejaculation onto Silvia's tongue she states in voice over, "And that was it. My life was over as I knew it. Things would never be the same again. I was now officially... [pause] ... a hooker." We discover later that here, "hooker" also means "vampire." The ensuing extended analogy crystallizes the parallels of vampiric transformation and sex worker stigma: "I had crossed a line—a line that could never be uncrossed." "But if you could uncross it, would you have?" asks the documentary interviewer. Silvia takes a long drag on her skinny cigarette: "I just knew I couldn't. What was done was done. But the one thing I did know was that my life would never be the same again. *I had changed* and this was only the beginning" (emphasis added). Silvia's vampiric change at the hands, or rather teeth (or penis? semen? cash? what is it that prompted Silvia's "change"?), of Vladdy is as permanent as the change brought about by exchanging cash for sexual services. Her life will never be the same, and the line cannot be uncrossed. In this way, the film makes explicit the impossibility of return from the societal category of "whore," framing this societal containment as a vampiric nighttime existence, as an actual change in blood, in body, and in species. Silvia inhabits three identities—vampire, sex worker, Asian American—that irrevocably Other her. The film integrates the three almost invisibly as a way of highlighting parallels of Otherness.

Born in the Philippines and of Chinese/Filipino descent, Lei is one of the most successful Asian American porn stars of all time. During her fourteen-year career, she performed in about 250 adult films. Her star power as a long-time Wicked Girl (2003–2005, 2007–2015) and her many lead roles in their feature films brings much to bear on the understanding of her performance as a vampire sex worker. Lei was a top star for many years and as Wicked Girl she connotes a particular level of glamour. Wicked Girls embody an ethos of strength, maturity, and sexual power. Current contract performers include jessica drake and Asa Akira; previous contract performers include Jenna Jameson, Sydnee Steele, and Stephanie Swift, women known for their strength of character, entrepreneurship, and dynamic sexual performances. Wicked Girls are also presented as intelligent and creative, often working as writers and educators in addition to being performers.[6] As an Asian American Wicked Girl, Lei, like Asia Carrera of Vivid, "reinscribe[s] the tradition of hypersexuality as essential to race" (Shimizu 165) even while she also resists them through self-authorship. She and other Asian porn superstars "pres-

15. Sylvia prowls the night in *The Accidental Hooker* (Wicked, 2008).

ent existing fantasies of Asian women as crucial to their self-perception and social legibility" (Shimizu 165). In performing the Asian high-class escort, Lei embodies one of these existing fantasies (the Asian "hooker") and builds upon it through the combination of sexually confident, self-possessed vampire and high-priced, self-employed escort.

As the title of the film suggests, Silvia finds her profession of sex work by accident. Her existence as vampire is similarly accidental, occurring as a result of a client who, it is revealed at the end, is Dracula. The revelation that Silvia is a vampire recasts the preceding sex scenes in a new light, but even without the revelation Silvia is portrayed as a commanding sexual presence. She, the sex worker, functions first as a student and then as a sexual overseer. She is the (unreliable) narrator and has control over the way her story is told. In addition, she is repeatedly presented as financially autonomous (demanding her standard sex-work fee from the flustered documentary crew whom she sees as simply another client) as well as someone who operates alone. Scenes of Silvia—alone, confidently walking the streets of Los Angeles at night, sipping on a soda and glancing around at her surroundings—are visual accompaniment to her lengthy voice-over narration. When she visits a sex worker to see how professionals do sex work, she sits masturbating and watches the woman fuck a client, enjoying the scene in both an erotic and educational sense. Throughout, she is a participant primarily through her gaze. Occasionally, she steps in for a kiss, quickly returning to her post to continue her education.

At the film's close, we discover that Silvia's clients have also been her victims. In turn, her subject position (and theirs) radically shifts. Through this twist, the film complicates the roles of sex worker and pimp, two forms of sex work that are traditionally highly gendered and arranged according to a simplistic, symbiotic power binary of owner and owned, pimp and "ho." Vampirism helpfully reveals this relationship as one of mutual dependency and oscillating power relations. Vampiric sex work reveals the complex navigations of sexual representation, gender, and power in connection to race. Vampirism, sex work, and race speak to each other throughout the film. Silvia and Vladdy's vampiric qualities of mastery, seduction, sexual desirability, and sexual exchange rearrange assumptions about race, gender, sex work, and power.

The Pleasures of Racialized Sexual Deviance

Stoker's novel is notorious for the way it presents female sexual aggression as monstrous and unclean. Lucy in particular is singled out as monstrous because she is female and sexually aggressive. Craft goes as far as describing Lucy's death-by-stake as "the novel's real—and the woman's only—climax" ("Kiss Me" 122), suggesting the slippage between sex and violence. Lucy's death is equivalent to her orgasm: her *petit mort*. Mina and Lucy are the two central women in the novel, representing what Phyllis Roth describes as "the dichotomy of sensual and sexless woman" (412). Mina represents all that is virtuous, yet strong-minded, while Lucy is flirtatious and, after being bitten, aggressive in a "voluptuous" and sensual manner. As Roth also observes, the novel is riddled with comments that reflect a late-Victorian anxiety over the strident, sexual, and independent New Woman, fear of the loss of "good women" who fulfill traditional subservient gender roles, and a reaction to "fallen women" (411). In other words, *Dracula* plays out the familiar dichotomy of Madonna and Whore. Yet hardcore typically celebrates fallen and dark women resulting in *Dracula* adaptations that flatten the dichotomy. After all, pornography is a medium that generally *requires* the always-sexual woman, and is one of the only sites of unquestioned and encouraged active female sexuality.

While some of the hardcore Dracula films offer a Mina-esque "good woman" for Dracula to fall in lust with, the films are typically more enamored of Lucy-esque bad girls. Even the pornographic Mina characters, such as the sweet and naïve Amira of *Voracious* (2012), are also sexually aggressive and vampiric. The character of Surka/Sally in *Dracula Exotica*, too, is depicted as pure in her former incarnation. As Sally, however, she does sex work in order to get information on her cases. Her "fallen" status has no impact on her desirability and indeed she is pursued by Leopold and is willingly vamped so they can be together for eternity. Centering the sexually rapacious, monstrous woman as simultaneously good and worthy of love is suggestive of hardcore's recuperation of the "whore" by blurring the lines of good and bad girls. Monsters are, after all, typically celebrated in porn. Even the monstrous women who are Dracula's nemeses, such as Del Rio's Vita Valdez, are shown to be desirous, desirable, and powerful. Indeed, Del Rio appears on much of the publicity for the film. Porn renders the monstrously sexual sexually good.

Key to these pleasures in vampire porn is the racialized woman and the perverse celebration of their deviant sexualities. If Mina and Lucy are the dichotomous female protagonists of *Dracula*, then Surka/Sally and Vita Valdez are their corresponding characters in *Dracula Exotica*. Vita Valdez embodies a societal fear of the conflated racial/gendered Other expressed in several Victorian vampire narratives, including both *Dracula* and *Carmilla*. Marilyn Brock observes that both nineteenth-century stories represent fin de siècle anxieties over racial Others, female sexuality, and the decline in patriarchal power signaled by the New Woman: "In both narratives, the concept of the racial other is inextricably linked with female sexuality by nature of the vampire's acts" (13). The various stakings in both stories are a way to contain these threats (130–31). Meanwhile, hardcore tends not to contain or demonize female sexual aggression. It is significant, then, that Vita Valdez, played by Latina porn icon Vanessa Del Rio, is the sexual threat that must be contained. Valdez is representative of the many pornographic vampires of color in that her vampirism serves as a technology with which to mobilize racialized and gendered pleasures, pleasures characterized by the erotics of power, submission, dependence, and autonomy that are the hallmark tensions of the vampire, and which are explored in pornography through race.

While Valdez is certainly a composite of Latin stereotypes (smuggling cocaine, sexually voracious, hyperbolic accent) her character is complicated by Del Rio's own star power and the racialized and sexualized hyperbole that is Del Rio's performative calling card. Her performances are defiant even as they appear to conform to stereotypes. As Juana María Rodríguez states, "Despite the roles she was offered, del Rio always brought her own brand of Latina glamour to the racial caricatures she was paid to play" (316). Through her star power, del Rio "conjur[ed] an alternate universe in which a young

Afro-Latina from Harlem could become an international porn sensation" (Rodríguez 316).

A cultural icon to both men and women from black and Latin communities alike, Del Rio has crafted an ethos of sexual aggression, authentic lust, and an embrace of all things slut. As detailed in her extravagantly mounted autobiography, *Fifty Years of Slightly Slutty Behavior*, she co-authored her images and performances from the start of her career (Hanson 194). Once she became a star, she would tell directors pre-scene, "Don't even tell me what to do" (Hanson 228). Described as having "the world's most carnal mouth; even in baby pictures her lips seem slightly obscene" (Hanson 12), it seems Del Rio was born to play a pornographic vampire. Indeed, Del Rio recalls her fantastical strategies of survival growing up in a dangerous neighborhood she was afraid of: "I'd conjure up demons, monsters, just to fight them off, to prove to myself that I was invincible" (Hanson 31). However, she asserts, "I don't have Victorian fantasies. I never see myself walking through a field of flowers before I'm ravaged. I see myself giving a blowjob before I'm ravaged [*laughs*]" (Hanson 271). And yet, in *Dracula Exotica*, she participates in a quintessentially Victorian fantasy, just not the flowery kind we sometimes associate with the Victorian period. This is the Victorian fantasy of sexually aggressive women, the pleasures of submission, deviant Others, queer fluid arrangements, and gender inversion. Del Rio is the embodiment of these particular Victorian qualities par excellence.

On a superficial narrative level, Vita is victim to containment, rape, and eventual extermination. At the same time, Del Rio's performance and star power together with the sexual numbers she performs complicate simplistic dichotomies of femininity through her oscillation between aggressive and passive woman. While Vita is punished, she is also dominant, exacts revenge, is artful in her schemes, and is a central erotic and identificatory touchstone in the film. Indeed, in line with porn's preferences it is Del Rio the troublemaking bad girl on the box cover, not fellow superstar good girl, Samantha Fox.

Del Rio's first sex scene in *Dracula Exotica* demonstrates her character's sexual and vocational dominance. Vita is introduced on the boat wherein Leopold is hiding himself. She is the leader of a gang of male cocaine smugglers and is immediately shown to be in control of her sexuality, in control of her gang of men, and sexually demanding of others. After sampling the cargo, one of the gang, Eric (Ron Hudd), starts groping Vita, and she knees him in the crotch, snapping, "No one fuck with Vita Valdez unless Vita want them to." Vita is sexually domineering in a way that Sally is not. Sally poses as a sex worker and goes along with the exploitative advances of Big Bird (Eric

Edwards), but Vita is in charge and refuses the men unless these advances are on her terms. As if to prove this fact, she demands that the three other men get undressed so they can have an impromptu orgy. Only Eric is left out, sitting at the sidelines while the others enjoy some preliminary sexual activity. Ultimately, however, Vita feels sorry for Eric and invites him to join in. Throughout this scene, Vita directs the sexual activity, telling the men to "hurry up" at the beginning, giving permission to Eric to participate, enjoying all three men as they orally pleasure her. She finally commands, "Fuck me Eric. Now." Vita sets the parameters, and the men obey.

Vita also inhabits submissive sexuality, first when under Dracula's hypnosis (she is unable to resist his sexual powers and allows herself to be bitten), and second when she is dead and in the process of becoming a vampire. In this latter scene, Rudy the morgue attendant rapes her on the morgue slab in a memorably unsettling sequence. Del Rio remains completely immobile and slack throughout, never breaking character to embody an active porn star persona. The vamping of Rudy that concludes the scene goes some way toward avenging her violation and further demonstrates the way vampire narratives mobilize the highly desirable passive and active sexual female subject. Valdez occupies oscillating positions, moving from dominant to submissive and back again throughout the film and sometimes within the same scene.

Men, too, occupy these oscillating positions. Leopold employs Vita, now a vampire, as his secretary, a typically feminine menial job in which she is supposed to be subservient to Leopold. In reality, she is using her stereotypical role to scheme against Leopold, and her role-playing is depicted as amusing, with Leopold the butt of the joke. Later, the newly vamped Vita takes her sexual revenge on the racist detective Blick (Roger Caine) who hates "spics." The subsequent BDSM scene, in which Vita treats Blick as the "piggy" he is, making him "oink" and serve her sexual wishes, indicates the oscillating power dynamics of the *Dracula* narrative and the pleasures of being a switch. These power dynamics are heightened by racial difference, a difference addressed through the metaphor of the vampire. Nothing in hardcore is truly as static or stationary as it appears, and the wildly pivoting and pleasurable nature of Del Rio's racialized sexual performance is starkly indicative of this. Vita Valdez's character exploits the vampiric exotic, while also creating a space for subversive performative racialization.

Del Rio utilizes her notorious Latina persona as a way of intimidating Blick, enacting what Jennifer C. Nash calls "race pleasure." Nash argues that women of color can generate pleasure through hyperbolic performances of race, while viewers of color can experience pleasure through these performances (93). Hyperbole and hyper-racialized performance can highlight the constructed, artificial nature of racialized representation and stereotype (Capino). Vita/Del Rio deploys this hyper-racialized performance to mock and intimidate her racist persecutor. Blick is initially confused by the apparent resurrection of a dead woman, but Vita deflects Blick's confusion by invoking his racism and using it against him: "You know what they say, that us Spics all look alike too." Blick is also confused by his mingled feelings of disgust and desire, foregrounding the hypocrisy of racist sexual fetishism, a conflicted attitude toward the sexually aggressive, exotic woman—an attitude that comes straight from the pages of Stoker's novel. As Vita grows increasingly predatory, Blick attempts to leave, exclaiming, "I don't like your filthy hands touching me . . . !" Mocking his racism, Vita exclaims, "Ooo-ee! I do believe you don't like us spics," and persists in her advances. Blick closes his eyes, grappling with his conflicting emotions, and the screen dissolves to a shot of him naked, with bloody bite marks on his neck.

As with so many other hardcore vampire narratives, the moment of vampiric penetration is absent. Hardcore's claim to speak the hypocritical silences of the Gothic Victorian text is again contradicted by heteroporn's coyness when it comes to penetration of the male, but also by society's condemna-

16. Vita Valdez orders Blick to oink like a pig in *Dracula Exotica* (1981).

tion of pornography's alleged violence and porn's subsequent self-censorship. Instead, Vita is shown in a black dominatrix outfit complete with bat wings, while Blick is entirely nude and on all fours. The role reversal is immediate and startling. The scene itself involves Vita's continued humiliation of Blick, forcing him to "Come to me like a pig," prompting him to "oink" repeatedly, kiss her feet, and perform cunnilingus on her. The absence of any penetration of Blick is compensated for by Vita's dynamic, dominant sexual exploitation of him. The dominatrix sex scene speaks the Victorian Gothic vampire bite that, ironically, porn cannot represent.

The power dynamics of the money shot are also subtly destabilized. Vita is on her knees in a traditionally submissive position, while Blick stands above her in a traditionally dominant position. Yet Vita aggressively demands the semen, complicating simplistic notions of feminine passive receptiveness, as she orders, "Cum in my face! Cum in my face!" She responds to the facial with fangs bared, growling and writhing. Vita oscillates between active and passive in a similar way to her treatment on the morgue slab. Even during the money shot, she is sexually aggressive, challenging simplistic cultural meanings of submission. While the enthusiastic and aggressive reception of a money shot is common in porn, it is the vampire mythos together with

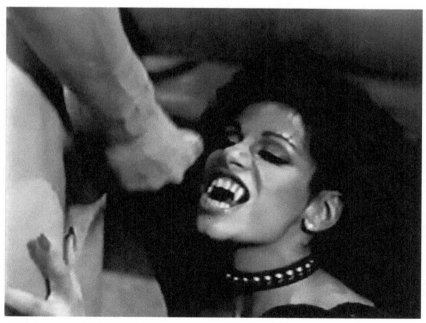

17. Vita Valdez demands the money shot in *Dracula Exotica* (1981).

del Rio's hyper-racialized performance that explicitly mobilize a challenge to simplistic ideas of passive femininity or exotic sexual deviance.

Pornographic representations of women echo the dueling sensations of pollution and eroticism evoked by Lucy and the vampire sisters in Stoker's *Dracula*. The rhetorical position of women in porn is emphasized dramatically in hardcore Dracula films that seek to expose the suppressed content of Stoker's novel. In the novel, Jonathan regards the vampire sisters as "both thrilling and repulsive" (42), while Lucy's changed state makes the Crew "shudder[] with horror" (187). Mina, during her precarious state of transition, repeatedly cries out that she is "'Unclean! Unclean!'" and has "'polluted flesh!'" (259). Blick's disgust with Vita echoes the disgust leveled at the transformed women in Stoker's *Dracula*, and more specifically the conflicting feelings of pleasure and horror Jonathan experiences. But there is nothing disgusting about Vita. Indeed, Blick is portrayed as a fool and the butt of Vita's racial jokes. In addition, Vita's sexual aggression is unchanged—she was sexually dominant before her transformation, and remains so in her altered state, only now with supernatural powers of control. The repulsion and confusion Blick experiences are not due to her sexuality alone, but also to her race. In this way, the gendered fear of reverse colonization is present in both novel and film. In the former, the reader is meant to fear the Other even as they may experience simultaneous desire. In the latter, the Other is desirable as a result of their sexual deviance, their monstrosity, their nastiness.

Blick's disgust and arousal is a highly gendered fear of reverse colonization, only here the audience presumably wants this "colonization" to occur. Just as men have occupied women's bodies, Vita is intent on occupying Blick's. The film mocks racism and celebrates active female sexuality even if the monster must be vanquished, in turn suggesting that erotic appeal and sexuality are closely tied up in racist attitudes and ideologies. Desire for and disgust toward the racial-female Other, the film suggests, work together seamlessly, just as in the nineteenth century. Vita also conjures late-nineteenth-century fears of racial impurity, suggesting that American fears of the (re)pollution of United States soil by immigrant "spics" is the 1980s version of this nineteenth-century angst. *Dracula Exotica* exemplifies how hardcore offers space to challenge social constructions of race and gender even while it also exploits the most hyperbolized manifestations of societal racism and misogyny. Ironically, performers and directors are able to provide surprisingly direct transgressive moments of "speaking back" due to the blatant intent to outrage that is part of hardcore's rhetoric.

The pervasiveness of pornographic Draculas is testament to the sexual power and ambiguous gender dynamics of Stoker's novel. Of all the texts discussed in this book, *Dracula* is surely the most overtly sexual, bordering on the pornographic, as so many scholars have observed. Yet, as with all neo-Victorian pornography, the use of an era unable to fully speak the sexual in order to stage pornographic transgression creates further silences and delicate navigations of the sexual content pornography claims to speak unabashedly. Merely by resexualizing Victorian novels in an unsimulated, explicit fashion, pornography claims to boldly go where Victorians could not. However, these hardcore films go boldly into terrain that is also carefully sanctioned by the generic demands of hardcore and its intricate and sometimes convoluted categories. Porn constantly navigates abject fluids, gendered bodies, and sexual identity; it monitors, separates, and conflates. Together with the invocation of vampirism as a technology of female sexual agency and racial subjectivity, these conflicting interests produce a queering effect. Hardcore Dracula films mine the rich silences in Stoker's novel and demonstrate the deviant and oscillating pleasures at the constantly mobile erotic intersection of race, gender, and power.

3

I'M GROWN UP NOW

Female Sexual Authorship and Coming of Age in Pornographic Adaptations of Lewis Carroll's Alice Books

"It was much pleasanter at home," thought poor Alice, "when one wasn't always growing larger and smaller, and being ordered about by mice and rabbits. I almost wish I hadn't gone down that rabbit-hole—and yet—and yet—it's rather curious, you know, this life! [. . .] There ought to be a book written about me, that there ought! And when I grow up, I'll write one—but I'm grown up now," she added in a sorrowful tone: "at least there's no room to grow up any more *here*."

—Carroll, *Alice's Adventures in Wonderland*

Drink me

—Carroll, *Alice's Adventures in Wonderland*

Eat me

—Carroll, *Alice's Adventures in Wonderland*

It is not difficult to see why many people (myself included) find Wonderland to be a terrifying, oppressive, violent, and controlling space for girls. Alice's contention that there is little room to grow up is borne out in further scenes from *Alice's Adventures in Wonderland* (1865), and particularly in the sequel, *Through the Looking Glass* (1871), in which Alice is variously verbally and physically accosted before she emerges in ambivalent spirit into the real world. At the same time, the many instances of eating, drinking, tunnels, and physical transformations create a sense of rebellious mobility, consumption, and metamorphosis that many scholars have interpreted through a feminist lens to represent sexual transgression. Once seen as the subject of a children's tale, Alice has grown up over the past decade. Victorianist Catherine Siemann describes the current form of this erstwhile innocent story as "unsuitable for children" (175). Pornographers, in hot pursuit of anything remotely suggestive of sex, but also attracted to icons and tropes suggestive of purity, have exploited the Alice narrative in dozens of films spanning five decades.[1]

Alice is a child of seven years old in Carroll's stories. The real Alice, Alice Liddell, is shrouded in mystery and troublingly linked to Lewis Carroll (writer Charles Dodgson's pen name) and his suspected pedophilia. In discussions of "pornography," the specter of "child pornography" often looms nearby. Considering Alice is the creation of a man subsequently suspected of pedophilic desires, and who certainly photographed pre-pubescent boys and girls,[2] the prospect of pornographers exploiting this character in sexually explicit ways understandably makes some people uncomfortable. In turn, pornographers are wary of invoking childhood while at the same time operate in an industry that (like all media) sexually exploits the iconography of youth. There is a contradiction in the way pornographers have adapted Alice: while hardcore adaptations of the *Alice* stories claim to reveal an inherent sexual quality to the stories, part of the appeal of adapting a children's fairy tale is also, as Jason Williams, production manager of *Alice in Wonderland: A XXX Musical*, puts it, "the polarity, the contrast" (*Alice in Wonderland* [1976]). As with all the neo-Victorian porn films discussed in this book, this seeming contradiction between a sexually suggestive source text that is also innocent and naïve is exactly where the pleasures of neo-Victorian porn rest.

In the case of Alice, pornographers seem drawn to interrogating a perceived Victorian paternal control of the female protagonist. In response to this perceived paternalism, a handful of hardcore adaptations explicitly Gothicize the tales, such as *Through the Looking Glass* (1976), *Tormented* (2009), and *Malice in Lalaland* (2012). These films situate Alice as an unwilling pawn in a masculine world populated by abusive patriarchs. In the first film, the protagonist, Catherine, is haunted by the incestuous abuse she suffered at the hands of her father and is gradually seduced by a demon (in the shape of her father) into a Looking Glass hell.[3] In *Tormented* and *Malice in Lalaland*, Wonderland is an illusory escape from the insane asylum where the female protagonist has been placed due to her inappropriate sexual appetites. Such implicit critiques of the Carroll tales are in the minority, however. Hardcore more commonly rescues Alice from Carroll's controlling grip, either releasing Alice into a joyful Wonderland of sexual development or turning the tables on Carroll and his cast of abusive characters.

If Dracula and his weird sisters reflect darkness and all the deviant delights therein, Alice represents light—white, English femininity—and the pleasures of transgressing that chaste boundary. Pornographers take the popular notion of Victorian white femininity as sexually repressed and socially oppressed and recast this feminine character as an active sexual subject. For while pornography routinely exploits the iconography of youth, hardcore adaptations of Alice opt to focus on an adult Alice, coming of age, and the process of maturity— more interested in adult female sexual subjectivity than the innocence of youth.[4] More specifically, the Alice narrative has become a popular canvas on which female and feminist pornographers develop explorations of guilt-free white female sexual agency and gendered power dynamics circulating in society. Alice, an ambiguously empowered little girl, becomes an adult fully in possession of her sexuality.

The cultural meaning and perception of Alice, both text and character, have been deeply influenced by a range of paratexts: Disney, Carroll's relationship with Alice Liddell, Carroll's photographs of nude children, psychoanalytic theory, and feminist interpretation that has explored the books for sexual symbolism. Alice and her Wonderland, the meaning of her image and journey, have become culture texts. In Will Brooker's exhaustive history of the many myths and permutations of Alice, *Alice's Adventures*, he notes, "Carroll and Alice currently circulate as cultural myths, cultural icons" (xiv), myths and icons that perform particular functions for twenty-first-century consumers. The same can be said of all the literary icons discussed in this book. Yet *Alice*, as Helen Pilinovsky argues, stands apart as a culture text due to "the taboo issue that is central to the cultural fixation with *Alice*: the circumstances surrounding its composition" (176). Pilinovsky alludes to the pedophilic associations with the books, associations that pornographers tiptoe around very carefully. Pornographic appropriations of *Alice* simultaneously invoke and displace these connotations and the sexual suggestiveness of Alice's journey, utilizing them as a way of exploring Victorian patriarchal control and exploitation of female sexuality. Hardcore filmmakers porn the subtextual content of the *Alice* books while simultaneously closing it up by denying any association between sexuality and youth.

While Carroll is at best ambivalent about Alice's maturation, and at worst resistant and controlling of it, pornography presents sexual stasis as not simply undesirable but outright destructive. In hardcore Alice adaptations, female sexual maturation is presented as a necessity and a pleasure, contradicting Carroll's insistence on retaining female innocence and youth. These adaptations approach Wonderland as a place that, in the words of Mistress

Alice of *Alice in Bondageland*, "gives license to almost anything because it is transgressive by nature. That's the whole point of Wonderland, that all rules must be broken. It's kind of the only rule. That lends itself to especially rich taboo fantasies with blanket permission." Pornographic adaptations of Alice reclaim Wonderland for Alice, literalizing the sexual symbolism of the novels while at the same time offering a transformed Alice who is free to author her own sexual coming of age.

A Proper English Girl: The Mid-1900s and White Femininity

The *Alice* stories are the only works of fiction from before the late nineteenth century addressed in this book. Published in 1865 and 1871, respectively, *Alice's Adventures in Wonderland* and *Alice's Adventures through the Looking Glass* are from a Victorian society a good fifteen years prior to the next-youngest novel in this project. *Dr. Jekyll & Mr. Hyde* (1886), *The Picture of Dorian Gray* (1891), and *Dracula* (1897) were all published within an eleven-year span and reflect a fin de siècle society with quite different understandings and fears regarding race, gender, class, and sexuality. Alice is of an era that knew nothing of the "New Woman" and had not yet been introduced to the word "homosexuality." The threat of women's liberation and anxieties over expansion of the British Empire had not crested and would not for a decade or more. Oscar Wilde's imprisonment for "indecency" under the Labouchere Amendment wouldn't occur for another thirty years. Likewise, the joys and apprehensions ignited by motorized vehicles, electric light, mechanized warfare, the telephone, skyscrapers, and radio were not to be felt for several years.

At the same time, technological advancements brought gas and, therefore, light to the streets of London that were themselves experiencing something of an overhaul. Gas lit, commercialized, mapped, and rerouted, the city streets were the site of a modernizing strategy. They were also teeming with a cross section of the populace. Consumer culture combined with a reinvented city, colonial rule, and developments in technology such as the photograph, transformed London into a bustling, multicultural, and (unsettlingly for some) diverse locale. The transformed city confronted citizens with the realities of the working classes, lewd women, obscene media, and traces of empire such as "oriental beggars and black street musicians" (Nead 152). Photography and other forms of low urban spectacle were associated with "the trash of the empire" (Nead 153). This burgeoning metropolis guaranteed that if an elite white flâneur went strolling and observing, he would likely be observed himself. White men were no longer the privileged voyeurs; by the mid-1860s they had a lot of company. In this social context, curious little Alice—blonde, white, and dressed in a pinafore—emerges as a symbol of Victorian innocence, and Carroll is loath to let her grow up too fast.

The 1860s were exciting, forward thinking, and yet also distinctly rooted in a pre-fin de siècle social consciousness imbued with innocence, uncertainty, and tradition. In this way, the Alice culture text has evolved in a way distinct from Dracula and his weird sisters, Dorian Gray, and Mr. Hyde. The late-nineteenth-century characters of interest to pornographers are by no means innocent. They are of an era bursting forth into the next century, technologically advanced, racially and sexually ambiguous, deviant in gender, traveling fast, on the cusp of the modern world, monstrous. Alice, on the other hand, appears to represent a prototypical white Victorian femininity, one that generates pornographic adaptations intent on rescuing and reclaiming this little girl from the grasp of patriarchal Victoriana. Pornographers ensure that Alice can grow up and seize control of her destiny.

"The Dream-Child": Sexual Pleasure and Womanhood in *Alice in Wonderland: A XXX Musical* (1976)

In her essay "Underworld Portmanteaux: Dante's Hell and Carroll's Wonderland in Women's Memoirs of Mental Illness," Rachel Falconer observes the ways in which the concept of an underworld Wonderland has served authors striving to embody a space "outside (or beneath) the normal spaces of social interchange" (9). Wonderland can serve as a space for something "other," the doppelganger to the norm, any niche or subgenre a pornographer wishes to explore. Wonderland functions in hardcore as what Steven Marcus calls a "pornotopia": a timeless, placeless (Gothic) space where everything is designed to connote and facilitate sex with no consequences; a space where it is "always bedtime" (269) and where language "is a prison from which [pornography] is continually trying to escape" (279). Similarly, Victorianist U. C. Knoepflmacher regards Wonderland as "an anti-linguistic otherworld" (153) where Carroll is able to indulge in "self-rejuvenation" (158), "regressive hostility to growth and sexual division" (5), and to use his heroine as an "authorial surrogate" (8). Scholar of Victorian literature and childhood sexuality James R. Kincaid argues, "The Alice books are, above all, about growing up, and they recognize both the melancholy of the loss of Eden and the child's rude and tragic haste to leave its innocence" (93). This focus on growing up, in tandem with a resistance to this process, is perhaps the most obvious reason for the popularity of the *Alice* books in hardcore pornography—the journey from girlhood to womanhood via experience and consumption holds much in the way of sexually suggestive imagery and concepts.[5]

Consumption of food and drink, for example, figure prominently in *Wonderland*, which can connote sexual desire, gratification, and its denial. Helena Michie observes that in Victorian culture, hunger "figures unspeakable desires for sexuality and power" (15), desires that film pornography is eager to speak. Alice is "a greedy little girl who tastes drinks and cakes as soon as she falls into Wonderland" (Talairach-Vielmas 49), making her a sexually voracious protagonist ideal for pornographic appropriation. Indeed, in her influential essay, "Alice in Wonderland: A Curious Child," Nina Auerbach muses in a footnote, "Does it go too far to connect the mouth that presides over Alice's story to a looking-glass vagina?" (39). In pornotopia, it does not. As *Playboy* magazine bluntly puts it in their review of *Alice in Wonderland: A XXX Musical* (1976), "Eat me, redefined" ("X-Rated").[6]

At the same time, Alice equivocates. She is not always greedy, active, and dominant. She is often passive, pushed around, and uncertain. She eats and drinks because she is told to. When she does eat or drink, her body often reacts in rebellious and uncontrollable ways. This has resulted in a body of scholarly criticism that attempts to situate Alice as either active *or* passive, when in reality she is both at different moments. For example, whereas Auerbach sees Alice as "explod[ing] out of Wonderland hungry and unregenerate" (46), Laurence Talairach-Vielmas sees Alice's "voyage into womanhood" as "a journey into powerlessness" (10). For Talairach-Vielmas, food is not a source of sexual agency and exploration; on the contrary, "the food she finds in Wonderland systematically seems to punish her acts of self-assertion, as if the luring treats which peppered her adventures were devised to tame her appetite from within" (10). Rather than escaping the prescriptions of femininity and proper gendered behavior, "[h]er dream does not enable her to escape reality and to enter a wonderland where she can give vent to her appetites" (Talairach-Vielmas 61). This conflict at the heart of Alice's journey is in large part why she works so well in pornography, a genre where the changeable, dynamic woman reigns supreme. Violation of the mainstream, shifting gender dynamics, and power play are the bread and butter of hardcore, so it should come as no surprise that Alice has been a staple of the genre since 1976.

Certainly, Alice is obsessed with food and drink, and her journey is a seemingly never-ending trail of edible items. These items often have a physical effect on her, and sometimes a psychical one. While she is certainly "curious," active and on the move, and consumes whatever edible things she comes across, it is difficult to fully embrace Auerbach's reading that Alice is in control of her own physical changes or that she emerges from Wonderland "hungry and unregenerate." Indeed, the Dormouse's cautionary tale of the children stuck in the treacle well initially engages Alice, as she "always took a great interest in questions of eating and drinking" (Carroll 49), and yet the story has a subordinating effect. Alice's attitude changes from that of anger to politeness and humble promises to stop interrupting. Her desire to hear the story stems from a desire to hear about food, and yet the story warns against consumption, and Alice's desire prompts her own self-silencing.

Furthermore, the trial of the tarts, which results in Alice's violent awakening from her dream, begins with further desirous thoughts and self-restraint on Alice's part: "In the very middle of the court was a table, with a large dish of tarts upon it: they looked so good, that it made Alice quite hungry to look at them—'I wish they'd get the trial done,' she thought, 'and hand round the refreshments!' But there seemed no chance of this; so she began looking at everything about her to pass away the time" (73). Alice's desire for the tarts goes unsatisfied, as Talailach-Vielmas observes, and yet Alice does not avert her eyes from "everything about her." Ultimately, her verbal outbursts and physical growth have the effect of disrupting and then dismantling proceedings, leading to the ambiguous "fright" and "anger" Alice experiences before waking up (Carroll 83). As Jennifer Geer, professor of children's literature, observes, "For an instant, Alice assumes a position directly contrary to those prescribed by domestic ideology or ideals of girlhood" (9). However, any lingering ambiguity regarding Alice's empowerment and subversive agency is quickly stifled by "a transition back into the domestic" (Geer 10) and the anonymous narrator's instruction that it was "a wonderful dream" (84). Alice's older sister envisions Alice as "a grown woman [. . .] how she would keep, through all her riper years, the simple and loving heart of her childhood; and how she would gather about her other little children, and make *their* eyes bright and eager with many a strange tale" (Carroll 86). Thus, the domesticating framework of the real world, not to mention the bullies she has been fending off throughout the narrative, defang Alice's subversive adventures.

A product of 1970s sexual revolution and counterculture, *Alice in Wonderland: A XXX Musical* (dir. Bud Townsend, 1976) consciously subverts the sexually condemnatory attitude that emerges from Carroll's *Wonderland*. The marketing rhetoric plays on the origins of the text as children's literature to exploit the risqué pornographic overturning of the Carroll text, situating the film as "an X-rated musical—but it's not for kids. It's a bedtime story—but it's not for kids" ("Alice in Wonderland [1976]"). A tagline for the film also plays on the double meaning of what goes on in bed, declaring, "The world's

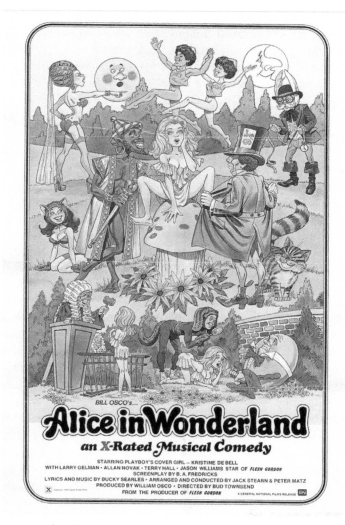

18. Poster for *Alice in Wonderland: A XXX Musical* (1976).

favorite bed-time story is finally a bed-time story" ("Alice in Wonderland [1976]").

While these advertising tactics draw on the childhood origins of Alice as a way of clearly positioning the film as "for adults only," in referencing the distinction in address between the novels and the film, the rhetoric also offers a reconciliatory notion of coming of age for girls. As Pilinovsky notes,

"Reversing the polarity of the original Victorian narrative, the 1976 *Alice* rejects the notion of a glorified childhood. This twentieth-century Wonderland conveys that maturity—physical, sexual, and emotional maturity—can be magical, and that there's little to fear from the inevitability of growing up" (182). Hardcore treatments of Alice are firmly grounded in the adult, exploiting the controversial nature of adapting children's literature through marketing but focusing on the pleasures of adult womanhood in the films themselves.

At the same time, while the XXX Wonderland segments are delightfully carnivalesque and prioritize Alice's autonomous and joyful sexual explorations, the narrative is bookended by segments that suggest a woman's "physical, sexual, and emotional maturity" merely involves putting out for one's boyfriend, a common feminist critique of sexual counterculture. This XXX Alice (Kristine De Bell) is a young and sexually inexperienced woman, "just not that kind of girl." As Alice's boyfriend observes, "The body is all grown up, but the mind is still a little girl's. . . . You've got all the right equipment, but you don't know how to put it to work." After leaving Wonderland a sexually experienced and grown-up woman, Alice puts her new-found knowledge "to work" by having sex with her boyfriend and achieving orgasm, a demonstration of the proper, heteronormative outcomes of female sexual awakening. The postscript also promotes monogamy, marriage, and children as the inevitable happy ending for a woman: "Alice settled down, got married, raised a family, in a house, with a white picket fence, filled with kids, and a little arf! arf! puppy."

With all that said, the postscript appears to be tongue-in-cheek, and even if it is not, the implication that Alice's sexual adventures do not preclude her entry into the patriarchal contract of marriage is surely something to celebrate. Wonderland is a joyous, singing-and-dancing adventure of sexual self-exploration for Alice, and one that has no ill effects on her real life existence. Indeed, Alice actively seeks to settle down with her boyfriend, raise a family, and have all the other trappings denied the fallen woman of the Victorian era. Wonderland offers much in the way of pleasure, self-satisfaction, and curious exploration that goes wholeheartedly unpunished. The real world is no place for a girl to attempt growing up. It stifles female pleasure. By entering XXX Wonderland, Alice has the opportunity to set things right—as she puts it, to "grow up all over again."

From the moment her boyfriend leaves her, Alice is a determined sexual agent. Crying out as if in warning, "Here I come!" XXX Alice leaps down the rabbit hole with gusto. Unlike Carroll's story, though, Alice's journey through

Wonderland is characterized by encouragement of sexual desires, which are conflated variously with growing up, exploring your imagination, trusting what feels good, and being yourself, all things that the real world tends to deny women. Sexuality and appetite are not condemned or punished. In fact, Alice is put on trial for her "chastity" and is found guilty. Moreover, the film self-consciously acknowledges the source text as a restrictive, controlling influence getting in the way of sexual abandonment. For example, the trial—the most condemnatory element of the film—is included solely because it appears in the Carroll book. In fact, the inhabitants of XXX Wonderland are bemused by such a punitive event. The Queen cries out, "Trial? A trial? Where is it written that we have to give you a trial?" The Hatter hands the King a copy of *Alice's Adventures* and exclaims, "It says so right here in this book."

The ensuing trial is thus framed as a perfunctory performance of the limiting and punitive nature of Carroll's text, begrudgingly included in order to satisfy the requirements of an adaptation. In addition, the fact that Alice is on trial for chastity ironizes Carroll's puritanical attitude toward sexuality. Roger Ebert, in his mostly positive 1976 review of the film, exclaims that it will have Carroll "spinning in his grave." While Ebert presumably meant this as a lazy joke about the explicit sex scenes, to bother Carroll is indeed the point of the film. The trial does not end with the court attacking Alice, as it does in Carroll's version. The Wonderland inhabitants have been nothing but supportive of Alice throughout the film. The trial is instead followed by a segment titled "Fun in Wonderland," a wacky montage of orgiastic imagery and visual jokes that frequently conflate food and sex. If the film must include Carroll's unpleasant trial, the film suggests, then it will be one that criticizes the very concept of female virtue, and concludes with a laughter-filled romp through Wonderland.

The sexual activities within Wonderland are rapid-fire, joyful, and queer. In a memorable scene, Alice enjoy interspecies sex with the Scrugs, a group of naïve and joyful abhuman creatures that helpfully lick Alice dry after she falls in the pool of tears. In another scene, a song-and-dance number reveals the Black Knight and White Knight (actual allusions to their race) to be same-sex lovers. And brother and sister, Tweedledee and Tweedledum, enjoy a harmonious sexual relationship with no concern for real-world notions of incest. Such transgressive sexualities abound in this pornotopian, musical Wonderland.

The overwhelming message of the film is to shake off the guilt and shame women internalize as part of their sexual coming of age. This Wonderland is a place where perversions mingle with naïvety, rendering any dirtiness clean or meaningless. The King, who has no understanding of Alice's meaning when she tries to explain her desire to wait until marriage, best expresses this. Alice tells him she cannot have sex because she wants to be "clean, unblemished, spotless." He assures her, "I won't put any spots on you. I like you just the way you are!" In this pornotopian Wonderland, such constructions of feminine virtue are meaningless. Furthermore, following Alice's emergence from her dream into the real world, she is able to assimilate into a normative sexual contract of marriage and monogamy in spite of, or even because of, her explorations in Wonderland. Thus, unlike the fallen women of the Victorian age, Alice is able to have her cake and eat it too.

"I Generally Hit Everything I Can See—When I Get Really Excited": BDSM Alices

Of all the texts analyzed in this project, the *Alice* books have the most adaptations and appropriations that fall under the fetish and BDSM categories: *Alice in Fetishland* (2000), *Alice in Bondageland* (2000), *Fetish Fairy Tails 3: Alice in Summerland* (2005), *Alice in Savageland* (2008), *Alice in Tickleland* (2009), and Mistress Alice's website, AliceinBondageland.com. Another film titled *Alice in Fetishland* was included in the 2013 CineKink Film Festival in New York City. While the popularity of Alice with this particular genre may at first seem unusual, in fact the punitive violence of Wonderland and Looking-Glass Land, coupled with Alice's variously dominant and submissive behaviors, make these particular appropriations more understandable. While Alice of the books is a reluctant plaything of Carroll's imagination, subject to "uncontrolled aggression" (Kincaid 93), hardcore fetish and BDSM pornographers overturn these formulations, throwing the gendered nature of domination and submission into flux and restaging Wonderland as a space that is very much controlled and negotiated. Moreover, the concept of a Wonderland and a Looking-Glass Land, where play, inversion, and the topsy-turvy seem possible, provides a play space for primarily female BDSM practitioners to hold court. Alice has become the dominatrix icon of this world, its mistress and author, with Carroll entirely removed from the equation. Through BDSM's staging of "sexual commerce as a theater of transformation" (McClintock 87), the gender and subjectivity of Alice and her cohorts are thrown into disarray, with Alice at the helm of their play-world.

While appearing to draw on and perpetuate a natural gender hierarchy, in reality BDSM "*performs* social power as both contingent and constitutive, as sanctioned neither by fate nor by God, but by social convention and invention, and thus as open to historical change" (McClintock, "Maid to Order" 91, italics in original). This is because anyone can inhabit the role of dominant or submissive, regardless of gender, and the submissive co-authors the scene. Likewise, philosopher and ethicist Patrick D. Hopkins frames sadomasochism as a simulation of power structures, rather than a replication of them. In this way, BDSM becomes "a site for the (partial) performative subversion of gender" in the sense that gender does not dictate power, and vice versa (Hopkins 135). "To the extent that sex and gender and sexual identities themselves are captured and manipulated and exposed by the 'scene,'" Hopkins explains, "they are made to seem less natural, less definite, less compulsory" (136). Furthermore, the BDSM *Alice* films tend to position men in submissive roles and Alice in the dominant role. This produces what Hopkins describes as "an image subversive to patriarchal sexual ideology" an ideology associated with Alice's submissive status under Carroll's controlling authorship and Victorian gender relations more broadly.

The popularity of BDSM Alices is likely the result of Alice's conflicted experiences of Wonderland. While Kincaid recognizes both "rootless hostility" and "free and uncompetitive joy," a world where "Alice is the object of love as well as fear" (92), Jacqueline Labbe regards Wonderland as "dangerous for Alice," a world where "submission is the only answer" (24). Indeed, Wonderland is a precarious and intimidating space. Following her leap down the rabbit hole, Alice quickly learns that she must navigate this new world and its unpredictable inhabitants, not to mention her own unpredictable physical changes, leading to her constantly oscillating position within the power relations of Wonderland. One moment she is replying "shyly" (27) to the Caterpillar, and a moment later she is "swallowing down her anger as well as she could" (28). At the tea party she speaks "angrily" and "with some severity" (44) but is soon "dreadfully puzzled" and speaking "as politely as she could," "cautiously" and "thoughtfully" (46). Interrupting the tale of the treacle well, Alice finds herself "beginning very angrily," but then asks the Dormouse "very humbly" (49) to continue, until finally finding the Hatter to be too rude to bear: "She got up in great disgust, and walked off: the Dormouse fell asleep instantly, and neither of the others took the least notice of her going, though she looked back once or twice, half hoping that they would call after her" (50). BDSM porn appropriates these power dynamics but does away with the hesitancy and care Alice takes in responding to these erratic characters. The BDSM adaptations seize control of the narrative, wresting it away from Carroll and placing it in the hands of Alice as participant and author.

While Alice's interactions with the Wonderland creatures are perhaps most memorably fraught with tension, she reserves her bitterest scoldings for herself. This finds an interesting parallel in the degree to which the submissive is author of the scene in BDSM. As Anne McClintock observes in "Maid to Order," "To argue that in consensual S/M the 'dominant' has power, and the slave has not, is to read theater for reality; it is to play the world forward. The economy of S/M is the economy of conversion: slave to master, adult to baby, pain to pleasure, man to woman, and back again" (87). To be sure, after scolding herself for crying, the narrator explains, "sometimes she scolded herself so severely as to bring tears into her eyes . . . for this curious child was very fond of pretending to be two people" (6). The "two people" Alice inhabits are the scolder and weeper, the masculine and the feminine, the dominant and the submissive. Such gendered, binary power relations characterize both Wonderland and Alice's psyche (which, after all, *is* Wonderland). BDSM pornographers can rupture and stage these Wonderland dualities, transforming gendered subjectivity in the process.

Two competing desires are at work within the text: "the adult's desire to dominate children and the child's desire to resist that domination" (Geer 7). While Geer's analysis centers around the narrator's framing poems, which seem to contradict Alice's adventures themselves, it is not so great a leap to gender such forces as masculine and feminine, or to dichotomize them according to power relations of dominant and submissive, power relations that can then become pleasurably performed, transformed, and ungendered in BDSM.

Alice rarely submits in the BDSM and fetish film appropriations. While in Wonderland she is helplessly resized and ordered about, in BDSM pornography the girls stage a takeover of Wonderland. The members of each various "land" are subject to Alice's whims and punishments, not the other way around. Linda Williams has observed that "although male submissives apparently outweigh dominators in real-life heterosexual sadomasochistic practice, the incompatibility of this role with the more traditional use of heterosexual pornography as confirmation of viewers' masculine identity inhibits its incorporation into hard-core narrative" (*Hard Core* 196). Yet the Alices of the fetish and BDSM titles are almost all dominant, the male characters almost all submissive. Summer Cummings's *Fetish Fairy Tails 3: Alice in Summerland* is a notably playful and reflexive light-BDSM fetish video, featuring four scenes in which Alice meets a character from Summerland: the White Rabbit, Cheshire Cat, the Caterpillar, and finally the Queen of Hearts (the only character to dominate Alice). *Alice in Summerland* establishes from the very title that this is Summer's Land. There is no confusion over authorship; Alice, Summer Cummings, and author are one. This is Summer's playground: she wrote, directed, and stars in the film.

The video, like much fetish and BDSM pornography, involves no conventional sexual intercourse of any kind, and only small amounts of genital contact. As Williams has noted, much of BDSM and its subgenres are characterized by a "lack of subordination to a genital goal of discharge or 'end pleasure'" (195). In this way, the video avoids much of the perceived imbalance of power relations signified by androcentric genital intercourse and yet simultaneously foregrounds power relations via constant verbal and physical power play. BDSM in general is not about one person being dominant and one person being dominated; rather, it is about a contractual power play, one in which power is not fixed (Williams, *Hard Core* 228), where the dominant might switch and become submissive, and where participants can confront gender and power, challenging the natural order of gender relations through simulation, staging, and "doing a scene" (Hopkins). Indeed, Summer's attraction to the Alice story is rooted in "the fact that she is both dominant and submissive in different parts of the story" (Cummings). Alice's oscillating power in the Carroll text offers up a rich canvas on which to play out the fluid gender positions of BDSM.

In Summerland, the characters of Carroll's stories attempt their punitive attitude toward Alice but are quickly put in their place. For example, on meeting the Caterpillar, Summer answers his question— "Who are you?"—with a tentative "I'm not really sure," similar to Wonderland Alice's "I—I hardly know, Sir" (27). Yet when the Caterpillar persists with the question, Summer's Alice snaps and yells, "I just told you, OK?! I'm Alice, and I need to get outta here!" Similar to this, when the White Rabbit asks if she is a girl, Alice doesn't hesitate to assert angrily, "Yes I am a girl! What, you don't have girls here?" In Wonderland, the Pigeon's question regarding Alice's species prompts an introspective query on Alice's part as to whether she is a girl, whether she is a serpent, and whether she eats eggs (35), but not so in Summerland.

Furthermore, in Summerland the Caterpillar—a somewhat intimidating and wise character in Wonderland—is reduced to an absurd broken record. Each time Summer asks for the way out, the Caterpillar returns to his cycle of stock phrases. This enrages Summer, who, after giving him ample warning, opts to reject any potential assistance, gags him with rope, and wraps his entire body in saran wrap like a cocoon, covering his mouth and silencing him before moving on to the next scene. Tenniel's illustration of Alice's encounter with the Caterpillar also stands in stark contrast to the composi-

19. Summer and the Caterpillar in *Fetish Fairy Tails 3: Alice in Summerland* (2005).

tion of the same encounter in Summerland. While Tenniel's Alice is barely tall enough to see over the mushroom on which the Caterpillar is seated, so that only her hands and eyes peeking over the edge can be seen, Summer—forty-three years old, stocky, loud, and with very large breast implants—is immediately physically dominant over the tubby and dimwitted Caterpillar. In Summerland, Alice is the one teaching lessons, and the violence and unsettling power relations of Wonderland become the source of staged gender and power play.

Alice also becomes the dominant in the website *Alice in Bondageland*, run by Mistress Alice. The tone of this site depicts smiling, laughing BDSM. Mistress Alice explains that at the time of the site's conception, she could not find any BDSM content that depicted "happy and healthy BDSM where it looked like participants were having fun" (Mistress Alice). Thus, *Alice in Bondageland* was created. Mistress Alice explains that when she began the site, she was disappointed in the BDSM porn on offer, so she sought to produce scenes that reflected the "joyful quality" of BDSM play that she witnessed in her personal life and in club settings: "We call it 'play' for a reason" (Mistress Alice). In this way, as with other hardcore adaptations of Alice, female sexual

20. Website banner from AliceinBondageland.com. Courtesy of AliceinBondageland.com.

agency becomes a guilt-free, celebratory endeavor, reclaiming and restaging the dark and ambivalent power struggles of Carroll's books.

Significantly, Mistress Alice explicitly identifies with Alice of Looking-Glass Land, "where she crosses the chessboard and then becomes the queen" (Mistress Alice). Alice's position as a pawn in a chess game is ambiguous in terms of agency, suggestive of both an anonymous player moving her around the board and the ways in which a pawn might escape the hands of this same player. In general, the relationship between Alice and her author is more fraught in *Looking-Glass*, authorial intentions more ambiguous, sinister, and domineering, and yet, as Mistress Alice observes, this is the narrative in which Alice is afforded the most agency. Carroll seems ambivalent about Alice's maturation; even though Carroll interrupts and overshadows his heroine, he also permits agency and authorship throughout the text. Hence, Knoepflmacher's contention that "The *Looking-Glass* Alice . . . is quite deliberately presented as a mirror image of the narrator who dominated the heroine of the *Wonderland* text" (209–10). Thus, while Carroll's presence is persistent, and he is reluctant to allow Alice to mature, the tone of his authorial presence is also pathetic and wistful in its understanding that she must come of age and become subject.

Perhaps most jarring is the narrator's aside regarding the White Knight who, it appears, represents Carroll himself saying goodbye to Alice as she goes off to become an adult woman. The narrator explains,

> Of all the strange things that Alice saw in her journey Through The Looking-Glass, this was the one that she always remembered most clearly. Years afterwards she could bring the whole scene back again, as if it had been only yesterday—the mild blue eyes and kindly smile of the Knight—the setting sun gleaming through his hair, and shining on his armour in a blaze of light that quite dazzled her. (125)

It is a melancholy scene, and one in which the desires of the narrator, or the White Knight, are palpable: for Alice to cherish this moment more than the others and to recall it in dazzling fashion. However, Alice does not shed the tears the Knight was expecting; instead, she runs off thoughtlessly rather than giving him an emotional goodbye. In this way, it is entirely understandable that Mistress Alice would align herself with Alice of Looking-Glass Land. As Mistress Alice puts it, "I did the 'through the rabbit hole' journey, that I read as kind of a coming of age and a sexual awakening story that's very fraught with Victorian sexual mores and peril and things like that. But Looking Glass Alice has a journey of moving into adulthood that I relate to a lot more now that I'm grown up, I guess you could say. So, that's the Alice I relate to from my femdom persona rather than the childlike Alice" (Mistress Alice).

Mistress Alice occasionally reads the Carroll stories to the characters themselves, enacting a bizarre and (in Mistress Alice's words) "ridiculous" metatext that acknowledges the fiction at the heart of the scene. These scenes also implicate Carroll and his text as a kind of torture device in a similar way to the frustrating and perfunctory inclusion of the book in *Alice: A XXX Musical*. In "Alice in Wonderland Chapter 2: Pool of Tears Sissy Bondage," Mistress Alice reads "The Pool of Tears" to a male sub dressed as Alice in the classic blue and white Disney costume. Speaking to the sub in the manner of a mother putting a child to bed, Mistress Alice makes it clear that she is the author, while the sub remains the "innocent" and "pretty" Alice of the original text in need of severe restraints because she has "a little trouble paying attention." By featuring two Alices of different sexes and coding them clearly as dominant and submissive, Mistress Alice creates a world where the fictions of Carroll's text are entirely malleable and where gender and text are revealed a fiction.

Like Summer, Mistress Alice dominates characters from Wonderland, feminizing and infantilizing them. Mistress Alice refers to this as "turning the tables" on those characters who so mercilessly ordered Alice around in the books. At the same time, indicative of the manner in which the submissive authors the scene, subs are allowed and encouraged to pick the Wonderland character they most identify with. While submissive Alice must be restrained because she has trouble paying attention, in "Cheshire Cat Saline Ball Busting," submissive Cheshire Cat must be locked up so as to limit his ability to appear and disappear. "You think you're quite the little escape artist, don't you?" Mistress Alice says mockingly, laughing in his face as she explains that the chains she is using are "enchanted," such that they will disable his magical abilities. In this Wonderland, Mistress Alice is able to invent her own rules and turn the tables on its inhabitants.

Mistress Alice is also aware of the complicated baggage surrounding Dodgson and his photographs of Alice Liddell and other children, viewing the

21. A still from "Cheshire Cat Saline Ballbusting." Courtesy of AliceinBondageland.com.

Alice culture text as a curious entry in the history of pornography: "The book and the character and the author already have this strange relationship with the dawn of modern porn, as you'd call it" (Mistress Alice). In this way, Mistress Alice recognizes this marginal sexual association and complex relationship between the novels, coming of age, and female agency. Her BDSM pornography seeks to recover this agency, a gesture Mistress Alice regards as empowering for women: "There's a certain amount of power in reclaiming those images for ourselves and particularly in my case the idea of Alice, reframing it in her own terms both as a character and also as a subject and artist relationship" (Mistress Alice). Here, Mistress Alice makes explicit what all of the adaptations under consideration suggest: pornographic Wonderlands offer Alice the opportunity to displace Carroll/Dodgson and author her own sexuality.

Hardcore adaptations of the *Alice* books vary significantly in genre and tone, offering a wide range of approaches, and yet all tap into the source texts' dealings with identity, femininity, patriarchal control, and sexual authorship, reclaiming Alice and permitting a celebratory sexual coming of age via an unruly Wonderland. Pornographers, many of them female, recognize the ambivalence surrounding female coming of age in the Alice books and stage a takeover, using porn to fill the gaps of the canonical text but also to answer it back and respond to it in complex ways that center Alice as author of her sexuality. Indeed, in the last decade, four hardcore films that adapt the *Alice* text have been produced, all of them written and/or directed by women: *Tormented* (2009), written by Stormy Daniels; *Erica McLean's Alice* (2010), directed by Erica McClean; *Malice in Lalaland* (2010), co-written by Nicki Heartache; and *Alice in Wonderland XXX* (2011), written and directed by Wendy Crawford. In porning Alice, these writers, directors, and performers do not merely expose the sexual suggestiveness of Carroll's texts and the cultural baggage surrounding them; they prove themselves sensitive literary critics. As with many of the texts under examination, the initial allure for pornography is deceptively simple: a female protagonist, a theme of emergence into womanhood, and an alternative realm where anything can happen. Yet what the adaptations show is more than simply the sexualization of youth and the ease with which a low-budget video can appropriate a familiar feminine image. The popularity and diversity of these adaptations and appropriations demonstrate the fraught nature of coming of age for girls and women, and the ways in which pornographic Wonderlands can offer space for women to speak back to a culture that attempts to contain and control sexual autonomy. In turn, hardcore Wonderlands reveal the extent to which pornography itself serves as a Wonderland for women (and men) to enjoy and enact explicit, unrepentantly deviant, and non-normative sexualities denied them in the real world.

4

RADICALLY BOTH

Transformation and Crisis
in Jekyll and Hyde Porn

The pleasures which I made haste to seek in my disguise
were, as I have said, undignified; I would scarce use a
harder term. But in the hands of Edward Hyde, they soon
began to turn towards the monstrous. When I would come
back from these excursions, I was often plunged into a
kind of wonder at my vicarious depravity. This familiar that
I called out of my own soul, and sent forth alone to do his
good pleasure, was a being inherently malign and villain-
ous; his every act and thought centered on self; drinking
pleasure with bestial avidity from any degree of torture to
another; relentless like a man of stone.

—Robert Louis Stevenson,
The Strange Case of Dr. Jekyll and Mr. Hyde

What is Hyde up to on these mysterious nighttime excursions? Many mainstream writers and directors have attempted to satisfy this question, visually
or in writing, with answers ranging from simple sexual desire to seeing child
prostitutes and/or killing adult prostitutes.[1] Stevenson himself offers some
insight, describing the brutal murder of Danvers Carew, and the trampling
of a child in the street.

Porn, we might imagine, with its singular and simple-minded sexually
transgressive agenda, would use Stevenson's plot to reveal that Hyde is the
sexual id to Jekyll's uptight gentlemanly ego. In fact, this is the stuff of Hollywood. Pornography grapples with Stevenson's perennially provocative novella in ways that foreground transformation itself as a desirable and erotic
process. The nature and consequences of the respective erotic transformation suggest the profound differences in social status according to gender

and sexual orientation and offer insight into the differing ways gay and straight pornographies have evolved. Here, I analyze three hardcore films representative of the different uses of Stevenson's narrative of transformation: *Heavy Equipment* (Tom DeSimone, 1977), a whimsical 3-D all-male film of the golden age; *Dr. Jerkoff and Mr. Hard* (Wash West, 1997), a hardcore gay comedy of the video age; and *Jekyll & Hyde* (Paul Thomas, 1999), a big-budget hardcore hetero thriller of the video age (though shot on film), produced by Vivid, perhaps the epitome of commercial heteroporn. These films, I argue, demonstrate the way pornography exploits the repression of sexual desires seen to be particularly Victorian, and utilizes the process of transformation to verbalize unspoken desires and anxieties of the particular cultural moment.

The duality enabled by transformation is porned to reveal the differing ways women and men inhabit, enjoy, and explore their sexuality. The gay male porn text skips directly over explicitly stating that Hyde was actually engaged in homosexual activities or that Jekyll himself enjoyed erotic homosocial bonds. Assuming the homoerotics of the novella via the porning itself, *Dr. Jerkoff & Mr. Hard* and *Heavy Equipment* suggest that the Stevenson mythos of dual natures can offer a pornographic homotopia for men who wish to be desired as objects. In contrast, Vivid's big-budget hetero feature, *Jekyll & Hyde*, returns the narrative of a sexually repressed daughter of Jekyll to the nineteenth-century fin de siècle, suggesting that the issues facing (middle-class, white, heterosexual) Victorian women at that time remain issues in the twentieth-century fin de siècle when the film was made. *Jekyll & Hyde* re-centers the absent or marginal women, particularly sex workers, of the original novella. It is a darkly postfeminist tale that uses the Stevenson narrative to reflect the persistent duality, marginalization, and dichotomization of women in and out of the sex industry. The contrasting nature of these two sets of films suggests that duality is not required for sexual desire in men but rather for enhanced self-esteem and the magnification of existing desire. Duality functions as a thrilling opportunity. Women, on the other hand, remain in grave need of a dual life in order to explore any sexual desire at all.

Porn: The Hyde to Mainstream's Jekyll

The porn consumer himself is described as a Jekyll & Hyde character in Rebecca Whisnant's essay on porn consumption and the normalization of misogyny. Whisnant argues that porn consumers who watch and masturbate to sadistic, abusive porn are not moral degenerates and sociopaths. Indeed, like Dr. Jekyll of Robert Louis Stevenson's *The Strange Case of Dr. Jekyll and Mr. Hyde*, they are "normal," everyday men who "manage the conflict between their self-image as decent, ethical people and their continued enjoyment of material that violates their own ethical standards" through a process of grooming on the part of pornographers (130). This grooming encourages a division of self: "The consumer can create a second self, one that exists in an 'extreme environment' that he regards as a realm of pure fantasy. This second self, rather than denying or minimizing abuse, can name it and revel in it" (130). Pornographers produce this second self, ready-to-wear, through rhetoric that both assuages and mocks ethical concerns.

Whisnant's argument is persuasive, yet it does little to illuminate the meanings that pornographers have made of the *Jekyll and Hyde* story. Her understanding of Jekyll/Hyde is faithful to Stevenson's text but reliant on simplistic assumptions about pornography, pornographer, and consumer. This is perhaps why she reads the logo and rhetoric of Jekyll & Hyde Productions in such a straightforward way. In understanding the logo—a divided male face, "normal" on one side, green and sinister on the other—as implicitly encouraging the consumer "to distinguish between his everyday self and his scary, dangerous porn-using self" (129), Whisnant fails to consider the way this divided self reflects not a simplistic reality but a critical response to societal attitudes toward sex and porn. A reaction against society's rigid norms is, after all, what prompts Dr. Jekyll to embark on his experiment in the first place. In addition, while his nighttime adventures are certainly violent in some cases, the unspoken vice Hyde engages in can also more broadly be regarded as Jekyll's venting of non-normative desires that are not abusive but that society condemns. It is this configuration of the divided self—a reaction to punitive societal attitudes and restrictive sexual arrangements—that hardcore primarily enjoys in the Jekyll & Hyde story. Porn, bastard cousin to the canon, identifies with Hyde. He serves as a monstrous but sympathetic avatar, cruelly ostracized by the Victorians and deserving of pornographic recovery.

The duality of Stevenson's protagonist combined with Victorian Gothic ambiguity promises an abundance of sexual interpretations as social propriety gives way to sexual adventure and loss of inhibitions. As Linda Dryden explains in her book *The Modern Gothic and Literary Doubles*, "Hyde may resemble an atavistic creature, but the reality is that he is the savage side of Jekyll, kept repressed through an imposed external morality" (32). The splitting of the self permits "unspoken 'pleasures'" (Dryden 31), and when something seems sexual but goes "unspoken," pornography has material to work with. Thus, adaptations of *Strange Case* perform the act of porning in similar ways to all neo-Victorian hardcore texts. They fill in perceived gaps in a sexually stifled era of literature. Indeed, Raven Touchstone, writer of the 1999 porn adaptation *Jekyll and Hyde*, remarks that what drew her to Stevenson's novella "as a sexual piece" was its representation of the duality of man: "Most of us do not live in our sexuality 24/7. We are all multi-faceted and in one of those facets dwells our sexuality. I think this is why the sex industry has loved to use Jekyll & Hyde [. . .] the prim and proper side giving way to abandoned sexuality" (Touchstone, email interview). The violence and cruelty of Stevenson's Hyde—the trampling of a child, the savage murder of Danvers Carew—is either integrated into sex via BDSM and sexually motivated murder, as in *Jekyll & Hyde*, or displaced by comparatively innocent sexual conquests, as in *Heavy Equipment* and *Dr. Jerkoff and Mr. Hard*. The overwhelming interest in all of these films is not violence and evil but rather the management of sexual desire and reconciliation of the sexual self.

Homo and Hetero Pornotopias

The social and historical significance of all-male pornography is quite different from that of heteroporn. Representations of romantic and sexual interactions between men and women, whether in novels, advertising, Hollywood films, or adult material, are taken for granted as a staple of media in heteronormative society. For this reason, while the porno chic era certainly posed a political challenge through the depiction of sexually aggressive women and unsimulated sex, gay male erotica has always meant something rather more profound for its audiences and creators. Gay male pornographies have historically been the only site of affirmative depictions of sexual intimacy between men. For this reason, gay pornography tends to present what David Seubert calls a homotopia. While the world of *Heavy Equipment* is explicitly framed as the queer space of West Hollywood within an otherwise heteronormative world, and Dr. Jerkoff lives in the even more queer-friendly late-1990s San Francisco, both films nevertheless present a world "where everything is imbued with sexual content, no one is straight and characters stumble into one sexual encounter after another without danger, fear, or for that matter, without even really trying" (Seubert). Heteroporn, however, has tended to pose sex as a problem complicated by gender difference and sex as something that needs negotiating.

The contrasting importance of pornographic materials to gay and straight men and the different needs and concerns when it comes to hetero and homo sex is reflected in the way gay and straight pornographies have adapted *Strange Case*. The gay films offer fantasy visions of a society in which sex between men is taken for granted and transformation is the key to becoming beautiful, desired, and whole. Straight films offer a less utopian world where female sexuality remains repressed, oppressed, and a source of trauma. As I show here, straight renderings of *Strange Case* offer women (and men) darkly erotic fantasies that, regardless of intended audience, anchor eroticism in a postfeminist Gothic reality.

"It's Him! It's Me!": Recoveries of Self-Love in *Heavy Equipment* and *Dr. Jerkoff and Mr. Hard*

Stevenson's *Strange Case* is an articulation of unspoken identities, vices, and sexualities during a time when these things were understood yet nameless, when "homosexuality" was still "the love that dare not speak its name." The Labouchere Amendment, nicknamed "the blackmailers charter," was passed in May 1885, just five months before Stevenson wrote *Strange Case*. It became law January 1, 1886, and prohibited sex between men, regardless of age, in either public or private places. *Strange Case* was first published January 5, 1886, just four days after the law went into effect. The Amendment does not specify "homosexuality," instead referring to "acts of gross indecency" between men. Similarly, during the Wilde trials the newspapers did not go into any detail about the "crimes" Wilde was on trial for. Still, the public seemed to understand the specifics of it (Cohen 4–5). Elaine Showalter notes that at this time, "the Victorian homosexual world had evolved into a secret but active subculture, with its own language, styles, practices, and meeting places" (106). For Showalter, Stevenson's novella "can most persuasively be read as a fable of fin-de-siècle homosexual panic, the discovery and resistance of the homosexual self" (107). Victorianist Susan Zieger goes so far as to call *Strange Case* "part of the gay canon" (164).

With *Strange Case*, Stevenson creates a homosocial fantasy world of bachelors. Wayne Koestenbaum describes the novella as part of a literary response to the Labouchere Amendment that he calls bachelor literature, in that it is concerned with "the male communal fantasies of resolutely unmarried men" (2). The literature of Stevenson, as well as others such as Oscar Wilde, celebrated a play space for boys and men without the complicating realities of heterosexual romance. Moreover, *Strange Case* celebrates undefined intimacies between men—intimacies that, ironically, became increasingly defined, labeled, and named as a result of the Labouchere Amendment. Gay

22. Promotional materials for *Heavy Equipment* (Bijou Films, 1977).

porn adaptations of *Strange Case* highlight the novella's homosocial erotics by crafting a hardcore homotopia, concretizing Stevenson's nebulous masculine intimacies. With *Heavy Equipment* and *Dr. Jerkoff*, DeSimone and West, respectively, realize the queer implications of homosociality and duality, directly addressing gay identity and culture and eroticizing the desire for a unified queer self.

While not explicitly sold as an adaptation of *Strange Case* in the same way as the other films discussed here, DeSimone's *Heavy Equipment* is undoubtedly a Jekyll & Hyde narrative. The film's protagonist is Chester, a nerdy young man who works at a bookstore and has a lust for men with "bodies"—that is, muscular bodies. Chester is given a book of magic by a mysterious man. At home, he finds the volume has been bookmarked at a page containing a spell that promises "self-transference" and "the image of your desire." Following the instructions, Chester takes magazine clippings of men that best depict the physical traits he desires, burns them, mixes them with soda, and drinks the resulting liquid. A flash of lightning appears on the screen—the signal to put your 3-D glasses on—and there in Chester's place, shirt torn by his bulging muscles, is gay superstar of the time Jack Wrangler. The remaining film is made up of the many sexual encounters—in the restroom at the beach, in the gym, and on the construction site—where Chester enjoys his new body and those of others. The film concludes with Chester quitting his job to embark on a life as/with his alter ego.

In West's more narratively developed adaptation, Dr. Jerkoff (Jim Buck) is a university professor who lives alone, is dedicated to his work and mother, and is effectively celibate, though not a virgin. After a student asks for "an extension" due to the distractions of his own rampant lust—"I always end up wanting more . . . more and more"—Jerkoff forces himself to wake up to his sexless reality: "I know what that fella' means," Jerkoff writes in his diary, which serves as voice-over narration, "I haven't had sex since the last Star Trek convention. And that was with a Klingon." Determined to try and turn his lonely life around, Jerkoff leaves his domestic space and visits the local gay bar, Hard. However, after being shunned by men who are put off by his awkward advances, he concludes sadly to himself, "That's not the place for me. It never will be. I'm a geek, a misfit. Even in the back room I'm as welcome as a fart in a space suit." Jerkoff feels his place is in the private, domestic sphere or the halls of the academy; the only other available option seems to be the opposite extreme of the club. However, going through his laundry the next morning, he discovers a flyer for Mama Guadalupe, ambiguously promising help with "nature" and "bad spirits." On visiting Guadalupe (Carmen), Jerkoff is told that he has a "river of lust" and a "volcano ready to erupt" inside him, and she gives him a potion that will help him realize these qualities. The remaining narrative revolves around his alter ego, Mr. Hard, a beautiful, sexually desirable, and emotionally unattached stud, complete with cock ring. Mr. Hard definitely fits in at the gay club and is in such demand that he can be arrogantly selective about his sex partners. Dr. Jerkoff/Mr. Hard eventually falls in love with one of his conquests. The narrative concludes by revealing that the potion was merely Pepto-Bismol, and that Dr. Jerkoff was Mr. Hard all along. Moreover, the nerdy appearance of Dr. Jerkoff was an artifice—he pulls off his wig and moustache to discover that he has always been a beautiful and desirable man and always had the capability to be a volcano of lust. He just needed to recognize it in himself.

These adaptations recuperate some of the regretful, tragic, and condemnatory residue of the late-Victorian novel. DeSimone and West enact what horror scholar Harry M. Benshoff has observed of many queer adaptations of gothic and horror fiction: "an attempt to draw out or exorcise the monster from the queer" (286). This particular "exorcism" involves a change in location from late-nineteenth-century London to West Hollywood in the 1970s and San Francisco in the late twentieth century. West Hollywood in the 1970s was a pre–HIV/AIDS queer utopia (relative to rest of the country). Late-twentieth-century San Francisco was (and remains) a fully realized LGBT mecca, one that exists in the context of a commodified and homogenized gay identity. These adaptations also present an identity crisis quite different

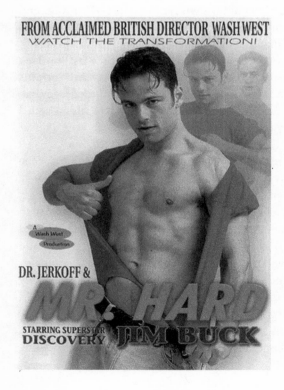

23. *Dr. Jerkoff & Mr. Hard* DVD box cover (BIG Video, 1997).

in nature from that with which Stevenson was concerned. One might assume that gay pornographers would present the Jekyll & Hyde story as one
in which a gay Jekyll finally emerges from his closet. However, this version
of the tale does not occur in any gay Jekyll & Hyde film. Rather, the narrative is used to articulate the desire to be desired, together with the pleasures
of transformation and importance of exploration. In both DeSimone's and
West's porned versions of *Strange Case*, the transformation is not one of
straight to gay, or closeted to out, but instead shy, nerdy, and unattractive
to outgoing, beautiful, and sexually desirable. These adaptations present an
affirming fantasy where, unlike Dr. Jekyll, gazing into the mirror—at one's
self, at another like one's self—is a source of guilt-free erotic pleasure rather
than abject horror.

The significance of voyeurism and male sexual spectacle overlaps with the
homoerotic tension of identification and desire. As Thomas Waugh notes,
Narcissus iconography is conspicuous to gay erotic imagery. Gay porn across
the decades is rife with doubles and reflections, a set of imagery used "to deal
with the gay problematic of sameness and difference" (*Hard to Imagine* 123).
Waugh argues that the tension between subject and object, identification and
desire, is particular to same-sex desire and subversive of heteronormative
systems of gendered sexuality:

> If heterosexual culture simplifies and rigidifies the dynamics of male subject
> and female object through the tyranny of gender difference, same-sex eroti-
> cism opens them up, rendering them ever more volatile. Same sex eroticism
> layers upon the individual erotic object choice the option of identification
> as well as voyeurism, projection as well as objectification: we (often) want to
> be, we often *are* the same as the man we love [. . .]. Transposed to same-sex
> representation, this pattern becomes a tension, even a confusion, between
> identification and desire. (44–45)

Or, as Christopher Craft observes, "The experience of reflection is queer
enough" ("Come See" 109). It should also be noted that in all adult film appropriations of *Strange Case*, the sameness, duality, and homoerotic tension
between self and other are exclusively channeled through white bodies. In
this way, the queer reflections and doubles assume gender unity as though
the erotics of sameness do not accommodate racial difference.

Jekyll of *Strange Case* struggles with the same tension between self and
other, sameness and difference. He has terrible trouble acknowledging Hyde
as his corporeal self, yet he also displays an enthralled desire for his physical
transformation—an enthrallment that Jekyll's friend Utterson finds deeply

disturbing. Jekyll's mirror is first mentioned following Jekyll's suicide. Utterson and the butler, Poole, break down the door to his chambers; while investigating the various cabinets and closets, they discover "the cheval glass, into whose depths they looked with an involuntary horror" (40). Poole remarks, "'This glass have seen some strange things, sir'"; Utterson stammers, "'For what did Jekyll'—he caught himself up at the word with a start, and then conquering the weakness: 'what could Jekyll want with it?'" (40). Showalter regards this reaction as an embarrassed acknowledgment of effeminacy and possible evidence of homosexual activity: "The mirror testifies not only to Jekyll's scandalously unmanly narcissism, but also to the sense of the mask and the Other that has made the mirror an obsessive symbol in homosexual literature" (111). Waugh would likely agree, noting the regular appearance of mirrors in gay porn, something he describes as "feminine iconography" (*Hard to Imagine* 123).

There are further references in the novella to discomfort related to self-adoration and the disturbing tension between identification and desire. While Hyde goes mostly undescribed in Stevenson's text, and his deformity cannot be precisely located, his hand becomes a sure way of demarking Hyde's body. Hyde's actual hand is described in greatest detail during the moment Jekyll wakes to find he has transformed involuntarily overnight and is waking up in Hyde's quarters. The homoerotics of such a scene—waking up and drowsily realizing he has gone to bed in a strange man's room, indeed is lying next to (inside of) a strange man—are obvious. Jekyll is unsure of where he is, or what has happened, until, he says, "my eye fell upon my hand" (54). Jekyll describes his own hand as "professional in shape and size: it was large, firm, white and comely. But the hand which I now saw, clearly enough, in the yellow light of a mid-London morning, lying half shut on the bed clothes, was lean, corded, knuckly, of a dusky pallor and thickly shaded with a swart growth of hair. It was the hand of Edward Hyde" (54). George E. Haggerty describes the "morning after" scene as reading "like an account of finding oneself in a strange bed after a night of sexual transgression," adding, "Henry Jekyll has participated in a night of transgression as Edward Hyde, not with him. Does this distinction really matter?" (127). Such blurring between being and having Hyde, particularly as a queer narcissistic desire, is articulated literally in the post-transformation masturbation sequences in both *Heavy Equipment* and *Dr. Jerkoff*.

Both transformations are enthusiastically voluntary. Indeed, Chester and Dr. Jerkoff alike go to great lengths to transform into an alternative self. They do so in order to become beautiful and therefore desired—something they struggle to achieve as nerdy and shy gay men who, they believe, do not possess the physical beauty required to attract men. At the same time, they want to become what they themselves sexually desire. The fusion of what Chester desires and what he desires to *be* is emphasized in the selection of male imagery used to create the magic potion, taken from the pages of beefcake magazines. In addition, the spell promises "the image of my desire," blurring the line between the image we desire in another and the image we desire as our own. This line is further blurred at the film's conclusion, as "Chester," in his new body, quits his job; he tells his puzzled boss, Mr. Cornelius, that Chester is "perfectly all right." "As a matter of fact," he says, "we're going away together." Due to the alter ego's beauty, Mr. Cornelius doesn't believe him: "That's preposterous. *You* and *Chester* going away together?" Chester's alter-ego responds with emphasis and a smile, "Together."

The moment of transformation is the erotic centerpiece of each film: the image of the man transformed is presented for the erotic pleasure of both the nerdy original, who lustfully enjoys his new body, and the spectator, who lustfully gazes at the screen. The performance of self-caressing, of becoming a spectacle for the self, is technically not a homosexual act. It becomes

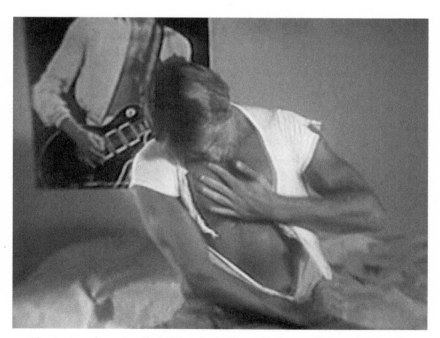

24. Chester transforms into Jack Wrangler in *Heavy Equipment* (Bijou Films, 1977).

a homosexual act through the technology of transformation and the movie screen. When Chester transforms into the gorgeous Jack Wrangler, he touches his face, then his arms and his chest. He tears his shirt open to touch his own skin, strokes his cock through his pajama pants and then rips these apart also. The scene is performed almost entirely for the camera. The scene is one of wonder and awe directed at the physical self and performed for the viewer, revealing the queer effect of reflection in relation to pornographic exhibition and performance.

The film is obsessed with doubles and reflections in a larger context also. Most strikingly, the film is presented in 3-D. Moreover, in its current DVD form the film can be watched only as a one-dimensional film with the lingering dual traces of the 3-D technology. When the flash of lightning appears on screen, we are meant to put on our 3-D glasses; yet in an unintentional and serendipitous transfer in technology, on DVD this lightning bolt warns us of the oncoming blurry green and red double images of the participants. Every 3-D scene is presented in blurry double vision. Moreover, marketing materials show that some screenings were accompanied by a featurette titled *Narcissus*, and posters emphasized the appearance of the Christy Twins, who perform their glory-hole scene on either side of a bathroom stall as if reflections of each other.

With the 1997 video *Dr. Jerkoff and Mr. Hard*, Wash West uses Stevenson's narrative of dual masculinities and transformation to enact a pornographic interrogation of late-twentieth-century "out" culture. Dr. Jerkoff is an academic nerd marginalized by a gay culture populated by buff, shirtless guys whose primary interests appear to be clubbing and fucking. Jerkoff's failures at sexual contact are not about being gay but rather about being "a geek." Hyde thus serves as a way for a nerdy gay man, insecure about his sexual appeal, to explore a more adventurous, sexual side of himself.

West takes Stevenson's ostensibly "straight" but ambiguous and silence-riddled source text and queers it. In this sense, the adaptation itself suggests the homoerotic implications of Stevenson's story. Indeed, West himself found Stevenson's story "dark and tantalizing" as a youth in a way that separated it from the other "more wholesome storybook narratives" in his possession (West). Discussing *Strange Case* and *The Picture of Dorian Gray*, West explains, "Both tales utilize a supernatural premise in service of an essentially homoerotic fantasy—I always regarded the heterosexual elements as a thin veneer, but I accept that this is a very subjective point of view—so they both made excellent candidates for adaptation into gay porno" (West). Through his adaptation, West casts off this thin veneer and produces a homotopia in which a man discovers erotic self-love through transformation.

Similar to that of *Heavy Equipment*, West's narrative is set in a world where same-sex desire is almost entirely normalized, and in which the crises of identity and sexual difficulties that Jerkoff must navigate have to do with self-esteem and confidence. As with *Heavy Equipment*, rather than focusing on the tension of nameless desire, West's interest lies in the erotics of transformation. West's vision departs from that of DeSimone's in the film's post-HIV, late-twentieth-century discord between an authentic but solitary life and that of a commercial gay identity, one that in part evolved through pornography. For West, the Jekyll/Hyde narrative offers a space for transformation that results in the potential reconciliation of identity and image. The character names are indicative of the meaning of their duality: Dr. Jerkoff suggests a solitary existence associated with a post-HIV cautious autoeroticism, whereas Mr. Hard suggests the importance of a hard body and a hard penis in an out culture that has recovered prolific, penetrative fucking. In this universe, there seems to be no space for dorky Dr. Jerkoff. Financial stability and academic prowess cannot replace the physical intimacy that Jerkoff desires, but, as the film ultimately suggests, neither can the selfish, emotionless, and obsessive sexual activity that Mr. Hard participates in. West indicates that Dr. Jerkoff feels he must become the hairless, buff sexual object of gay commodity culture in order to fulfill his desires, but he finally shows that this need not be the case. Self-love—emotional and erotic—discovered through fantasy and exploration, is at the heart of this film.

The transformation sequence is uncannily similar to that of *Heavy Equipment*. Having swallowed a dose of the potion, Jerkoff falls to the floor coughing, and gradually transforms before the camera into a shaved, muscular beauty. Looking in the mirror, he exclaims, "So fucking beautiful . . ." and touches his reflection. In awe of his own beauty, Mr. Hard caresses his own body, kissing his own reflection, and anally pleasuring himself. Emphasizing the erotics of reflection, West cuts to close-ups of Mr. Hard's penis kissing its own reflection. Towards the end of the scene, the camera shifts so as to capture a fragmented reflection that offers three bodies—two reflections and the "real" Mr. Hard. The money shot is also shown in triplicate, as Mr. Hard looks on in lust.

This scene renders a "straight" sex act—one that self-identified heterosexual men presumably participate in on a regular basis—homoerotic. While

25. Dr. Jerkoff transforms into Mr. Hard in *Dr. Jerkoff & Mr. Hard* (BIG Video, 1997).

this is also true of *Heavy Equipment*, in West's version the concept is multiplied quite literally through the extensive use of the mirror. In both films, the male body is portrayed as an erotic spectacle, but in *Dr. Jerkoff* the mirror more explicitly frames the male body as an erotic spectacle for itself. Mr. Hard does not masturbate facing us, the spectator; instead, he is turned away, toward the mirror while his reflections face toward us. In this way, the scene replicates the idea of Jekyll/Hyde as a homoerotic relationship within one man—"closer than a wife" (Stevenson 61). The popularity of self-adoration and solo masturbation in gay porn is not only due to same-sex desire but also to the empowering image of a man comfortably facing himself head-on, embracing his own body and form sexually, without shame.

Dr. Jerkoff thrives as Mr. Hard, yet instead of promoting sexual transgression and promiscuity, West chooses to offer a moral that might seem antithetical to porn: emotionally meaningful relationships are the paths to happiness. However, the journey to this discovery may well involve a good deal of adventure and experimentation; as well, an emotionally meaningful, committed relationship does not necessarily preclude further adventures. In a queer context, this conclusion functions as affirmative in the face of homophobic society.[2] This is a similar moral as the 1973 hetero adaptation, *The Erotic Dr. Jekyll* (dir. Victor Milt), which posits that deviant, excessive swinger lifestyles of the 1970s are no substitute for the loving, monogamous, domestic arrangements of heterosexual marriage. Indeed, gay or straight, the majority of hardcore adaptations of *Strange Case* seem to conclude with lessons in love or offer, as in *Jekyll & Hyde* (1999), dark meditations on the impossibility of escape from the Madonna/Whore dichotomy. Evidently, pornographers retain a Victorian domestic streak even as they porn these Victorian texts.

The focus on Jerkoff's initial loneliness stands in contrast to the homosocial network of peers in *Strange Case*, men who "keep each other's secrets and intimacies" (Zieger 169). As William Veeder has pointed out, "the repression of *pleasure* is not the principal dilemma in *Jekyll and Hyde*" (109); indeed, as Veeder demonstrates, Jekyll and his male friends engage in all manner of "traditionally sanctioned social 'forms'—friendship and professionalism—to screen subversive drives directed *at one another*" (109, italics in original). Whereas Jekyll foresaw a future as Hyde in which he is destined to become "despised and friendless" (55), Jerkoff is the one mocked or ignored, living alone, unable to participate in the socially established category of urban homosexuality where Mr. Hard excels. Jekyll's homosocial network of convivial friends, which "provide certain paradoxical opportunities for homoerotic expression" (Zieger 194), is absent in this homotopic twentieth-century fin de siècle as men at the gay club Hard pass judgment and reject Jerkoff based on his appearance and manner. It is only as Mr. Hard that he is able to fit in to this socially bracketed and signaled site of gay male bonding. It proves to be an experience as superficial and dissatisfying as it is pleasurable, one that Jerkoff hazily recalls as both "incredibly revolting" and "exciting" yet not something on which he is willing to waste his final dose.

While Jekyll/Hyde "is never offered the possibility of love" (Haggerty 128), Jerkoff/Hard does find love, or at least an emotionally meaningful and satisfying sexual experience. Jerkoff has one more dose of potion before returning to "the demure thrill of academia," and decides he will use it wisely: "There is one man I desire above all others. It is he I will pursue." The final dose, then, will go toward a meaningful relationship, as opposed to what Mr. Hard has up until this point been participating in: arrogant and emotionless sex with the physically gorgeous men he picks up at the club. The man he desires is one of the homeless boys, Brad, whom Jerkoff encountered at the beginning of the film. Brad is the only character in the film who has acknowledged any positive qualities in Dr. Jerkoff, describing him as "pretty cool" for giving him twenty dollars. Nevertheless, Jerkoff cannot accept that Brad would be interested in him, assuming he is only desirable as Mr. Hard. On finding out his mother has swallowed the remaining potion, Jerkoff once again visits Mama Guadalupe to beg for more.

Mama Guadalupe refutes the perception that man has a "dual nature." She reprimands Jerkoff's desire for more potion as the product of his own lack of self-knowledge, invoking white San Francisco queer culture as a source of the problem. She snaps, "You white boys! You are sexual, you are sensual . . . you need to be whole and sensual, you need to be whole and complete." Unbeknownst to Jerkoff, the potion is merely a Pepto-Bismol placebo that draws out the sexual confidence that has always resided within him but that he repressed. Guadalupe removes Jerkoff's glasses, then his mustache, and finally his wig, which humorously prove to be fake accessories; Dr. Jerkoff's public persona is a costume, while underneath he is and always was the beautiful Mr. Hard.

Guadalupe's reprimands indicate, much as Stevenson does, the necessity for a united and whole sexual identity. It is the failure to commit to this unity that results in Jekyll's downfall, a defeat that Stevenson scholar Katherine Linehan is less than sympathetic toward:

> We see Jekyll struggling in anguish to preserve what he intuitively feels to be the shrinking remains of his soul and clinging to an awareness of the element of a genuine love of virtue in himself as a sign that he is no hypocrite; we are little inclined to dwell on the fact that the self-estranged doctor, poor devil, is shrinking from ownership of the side of his being that flourished in the licentiousness he himself granted it. (212)

Indeed, it is Jekyll's desire to separate his undignified characteristics from his virtuous ones, the wish that they "be housed in separate identities [so] life would be relieved of all that was unbearable" (Stevenson 49), and the commitment to social norms that prohibit certain behaviors in a man of his social class, which lead to his downfall.

Jerkoff is living in a different time and place, though, attempting to conform to a licentious culture he feels drawn to but also pressured to conform to. In turn, it is Jerkoff's understanding of the perils of an attitude such as Jekyll's that saves him. The moral, then, isn't simply that meaningful and committed relationships are best. The moral is that in order to be desired, one need not be a perpetually hard, perpetually sexual being. The transformative neo-Victorian Gothic offers space for staged transgression as well as monstrous recovery and unity of the queer self.

Looking in the mirror at the end of the film, Jerkoff exclaims, "It's him! It's me!" in direct contrast to Jekyll's, "He, I say—I cannot say, I" (Stevenson 59). Jerkoff's utterance acknowledges a unity of self and sexuality that in Stevenson's time was socially not an option. West's film suggests that, in contrast to a nineteenth-century context, same-sex desire has reached a level of acceptability that leaves it vulnerable to the rigid social norms experienced in heterosexual relationships. The irony here is that the film cannot capture the same sense of charge and excitement as the ambiguities and silences of Stevenson's text. Indeed, modern pornographies claim to have no use for such silences. In porning *Strange Case*, DeSimone and West skirt right around the tensions of the closet, instead humorously eroticizing the fantasy of transformation. DeSimone offers a fantasy of absolute transformation and carnal unity of self that suggests the right body—a hot one—can provide an erotic solution to internal and external discord. In the case of post-HIV, post-sexual revolution, West suggests that unity of the erotic self in a sexually commodified, late-twentieth-century homotopia requires a more authentic self-discovery. Chester was quite happy to permanently become his alter ego whom he also viewed as his lover, whereas Dr. Jerkoff had to reconcile with himself in order to realize that there was no actual discord in physical self, merely a misguided self-loathing. In the modern era, West suggests, self-love and a beautiful body can be achieved internally and without magic through a reconciliation of internal and external that was always there for the taking.

A New Fin-De-Siècle: Femininity, Monstrosity, and Heterosexuality in Thomas's *Jekyll & Hyde*

What would happen if Jekyll were a woman? Very few adaptations, porn or otherwise, have explored this question. With *Jekyll & Hyde* (1999), writer Raven Touchstone and director Paul Thomas make a valiant attempt. In stark contrast to affirmative and homotopian adaptations, Thomas's big-budget Vivid feature presents a darkly pessimistic view of social attitudes toward female sexuality. The dual self here is not explored in a utopian society. Rather, the action is explored in the nineteenth century, when, as today, gendered sexual double standards rule. Through Molly (daughter of Jekyll and inheritor of his estate and legacy), Thomas and Touchstone offer a commentary on the false dichotomy of Madonna/Whore and the traumatic experience of attempting to be both. Flora's forbidden sexual desires find an outlet in Molly, the film's version of Hyde, who carries out her sexual adventures within the pre-constituted parameters of prostitution. For women of the twentieth century, the film suggests, the fraught sexual duality of the nineteenth century is far from over. The late-nineteenth-century setting constitutes a degree of removal that paradoxically highlights the pertinence of the Jekyll/Hyde narrative for post–sexual revolution women. In turn, the film suggests parallels between the work's narrative and the place of women in the sex industry.

Jekyll & Hyde picks up Stevenson's story in 1887 Budapest soon after the mysterious death of Dr. Jekyll (Mike Foster). His daughter, Molly (Taylor Hayes), has returned home from school for her father's funeral and begins to investigate the circumstances of his death. She also begins assisting Utterson (Frank Gunn) in the settling of Jekyll's estate. In the process, she discovers and restarts Jekyll's experiments, transforming into Flora and infiltrating the streets of London at night as a murderous prostitute. Throughout this narrative, Jekyll reads his diaries in voice-over, exposing the ambiguously wrought "infamy" and "vicarious depravity" Dr. Jekyll indulges in the novella (Stevenson 53). The film integrates Flora's exploits with those of her father, cutting from Flora's present-day adventures to flashbacks of Jekyll's. This fractured narrative creates a tapestry of father and daughter sexual indulgences and violent acts. As Flora, Molly acts out sexually as a woman of the streets. Molly soon wishes to reverse the effects of the potion so as to conform to the virginal female archetype and maintain a relationship with her childhood friend and servant, Jack (Julian). She attempts to find her father's missing manuscript pages, held by Utterson, in order to learn how to stave off transformation. During these attempts, Molly (as Flora) kills Utterson and brings the manuscript pages home. The narrative concludes in tragedy: while making love to Jack, Molly discovers she is transforming involuntarily during sex and, horrified, retreats into the dungeon laboratory in an attempt to discover an antidote from her father's manuscript. Failing this, and learning of her father's fate from his own statement of the case, she kills herself.

Such a grim denouement may appear surprising within the genre of heteroporn, a media space where, as Linda Williams observed in 1991, women are almost never punished for their sexual desires ("Film Bodies" 274). Pornography tends to celebrate the whore over the virgin, the monstrous over the pure, the bad girl over the good girl. "Bad" girls, such as women of the night, occupy an important but marginal role in Stevenson's novella. This spectral presence has generated several mainstream and pornographic adaptations that suggest Jekyll/Hyde and possibly others in his homosocial circle visited sex workers. In *Jekyll & Hyde*, Touchstone and Thomas foreground these marginal women, crafting a story that privileges the silenced sex worker but also provides no utopian promise of unbridled, aggressive female sexuality without social consequence.

In *Jekyll & Hyde*, sex workers become agents of narrative—not only the narrative of the film, but also the narrative of the deceased Jekyll/Hyde, of whose visitations they have intimate knowledge. In resituating the women of the sex trade, Touchstone and Thomas privilege a depiction of the oft-ignored labor, experience, and knowledge of sex workers, eroticizing female divergence from normative heterosexual roles. In turn, they explore the duality of pure and fallen that women are expected to inhabit, the tenuous privileges afforded to each strictly dichotomized group, and the punishments that ensue for those who dare occupy both.

Victorian London had a thriving sex-work community. By around the 1840s, the prostitute became a publicly recognized figure of interrogation appearing in newspapers, novels, and political discourse (Walkowitz 22). She was too visible, too revealing of the collapse in gender and class boundaries, so in 1864 the government finally acted on public discomfort by introducing the Contagious Diseases Act, a response to the spread of venereal disease in the armed forces, allowing police to arrest and physically inspect any woman suspected of being a prostitute. If she were discovered to have a venereal disease, she would be forcibly confined to a hospital for treatment. Initially, the law applied only to port towns, but by 1869 such arrests were permitted in eighteen districts, and the maximum term of imprisonment increased from three months to a year (Walkowitz 22–23). Furthermore, the statute did not only police women in order to contain disease, it also sought "to contain the occupational and geographic mobility of the casual labouring poor, to clarify the relationship between the unrespectable and respectable poor, and to force prostitutes to accept their status as public women by destroying their private associations with the poor working-class community" (Walkowitz 23). In other words, the law was designed to contain the prostitute. The act was repealed in 1886, the same year Stevenson published *Strange Case*.

Discomfort concerning prostitution soon developed into sensational fears concerning child prostitution and what was then termed "white slavery" and is now termed "modern slavery" or "sex trafficking." The epitome of sensational journalistic inquiry into child prostitution and the earliest journalistic equation of prostitution and slavery was William T. Stead's "The Maiden Tribute of Modern Babylon," published in the *Pall Mall Gazette* in four installments in July 1885 (Soderlund 24). Stead's report prompted outrage that resulted in the Criminal Law Amendment Act of 1885. The Act raised the age of consent from 11 to 16, expanded the power of law enforcement in arresting prostitutes, and made indecent acts between men illegal (Soderlund 24). Stevenson had received the collected pages of Stead's scandalous article the same July it was published, just months before completing *Strange Case*.

Because of this, it is highly likely that Stead's provocative and sensational narrative of metropolitan sexual commerce and danger was a powerful influence on the direction of Stevenson's novella.

The labyrinthine and threatening streets of Stevenson's London combined with the duality of a supposedly respectable gentleman echo the exposé, and yet the women and girls so central to Stead's narrative and to popular London narratives of the East End in general are nearly absent in *Strange Case*. One or two do show up, in appropriately veiled and ambiguous form, and in ways that indicate the creeping instability of privileged, upper-class masculinity. In the early hours of the morning, Mr. Enfield observes a man he later discovers to be Mr. Hyde run into "a girl of maybe eight or ten": "the man trampled calmly over the child's body and left her screaming on the ground" (9). We might wonder what an eight-year-old girl is doing out at 3:00 A.M., but we should also question the nature of Mr. Enfield's activities, as he is "coming home from some place at the end of the world" himself (9). A group of women "wild as harpies" attack Hyde in response, frightening him (10), representative of the new social actors contesting the privilege of the elite flâneur.

Women are not only glimpsed in the street but also in indoor spaces of vice. Later, Mr. Utterson witnesses the surroundings of Mr. Hyde's house in a "dismal quarter of Soho" (23). This "district of some city in a nightmare" features "a gin palace" populated by "many women of many different nationalities passing out, key in hand, to have a morning glass" (23). It is soon after this that Utterson is confronted with "an ivory-faced and silvery-haired old woman" with "an evil face, smoothed by hypocrisy" who keeps Hyde's house. Finally, in his "Full Statement," Jekyll recalls himself as Hyde walking the streets "when the night was fully come": "Once a woman spoke to him, offering, I think, a box of lights. He smote her in the face and fled" (59). The remaining women featured in the text include maids and other domestic workers. As Stephen Heath notes, "All these women are simply found in the streets or are glimpsed as servants of one kind or another; the brevity of their appearance goes along with their lowness of class which itself in turn runs into their marginalisation in the given middle-class male story-world" (94). In other words, these women are outside the bounds of the "respectable," for they are outside of the spatial bounds of the respectable domains of home and/or middle- and upper-class neighborhoods, thereby signaling deviant femininity.

G. M. Hopkins seems to have picked up on the novella's metaphors, writing to Robert Bridges in 1886, "The trampling scene is perhaps a convention: he [Stevenson] was thinking of something unsuitable for fiction" (qtd. Heath 93). Likewise, in his psychoanalytical essay titled "Children of the Night: Stevenson and Patriarchy," William Veeder crudely observes of the woman struck by Hyde that "[a] woman who walks the streets late at night asking men if they need a light is offering quite another type of box" (141). All of the women present in the novel, though, are either disreputable due to their presence on the streets of London, or marked by their servitude and "downstairs" status. Victorian female servants, of course, were often vulnerable to sexual exploitation by their masters, and some supplemented their meager incomes by becoming so-called dollymops (part-time or amateur prostitutes). In this way, the specter of Stead's prostitute and woman of the streets haunts the margins of the Stevenson text.

In her analysis of adaptations of *Strange Case*, Elaine Showalter queries the possibility of an "Edie Hyde": "But is the divided self of the fin-de-siècle narrative everybody's fantasy? Can women as well as men have double lives? Can there be a woman in Dr. Jekyll's closet?" (118). The answer, according to director Paul Thomas and screenwriter Raven Touchstone, seems to be yes, though under highly disparate circumstances and a significantly different set of rules. For, as Showalter argues, "While Victorian gentlemen had the prerogative of moving freely through the zones of the city, Victorian ladies were not permitted to cross urban, class, and sexual boundaries, let alone have access to a nighttime world of bars, clubs, brothels, and illicit sexuality as an alternative to their public life of decorum and restraint (118–19). During Stevenson's time, however, women were moving through the city, thanks to a quickly developing middle-class consumer culture and shifts in technology, work, and industry. The vast changes in London society at this time ensured that the city was no longer a privileged masculine site but, rather, one increasingly populated by a diverse cross section of London. Of course, these changes were met with a concomitant effort to control such blurring of social lines.

Jekyll & Hyde (1999) suggests that female mobility was and remains restricted by dichotomies of good and bad womanhood. Female mobility is possible, the film argues, if the lady in question embodies not a monstrous Mr. Hyde but a beautiful and also monstrous sex worker. Showalter's main objection to the idea that an "Edie Hyde" could exist lies in the fact that a "working-class Edie Hyde wandering the docks alone in the early hours of morning would have been taken for a prostitute or killed by Jack the Ripper" (119). Evidently, Showalter did not consider that in a postfeminist neo-Victorian Gothic world, Edie Hyde might be both a prostitute *and* the Ripper.

26. Flora works the streets in *Jekyll & Hyde* (Vivid, 1999).

Rather than operating outside of the supposedly masculine sphere of mainstream pornography, Touchstone is working from within it, contributing to what Susanna Paasonen calls "alternative" pornographies that exist within commercial product. These alternative pornographies subvert "the standard, and the generic" in which they are housed by rendering its potential limits to creative expression "elastic enough to encompass all kinds of peculiarities" (*Carnal Resonance* 7). Touchstone thus serves as an example of the undervalued female participation in—and feminist implications of—mainstream porn. *Jekyll & Hyde*'s process of re-vision occurs within and without dominant cultural production, developing a discourse between the two, and complicating simplistic assumptions about the sexual politics found in "commercial" (bad) and "independent" (good) porn. *Jekyll & Hyde*'s narrative of women traveling through masculine urban spaces, breaching the culturally imposed divide between "good" and "bad" femininity, reflects a larger subversive project within pornography that too often goes unremarked upon. Through the original subtitle, "The rest of the story . . . ," Touchstone presents the film as a *continuation* of the narrative. She is not re-visioning the source text but leaving it in place, offering a female-centered extension of the masculine narrative. Women—Flora, Molly, the ladies of the night, Taylor Hayes, and Touchstone—have inherited the strange case.

27. Molly transforms into Flora in *Jekyll & Hyde* (Vivid, 1999).

Unfortunately, large portions of *Jekyll & Hyde* were destroyed in development and had to be re-filmed. Many scenes, most of which dealt with Molly's struggle with her dual self prior to her transformation, were simply lost. The original screenplay depicts one of these lost scenes in which Molly, reflecting on the discovery of Jekyll's papers, wonders aloud about man's duality, constantly engaged in a "war between the spiritual and the carnal, morality and lust." Molly asks Jack whether women "have that dual nature too." Jack does not deem this possible because he holds categorically that "there are good women and bad ones. The good don't entertain impure thoughts" (Touchstone, *Jekyll & Hyde* 13). Jack's belief in the virgin/whore dichotomy prompts Molly to admit that she has impure thoughts "all the time" (13), but her efforts at masturbation thereafter (retained in the film in fragmentary form) are thwarted by internalized shame:

> As her excitement builds, she hears the voice of the Good Girls, the Voices
> of Society, whispering, echoing . . .
>> VOICES (V. O.)
>> Shame . . . shame . . . evil, sin . . .
>> You'll go insane . . . shame, girl . . .
> The voices get louder & louder until Molly cries out:
>> MOLLY
>> Oh shut up!!!

She pulls her drawers back up and starts getting into her dress again, angry, torn by her own desires. (14–15, ellipses in original)

The duality of woman is rooted in the condemnation of her desire and the struggle with the impossible dichotomy of good and bad femininity—similar to that of Stevenson's Jekyll, then, yet different in significant ways. The manner of release and technology of transgression takes on a necessarily different form in a woman; while Hyde may go about town frequenting whorehouses, Molly must become the whore in order to safely and anonymously explore her desires.

Thomas and Touchstone suggest that the Victorians are, in Kohlke and Gutleben's words, "our threatening doubles and distorted freak-show/funhouse mirror images, disclosing something akin to rejected atavistic or archetypal selves, our superseded progenitors who are nonetheless still with us, if only as an evolutionary vestige" (4–5). In this way, the Victorians constitute the other half of our dual self, like Hyde/Flora, but they also function as a paternal, maternal, or sovereign figure, an authoritarian presence that is simultaneously regressive and uncomfortably close to our modern selves. Molly is the direct inheritor of her father's property, his drive toward scientific experimentation, and his crisis of self. At the same time, as a neo-Victorian product, the film suggests that by virtue of being a woman, Molly has inherited punitive moral cultural beliefs regarding female sexuality, beliefs popularly understood to have been handed down to us from the Victorians.

Molly/Flora is represented specifically as the offspring of her father, the imitator of his practices, and the present-day embodiment of his actions and words. As Molly's father describes his transformation in voice-over, of how he "approached the mirror and saw for the first time the appearance of Edward Hyde," so Molly returns his words, approaching the mirror and uttering, "Papa, papa, what have you done?" In voicing this query, Molly asks something of the patriarch, wondering aloud what exactly the father has passed down to the daughter. The film also asks what, precisely, the Victorian era has passed down to its inheritors a century later, implicitly indicting the Victorian patriarchy for the sufferings of the twentieth-century woman. While the modern-day woman may enjoy the illusion of passing seamlessly between domestic and urban spaces, this film reminds audiences of the limits (and pleasures) of transgressing gendered sexual boundaries experienced within and upon the (female) body. In this sense, the female sex worker (including the pornographer and porn performer) is arguably the ideal embodiment of neo-Victorian concerns, a point of convergence between the Victorian and our postmodern selves. In *Jekyll & Hyde* she mobilizes and disturbs the fantasy formations we have come to construct around sexual attitudes in the nineteenth century and now.

Molly follows in the footsteps of her father even in her manner of death: she commits suicide, prompted by her involuntary transformation while making love to Jack on the staircase of her father's mansion. It is a profoundly disturbing experience for Molly when the monstrous Flora of the city streets suddenly invades the domestic interior of the home, the interior of herself. The shame, it would appear, is unbearable. Showalter's observation that "transgressive desires in women seem to have led to guilt, inner conflict, and neurotic punishment, rather than to fantasies or realities of criminal acting out" is thus partially borne out by the film's conclusion (120).

However, this conclusion also enacts what Sarah E. Whitney calls the "postfeminist Gothic." Speaking of postfeminist gothic novels, Whitney argues that this "powerful but underacknowledged strain of American women's fiction [. . .] violently intrude[s] on the well-constructed fantasy of a safe and equitable world. They feature abject protagonists who are socially invisible, physically broken, or speaking from the grave. Emphasizing women's *dis*empowerment, [postfeminist gothic fiction goes] against the grain of a victim-resistant, empowerment-oriented age" (2). Through the film's dual narratives, explicit invocation of inheritance, and Molly's horror at the uninvited reappearance of Flora, Touchstone and Thomas indicate a legacy of sexual double standards and whorephobia. Sex workers, particularly women, are subject to profound stigma: "Prostitution for women is considered not merely a temporal activity [. . .] but rather a heavily stigmatized social status which in most societies remains fixed regardless of change in behaviour" (Pheterson 399). For the highly visible porn performer, this stigma is especially hard to escape. As porn performer Lorelei Lee explains, "After you have made pornography, it will be viewed as a part of you forever" ("Once You Have Made Pornography"). There's no going back from porn. If societal attitudes are to be believed and, as Lee indicates, we do not have much of a choice in acknowledging the reality of these attitudes, porn has a metamorphic affect. Like swallowing a magic potion or being bitten by a vampire, "Pornography will change your life, and there will be no way to know, when you start, all of the ways that this will happen." Sex work stains the worker: "Anyone who knows you have done it sees a mark on you" (Lee, "Once You Have Made Pornography"). Sex workers are "fallen women" today just as they were in the nineteenth century, only now technologies have evolved to democratize speech. The sex worker can now speak for herself.[3]

Molly's suicide is framed as a tragic ending, one that sheds light on a troubled present. In addition, Molly's monstrosity, unlike her father's, incites desire as well as disgust. In this way, the film encourages viewers to "inhabit women's experiences of suffering" (Whitney 2). Molly's emotions—pleasure and trauma—and those of her fellow sex workers are the focus of this story. It is societal shame, internalized and *inherited* from culture at large—inherited from her Victorian forefathers—that leads her to become "a self-destroyer" (Stevenson 39). While there is nothing funny about Thomas's *Jekyll and Hyde*, it is riddled with transgressive and Gothic pleasures. These pleasures come with a price when acted out, however, if one wishes to return untarnished.

Pornographic film adaptations of *Strange Case* explore the pleasures of transformation and alternate physical, sexual identities. They also explore the downfalls that such transformations can engender. Yet in spite of the many differences between these films, particularly between the hetero and all-male titles, there is a parallel moral thread running through each. Each film suggests that duality of self or the desire to transform is not, in itself, wrong. Indeed, with *Heavy Equipment* we are left to imagine that you could live happily ever after with your dream man . . . who also happens to be you. West offers a subtle departure from 1970s utopian thinking with *Dr. Jerkoff*, positing that these transformations are an illusion—a pleasurable and exciting illusion, but an illusion nonetheless. Dr. Jerkoff required the illusion—the transformation—in order to discover that he needs no double. Indeed, he is and always was the man he wished he could be. Finally, with *Jekyll & Hyde*, Touchstone and Thomas propose the impossibilities and agonies of inhabiting both sides of a misogynistic sexual dichotomy for a white, middle-class woman of the late-nineteenth century . . . and possibly also today. DeSimone, West, and Touchstone/Thomas utilize Stevenson's *Strange Case* to explore different paths toward internal harmony at different moments in time and for different audience needs. What the three films seem to say in unison is that transformation can be productive and pedagogical, even when it results in tragedy.

The marginalized, the stigmatized, the monstrous—the Hydes of society—come to the fore of these Jekyll & Hyde narratives, hoping for redemption. Whether utopian or dystopian, pornographers analyze marginalization through the lens of gothic transformation and implicate the viewer in the need and desire for such a metamorphosis. The Victorian Gothic double functions as a technology with which pornographers can address and critique the social framing of gender, sexuality, and sex work. In the case of gay porn, the double mobilizes era-dependent fables of wish fulfillment and self-discovery, while in straight porn the double provides a way to explore women's fraught relationship to sex and sex work. In all cases, however, the Jekyll & Hyde narrative provides a canvas on which to play out fantasies of sexual and spatial transgression that might conclude with immersion in that fantasy, reconciliation with reality, or death. Whether resulting in homotopian pleasure or hetero-dystopian tragedy, pornography uses the Jekyll & Hyde narrative of duality and transformation as a form of socio-sexual critique that recovers and re-centers the conflicted sexual deviant.

5

STRANGE LEGACIES OF THOUGHT AND PASSION

Technologies of the Flesh and the Queering Effect of Dorian Gray

> I wanted to make a movie that Oscar Wilde
> would want to get off to.
> —Wash West, director of *Gluttony*

> Often, on returning home from one of those mysterious and
> prolonged absences that gave rise to such strange conjecture
> among those who were his friends, or thought that they were
> so, he himself would creep upstairs to the locked room, open
> the door with the key that never left him now, and stand,
> with a mirror, in front of the portrait that Basil Hallward had
> painted of him, looking now at the evil and aging face on the
> canvas, and now at the fair young face that laughed back
> at him from the polished glass. The very sharpness of the
> contrast used to quicken his pleasure.
> —Wilde, *The Picture of Dorian Gray*

Dorian Gray's nighttime pursuits are as ambiguous as Hyde's. Like Hyde's, some of Gray's activities are suggested (smoking opium, mistreatment of friends and romantic partners, blackmail of a former male lover, murder of Basil, the man who painted his portrait), while others remain whispered rumors in his social circle. We can only guess the full extent of what Gray does based on the horrors we know he has committed. Still, it is Gray's portrait—kept up in his secret attic where it lies in wait of Gray's desirous gaze—that most engages our fascination as a culture. We are captivated by his beauty and youth, as are Gray and his familiars. Of the novels discussed in this project, *The Picture of Dorian Gray* is perhaps the one with the fewest gaps and holes to fill. It is the canvas itself—the *media*—that intrigues pornographers, enamored as they are of the medium of pornography itself. Indeed, Gray himself is captured on canvas. Throughout this book, I have addressed the use of a specific period—the nineteenth century—as a canvas. Here, an actual canvas is at the pornographer's disposal. At the same time, Oscar Wilde, the man, the character, and the culture text, operates as a queer spectral presence that haunts pornographic adaptations of *The Picture of Dorian Gray*. Both films discussed here extend the late-nineteenth-century narrative into the present day as part of a larger legacy of sexual representation and technology originating with Gray's representation on the magic canvas. In his all-male video feature, *Gluttony* (2001), also known as *The Porno Picture of Dorian Gray*, Wash West uses different media effects to reimagine and queer porn history and porn studies. Meanwhile, with the 1970s hetero feature *Take Off* (1978), Armand Weston uses the tangible technologies of sexual representation together with parodic recreations of Hollywood film to speak the mainstream's sexual silences and to queer American hetero history. In both features, the *Dorian Gray* culture text becomes a technology itself, mobilizing a queer legacy of sexual representation.[1]

Oscar Wilde: Queer Culture Text

The name Oscar Wilde carries connotations of homosexuality as a cohesive identity in Western culture, perhaps worldwide. This is thanks to the enduring legacy of his trials that exposed his private life, dissected his literary work, and led to a reformulation of "homosexuality" as a public personal identity. In February 1895, Marquess John Douglas, the father of Wilde's lover Lord Alfred Douglas, left a calling card suggesting Wilde was a "sodomite." Wilde pursued this incident as libel and took the Marquess to court. Wilde lost the case and was arrested for sodomy and gross indecency. He was convicted in May of that same year and sentenced to two years' hard labor, the maximum permitted under the Labouchere Amendment.

Eve Kosofsky Sedgwick refers to the Wilde trials and their consequences as initiating "a sudden, radical condensation of sexual categories" (9). Likewise, Ed Cohen notes that "by the time of his conviction, not only had Wilde been confirmed as *the* sexual deviant for the late nineteenth century, but he had become the paradigmatic example for an emerging public definition of a new 'type' of male sexual actor: 'the homosexual'" (1–2). The Wilde trials took place in the wake of the Labouchere Amendment (1885) and the Cleveland

Street Scandal (1889). The Labouchere Amendment outlawed the practice of ambiguously defined acts of "gross indecency" between males (Hall 39), while the Cleveland Street Scandal exposed "a hidden world of Victorian homosexuality" (Hall 48) involving upper-class male uses of working-class male prostitutes.

Homosexuality was perceived as a threat in terms of exposing the upper classes but also in terms of the implications it might have for ostensibly heterosexual male relationships. The Wilde trials condensed growing anxieties circulating around male intimacy for the previous ten years. As Lesley Hall notes, "The Wilde debacle collapsed a number of transgressive male possibilities (effeminacy, decadence, aestheticism, bohemianism, dandyism, self-indulgence, and excess), in practice pertaining to heterosexual men, into one monstrous cautionary figure" (54). This can be seen in reflections made by the *New York Times* in 1890 that British panic over *The Picture of Dorian Gray* was likely due to the previous year's scandal, prompting Englishmen to be "abnormally sensitive to the faintest suggestion of pruriency in the direction of friendships" (Gillespie, "Reviews and Reactions" 353). In Sedgwick's words, "Oscar Wilde virtually *means* 'homosexual'" (165). Even when adaptations of *Dorian Gray* aren't explicitly articulated as homoerotic, the source text connotes a secret and transgressive sexuality, with, as Wash West describes it, "secret pockets."[2] Following the neo-Victorian porning impulse, adaptations of *Dorian Gray* seek to expose the secrets kept in these pockets, rhetorically suggesting that hardcore can speak the sexual content Victorians could only convey in metaphor.

Dorian Gray engages a host of Gothic concerns: physical transformation, the delights and crises of duality, deviant pleasures, unspoken vice, and the secret worlds in which these adventures play out. *Dorian Gray* is also about age. While the *Alice* adaptations displace issues of individual age, hardcore *Dorian Gray* adaptations actively confront age—historical and cultural, as well as individual—connecting it to sexual representation and its pornographic and mainstream genealogies. In doing so, these adaptations suggest that our corporeal selves constitute and are constituted by such representations, held in stasis and erotically moved by the material technologies enabling these same representations.

Technology occupies a special place in pornography. Almost every significant evolution in technology has become, accurately or not, attributed in some way to porn. The notorious failure of Betamax, for example, is consistently attributed to Sony's refusal to carry pornography. This is inaccurate, and yet it continues to be repeated as a truism in mainstream media. Porn is also credited with the thriving of the internet, which in popular culture is facetiously noted to be "for porn."[3] Alongside this perception of porn's savvy appropriation and development of new technologies, porn is also ridiculed and dismissed for its clumsy, derivative, and amateurish attempts at being "real film." Still, pornographers have an enduring interest in technology and its role in sexual representation across the decades. Joseph W. Slade argues that the sloppy nature of porn filmmaking is a conscious and integral element of the genre that signals defiance and generates the special pleasure of pornographic "Othering"—the pleasure of seeming authenticity vis-à-vis a trashy, anti-mainstream aesthetic. As Slade puts it, porn exhibits "clumsiness bordering on incompetence, a wholly deliberate devotion to anachronism as opposed to rapidly developing technological sophistication in the legitimate cinema" (37). According to Slade, this "technological regression" reflects a few possible things: a genuine ineptitude due to the lack of professional filmmakers involved in pornography, a desire to flaunt outlaw status, nostalgia for the "look" of illicitness, a "lack of economic motivation" due to lack of market, the "evocation of raw blue-collar sexual tastes" that results from such a class-leveling technology, a desire to minimize the capacity of such a powerful technology as a way of preserving the potency of the body, and, finally, some kind of inherent eroticism in primitive media (37–41). Even during the Golden Age, which lasted approximately fifteen years, when porn attempted to model itself on legitimate cinema, these glossy features rhetorically positioned themselves in opposition to the mainstream. The films discussed here address the legacy of technology and the screen, their relationship to corporeality and mortality, and the ambivalent erotics of visual representation.

The two films, *Take Off* (dir. Armand Weston, 1978) and *Gluttony* (dir. Wash West, 2001), use the *Dorian Gray* text to articulate pornographic and cinematic legacies of sex. Both films implicitly speak the implied sexual content of the *Dorian Gray* text simply by showing the sex the novel sublimates. In turn, the *Dorian*/Wilde culture text queers even the ostensibly "straight" porn films. However, these adaptations also offer their own revisionary, critical theses regarding sexual representation. In the case of *Take Off*, Weston not only speaks the sexual absences in *Dorian Gray*, he also demonstrates the unspoken sexual content of Hollywood cinema, critiquing Hollywood's habit of "invoking but never delivering sex" (Patton 132). As the film's tagline states, "Where Hollywood left off, *Take Off* takes it all off."

Meanwhile, with *Gluttony* West presents an explicit re-queering of *Dorian Gray*, wresting the veiled homoeroticism from the novel and rendering the

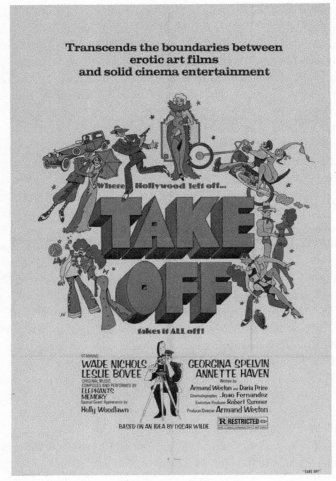

28. Poster art for *Take Off* (Distribpix, 1978).

narrative unambiguously gay. As West puts it, he wanted to make a film "that Oscar Wilde would want to get off to," suggesting that West envisages his film project as a twentieth-century gift to a man unable to fully realize his sexual orientations on the page. At the same time, West reclaims another legacy: gay porn. *Gluttony* recasts the history of pornography, so often couched in heteronormative terms, as queer. Both films, however, share an interest in the technologies of representation—the *screen*—that are foregrounded as an important conduit of sexuality and subjectivity. The scenes in each film envision different historical moments in which the Dorian character does not age, situating histories of sexual representation within tangible media forms and technologies of exhibition. Both Weston and West demonstrate the importance of these technologies to establishing sexual subjectivity by offering a defiant rewriting of sexual screen histories. Moreover, these films suggest the pornographic screen, its meanings and representations, is not static or solidified and occupies a central place in technologically produced sexual subjectivity. Seemingly timeless or forgotten images are in fact part of a legacy that goes back to the nineteenth century and, it seems, continues to unfurl and metamorphose endlessly before us.

Both Weston's *Take Off* and West's *Gluttony* use Wilde and the Dorian Gray narrative as a combined culture text to highlight the ways in which history is viewed through technology. They suggest that the history of America is a sexual one, mediated and perhaps constituted by the evolution of technology. These films suggest that technology and pornography create sexual subjectivity and shape desires, that the distance between subject positions in pornographic creation and spectatorship is smaller than it is for other genres. In turn, the specter of Wilde, and the use of *Dorian Gray* in Wilde's trial as damning evidence of sodomy, irretrievably queers Dorian adaptations. This results in what Sedgwick calls "camp"—"the moment at which a consumer of culture makes the wild surmise, 'What if whoever made this was gay too?'" (156)—even when the sexual activity is ostensibly heterosexual.

The Dorian Gray text appears to mobilize this question, particularly in the case of pornography. The two films ask the camp question of Wilde's text, but they also ask it of pornography, even of the ostensibly "straight" type. Despite what seems to be a deeply British narrative, both films' utilization of *Dorian Gray* results in the (homo)eroticizing of American culture and history, including porn and porn scholarship. On a narrative level, *Take Off* fills in the sexual gaps left by Hollywood. On another more meta level, *Take Off* fills in gaps left by Wilde queering the straight porn text itself. In *Gluttony*, American history is related as and through porn history. Pornography is recast to deflect the heteronormative lens through which we fans and scholars tend to view it, understand it, and theorize it. Both films are marked by the erotics of particular technologies of the age and serve as pornographic film treatments of the "strange legacies of thought and passion" that Gray recognized and identified with in queer artistic and literary texts (119). In this way, the films signal the affective relationship between the textures of visual technology, American culture, and sexual subjectivity, extending Wilde's narrative and bringing the immortal Dorian Gray into the twentieth and twenty-first centuries. Gray leaves his static place on the canvas and is mobilized through the moving image in a way that conjures a melancholy meditation on mortality and the erotic screen.

Both films center pornography as the starting place for sexual moving-image media by replacing Gray's portrait with the earliest form of hardcore film: the stag film. Like Gray's portrait, stags were illicit and secreted away, described by Dave Thompson as "the monstrous relative walled up in the attic" (7). *Take Off* is set in its own present, the late 1970s, where a mysterious man, Darrin Blue (Wade Nichols), is hosting a lavish party. A guest, Linda (Leslie Bovee), finds and watches an old stag film from 1925 that depicts an elderly man having sex with a young aristocratic woman. Darrin realizes she has seen the stag film, invites her for a drive, and tells her over the course of the day the curious story of a young man surreptitiously filmed having sex with his lover and mentor, Henrietta Wilde (Georgina Spelvin). Indeed, Henrietta had orchestrated the secret filming as part of her efforts to convey the importance of beauty. She wanted Darrin to see just how beautiful he was. After he saw his own moving image on film, Darrin wished he would stay young while the image in the film would grow old. He soon realized this wish had come true. The film is a "take off" of not only Wilde's novel but also, as adult film critic Jim Holliday puts it, of "motion pictures, film stars, and social climates through the decades" (71). The subsequent sex scenes are depictions of Darrin's exploits as a perpetually young man, embodying iconic Hollywood characters and tropes from different decades: James Cagney and gangster pictures of the 1930s, Humphrey Bogart and film noir of the 1940s, Marlon Brando and teen rebellion of the 1950s, a free love hippy of the 1960s, and, finally, a concluding love scene with Linda in the contemporary 1970s. This final love scene is recorded on CCTV by an aged Henrietta[4] and seems to break the spell of the first love scene recorded on a hand cranked motion picture camera. Darrin transforms back to his true, aged self and departs as an elderly man with his equally elderly lover, Henrietta Wilde.

Wash West's 2001 video, *Gluttony*, is a faux documentary in which undergraduate student Cyril Vane (a male version of Gray's love object in the novel, Sybil Vane) embarks on a search for mysterious and elusive porn star Dorian, who, after a wildly successful career as a performer, director, and chef, has disappeared from public view. Rumor has it he's never aged. As part of Vane's documentary narrative, he includes Dorian's various excursions in porn, which constitute *Gluttony*'s film-within-a-film sex scenes. Each scene depicts a different historical period in pornography from the 1960s to the

1990s, using digital effects to recreate the look of visual pornographic technologies from those eras. Cyril eventually finds Dorian and discovers he has indeed not aged, whereas his image in a stag film hidden in an attic has. In a similar gesture to that of *Take Off*, *Gluttony* ends with Dorian making love to Cyril, thereby breaking the spell and reverting to his aged self, an aged self that Cyril warmly encourages. Both films recover the monstrous Dorian Gray, offering him a romantic denouement that suggests aging is something to treasure. In understanding the importance of change and the destructive effect of stagnation, Dorian reconciles with his "loathsome visage" (Wilde 184) and avoids the necessity of self-destruction. These films suggest that the disappearing image need not be mourned; at the same time, they offer a profoundly haunting and melancholy metanarrative that invokes corporeal decay, the HIV/AIDS pandemic, and the mortality of media.

Melancholy Static: The Erotics of the Moving Reflection

Even before Gray spends hours in his attic gazing at the portrait that holds his deteriorating image, other men cannot take their eyes off Gray. Wilde's novel opens with Basil Hallward, the artist, gazing at the portrait in pleasure, "looking at the gracious and comely form he had so skillfully mirrored in his art" (6). In the same scene, Basil's friend and provocateur, Lord Henry, describes Gray as "a young Adonis, who looks like he was made out of ivory and rose-leaves" and "a Narcissus" (7). Gray is thus introduced as a beautiful, brainless object, valuable for the pleasure of gazing upon. These pleasures are primarily reserved for the men of the novel, including Gray himself. As with gay *Jekyll & Hyde* adaptations, *Take Off* and *Gluttony* depict the queer experience of reflection through the use of the double or the alter ego, but here this reflection is emphasized through the experience of watching oneself not just in the mirror, but also on the pornographic screen. The physical media of film itself becomes a kind of skin, a fleshy, sensory media articulation of the sexual self. While the mirror reflects back the self in real time, the screen—whether a cinema screen, a television screen, a computer monitor, or a spool of film held up to the light—captures a static and unchanging image. Except, in this case, it doesn't. Just as film, videotape, and other visual media suffer the ravages of time via deterioration, neglect, damage, and destruction, so Darrin's and Dorian's images in the stag films within these two features age, accumulating the aging process that the silver screen seems to defy.

Throughout this book I speak of the Victorian as a constructed canvas on which pornography projects its transgressions. *The Picture of Dorian Gray* deals more literally with a canvas that stages its protagonist's transgressions. A static visual technology, the painter's canvas, like film, is meant to time-lessly capture the body. While in the novel Gray's many horrific sins inflect the portrait, in the pornographic film adaptations it is only the ravages of time that are captured on the visual technology of film, his sins reduced to mere sexual indulgence and cavalier treatment of sexual partners. Indeed, these films are less concerned with crimes of the spirit and are instead pre-occupied with both the aging process of the corporeal body and the media on which this body is recorded. Gray's portrait in the novel (which, lest we forget, is his actual corporeal self) and the stag film, magazine pictorials, feature films, and videotapes of *Take Off* and *Gluttony* are what Laura U. Marks (no relation) calls "conductive," in that they create cultural memory and leave traces.

Marks's theory of sensory media and "loving a disappearing image" is particularly profound when applied to porn and is helpful in revealing the erotic work vis-à-vis Gray/Wilde performed in *Take Off* and *Gluttony*. As physical media deteriorates, we are reminded of the deteriorating bodies off screen. So many of these actors performing on the screen are dead, aged, or disappeared. When Marks speaks of "the physical fragility of the medium" (97), I am also reminded of the fragility of the porn performer's presence in the medium. Many porn performers make a career while others are "one-and-dones" or simply disappear from the spotlight, never to be heard from again. Performers from the early twentieth century stags are mysterious fig-ures, their motivations and circumstances unknown (Thompson 39–40). The same can be said of so many performers of the golden age who worked under pseudonyms and have long since evaporated into obscurity.[5]

Then there are the industry victims of the HIV/AIDS pandemic, most of them men performing in all-male features. Watching vintage porn involves a degree of mourning that is intimately connected to technology and the textures of film and video. As Marks explains, "To love a disappearing image one must trust that the image is real in the first place; that is, that it establishes an indexical link between the long-ago objects recorded by a camera and the present-day spectator. We mourn the passing of the young lovers/actors because we are sure that they existed: the photograph is a sort of umbilical cord between the thing photographed *then* and our gaze *now*" (*Touch* 96).

Gray mourns his decaying, disappearing image captured in the magic portrait; likewise, the Dorians of *Take Off* and *Gluttony* mourn their own decaying image—their decaying self captured in the image—only to be res-cued from mourning through a recuperative conclusion. Gray murders himself, severing the umbilical cord, while Darrin and Dorian of *Take Off* and *Gluttony*, respectively, are restored to their real, decayed selves and saved by true love that accepts age. In both cases, the monster is exorcized from the queer, while the spectator is left to meditate on decaying media and mourn the decaying body.

West explains that he has always been interested in "the textures of vintage pornography," and *Dorian Gray* (itself deeply concerned with the textures of the portrait) provided West with an opportunity to explore these textures in connection to legacies of pornographic film representations (West). These textures are in their own way tactile, corporeal, a "skin" and a sensory media experience. This tactility is a way of making an irrevocable, imagined past immediately sensually graspable. Indeed, West saw the *Dorian Gray* narrative as an opportunity "to do a movie that had a scene in every decade" (West). Weston appears to have found the same inspiration in creating *Take Off*, offering a scene from every decade of Hollywood up to the 1960s. In this way, *Dorian Gray* mobilizes a confrontation with *age* in all its forms, including ages of technology, aging bodies, the seeming agelessness of bodies on film, and the ways in which different film technologies act as "a membrane that brings its audience into contact with the material forms of memory" (Marks, *Skin of the Film* 243). Dorian Gray, the culture text, generates a pornographic corpus that addresses legacies of sexual representation, the *screens* on which these legacies are documented, and the melancholy residue of this very same legacy.

Both films take the stag as their origin point. Wilde situated Gray's soul in a portrait, whereas both Weston and West situate the soul in the stag film, a type of hardcore sex film that originated around the same time as the publication of Wilde's novel. "Stags," sometimes also referred to as "smokers," were one-reel silent pornographic films first produced at the end of the nineteenth century. Filmed and distributed illegally, they flourished in brothels and frat houses in the first half of the twentieth century, particularly before and immediately after World War I, and continued to enjoy an illicit trade up until the 1960s. They typically offered a simple narrative framing device, often involving humor; although primitive in form, they cemented particular pornographic tropes such as genital close-ups that remain surprisingly unaltered in the hardcore of today (Di Lauro and Rabkin; Thompson xvi). Very few stags survive today, suffering the natural stages of film decay, fearful or ashamed destruction at the hands of family members in the wake of a collector's death, or the cavalier disposal of what was (and is) deemed trash. Many stags may also linger anonymously, gathering dust in someone's attic. Stags inhabit an important place in the history of pornography because they are the first motion picture pornographies—the (often missing) link in a trajectory of sex on film that has been and remains patchy and incomplete. Stags are also significant because they are representationally consistent with their present-day inheritors. In this sense, the stag is the natural pornographic heir of Gray's portrait: an elusive, illicit technology of sexual subjectivity, secretive and hidden, occupying a mysterious and mythical place in the history of sexual representation.

Both *Take Off* and *Gluttony* present film as a sensual, tactile, and moving form of "portrait"—a canvas or skin that is not supposed to age but, like Gray's portrait and the bodies of Darrin and Dorian captured on celluloid, will indeed age and decay. The porned *Dorian Gray* narrative offers a meditation on the precarious state of film, the corporeal bodies captured on that film that are also vulnerable to decay, and the temporal, ever-changing formats, platforms, and machinery that host visual media and thus can carry the image to an endless array of time periods and contexts. In the process, we are led to ponder where the image is housed and what constitutes the *physical*.

Touching One's Self: *Take Off* (1978)

Weston's *Take Off* is interested in the textures and sensual experiences of cinematic and sexual legacies. The film was shot in the late 1970s, the pinnacle of porno chic. Budgets were bigger, filmmakers more accomplished, and the industry more established. *Take Off* is an example of the hopes some pornographers had for a blending of mainstream and pornographic. It is a whimsical, sometimes silly, and ultimately quite moving comedy that riffs on popular Hollywood tropes and boasts high production values, fine acting, a witty and romantic script, and beautifully handled direction by Weston.

The discovery of the stag film sets these questions in motion and indicates the sensual and erotic nature of the screen and the machinery surrounding it. Linda and fellow partygoer Roy discover a secret room in Darrin's house. Following a generic but loving and erotic scene between them, they discover and watch an old black-and-white porn film. In this film, a woman (Georgina Spelvin) walks across a lawn dressed in fine white clothes and carrying a white parasol. "Hey, we're going to the movies, honey!" cries Roy, as they settle down to watch it. From their mid-1970s vantage point, the couple are amazed at the antiquity of the film, surmising "it must be a collector's item." The film shows a picnic, where an old man is gradually and playfully remov-

29. The stag film that holds Darrin's true self in *Take Off* (Distribpix, 1978).

ing the stockings and clothes of the young aristocratic woman. "I didn't know they made stag films in them days," asserts Roy, adding, "That's practically an instant replay!"—a cheeky reference to the lovemaking they themselves indulged in moments before, as well as to a legacy of sexual representation of which they are now a part. The 1970s bodies we just watched making love remain ageless on our screen, yet the stag film points toward inevitable decay and the shifting notions of the past.

The interaction between Linda and Roy and the stag film, and between us the viewers and Linda and Roy, points toward the especially pronounced sensual relationship between pornographic spectator and pornographic image. This relationship is intensely corporeal, one of Linda Williams's "body genres" that elicits a physical "jerk" in its audience ("Film Bodies" 271). More-over, the interaction with pornography is not passive—simultaneous to the physical sexual activity assumed to occur before and alongside the image, the technology itself becomes part of the erotic encounter, whether that involves feeding the filmstrip into the projector or rewinding and pausing on the VCR player. These modes of viewing obscure decay by conveying immortalized bodies and creating a sense of authorial control, at the same time contribut-ing to decay through using the tape or film, leaving immediate traces. The very concept of "replayability" indicates the threat of wearing out an erotic spectacle until it no longer excites.

Linda and Roy's conversation emphasizes our expectations of immortality on film. Lit up by the flickering light of the projector, Linda grimaces, "Ugh, what's she doing with an old buzzard like *that*?" Roy grins and quips, "The same thing you was doing with me, sugar pie." "Yeah, but he's such a dirty old man," she replies. "Yeah, well I reckon I will be too someday," Roy states. This dialogue sets up the viewer to discover the story of the mysterious Darrin Blue, but it also poignantly highlights the relation of aging to technology. Here we, the spectators, see two young, beautiful, recently acquainted lovers, post-coitus, gazing up at a cinema screen and verbally connecting their soon-to-be aged bodies with those on screen; two beautiful pornographic actors who are themselves forever young and beautiful on our screen, once contained on reels of film, on the cinema screen, then on the television screen, and now available for any viewer's pleasure, at any time, on a variety of devices, on instant replay in the digital age.

Pornography is particularly susceptible to and suitable for consumer manipulation—replayability is a treasured quality in porn, while the rewind, fast forward, and pause buttons are infamously associated with hardcore media. In 1978, when *Take Off* was released, the majority of spectators had to attend

30. Roy and Linda watch the stag film in *Take Off* (Distribpix, 1978).

a theater and had no control over the text in the way they would during the ages of VHS and digital media. Even so, these viewers could choose to enter or leave the theater, duck out of particular scenes for a blowjob, or remain seated during a particularly hot scene to masturbate. The pornographic theater was a much more interactive and viewer-manipulated space than that of its mainstream counterpart.[6] *Take Off* eerily anticipates and confronts the shifting manner of porn consumption and its relationship to the bodies and sexual subjects on screen. The multimedia transformation of Wilde's novel emphasizes the changing meanings and media of pornographic representation even while the bodies on screen remain perpetually static and timeless. The result is a film that feels like a media kaleidoscope or ripple—the skin of the film, the bodies projected over and over within, transferred onto subsequent media textures, and consumed by generations of consumers on newly emerging platforms, generating new forms and styles of consumption. Darrin's aged, decrepit body on 8mm is the fleshy, corporeal representation of these ageing and changing media platforms. His body cruelly reflects the vulnerable, temporal nature of media and the human bodies captured on its screens.

Darrin's intimate, sentimental relationship with the technology that holds his true self emphasizes the texture and tangible nature of film media. In addition, this relationship signals the difference between art of the nineteenth century and art in the age of mechanical reproduction. Machinery mobilizes visual images, making the tools required to exhibit the image as sentimental and fascinating as the image itself. Like Gray, Darrin's true image is captured in his portrait, the moving-image stag film, and as such constitutes his flesh. Once Linda and Roy nervously sneak out of the viewing room, Darrin Blue, the mysterious host of the party and owner of the property, walks silently down into the room and stands with his hand on the projector. The narrative purpose of this scene is to show Darrin feeling for warmth—feeling for evidence of a screening—but there is something more literally touching and intimate about his connection with the machine that assists in depicting his true self.

Darrin stands with his hand resting on the projector, gazing past off screen, presumably at where the stag would be projected, gazing at where his own image would be—the image that haunts that space and appeared there only moments before. Unlike a painting, which is perpetually on display, which Gray must contain in a locked attic and cover with a drape, the film image requires further technology to be exhibited. This technology initiates a change in light and sound, and makes a tangible sensory difference to the machine that produces the image. Darrin gazes at the empty space that held his me- chanically reproduced image—a space that theoretically could be anywhere, as all that is required is empty space on which to project—while his hand absorbs the heat of the projector, a sensory inverse of what Gray experiences with his painting. Darrin can only see space, but can feel the heat that is a synecdoche for his image. Through touch, through sensory connection to the device, Darrin conjures the spectral portrait in his mind's eye.

Darrin attempts several tactile connections with the various media that hold and project his image. Through looking and touching, Darrin's con- nections with the media constitute a gesture of self-love and melancholy awe that bring the self-objectifying queerness of the novel to bear on the (ostensibly) hetero porn film.[7] Gray gazes at his changed portrait in horror: "The quivering, ardent sunlight showed him the lines of cruelty around the mouth as clearly as if he had been looking into a mirror after he had done some dreadful thing" (Wilde 77). Yet Darrin has not "done some dreadful thing," he has merely been immature and sullen, and sees no "cruelty around the mouth." In fact, as Darrin touches the screen onto which his moving im- age is projected, the projected mouth he touches is gaping in ecstasy.

31. Darrin touches his portrait, the stag film, in *Take Off* (Distribpix, 1978).

He is watching the film because he misses Henrietta, who has left him after two years of romance, yet this seems to be a camouflage for the real object of his gaze: his own sexually ecstatic performance. Darrin explains to Linda in voice-over, "As he watched, he thought he noticed something peculiar. *He was distracted away from Henrietta* and thought he detected small changes in his own image" (italics added). Darrin then turns to the mirror using a magnifying glass to gaze in ever greater detail. He gazes at his image on the actual filmstrip, his celluloid skin, which he holds up to the light in wonder. Darrin's portrait is not singular, as Gray's was. Darrin's portrait is a film within a film, but also more literally, *film*—celluloid—within the film. Usually hidden within a machine, Darrin's move from projected image to celluloid miniature reveals the multilayered media involved in the pornographic portrait.

Set in the context of Gray's illicit portrait and the same-sex eroticism it engenders, West's film takes up a Wildean legacy that reimagines histories of sexual representation as queer and sets these histories in motion. West and Weston highlight the fleeting nature of the present and what Church calls "the sliding ground of nostalgia" as we, the viewer, already view these texts as "the past." Both *Take Off* and *Gluttony* create an uncanny sense of moving past the present, of imagining and mobilizing an inevitable future—a future of sexual representation that we, the viewer, already inhabit.

Our Pornographies, Ourselves: *Gluttony*

While *Take Off* unsettles the orientation of spectator, sexual image, and sensual screen, with *Gluttony* Wash West offers a revisionist history of pornography that rewrites gay male porn back into our popular and academic discourse. West does this through the fictional discovery of the first stag film, the first money shot, and many more firsts in the genre of porn, all of which are revealed to be gay. While these discoveries occur in a faux documentary, the revisionism articulates truths: when we say "porn" we usually mean heteroporn; when we discuss the origins of porno chic with the first feature, *Deep Throat* (1972), we ignore the gay feature *Boys in the Sand* from the year before.

Gay porn complicates the rote, heteronormative procedures of analyzing "porn." Discussions of porn spectatorship often ignore the men in the theater or the peep booth who were more focused on sexual activity they engaged in with each other than that which was occurring on screen.[8] Also, porn that features only men obstructs our preoccupation with the treatment of women, leading to bad-faith arguments such as when Dines claims in her anti-porn book, *Pornland*, that "to ensure that this is *an accurate reflection of all porn available on the Internet,* and not one that focuses on only the most excessive, I started my search by typing 'porn' into Google and clicked on some of the sites that appeared on the first page" (xviii, italics added), yet adds in a footnote, "I did not look at gay porn as it has its own specific representational codes and conventions" (169). West satirizes such heteronormative and agenda-driven exclusion of all-male pornographic film and media, envisioning a heteronormative world that suddenly discovers that gay porn is the origin point of the media we have assumed to be hetero dominated.

West's revisionist history speaks to the absences and silences in Wilde's novel, as well as the absences and silences in academic discourse. Rather than reimagining the past through a queer lens, West reimagines a present that suddenly discovers this past is queer. In doing so through pornographic media, West conveys the importance of illicit sexual media to the visibility and validity of queer sexual orientation, as well as the visibility and validity of queer sexual media itself.

Gay porn shapes, reflects, and recovers gay sexual identity, historically providing one of the only sites of affirmation in visual culture. In this way, it occupies a distinctly different cultural place for gay men than straight porn does for straight men and women. As Tom Waugh reflects, "Somehow these images have meant more to us, for all their furtiveness, than girlie-pictures to straight men. Fuck photos have always had to serve not only as our stroke materials but also, to a large extent, as our family snapshots and wedding albums, as our cultural history and political validation" (*Hard to Imagine* 5). Burger calls the work that gay porn does "one-handed histories," arguing that many gay porn films actively recast American history to visualize gay places within straight spaces, as well as gay-specific sites and roles (34). These revisionist histories, Burger asserts, "are reparative. They make room for new historic truths, whether these be the ones they proffer or ones the viewer invents on his own" (37). For Burger, gay pornographic film as a whole is "history writing beyond the limits of academia" (34), "a warehouse of our cultural heritage and memory, as well as an important site for the production and modification of this heritage and memory" (x). Visualization of gay male sexual practices, then, is political work. For writers such as Burger and Waugh, it is not an exaggeration to say that gay pornography and erotica are an integral part of gay sexual identity and community. Moreover, gay porn is an important site of retroactive storytelling for those whose tales go untold. West enacts this work explicitly, directly addressing the oversights in academic and popular understandings of porn. Indeed, just as *Dorian Gray* and Wilde serve as present-day history lessons in nineteenth-century sex, sexuality, society, and law, so *Gluttony* in its documentary format serves as a hardcore history lesson in gay sexual representation.

Up until the mid-twentieth century, gay pornographies also differed from hetero pornographies in terms of media. During much of the first half of the twentieth century, beefcake photos and men's physique magazines were the primary sources of male same-sex erotic imagery. These images used such scenarios as men in Greek trappings, muscle flexing, and other forms of sport and exercise poses (Waugh, *Hard to Imagine* 215–83). It was not until the 1950s that these illicit pornographies developed into moving pictures.[9] Short films of the mid-twentieth century used similar themes of physical activity and Greek iconography that were used in the magazines, and in an important way in *Dorian Gray*.

Gay pornography has a fraught history characterized by the covert generation of images and pornographies that could be disguised as properly heterosexual and masculine. In this way, gay porn itself mirrors the perceived inability of Wilde to articulate homoeroticism without the use of metaphor. Covert imagery such as bodybuilding pictorials reflects a larger cultural alibi in which men are permitted to pose and/or look at other men as long as there is physical activity. Other handy alibis included the mediating influence of Greek imagery, which was especially popular in the Victorian period. Sedgwick explains: "Synecdochically represented as it tended to be by statues of nude men, the Victorian cult of Greece gently, unpointedly, and unexclusively positioned male flesh and muscle as the indicative instances of 'the' body, of a body whose surfaces, features, and abilities might be the subject or object of unphobic enjoyment" (136).

However, this alibi did not fool authorities in a post-Wildean era, and in 1948 the U.S. Post Office clamped down on mail-order advertisements for this type of material that could be found in the back of magazines (Escoffier 17). While the non-explicit male physique mail-order ads were not technically illegal, the magazines containing them erred on the side of caution and banned them. In response, Bob Mizer, one of the primary producers of these ads, created his own magazine, *Physique Pictorial*, and in 1958 started making black-and-white short films—effectively, moving images of beefcake photography: "the same young men cavorting by the pool or dressed in Greek tunics. [. . .] [T]he films employed simple story lines in which the youthful performers usually played stock characters—athletes, sailors, prisoners, and blue-collar workers" (Escoffier 18). These short films became known as "danglies" or "backyard cock danglers" (Escoffier 52) and represent, along with the magazines that sold them, the first mass-produced gay pornographic images of any substantial, widespread influence. Escoffier notes that "the cult of male beauty that the physique magazines fostered helped shape gay men's physical ideals before there was any common culture" (18). While sexploitation and beaver films were screened in cinemas for men and women who desired to look at the female form, men who wished to look at men were quietly stashing beefcake magazines.[10]

In *Gluttony* West consciously references these illicit pornographic origin points, beginning his faux documentary with Cyril Vane's retelling of his discovery in the 1980s: images of legendary porn star Dorian from the 1960s physique magazines that his closeted father had stashed under the mattress.

Dorian makes a deep impression on the young Cyril: "his image burning into my brain like a brand," and now he is "attempt[ing] to trace the life of a man that was there at the very beginning of my sexual self. I'm hoping to find out who he is, who he was, and at the same time maybe find out about myself." For Cyril, discovering truths about an iconic pornographic figure is a pathway to discovering truths about himself much in the same way that

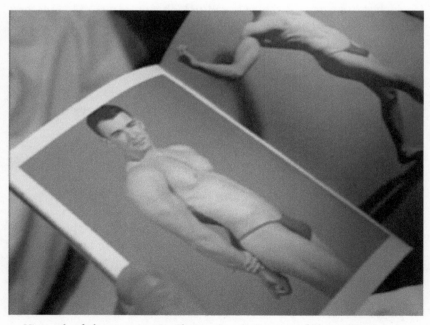

32. Vintage beefcake magazines in *Gluttony* (2001). Courtesy of Channel One.

early all-male erotic imagery served an important function in gay male self-actualization. This journey speaks to the closeted forefathers—our own fathers or symbolic ones such as Wilde—who produced, kept, and continue to keep valuable archives of homoerotic and same-sex erotic material (Waugh, *Hard to Imagine*; Gee).

In the course of the faux documentary, Cyril interviews various people who knew or knew of Dorian—co-stars, directors, academics, and industry affiliates—piecing together a narrative and a character through the fragmented authorship of artist, performer, and consumer. West deploys digital effects that recreate visual and communication technologies of different eras, explicitly marking the medium as a conductor of eroticism. West reproduces the style of film from the 1960s and 1970s, video of the 1990s, and the plentiful twenty-first century digital and analog technologies Cyril uses to search for and exhibit the information (email, databases; film projectors, video players, computer screens). West suggests that sexual subjectivity and desire is made up of profoundly fragmented and democratic media as much as it is of corporeal bodies themselves.

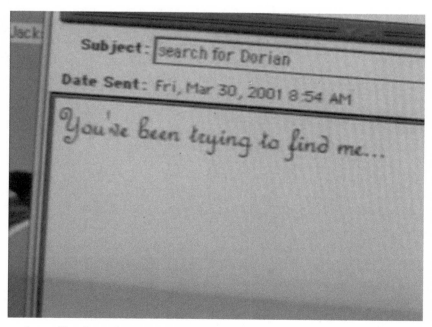

33. An email exchange between Dorian and Cyril in *Gluttony* (2001). Courtesy of Channel One.

In porning a late-Victorian classic, West enacts a similar move to those setting the action in the nineteenth century in that he invokes Gothic nostalgia for a more "innocent" cultural moment where players can indulge in deviant and unspoken desires. At the same time, he inserts modern-day sexual explicitness into those innocent spaces, flattening out linear trajectories of sexual representation. West actively defies historicity even as he offers a kind of queer-history lesson. For example, after discovering an old film called *Original Sin*, starring Dorian, Cyril explains the early days of gay pornography: "The movies of the '50s and '60s were called smokies. They were usually shown in smoke-filled backrooms. They were often about exotic themes, using imagination to turn people on in the absence of graphic images." The film shows Dorian and another man jumping up and down on a trampoline in nothing but briefs. As Cyril narrates, "The fine muscled young specimens paraded around, and viewers were left to imagine what lay beneath the g-strings." However, *Original Sin* turns out to be a "groundbreaking" discovery: "It goes places that movies never went back then. There's nudity, there's unabashed sex, even a cum shot." The scene unfolds in just this manner, providing modern sexual explicitness in a genre that is marked by its necessary coyness regarding sex. In this way, West is engaging in wish fulfillment. Viewers can bask in the glow of nostalgia but also get to see the kind of explicit content denied to the smokies' contemporary viewers.

However, in another more profound way, he is revising pornographic history to foreground gay porn as *porn*. In the above paragraph, the smokies discussed are *gay* and thus contradict the information I have provided thus far concerning "stags" and "smokers"—by which I almost always assumed the appendage, "straight." In West's universe, "porn" no longer means "straight porn." Gay porn is no longer the Other in porn discourse.

The absence of gay porn in popular and academic conversations about "porn" is symptomatic of a broader silencing and marginalization of same-sex desire. West recovers the significant contributions of gay pornographers, queering the standard heteronormative discourse around porn. If porn features only men, then it is "gay porn," not "porn." Cyril interviews fictional professor Reina Rica, a thinly veiled parody of porn studies legend Linda Williams, who excluded all gay porn from her groundbreaking 1989 book *Hard Core*, citing "a variety of practical, theoretical, and political reasons" (6), among them her desire to offer analysis of what we deem "representative" of porn. While in the second edition of the book she shame-facedly acknowledged this exclusion and its attending excuse, and has indeed covered gay pornographies in subsequent work, in the first issue she argues, "It seems important to begin a generic discussion of film pornography with an analysis of the general stereotype of the genre" (7). In other words, gay porn is marginal to the dominant "Porn" with a capital P.

West challenges the academic assumption that gay porn is peripheral to porn proper. Prof. Rica tells Cyril in an authoritative tone that the first recorded cumshot is from the heterosexual white coater,[11] *Sexual Freedom in Denmark* (dir. Alex DeRenzy, 1970). In response, Cyril informs her of his discovery of an earlier recorded cumshot, and she immediately calls her publisher to add a footnote to her forthcoming publication. Similarly, as the documentary goes through subsequent films and decades, various heterosexual milestones, such as the minor "talking pussy" subgenre and Russ Meyer films, are rediscovered as being spearheaded by all-male affairs. These gestures constitute an effort to reclaim pornographic history from an academic and popular sphere that routinely uses the term "porn" to mean "heterosexual porn." In literature on porn, gay porn is othered, whereas in West's film "gay porn" is rendered "porn."

Wilde's Ghost and the Specter of HIV/AIDS

While Joyce Carol Oates suggests that in another era Wilde's tale might be "a tragedy of the violent warring of consciousness with itself" (421), the tale becomes a comedy in *Take Off* and a satire in *Gluttony*. At the same time, both are tragic romances with traumatic spectral contexts. A legacy of cultural baggage makes these texts mean different things in different spaces and times. The films accrue histories that merge with the films and expand them, taking on nuanced and extra-textual resonances—both culture text and paratext. Both adaptations are touched by the tragic fate of Oscar Wilde and haunted by post-HIV pornography and culture.

Dorian Gray is now tinged with an uncanny sense of foreboding thanks to our knowledge of the trials and the role Wilde's subsequent imprisonment played in his early death. *Dorian Gray* was used in the trial as evidence of Wilde's homosexuality, giving the novel a dark sense of dual narrative. On May 25, 1895, Wilde began his two-year jail sentence. The hard labor he was sentenced to would involve six hours a day on a treadmill (twenty minutes followed by a five-minute rest) constituting an ascent of six thousand feet. Food was meager and sleeping conditions were a strain. He slept on "a bare board raised a few inches from the floor" (Pearce 340). Later, Wilde was assigned tailoring, sewing, and picking oakum (separating old rope into strands for use in ship building). As biographer Joseph Pearce explains, Wilde was physically unaccustomed to such work and his health quickly declined. Just two weeks after his imprisonment, he was visibly changed. On June 9, 1895, the *Reynolds News* reported, "Already Wilde has grown much thinner [. . .] and since his conviction he has preserved, it is said, a settled melancholy and reticence. He has had great difficulty in getting sleep, and from time to time he loudly bemoans the bitterness of his fate" (qtd. in Pearce 340).

The following October, Wilde was suffering from dysentery. Wilde's sister-in-law, Lily, visited him and described him as "very altered in *every* way" (qtd. in Pearce 343). Alarmed by reports, More Adey wrote to Wilde's wife, Constance, saying her husband was "evidently much changed for the worse both mentally and bodily. He is looking frightfully emaciated, his hair is falling off and is streaked with white, and his eyes have a vacant expression" (qtd. in Pearce 344). While still imprisoned, Wilde's mother died, worsening his despair. When Wilde was finally released in 1897, he was financially ruined. He spent the majority of his last years in France surviving on the charity of others, much of which he begged for. He died from cerebral meningitis in November 1900, just two years after being released from jail. If Frank Harris is to be believed, Wilde's end was horrifying. Harris describes the awful physical condition Wilde was in during his last days, remembering that "mucus poured out of Oscar's mouth and nose, and—Even the bedding had to be burned" (539). Harris darkly posits, "All those who live for the body shall perish by the body, and there is no death more degrading" (539), situating Wilde as an agent of his own demise by virtue of his ideological and sexual practices. Similarly grotesque moral judgments have been leveled at gay men during the HIV/AIDS pandemic.

Just as Wilde's corporeal decay haunts the margins of the novel used to condemn him to ignominy, imprisonment, and death, so the devastation wrought by the HIV/AIDS pandemic haunts the margins of gay porn. Escoffier calls the post-HIV era "gay noir," the period between 1985 and 1999 in which "the gay male community [was] populated by traumatized men whose sexuality was hemmed in by death, religious bigotry, and homophobia" (280). *Take Off* is haunted by the fate of Wade Nichols, who died in 1985 from a self-inflicted gunshot wound after he had contracted HIV/AIDS.[12] Nichols's appearance also conjures the memories of the many, many performers who so rapidly succumbed to the illness. What makes the pornographic film distinct from mainstream is that porn shows unsimulated, unprotected sexual activity—activity associated with the death of the participants. Gay porn superstar Al Parker remarked in 1988, "There are so many models who are dead now, who died of AIDS. You watch them in these old movies, and they squirt into somebody's mouth, and you're shouting at the screen, 'Don't do that!' It makes you cringe" (qtd. in Escoffier 198). Similarly, as a post–HIV/AIDS gay porn video produced at a time where condoms are the norm in gay porn, *Gluttony* is haunted by the specter of the disease. These texts take on complex and intersecting cultural threads and contexts from the nineteenth century to the present, constituting a troubled legacy of pleasure scarred by tragedy.

Reflecting on his 1985 essay, "Men's Pornography: Gay vs. Straight," in which he argued gay porn's "hard won centrality" to gay culture, Waugh contends that "from the point of view of the early 1990s, centrality seems like an understatement: the HIV pandemic has done nothing to stem the boom in the cultural ubiquity of sexual images within gay male communities" (4). While porn continued to operate and became increasingly industrialized, HIV/AIDS forever altered the pornographic landscape. Both *Take Off* and *Gluttony* carry the devastation of the pandemic—the devastation to men who have sex with men—at the edges of the text, much as the devastation of anti-gay legislation and the fate of Wilde permeate the edges of *Dorian Gray*.

Gay porn as an industry addressed the HIV/AIDS pandemic incredibly early, joining forces with activists and playing a vital role in the fight for medical research, efforts to combat stigma, and safe-sex education. In the early 1980s the gay porn industry took stock of their responsibility to society and joined forces with HIV/AIDS activists in order to assess what might be done. Around 1985, producers and activists were considering the extent to which condom usage might be eroticized on film and how porn stars might become role models for safe sex practices. In 1987, after much discussion and discord, the industry made the decision to go condom-only (Burger 22). Meanwhile, the straight industry opted for a system in which performers are regularly tested and typically do not use condoms (Escoffier 191). Wicked Pictures is the exception, as was Vivid between 2004 and 2006, prompted by the 2004 HIV outbreak. Both of these heterosexual studios went condom-only following the 2004 HIV scare; only Wicked remains exclusively condom-only. Following the multiple efforts to mandate condom use in straight porn, however, several studios have started to use condoms. Furthermore, queer and "ethical porn" studios such as *Pink & White* use safe-sex practices, including condoms as well as latex gloves and coverings for sex toys. Nevertheless, the gay porn industry is generally distinct from straight in its use of condoms.

A timely piece of evidence reflecting the break in pre- and post-HIV gay porn culture arrived in the form of a "Safe Sex Policy" printed on a piece of paper tucked into my DVD copy of *The Portrait of Dorian Gay* (1974) from Bijou Video. This policy, signed by president and founder of Bijou, Steven Toushin, provides a brief history of condom use in gay porn. This text demonstrates the way gay pornography, historical narrative, social responsibility, sexual subjectivity, and a sense of legacy intersect in a way that is distinct from hetero-porn. The policy notes,

> Bijou Video distributes films that were made in the pre-AIDS, pre-condom era of the 1970s and 1980s. HIV/AIDS emerged on the scene in 1980. By 1985, the gay porn industry was vigorously debating the use of condoms. By 1991–1992, all gay companies had adopted a safe-sex, condom-only policy for the models making gay sex films. I believe that gay films have an influence both on how gay men see themselves and on their sex practices. Remember as you watch our vintage, classic pre-condom films that they were made in a different era.

Toushin concludes with the chilling reflection, "I hate the idea that having sex might leave a person in a physical state in which they need drugs to stay alive." The idea that such a note might appear with a DVD from one of the current hetero-porn companies is unimaginable. The discourses of death, suffering, and abuse surrounding both *Take Off* and *Gluttony* create a ghostly sense of tragic legacy, with Wilde a ghostly figurehead.

West addresses the HIV/AIDS pandemic in a subtle way through absences and slight alterations to the sex acts depicted in each period. The versatile performer (men who penetrate as willingly as they are penetrated) became "erotically, the ideal man of the seventies" (Escoffier 185) due to the perception that such behavior represented a confident, free gay sexuality in the wake of the sexual revolution. Post-HIV/AIDS, sexual versatility became associated with an era characterized by sexual promiscuity that contributed to the pandemic. For this reason, performers tend to market themselves as either "tops" or "bottoms" and for the most part do not deviate from these categories. *Gluttony* relays these stories through the history of pornography. For example, the decrease in versatility is reflected in the fact that the performers in the 1960s scene act as both top and bottom, while the performers in the post-1980s scenes are strictly either top or bottom.

Furthermore, the narrator, Cyril, informs us, "We lose track of Dorian for a while" between 1978 and 1990, the period in which HIV/AIDS was discovered and seemingly overnight decimated a population of people, infecting and killing a shocking number of porn performers. While West narratively incorporates fluctuations in pornographic practice by including sexual versatility, he does not break with the twenty-first-century convention of condom usage, even in the 1960s scene. The ahistorical usage of condoms highlights what Escoffier terms "the strange doubleness of porn—it is *both* a fantasy created by actors *and* an enactment of the fantasy through real sex" (243). Even while West depicts the sexual freedoms of the 1960s, he is cautious to remind the viewer of the realities of the twenty-first century. West's film demonstrates the degree to which pornographic and pornotopian content is shaped by cultural realities and fuses cultural baggage with the text.

Exorcising the Monster

The Picture of Dorian Gray is a novel about the senses, both indulging in them and morally equivocating over them. Gray's crimes and craving for sensation result in his suicide-murder. In general, the novel is ambivalent about pleasure, both physical and spiritual. Michael Patrick Gillespie remarks, "*The Picture of Dorian Gray* articulates, without offering a clear resolution, the conflict that arises as a result of the struggle within an individual's nature between the impulse toward self-gratification and the sense of guilt that is a consequence of acting upon that inclination" ("Preface" ix). In addition, Gillespie locates a strong degree of pleasure for the reader in such ambiguities ("Picturing Dorian Gray" 393), ambiguities that pornography takes pleasure in claiming to unravel. In *Take Off* and *Gluttony*, the Dorian characters pursue pleasure in an indulgent and promiscuous way that is distinct from the more sinister suggestions of the novel, and for the most part without penalty. At the same time though, there is a sadness and ambivalence regarding the pornographic performer, a feeling that is compounded by the subsequent suicide of *Take Off*'s Nichols, and also reflected in West's bitter tribute to the world of gay video pornography in his later mainstream film, *The Fluffer* (2001).

Gray of the novel pursues sensations and pleasures that are ambiguous in many cases yet irrefutably damaging to others, resulting in murder, suicide, drug addiction, blackmail, and other unspoken atrocities. He believes in Lord Henry's "new hedonism," and in its aim: "experience itself, and not the fruits of experience, sweet or bitter as they might be" (108). As Oates observes, Gray's sin is constituted by "the fact that he, without any emotion, involves others in his life's drama 'simply as a method of procuring extraordinary sensations'" (419). In contrast, Darrin does not milk others for "extraordinary sensations," instead simply embarking on sexual adventures with willing participants. He is a basically sweet-natured man, vain and immature as a youth, later jaded and wise as a man who has lived too long. He simply has sex in different eras and is deeply regretful of his decision to stay forever young. Dorian of *Gluttony*, too, is no monster. He merely uses people for sex and "discards them like Kleenex," as one interviewee recalls. He is ultimately lonely and exhausted, just like Darrin.

Darrin and Dorian of the porn adaptations recognize the lesson at the core of Wilde's novel, which Gray never does: that, as Elana Gomel puts it, "desire turns out to be the function of time and loss" (83)—or, in Darrin Blue's words, "that nothing can remain the same, that change is the essence of life, and that aging is the proof. And that the lack of change is the real death." As a result, Darrin and Dorian are transformed from "textual construct" (image on the screen) to "the real" (Gomel 84) without the necessity of death. Indeed, both Darrin and Dorian are rewarded with love. In both films, the spell of the magic stag is broken—in *Take Off* through filming him have sex again, and in *Gluttony* through sex infused with love—and Darrin and Dorian are returned to their aged selves. Darrin disappears with an equally aged Henrietta Wilde, while the youthful Cyril warmly accepts the aged Dorian. Weston and West redeem the monstrous Dorian Gray, then, forgiving the "sin" of sexual indulgence and validating the embodiment of the real rather than the reproduction.

Both *Take Off* and *Gluttony* depict men who have certainly transgressed but are forgiven and happily shift into romantic relationships with an accepting partner. This generic trope of the acceptance of transgression is perhaps unique to pornography. In addition, given pornography's reputation as socially and sexually transgressive, it is surprising how many pornographic features end in such a manner. In these films, as with others, sexual abandon is not as appealing when put into practice; sexual commitment and true love are more desirable in the long term. Let us not forget, however, that this longing for stability comes at the end of a raucous indulgence in hedonistic sexual pleasure. Moreover, visions of romantic love and stability constitute an intervention in heteronormative portrayals of love. In pornography, the neo-Victorian opens a space for deviant pleasure and just as easily accommodates a seemingly discordant romantic denouement.

Take Off and *Gluttony* conjure anxieties surrounding what Church calls "the lived costs for those performers whose indexical bodies are lent to the genre's enactment of erotic fantasies" (*Disposable Passions* 211). These lived costs are not restricted to disease. Many of these stars died broke, are living with illness, surviving on Social Security, and largely ignored for their art and their contributions (whether actively or incidentally) to freedom of speech and sexual politics. Some of the biggest stars of the golden age have suffered homelessness, crippling illness, and financial destitution, and have reached out to their fans for support. The existence of the Golden Age Appreciation Fund—an organization that raises money to "help participants from the 'Golden Age' of adult films (1968–1988) in their time of need," whether that be for housing, transportation, or pet care ("About the Fund")—indicates of how little the stars of erotic film are recognized by larger society for their cultural contributions.

These films are celebrations of momentary transgression, mobilizing indulgent, hedonistic sexual journeys that ultimately exhaust the traveler. These transgressions are made all the more pleasurable by the eventual return to normality, much in the same way as the cinema spectator emerges from the darkness into the daylight, or the masturbator resurfaces following climax. Both *Take Off* and *Gluttony* revise the sexually indulgent, narcissistic monster. They claim to reveal the "truths" behind the silences, gaps, and metaphors of Wilde's novel, and offer the protagonist redemption. In the process, West and Weston provide texts that, like a cypher, accrue layers of meanings, contexts, and spectral presences generated by a quite specific legacy of sexual and technological discourse surrounding *Dorian Gray* and its author. These are corrective and *collective* narratives, ones that implicate the spectator in their queer kaleidoscope of screens, images, and mechanical exhibitions of the body, and also in that spectator's own corporeal relations to the image and the decay of the bodies and media they enjoy. The men of these films take pleasure and pain in gazing at themselves, pleasure and pain that touches the viewer as they gaze back and touch themselves. The anxieties and pleasures at the heart of much of pornography's repetition and restraint are generated by the anxieties and pleasures of the screen, the bodies contained on those screens, and the bodies that respond to those screens. The *Dorian Gray* narrative mobilizes the melancholy erotics of fleeting images and media, fleeting life and love, and the recovery of and interaction with these temporal pleasures on new and emerging media.

Porn is a genre engaged with hedonism, fantasy, and pleasure. It celebrates that which we are encouraged to silence, fear to speak, and thrilled to encounter. Yet, as the films discussed here show, it is also a profoundly self-reflective genre unafraid to engage with loss and melancholy. Moreover, pornographers and pornography consumers recognize the centrality of pornographic media in exploring, speaking, and processing this loss. Pornography accrues loss and melancholy over time in the very fiber of the media even as it also accrues greater social meaning in connection to the sexual injustices of the world at large. Such legacies of the flesh—legacies composed of media, technology, representation, spectatorship, and illicit documentation—reveal the intimacy we enjoy with the Victorians through pornography. Such legacies point to the fact that pornography is a critically important space for Gothic reflection and introspection even while it simultaneously functions as an erotic outlet and tool in constructing our sexual subjectivities.

CONCLUSION
Fueling the Lamps of Sexual Imagination

Opinion pieces are fine, but I'm hungry for something more.
—Lorelei Lee, "Cum Guzzling Anal Nurse Whore:
A Feminist Porn Star Manifesta"

I share Lee's hunger for "something more." In her 2013 manifesta, Lee bemoans the recent surge in sensationalistic, tabloid-style think pieces concerning the dangers of porn. There has been a similar surge in academia that is
at once influential and unnerving to the extent that this superficial research
threatens to turn back the tide on porn studies. As Lee observes, "After reading the recent crop of antiporn books and articles, I'm left with the impression
that many of the people in this country start from a place of assumption that
to work in pornography is, for women, a fate close to death. It seems to me
that this attitude is directly related to attitudes that describe sexually active
women as 'fallen' or 'disgraced'" (211). Indeed, nineteenth-century rhetoric
permeates the latest moral panics casting neo-Victorian pornographies in
a rather revealing light.

This project reveals the myriad ways pornography tries to stabilize itself
and generate sexual excitement through the ongoing, obsessive process of
transgression and dissolution of boundaries. It has also been an exploration
of the ways pornographers toy with the Victorian Gothic in order to mobilize
dynamic visions of gender, race, class, and sexuality. The fallen woman, the
deviant, the homosexual, the Other—these are the heroes and monsters of
pornographic media.

Pornography requires a perceived gap in speech to fill or a socially constructed taboo to violate in order to play out its various transgressive moves.
Subsequently, pornography presents itself as a medium that appears to cross
boundaries, speak the unspoken, and challenge the status quo. Yet these

obsessive transgressions ultimately enact, protect, and contain visual articulations of certain gender, sex, and identity norms even as they offer up productive sexual spaces. The Victorian Gothic offers a particularly appealing and fraught gap in speech, one that we obsessively return to as if to a primal scene. As Wash West elegantly explains, "Although our society today is relatively liberated, Victorian ideas about sex are still there lurking underneath—like a seam of coal tar that can be mined and used to fuel the lamps of today's sexual imagination." As I have demonstrated, the Victorian persists in fueling the lamps of pornography, serving as an important canvas on which to stage its transgressions. Indeed, as West's comment suggests, the Victorian and the Gothic constitute a crucial driving force behind twentieth- and twenty-first-century sexual pleasures and a potent framework for pornographers.

Umberto Eco argues, somewhat facetiously, that a porn film is recognizable by how much time it wastes:

> The pornographic movie must present normality—essential if the transgression is to have interest—in the way that every spectator conceives it. Therefore, if Gilbert has to take the bus and go from A to B, we will see Gilbert taking the bus and then the bus proceeding from A to B. This often irritates the spectators, because they think they would like the unspeakable scenes to be continuous. But this is an illusion on their part. They couldn't bear a full hour and a half of unspeakable scenes. So the passages of the wasted time are essential. (224–25)

These "passages of wasted time," if we expand the notion beyond Eco's bus travel, would be the substance I have addressed in this project: clothing and costumes, dialogue, architecture, writing and letters, plot. In many of the gonzo scenes of today, the "wasted time" would be the tease, preliminary interviews, brief set-ups (as in vignettes), or even the behind-the-scenes featurettes. Most anything that is not "just fucking" might be considered a waste of time if one regards pornography in such a superficial manner. Eco is correct: it is his terminology that is off. These "passages of wasted time" are actually the text, context, and paratext of porn, the critical canvas without which eroticism and transgression would be more difficult to stage. Passages of wasted time render performers subjects, establish humanity for sexual dissolution, and infuse the pornographic space with a heady mix of reality and fantasy.

I have argued in the preceding pages that the Victorian Gothic is one of the more appealing and useful stages on which to play out the diverse functions and pleasures of pornographic film. Regarded as, at best, a simplistic and superficial genre solely in pursuit of climax, or at worst a poisonous genre that inflicts real harm on people, especially women and children, pornography is actually a wildly unstable genre, veering into unexpected territories and offering a constellation of sexual perversions and gender arrangements. While the tantalizing boundaries and thresholds that the Victorian appears to erect are enticing to cross over, the Victorian also contains dark and ambiguous spaces populated by shifting, monstrous beings. These beings promise much in the way of perversion, fluidity, deviance, and disruption—interventions inherent to pornography that, consciously or unconsciously, generate rich pleasures. Neo-Victorian porn draws these monstrous pleasures more clearly to the surface.

Pornography is haunted by a particular malleable, "plastic" Gothic Victorian world inhabited by strict binary divisions (Halberstam). Each porned text is representative of deep anxieties over sexual identity, gender fluidity, authorship, duality, perversion, and shifting social structures reflective of a rapidly changing nineteenth-century culture. This visioning is deeply sexually perverse, yet also sexually repressed—a world where homosexuality is forbidden and silenced, yet is everywhere in discourse, where women are active narrative agents and sexually bold, yet part of a genre and culture in which meaning is inscribed onto female bodies. In short, pornographic representation and desire are about transgressing boundaries that are exciting for the very transgression. This transgression is an anticipated and understood component of pornography. Dismantling boundaries is not necessarily the goal; boundaries are, in fact, sexually thrilling. Achieving sexual enlightenment is also not necessarily the goal; the staged sense of illicit discovery is.

Neo-Victorian Panic

Pornography thrives on crossing boundaries. Ever since its modern incarnation, society has attempted to halt these crossings and restrict pornographic media and other forms of adult entertainment to specific locations. The internet has made these efforts particularly difficult, inspiring redoubled efforts that conflate pornography with addiction, child abuse, trafficking, and the moral decline of a global community. Over the last few years, fears over internet pornography have grown to fever pitch. Young people, we are told, are learning about the wrong sort of sex. Pornography is destroying marriages. Men are growing addicted to online porn, resulting in a wide range of problems including lower libido, erectile dysfunction, marital strain, and toxic sexual behaviors. Like a Gothic plot, internet porn has become a monstrous technology that "exerts a dehumanizing power that will kill us, or enslave us. . . . It must remain passive and conquered for us to rule, and yet it always threatens us with revolt" (Edwards "Introduction: Technogothic" 2). As of last year, politicians and activists began declaring porn a "public health hazard," with several state legislators adopting the language and pushing for regulation.

The Utah resolution that introduced this political platform declares not only that "research indicates that pornography is potentially biologically addictive" but also that pornography "increases the demand for sex trafficking, prostitution, child sexual abuse images, and child pornography" (Utah Leg.).[1] Terminology is key here. For many, "trafficking" is a catchall term for any form of sex work. For example, Laura Lederer is quoted as saying, "We should not say that pornography *leads* to sex trafficking; pornography *is* sex trafficking" (Trueman). Ambiguous and vague sex trafficking rhetoric is deployed to regulate immigration and deport immigrant workers, to regulate strip clubs and even adult bookstores (Litten), and more broadly to abolish and severely punish all forms of sex work.

These developments have the distinctive whiff of Victorian regulation of the public space, particularly in terms of maintaining class and race segregation and resisting migrant workers. As Karen E. Bravo asserts, "The specter of involuntary sex and of despoilment of innocent white maidens seized the world's attention in the late 1800s and the early 1900s. Overtones of that appalled, fascinated, and condemnatory prurience continue to pervade public and institutional perceptions of the traffic in human beings in the early twenty-first century" (221). Indeed, anti-trafficking rhetoric has its roots in the late nineteenth century. In the mid-1800s, prostitutes were regarded as fallen women— that is, they were regarded as "simultaneously agents of their own destruction and objects of pity, unfortunate sinners with the capacity for redemption" (Soderlund x). By 1907, these women had been rhetorically transformed in the press and in the eyes of society into "trafficked victims." As Gretchen Soderlund explains, thanks to journalism such as Stead's 1885 "Maiden Voyage," "An image of a vast and coordinated system forcing unsuspecting white girls into sexual servitude replaced the earlier image of the dissolute, fallen woman" (xi). Then as now, there was very little evidence of this supposed crisis, and in fact "the level of specificity of the stories waned as the scale of the perceived problem grew" (Soderlund xi). Emotionally provocative rhetoric replaced hard facts, and trafficking rhetoric became "the dominant framework for understanding and regulating prostitution" (xi). This framework persists, only now it is used to legislate any and all forms of adult entertainment.

Likewise, dire projections regarding the physical, spiritual, and psychological ills of pornography bear an uncanny resemblance to a series of mid-nineteenth-century fears: the masturbation panic, young people and their access to lewd materials, visual media consumed by the poor and uneducated, and a thriving sex-work industry that threatened to spill out into middle-class society. Recently in the United Kingdom, particularly draconian pornography legislation has successfully been written into law. Starting with the extreme porn law of 2008, which criminalized the possession of "extreme porn," the country has only grown increasingly censorious as far as internet porn goes. The extreme porn law defined "extreme" porn as

> material that has been produced "solely or principally for the purpose of sexual arousal", which is grossly offensive, disgusting or otherwise obscene and that explicitly and realistically depicts (so that "a reasonable person looking at the image would think that any such person or animal was real"):
> - An act which threatens a person's life,
> - An act which results, or is likely to result in, serious injury to a person's anus, breasts or genitals,
> - An act which involves sexual interference with a human corpse, or
> - A person performing an act of intercourse or oral sex with an animal (whether dead or alive). (Rackley and McGlynn)

The law proved ineffective and flawed due to its subjective language that does not allow for nuance or BDSM practices. Indeed, many of the films discussed in this book could be subject to prosecution under this definition.

Since 2008, the government has made several gestures that further censor pornographic representation on the internet. As of 2013, internet access is by default filtered by the user's ISP. Here, too, the parameters were so ambiguous that sex education sites, child protection services, and suicide prevention were among the blocked sites (Smith "Porn Filters"). Senator Weiler, he of the Utah "public health hazard" resolution, has also made moves toward filtering software, citing the United Kingdom as the inspiration (Golden). Other states have followed suit, again citing trafficking concerns (Clark-Flory; Gross).

Most notoriously, the Audiovisual Media Services Regulations 2014 required that online streaming content conform to the regulations of the British Board of Film Classification that provides ratings on mainstream film. Unacceptable content includes face sitting, female ejaculation, caning, and verbal abuse. Male ejaculation was not infringed upon, and indeed many commentators observed what appeared to be a crackdown on female sexual pleasure and the content typically found on queer and feminist porn sites. Pandora/Blake notes, "The banned acts disproportionately refer to acts of female sexual pleasure, female dominance, and queer, ungendered or non-phallic sex acts. I see these laws as an attempt to control sexuality and limit us to patriarchally approved, heteronormative sex" (Gander).

Such measures are a reaction to the intersections of pornography and technology, specifically the internet, a frighteningly accessible space of unknown content that sits outside of the Obscene Publications Act of 1857. These measures are, predictably, framed as a way to protect children. When it comes to pornography and sex work, it appears we are at this very moment in the process of crafting a doppelganger. Simon Joyce's observation that Victorians are in our rear-view mirror, closer than they may appear, remains pointed. We are ostensibly far removed from the Victorians and yet here we are, returning once again to the very same sexual politics and reactionary rhetoric that, when attached to the Victorians, seems terribly naïve and laughably sensational. Perhaps now is the time to look more closely into that mirror of Joyce's.

In this environment, pornographic interventions that highlight cultural hypocrisy remain relevant and necessary. Supposed "pornified" culture is starting to feel more precarious for erotic artists than it has since the 1980s. Former president of the ACLU, Nadine Strossen, argued in 1995 that censorship would inevitably target the marginal voices of society: women, feminists, LGBT individuals, people of color, and those deemed "deviant" in their sexuality. In 2018, Strossen's contention holds true. Blake has written extensively of her struggles with ATVOD and Ofcom, the regulating bodies that ensure compliance with content restrictions and age verification. In August 2016, ATVOD forced Blake to shut down her spanking site because spanking was now a restricted act. Happily, Blake won her appeal and reopened the site in 2016—only to face the Digital Economy Act that was signed into law in 2017. This law requires age verification on all adult websites, a requirement that costs the owner a significant amount of money per user. As Blake points out, this means that those sites that don't earn as much revenue—typically feminist, queer, and alternative sites—will struggle to remain online (Blake). Furthermore, according to Blake, the content that officials latched on to tended to be scenes in which men were spanked, revealing a heteronormative anxiety at the heart of the investigation. Other sites that featured exclusively female asses being spanked did not attract the same level of scrutiny (Blake).

The Importance of Porn Literacy

Ironically, the censorship, silencing, and shaming that superficial anti-porn and anti-trafficking efforts mobilize are the very things that hinder education and literacy in sexual practices and representations, including safety, understanding of consent, and healthy, happy sexual intimacy. Porn literacy—open, honest, nonjudgmental education and discussion that, in Shira Tarrant's words, "decodes porn"—is sorely needed in this era of smartphones and the internet. Tarrant asserts,

> pornography is a crucial component in developing critical media literacy skills beginning from the position that porn literacy promotes stronger abilities to navigate sexual and gender politics in the 21st century. Pornography is an important media genre for both questioning normative expectations and exploring forms of resistance that challenge racism, classism, ageism, and related intersectional subjugations. (417)

Porn literacy is also crucial if we believe that understanding media representation and hidden labor is crucial. I believe this is particularly important with pornography, where so much labor occurs off screen. Moreover, the labor on screen can appear so spontaneous, so "real," that the labor of performance can also go unseen. These concerns apply to mainstream media in a less serious way. The difference is that while we are raised in a culture that openly and casually discusses the generic aspects of action films, and we generally come of age understanding that the car chases in said action films are staged and performed by professionals, very rarely do we gather a similar understanding of pornography.

Part of this has to do with parental squeamishness or related fears concerning charges of inappropriateness. But another significant part of the problem is the shallow yet self-righteous rhetoric surrounding pornography that tends not to engage with specific texts, frames pornography as a pernicious threat that cannot be "used" in a healthy manner, trivializes and dismisses the complex experiences of sex workers, and demonizes so-called deviant sexual proclivities. Constance Penley observes, "As a society, we debate, legislate, regulate pornography in almost a total vacuum of knowledge about what it really consists of historically, textually, institutionally" (qtd. in Tarrant 422). Pornographers, as I have shown here, are well aware of the historical and technological contexts of pornography. Yet for the average consumer or anti-porn activist, there is little distinction between texts, genres, studios, or eras.

I recently went for dinner with an academic who had requested we meet, as she was hoping to pursue porn studies as part of her present research. I quickly realized that she knew next to nothing about porn and, moreover, did not feel that acquiring such knowledge was all that important. Upon quipping that porn music was "unsexy" and bad, I replied that there is plenty of music in porn that is quite wonderful and certainly sexy. I noted that I owned the soundtrack to *The Devil in Miss Jones* on vinyl. She replied that *The Devil in Miss Jones* was old, indicating that it did not count as part of her claim. Later in the evening, she appeared to find it a surprising and novel idea to draw up a list of pornographic films she should watch in order to gain a richer understanding of the genre.

The notion of an academic thinking it initially unnecessary to engage with the texts he or she will ostensibly be studying is shocking to me. Nevertheless, I have encountered this attitude several times with students and faculty who seem taken aback that they might be expected to watch porn if they are writing a paper about porn. I imagine they think there isn't much to see—it is just fucking, after all. These interactions are evidence of a common trend—that is, making sweeping, ahistorical, and unspecific claims based on little to no research; believing that one need not watch porn in order to have a concrete opinion on it; and, in the face of contradictory evidence, qualifying that opinion by moving the goalposts.

Porn studies and porn pedagogies are crucial in that pornography is ubiquitous, yet "for all the punditry and moral panic about young-adult sexuality, there is little opportunity for teens and young people to discuss how to critically watch and think about pornography" (Tarrant 419). How are we to empower internet users to engage thoughtfully and ethically with pornographic media without the tools offered by porn literacy? How are we to demystify and educate on porn if we refuse to address it with any complexity or willingness to actually watch, absorb, and unpack the genre in question? The answer, I fear, is that many have no interest in demystifying and educating on porn. They want it to go away, or they want to pretend their children don't watch it, or that it doesn't exist, all the while consuming it surreptitiously behind closed doors. This is not simply hypocritical; it fosters silence and shame surrounding sexual health, desires, and practices.

Porn: Forever the Outlaw

You may have noticed during this book that at times porn seems more interested in itself than anything else, even with the pretense of a neo-Victorian response to the canon. Porn is indeed supremely insular and self-referential—

some might say narcissistic. It is also a self-Othering genre, relishing in its marginal outlaw status at the same time as it probes its heritage and parallels with the mainstream. These components work together to create rich opportunities for transgression while never quite dismantling the social norms it rhetorically claims to violate. Paasonen astutely observes that "by recurrently transgressing the boundaries of social categories, good taste, and disgust, porn works to construct and reiterate them. Some of these boundaries are explicitly anachronistic, others are more or less like self-parody in their excessiveness, while yet others seem difficult to decouple from social hierarchies and relations of power" (61). This reiteration, and the entailing confusion and instability, constitutes the films discussed in this book. However, as I have argued, these reiterations also constitute erotic fantasy spaces for working out and intervening in legacies of gender, class, race, and sexuality and the erotic tensions that punctuate them. Neo-Victorian pornographies rekindle desires, creating fantastical and nostalgic spaces where the transgression feels doubly thrilling. In turn, the neo-Victorian porn film looks back fondly, if ambivalently, constructing and articulating legacies of shared technology, art, culture, and anxiety. Most important, these films speak an inherited sexual discourse. These staged legacies situate pornographic discourse in historical context even as they also create a sense of timelessness.

Susanna Paasonen cautions that "porn futures need to be thought of as plural" ("Epilogue" 109). We should think of porn pasts as plural also. Pornographic film tackles plurality as part of its generic impulse, fracturing and complicating "Porn" with a capital P in the process. Constantly evolving pornographies of the twenty-first century—camming, CG monster porn, microporn (gifs), custom videos, sidebar ads, virtual reality, restored HD copies of 1970s classics, to name a small handful—represent a fragmented, mobile, and versatile Gothic engagement with the erotics of trespass and transformation. The media itself is alive, plastic, monstrous, and migratory. When the beast threatens to permeate the legitimate (its favorite pastime), it must be restricted. Hydes should be segregated from civilized society, beastly portraits kept in the attic, sexually voracious women rescued for their own good. Do we take pleasure in deviant doubles? Certainly, but only behind closed doors. And just like the monster, porn will never stay behind closed doors. It metamorphoses, escapes, changes direction, and is bolstered and inspired each and every time restriction and exorcism rear their ugly heads. Porn speaks back, and in that speaking back it develops a more dynamic outlaw ethos with which to eroticize this ongoing discourse.

NOTES

Introduction: Skin Flicks

1. It would be impossible to list every hardcore film in each of these genres—there are literally thousands of hardcore films that intersect with mainstream genres, some of which function as hybrids. Contrary to the perception that generic complexity and narrative have entirely fallen away from hardcore, pornographers persist in seeking new angles and approaches to hardcore product. See I. Q. Hunter's "Adaptation XXX" for a helpful overview of the myriad pornographic uses of mainstream and Hollywood genre.

2. It is too great a digression to go into how the stigma and shame attached to the workers performing these sexual convulsions and transformations render them abhuman in the eyes of society also. For further discussion of this, see the documentary *After Porn Ends* and the books *Coming Out Like a Porn Star* (edited by Jiz Lee), *Sex Workers Unite* (by Melinda Chateauvert), *Live Sex Acts: Women Performing Erotic Labor* (by Wendy Chapkis), and *Playing the Whore: The Work of Sex Work* (by Melissa Gira Grant).

3. The Disney film *The Rescuers* famously includes two frames from a pornographic film during the scene where the two protagonists take off on a pelican (Mikkelson). In 2009 the Arizona broadcast of Super Bowl XLIII was interrupted by thirty-seven seconds of hardcore pornography. Frank Tanori Gonzalez was arrested on charges of computer tampering. Some viewers were outraged. To make up for it, Comcast offered $10 credits to all service users (Hickey).

4. It is important to note that Penley's argument concerns *white* trashing and is concerned in an important way with class and white-trash aesthetics. Here, I hope to expand the notion of trashing so that it incorporates race. Porn is trash, but as Mireille Miller-Young observes, black women are seen as trashy even within this trashy genre. The trashing gesture is productively complicated by race.

5. Gail Dines suggests that those who teach pornography in a porn-critical fashion are merely providing "a captive audience for capitalists to push their products." See "The Shocking Suspension of Dr. Jammie Price." Those who are in favor of the full decriminalization of sex work, and even those who advocate for sex workers, have been described as part of a "pimp lobby." See Meghan Murphy's *Feminist Current* article "Who Gets a Say?" in which she uses the more palatable phrase "sex work lobby."

6. Here I use the term "porning" in a distinctly different way from Carmine Sarracino and Kevin M. Scott in their book, *The Porning of America*. While never exactly defining the term, Sarracino and Scott use "porning" to describe the insidious rise of porn culture that permeates mainstream culture. They also explain that the term can be deployed metaphorically: "'porning' can be understood as a cultural metaphor that applies to areas apparently disconnected from actual porn" (114). In this way, "porning" for Sarracino and Scott seems to mean the culture of sexualization, violence, and humiliation.

7. Brian McNair makes an interesting and persuasive case for the radical importance of capitalism. Capitalism, typically characterized as a corrupting influence on true radical, political work, is to McNair a vital component of social change.

8. It is notoriously difficult to ascertain how much money porn studios make. One thing that seems certain is that porn is not the multibillion-dollar industry people love to cite, especially not now. Performer wages are decreasing, studios are closing left and right, and the "extreme" and therefore expensive acts such as gangbangs and bukkakes are not as common. See Dan Ackman's 2001 *Forbes* article, "How Big Is Porn?," Carrie Wiseman's 2016 *Salon* article, "The Porn Industry Is a Lot Less Lucrative than You Might Think," and Jon Ronson's excellent 2017 Audible series, *The Butterfly Effect*, which traces the impact of tube sites and piracy on the adult industry.

9. See for example *Romance* (dir. Catherine Breillat, 1999), *Baise-Moi* (dir. Virginie Despentes and Coralie Trinh Thi, 2000), *The Idiots* (dir. Lars Von Trier, 2000), and *Shortbus* (dir. John Cameron Mitchell, 2006). These films feature unsimulated sex, but within a narrative that deals with dissatisfaction, neurosis, murderous rage, and other narrative tools that "elevate" the sex from porn to art. Hardcore sex is also not a punctuating, organizing, and consistent element of the film as it is in what we call porn. Even these films, however, are filtered by imdb.com, are certainly not shown on cable television, and are only carried by indie/art cinemas and video retailers.

10. For a detailed study of the erotics of the magic lantern and the importance of this device to visual culture and literature, see Jones, *Sexuality and the Gothic Magic Lantern*. For a discussion of the stereoscope and its role in the evolution of pornography see Williams, "Corporealized Observers.'"

11. At the time of our interview, Blake was presenting as a cis woman in porn work and used the accompanying pronouns and gender identifiers. Since then, Blake has come out as non-binary and uses the pronouns they/them/theirs. In accordance, and having consulted Blake on the matter, I use their preferred pronouns but, when discussing scenes in which they present as a cis woman, I refer to them as such.

Chapter 1. Behind Closed Doors: Neo-Victorian Pornographies

1. It is important to note that many seemingly random choices made by pornographers are related to random props and locations made available through friends and other connections. Eric Edwards told me that the idea for *Memoirs of a Chambermaid* was first planted in his mind after seeing the house. The script developed around the architecture and house interiors. Likewise, *E.T.: The Porno* is filmed in the same house as *Jekyll & Hyde* (1999), discussed in chapter 4. This indicates that whoever owns the house was perhaps connected to someone in the porn industry, made it available for filming, and the filmmakers decided to use the period architecture as a central aspect of the film. This would also mean they happened across an incredibly realistic E.T. suit and a wardrobe of nineteenth-century costumes, which perhaps is a stretch. In my opinion, the often-bizarre choices made in porn films are nearly always a combination of intent, luck, and accident (an aspect of porn that I find extremely appealing), and in the case of *E.T.: The Porno* we may never know exactly how the project developed.

2. Sarah Waters enacts a similar gesture through queering Victorian domestic space in her neo-Victorian novel *Tipping the Velvet*. While not a "pornographic novel," *Tipping the Velvet* is certainly erotic and relatively explicit.

3. While the majority of the sex scenes feature black men and white women, black women are also positioned as sexually desirable to the black men. The film opens with the slave women cheekily displaying their asses and vulvas to the slave men, who respond with hoots and whistles of gratitude. Women of both races also express desire for one another in sex scenes. While arguably a minor observation all things told, these moments do seem important in interrupting the standard IR approach that privileges the white woman as singularly desirable. In fact, the only bodies not lusted after (or even shown naked or engaged in sexual activity) are those of the cuckolded white men.

4. One of the more popular new porn websites is Greg Lansky's *Blacked*, a glossy interracial site established in 2014 that offers narratively framed scenes of black men with white, typically slender, often blonde, and nearly always modestly chested women. The narrative set-ups often involve some form of cheating, revenge on a white husband, or playful coercion (such as the woman having sex with the man after a lost bet). This site was so successful, Lansky created two more sites, *Tushy* (anal themed) and *Vixen* (boy/girl quite broadly). Neither site appears to be as popular as *Blacked*, which seems to have filled a gap in the market: interracial porn that trades in the erotics of miscegenation but with high production values, little to no roughness, and no explicit invoking of racialized rhetoric. Recognizing the appeal of this approach, in 2015 gonzo auteur Mason launched *DarkX*, an interracial addition to her existing labels, *HardX* and *EroticaX*, that adopts the *Blacked* sensibility through the gonzo lens that Mason has become known for. As she put it in the press release, "O.L. Entertainment is presenting me with the opportunity to continue to explore creatively in a new market. [. . .] DarkX will continue to feature intense and passionate exchanges that our studios are known for, while not shying away from anal, DP's and Gangbangs" ("Mason's New IR Studio").

Chapter 2. I Want to Suck Your . . . : Fluids and Fluidity in Dracula Porn

1. For the most comprehensive listing of all representations of Dracula in popular media to date, and with a section devoted entirely to the myriad X-rated Dracula films, see John Edgar Browning and Caroline Joan (Kay) Picart, eds. *Dracula in Visual Media*.

2. Over the past three or four years, rimming has emerged as an unexpectedly popular sex act when performed by a woman on a man. Not only does this sex act acknowledge the male anus as an erogenous zone, it also requires a physical position on the part of the man that might be seen as prone, vulnerable, or otherwise feminine. Moreover, rimming often involves penetration with the tongue. This new trend is rarely labeled to alert consumers, meaning it is fast becoming a normal part of mainstream porn repertoire.

3. It is also possible that the actor, Barrett Blade, simply did not want to eat his own semen, an understandable line in the sand.

4. Costello asserts that the writer, Schwartz, "lift[ed] the story from the screenplay of *Love at First Bite*, which had done very good box office six months earlier. Schwartz vehemently denied any connection, but the similarity was too extreme to be coincidental." E-mail interview, April 12, 2012.

5. The film does not specify its period setting, but based on Leopold's narration, which asserts that as of 1980 he has lived in his castle for four hundred years, it is reasonable to assume that his romance with Surka happened roughly four hundred years prior.

6. The accomplishments and specific talents of Wicked contract stars are numerous and too extensive to list completely. Of the currently signed stars, Stormy Daniels was the first woman contracted to write, direct, and star in an adult film (critically acclaimed *Camp Cuddly Pines' Powertool Massacre* [2005]). jessica drake directs the Wicked sex ed line, *jessica drake's Wicked Guide to Sex*. drake also participates in academic circles, while Daniels considered running for a U.S. Senate seat in her home state of Louisiana, against David Vitter. She is now even better known on an international scale for publicly taking on President Donald Trump. Asa Akira, one of Wicked's most recently signed stars, wrote a well-received memoir, *Insatiable*, and prior to signing with Wicked had directed *Gangbanged 6* for Elegant Angel. She also co-hosted and served as a mentor on the reality show *Sex Factor*. drake and Akira openly identify as feminists, while Daniels is conflicted over the label but nevertheless believes in the importance of female-crafted pornographies (Milne).

Chapter 3. I'm Grown Up Now: Female Sexual Authorship and Coming of Age in Pornographic Adaptations of Lewis Carroll's *Alice* Books

1. I regard the *Alice* books as Gothic texts. Though they are not typically described as such, these novels contain many elements of Gothic fiction, such as abhuman characters, duality, doppelgangers, insanity, the Gothic space, and what Catherine

Seimann calls "controlled menace" (175). Moreover, these texts have been reimagined into explicitly Gothic films, videogames, and graphic novels, suggestive of the latent Gothic elements in the original books. I have always regarded these books as darkly Gothic tales of terror for little girls, though Carroll's intention may not have been so.

2. See Brooker's chapter titled "The Man in the White Paper" (49–75) for a thorough overview and analysis of the various critics who have asserted and refuted Carroll's sexual desire for little girls.

3. For an excellent analysis of *Through the Looking Glass* as a feminist text, see Neil Jackson's essay and interview with the director, "Joseph Middleton: Reflections on *Through the Looking Glass*."

4. There are no invocations of preteen youth in *Alice in Wonderland: A XXX Musical*. The Kristine DeBell *Playboy* cover, however, deliberately exploits the iconography of adolescence. The cover depicts DeBell in the familiar Alice dress, pouting innocently and holding a teddy bear. This image misrepresents the content of the film, yet it is suggestive of what *Playboy* thought would sell copies. Likewise, the dark thriller, *Through the Looking Glass*, co-stars Laura Nicholson who was sixteen years old at the time. She does not perform in any sexually explicit scenes, and the film does not trade in her youth even while the plot centers around childhood sexual abuse. The poster, however, proudly announces, "Starring 14-year-old [*sic*] starlet, Laura Nicholson."

5. Rather intriguingly, a book titled *Alice in Wonderland: A Masterpiece of Victorian Pornography?* by David Hunter was published in 1989. The book is out of print, and the only trace of it I can find is a listing on Amazon.com. All of my efforts to find a copy or even a blurb have failed. Ronald Pearsall makes another interesting connection between Lewis Carroll and pornography in his foundational book, *The Worm in the Bud: The World of Victorian Sexuality*. In discussing the "quintessence of pornographic verse," the 1870 parody *Cythera's Hymnal*, Pearsall remarks, "The greatest master of the parody was Lewis Carroll, and *Cythera's Hymnal* was published when Carroll was at his peak, midway between the two *Alice* books. [. . .] Some of the parodies are so good that one is tempted to assign them to Lewis Carroll, though there is no evidence that he did have a hand in any of them, as all kinds of smut were alien to the mathematical don" (374).

6. The film was shot in 1976 and released that year in a semi-soft cut. Adult film producer and sometime director Chris Warfield later acquired the rights, added the hardcore back into the cut, and shot and inserted additional hardcore footage. He released this version through Essex Video in 1979. Thanks to Joe Rubin for these important details.

Chapter 4. Radically Both: Transformation and Crisis in Jekyll and Hyde Porn

1. See *Mary Reilly*, by Valerie Martin, and *Hyde*, by Daniel Levine.

2. Thanks to Wash West for pointing this out. I had initially read the romantic ending as both monogamous and conservative. However, West pointed out that neither

is necessarily true. Monogamy is not assured and, even within monogamy, sexuality continues to evolve. Moreover, as he rightfully asserted, these representations of committed, loving relationships mean something quite different in the context of queer history.

3. For an insightful analysis of the role of stigma in pornography—not just the harms of stigma but also the way pornography trades in stigma as part of how it rhetorically positions itself—see Georgina Voss, *Stigma and the Shaping of the Pornography Industry*.

Chapter 5. Strange Legacies of Thought and Passion: Technologies of the Flesh and the Queering Effect of Dorian Gray

1. There are many similar and overlapping names in this chapter. With this in mind, I will refer to Dorian Gray of the novel as Gray and Dorian of *Gluttony* as Dorian. I will also sporadically refer to Wash West and Armand Weston by their full names more so than I normally would so as to avoid confusion.

2. There are six adaptations: *The Portrait of Dorian Gay* (J. J. English, 1974), *Doriana Gray* (Jesus Franco, 1976), *Take Off* (Armand Weston, 1978), *A Portrait of Dorian* (Michael Craig, 1992), *Spiegel Der Luste* a.k.a. *Mirror of Lust* (Moli, 1992), *Bildins der Leidenschafte* a.k.a. *Portrait of Passion II* (Moli, 1992), *Portrait of Dorie Gray* (Jim Enright, 1997), and *Gluttony* (Wash West, 2001). Aside from these adaptations, two videos utilize the character name—*Fixation* (Jim Enright, 2004) and *Getting Personal* (Jim Enright, 2005). There are five adult-film performers who riff on Wilde/Dorian: gay performers Dorian Black and Dorian, and straight performers Wilde Oscar, Dorian Grant, and Dorian Velt. Of the five *Dorian Gray* adaptations, two are gay—*Gluttony*, *Portrait of Dorian Gay* (J. J. English, 1974)—and two recast Dorian as a woman (*Doriana Gray*, *Portrait of Dorie Gray*). In addition, one of the "straight" films, *Take Off*, stars an openly gay or bisexual man who previously worked in gay porn, while another, the barely hardcore *Doriana Gray* (Jess Franco, 1976), features only women.

3. For a thorough analysis of the way pornographers have invented and/or popularized everyday technologies such as streaming video, online-store recommendations, and other aspects of our online life, see *The Erotic Engine: How Pornography Has Powered Mass Communication from Gutenberg to Google* by Patchen Barss.

4. David Church states that Darrin is the one who films the scene and thus breaks the spell (*Disposable Passions* 209), yet it is clearly Henrietta at the helm of the CCTV panel. Joe Rubin told me he thinks the film leaves the authorship of the spell-breaking film ambiguous, suggesting Darrin and Henrietta may have been in on it together, but I strongly believe this is Henrietta's work alone. She is, after all, the one who secretly filmed Darrin back in the 1920s. Furthermore, the way Weston lets the sex between Darrin and Linda unfold for some time before cutting to the CCTV room and the mysterious hands at the controls suggests an illicit recording unknown to Darrin. There is nothing in Darrin's demeanor that suggests he is in on this.

5. Many of these performers do not want to be contacted, understandably wishing that their past not return to interfere with their present. These performers might have children, careers, or any number of reasons for simply not wanting their time in the industry dredged up. Others are completely unaware that anyone cares about the work they did. Podcast *The Rialto Report* is an indispensable resource when it comes to this subject, as many performers requested by fans do not wish to appear. Many do, of course, and often articulate their bewilderment that anyone would think their work is of value.

6. For examples of the ways in which viewers would manipulate and negotiate their viewing experience in the theater, see Samuel R. Delany's *Times Square Red, Times Square Blue* and John Champagne's "Stop Reading Films!" It is also worth noting that in the documentary *Wrangler: Anatomy of an Icon*, a friend remembers that gay porn theaters would screen Wrangler's straight films, advertising the times at which his scenes would occur. In this way, the theater owners and patrons mutually manipulated (not to mention queered) the pornographic feature film.

7. This queering affect is couched in a larger queer project implicated by Weston's casting choices. Lord Henry/Oscar Wilde undergoes a gender switch, conflating these characters into one woman: Henrietta Wilde. Ironically, the film consummates the homoerotic romances of the novel in a hetero scene, channeled through the bodies of a woman and a man. Furthermore, Wade Nichols, a gay or certainly bisexual man who performed in gay porn prior to his star status in straight porn, queers the character of the already-queer Gray, and is coupled with Georgina Spelvin, a lesbian or certainly bisexual woman who, while an iconic star of straight porn, is considered by many (myself included) to be part of the queer porn canon (Butler 174–75). Nichols and Spelvin and the characters they play re-queer the Dorian Gray text through an ostensibly hetero scene.

8. See John Champagne's "Stop Reading Films!"

9. In his exhaustive history of gay male erotic imagery, *Hard to Imagine*, Thomas Waugh discusses fifteen stags he uncovered that feature male-male sexual activity. Indicative of the titillating, queer associations of Wilde and the early porning of Victorian texts, the screenplay of one of these stags, *Surprise of a Knight* (ca. 1930, U.S.) is credited to "Oscar Wild" (313).

10. It is important to note that during this time art cinemas screened the films of Kenneth Anger and, later, Andy Warhol and Paul Morrissey. These films, while serving as important origin points for gay porn, were also partially sanctioned and more safely couched within the "art" nomenclature. Regardless, these films still faced obscenity charges and raids. My point here is that while there are important intersections and overlaps between homoerotic art, experimental film, and gay pornography, homoerotic art and experimental film are not regarded or encountered in the same way as "smut" and "filth," and subsequently Wash West does not acknowledge them in his revisionist history of porn.

11. A white coater is a hardcore pornographic film masquerading as a sex documentary. It is a genre that peaked in the 1960s and 1970s and developed as a way of
skirting around obscenity law.

12. Nichols is often incorrectly cited to have died from AIDS. In reality, he killed
himself before AIDS could. So many pornographic actors and filmmakers, gay and
straight but predominantly gay, died from HIV/AIDS, that it would take too much
space to list all of them. Notables include porn superstar John Holmes (1988), the first
gay porn star Casey Donavan (1987), gay, queer, and crossover performers Marc "10
½" Stevens (1989), Arthur Bressan (1987), Joey Yale (1986), Eric Stryker (1988), Paul
Vatelli (1986), Mike Davis (1986), J. W. King (1986), Al Parker (1992), Scott O'Hara
(1998), Karen Dior (2004), Joey Stefano (1994), Chuck Holmes (2000), Richard Locke
(1996), Kip Tyler (1995), acclaimed director Chuck Vincent (1991), and cinematog-
rapher Nick Elliot (1990). For a discussion of the devastating impact of AIDS on the
gay porn industry and gay community at large, see Escoffier's chapter, "Porn Noir,"
in *Bigger than Life*. In addition, rame.net keeps a list of porn industry deaths: http://
www.rame.net/faq/deadporn.

Conclusion: Fueling the Lamps of Sexual Imagination

1. None of these claims come with references to research. However, the insistence
on porn addiction as akin to crack cocaine addiction has been repeatedly debunked.
Notions of porn addiction have instead been tied to societal shame and self-loathing
in connection to sex and porn consumption. There is also no evidence to show the
mainstream porn industry has ties to trafficking or child pornography. See Ley,
Prause, and Finn, "The Emperor Has No Clothes."

BIBLIOGRAPHY

"About Pink & White." *Pink & White Productions*, n.d., http://pinkwhite.biz/about.

Albrecht, Thomas. "Same and Other Victorians." *Porn 101: Eroticism, Pornography, and the First Amendment.* Ed. James Elias, Veronica Diehl Elias, Vern L. Bullough, and Gwen Brewer, Jeffery J. Douglas, and Will Jarvis. New York: Prometheus, 1999. 545–50.

"*Alice in Wonderland* (1976): What Really Happened?" *Rialto Report.* Mar. 22, 2015.

Alilunas, Peter. *Smutty Little Movies: The Creation and Regulation of Adult Video.* Oakland: U of California P, 2016.

Andrews, David. "What Soft-Core Can Do for Porn Studies." *Velvet Light Trap: A Critical Journal of Film and Television* 59 (Spring 2007): 51–61.

Anonymous. *The Autobiography of a Flea.* 1887. Hertfordshire: Wordsworth, 1996.

Anonymous. *The Way of a Man with a Maid.* Erotica Ebook, 2012.

Auerbach, Nina. "Alice and Wonderland: A Curious Child." *Victorian Studies* 17.1, "The Victorian Child" (Sept. 1973): 31–47.

Barss, Patchen. *The Erotic Engine: How Pornography Has Powered Mass Communication, from Gutenberg to Google.* [Toronto], Canada: Doubleday, 2010.

Benshoff, Harry M. *Monsters in the Closet: Homosexuality and the Horror Film.* Manchester: Manchester UP, 1997.

Beville, Maria. "Gothic Memory and the Contested Past: Framing Terror." *The Gothic and the Everyday: Living Gothic*, ed. Lorna Piatti-Farnell and Maria Beville. London: Palgrave Macmillan, 2014. 52–68.

Blake, Pandora. "How Will the Digital Economy Bill Affect Sex Workers?" *YouTube.* Apr. 25, 2017.

———. Phone interview. May 17, 2017.

Brock, Marilyn. "The Vamp and the Good English Mother: Female Roles in Le Fanu's *Carmilla* and Stoker's *Dracula*." *From Wollstonecraft to Stoker: Essays on Gothic and Victorian Sensation Fiction*, ed. Marilyn Brock. Jefferson, N. C.: McFarland, 2009. 120–31.

Broderick, Sarah. "Some Vampires Are Real: Racial Stereotypes and Dominant Fears (Re)Presented in the Black Vampire of American Popular Film." *Gnovis: A Journal of Communication, Culture, and Technology.* Nov. 21, 2011, n.p.

Brooker, Will. *Alice's Adventures: Lewis Carroll in Popular Culture.* New York: Continuum, 2005.

Browning, John Edgar, and Caroline Joan (Kay) Picart, eds. *Dracula in Visual Media: Film, Television, Comic Book and Electronic Game Appearances, 1921–2010.* Jefferson, N.C.: McFarland, 2011.

Burger, John R. *One-Handed Histories: The Eroto-Politics of Gay Male Video Pornography.* New York: Haworth, 1995.

Burt, Richard. *Unspeakable Shaxxxspeares: Queer Theory and American Kiddie Culture.* New York: St. Martin's, 1998.

Buscombe, Edward. "Generic Overspill: A Dirty Western." *More Dirty Looks: Gender, Pornography and Power,* ed. Pamela Church Gibson. London: BFI, 2004. 27–30.

Butler, Heather. "What Do You Call a Lesbian with Long Fingers? The Development of Lesbian and Dyke Pornography." *Porn Studies,* ed. Linda Williams. Durham, N.C.: Duke UP, 2004.

Cadwalladr, Carole. "Editors of Sex Studies Journal Attacked for Promoting Porn." *The Guardian,* June 15, 2013.

Carroll, Lewis. *Alice's Adventures in Wonderland.* New York: Dover, 1993.

———. *Through the Looking-Glass and What Alice Found There.* London: Puffin, 2003.

Carter, Angela. *The Sadeian Woman: An Exercise in Cultural History.* London: Virago, 2006.

Capino, José B. "Asian College Girls and Oriental Men with Bamboo Poles: Reading Asian Pornography." *Pornography: Film and Culture,* ed. Peter Lehman. New Brunswick, N.J.: Rutgers UP, 2006. 206–19.

Chapkis, Wendy. *Live Sex Acts: Women Performing Erotic Labor.* New York: Routledge, 1997.

Chateauvert, Melinda. *Sex Workers Unite: A History of the Movement from Stonewall to Slutwalk.* Boston, Mass.: Beacon, 2013.

Church, David. *Disposable Passions: Vintage Pornography and the Material Legacies of Adult Cinema.* Bloomsbury, 2016.

———. "Stag Films, Vintage Porn, and the Marketing of Cinecrophilia." *Cinephilia in the Age of Digital Reproduction,* ed. Scott Balcerzak and Jason Sperb. Vol. 2. London: Wallflower, 2012. 48–70.

Clark-Flory, Tracy. "Meet the Man Who Wants to Block Porn across the U.S." *Vocativ.* Dec. 31, 2016.

Clover, Carol J. *Men, Women, and Chainsaws: Gender in the Modern Horror Film.* Princeton, N.J.: Princeton UP, 1992.

Cohen, Ed. *Talk on the Wilde Side.* New York: Routledge, 1993.

Costello, Shaun. Email interview. Apr. 12, 2010.

Craft, Christopher. "Come See about Me: Enchantment of the Double in *The Picture of Dorian Gray.*" *Representations* 91 (2005): 109–36.

———. "'Kiss Me with Those Red Lips': Gender and Inversion in Bram Stoker's *Dracula*." *Representations* 8 (Fall 1984): 107–33.

Cruz, Ariane. *The Color of Kink: Black Women, BDSM, and Pornography*. New York: New York UP, 2016.

Cummings, Summer. Email interview. Dec. 27, 2015.

Dau, Duc. "The Governess, Her Body, and Thresholds in *The Romance of Lust*." *Victorian Literature and Culture* 42 (2014): 281–302.

Davis, Paul. *The Lives and Times of Ebenezer Scrooge*. New Haven, Conn.: Yale UP, 1990.

Dee, Noble. *PIMP: Reflection of My Life*. Self-published. 2013.

Delany, Samuel R. *Times Square Red, Times Square Blue*. New York: New York UP, 1999.

Di Lauro, Al, and Gerald Rabkin. *Dirty Movies: An Illustrated History of the Stag Film 1915–1970*. New York: Chelsea, 1976.

Dines, Gail. *Pornland: How Porn Has Hijacked Our Sexuality*. Boston: Beacon, 2011.

Doane, Janice, and Devon Hodges. "Demonic Disturbances of Sexual Identity: The Strange Case of Dr. Jekyll and Mr/s. Hyde." *NOVEL: A Forum on Fiction* 23.1 (Autumn 1989): 63–74.

Dryden, Linda. *The Modern Gothic and Literary Doubles: Stevenson, Wilde, and Wells*. New York: Palgrave, 2003.

"E.T. The Porno." *The Cinema Snob*. The Cinema Snob, Jan. 4, 2010. Web. July 5, 2015.

Ebert, Roger. "Alice in Wonderland." *Chicago Sun Times* Nov. 24, 1976. http://rogerebert.suntimes.com/apps/pbcs.dll/article?AID=/19761124/REVIEWS/611240301/ June 6, 2011.

Eco, Umberto. "How to Recognize a Porn Movie." *How to Travel with a Salmon and Other Essays*. Orlando, Fla.: Harcourt, 1992. 222–25.

Edwards, Eric. Email interview. Feb. 27, 2013.

"Erotic Film Directing." *Spokesman Review*, Nov. 21, 1976. *Google Newspapers*.

Escoffier, Jeffrey. *Bigger than Life: The History of Gay Porn Cinema from Beefcake to Hardcore*. Philadelphia: Running, 2009.

Falconer, Rachel. "Underworld Portmanteaux: Dante's Hell and Carroll's Wonderland in Women's Memoirs of Mental Illness." *Alice beyond Wonderland: Essays for the Twenty-First Century*, ed. Cristopher Hollingsworth. Iowa City: U of Iowa P, 2009. 3–22.

Faludi, Susan. *Backlash: The Undeclared War against American Women*. New York: Doubleday, 1991.

Flint, Kate. "Seeing Is Believing? Visuality and Victorian Fiction." *A Concise Companion to the Victorian Novel*. Ed. Francis O'Gorman. Oxford: Blackwell, 2005. 4–24.

Foucault, Michel. *The History of Sexuality: An Introduction*. Vol. 1. New York: Vintage, 1990.

———. "A Preface to Transgression." *Language, Counter-Memory, Practice: Selected Essays and Interviews*. Ed. Donald F. Bouchard. Ithaca, N.Y.: Cornell UP, 1977. 29–52.

Frank, Jonathan. "Interview with Sharon McNight." *Talkin Broadway*. Talkin Broadway Inc. n.d. Web. Apr. 15, 2015.

fu_q. "Can't Be Roots: XXX Parody." *Adult DVD Talk*. AdultDVDTalk.com, Oct. 15, 2016. Web. Jan. 5, 2018.

Gander, Kashmira. "Feminist Porn Director Pandora Blake Wins Right to Reinstate Fetish Website in Landmark Ruling." *The Independent* June 6, 2016.

Gee, Alastair. "The Moving Revelations of Gay Home Movies." *New Yorker* May 11, 2016. Web. May 31, 2016.

Geer, Jennifer. "'All Sorts of Pitfalls and Surprises': Competing Views of Idealized Girlhood in Lewis Carroll's *Alice* Books." *Children's Literature* 31 (2003): 1–24.

Gibson, Ian. *The Erotomaniac: The Secret Life of Henry Spencer Ashbee*. New York: De Capo, 2001.

Gillespie, Michael Patrick. "From Edward Carson's Cross-Examination of Wilde (First Trial)." *The Picture of Dorian Gray*. New York: Norton, 2007. 382–89.

———. "Picturing Dorian Gray: Resistant Readings in Wilde's Novel." *The Picture of Dorian Gray*, ed. Michael Patrick Gillespie. New York: Norton, 2007. 393–409.

———, ed. "Preface." *The Picture of Dorian Gray*. New York: Norton, 2007. ix–xiii.

———. "Reviews and Reactions." *The Picture of Dorian Gray*, ed. Michael Patrick Gillespie. New York: Norton, 2007. 351–57.

Gilroy, Paul. *The Black Atlantic*. London: Verso, 1993.

Golden, Hallie. "Utah Lawmaker Wants Porn Filtered from Internet, Anti-Porn Software Installed on all Cellphones." *Salt Lake Tribune* May 20, 2016.

Gomel, Elana. "Oscar Wilde, *The Picture of Dorian Gray*, and the (Un)Death of the Author." *Narrative* 12.1 (2004): 74–92.

Grant, Melissa Gira. *Playing the Whore: The Work of Sex Work*. London: Verso, 2014.

Green-Lewis, Jennifer. "At Home in the Nineteenth Century: Photography, Nostalgia, and the Will to Authenticity." *Victorian Afterlife: Postmodern Culture Rewrites the Nineteenth Century*. Ed. John Kucich and Dianne F. Sadoff. Minneapolis: U of Minnesota P, 2000. 29–48.

Gross, Daniel J. "Bill Seeks to Put Porn Block on Computers Sold in SC." *Go Upstate*. Dec. 17, 2016.

Gutleben, Christian. *Nostalgic Postmodernism: The Victorian Tradition and the Contemporary Novel*. Amsterdam: Rodopi, 2001.

Hadley, Louisa. *Neo-Victorian Fiction and Historical Narrative: The Victorians and Us*. New York: Palgrave, 2010.

Haggerty, George E. *Queer Gothic*. Urbana: U of Illinois P, 2006.

Halberstam, Jack [as Judith]. *Skin Shows: Gothic Horror and the Technology of Monsters*. Durham, N.C.: Duke UP, 1995.

Hall, April. "Nina Hartley: The Importance of Being (With) Earnest: Podcast 47." *The Rialto Report*. Feb 22, 2015.

Hanson, Dian, and Vanessa Del Rio. *Fifty Years of Slightly Slutty Behavior*. Cologne: Taschen, 2010.

Harris, Frank. *Oscar Wilde: His Life and Confessions Vol. II*. Self-published. 1916. Google Books.

Heard, Mervyn. "A Prurient Look at the Magic Lantern." *Early Popular Visual Culture* 3.2 (2005): 179–95.

Heath, Stephen. "Psycopathia Sexualis." *Critical Quarterly* 28 (1986): 93–108.

Heilmann, Ann, and Mark Llewellyn. *Neo-Victorianism: The Victorians in the Twenty-First Century, 1999–2009*. New York: Palgrave, 2010.

Hickey, Brian. "Man Arrested for Allegedly Inserting Porn Clip Into 2009 Super Bowl Broadcast." *Deadspin* Feb. 5, 2011. Web. June 1, 2016.

Holliday, Jim. *Only the Best: Jim Holliday's Adult Video Almanac and Trivia Treasury*. Van Nuys, Calif.: Cal Vista, 1986.

Hopkins, Patrick D. "Rethinking Sadomasochism: Feminism, Interpretation, and Simulation." *Hypatia* 9.1 (1994): 116–41.

Hunt, Lynn. "Introduction: Obscenity and the Origins of Modernity, 1500–1800." *The Invention of Pornography: Obscenity and the Origins of Modernity, 1500–1800*. Ed. Lynn Hunt. New York: Zone, 1993. 9–45.

Hunter, I. Q. "Adaptation XXX." *The Oxford Handbook of Adaptation Studies*. Ed. Thomas Leitch. Oxford: Oxford UP, 2017. 424–440.

Hurley, Kelly. *The Gothic Body: Sexuality, Materialism, and Degeneration at the Fin de Siècle*. Cambridge: Cambridge UP, 1996.

Jackson, Neil. "Joseph Middleton: Reflections on *Through the Looking Glass*." *Video Watchdog: The Perfectionist's Guide to Fantastic Video* 167 (Mar/Apr 2012): 26–39.

"Jane Austen Style Porn Just for the Ladies?" *Adult DVD Talk*. AdultDVDTalk.com, July 20, 2011. Web. July 5, 2015.

Jennings, David. *Skinflicks: The Inside Story of the X-Rated Video Industry*. Bloomington, Ind.: AuthorHouse, 2000.

Jones, David J. *Sexuality and the Gothic Magic Lantern: Desire, Eroticism, and Literary Visibilities from Byron to Bram Stoker*. New York: Palgrave, 2014.

Joyce, Simon. "The Victorians in the Rearview Mirror." *Functions of Victorian Culture at the Present Time*. Ed. Christine L. Krueger. Athens: Ohio UP, 2000. 3–17.

Juffer, Jane. *At Home with Pornography: Women, Sex, and Everyday Life*. New York: New York UP, 1998.

Kendrick, Walter. *The Secret Museum: Pornography in Modern Culture*. Berkeley: U of California P, 1996.

Killingray, David. "Tracing Peoples of African Origin and Descent in Victorian Kent." *Black Victorians/Black Victoriana*. Ed. Gretchen Holbrook Gerzina. New Brunswick, N.J.: Rutgers UP, 2003. 51–67.

Kincaid, James R. "Alice's Invasion of Wonderland." *PMLA* 88.1 (Jan. 1973): 92–99.

King, Charles. "Themes and Variations." *Strange Case of Dr. Jekyll and Mr. Hyde*. Ed. Katherine Linehan. New York: Norton, 2003. 157–163.

Kipnis, Laura. *Bound and Gagged: Pornography and the Politics of Fantasy in America*. Durham, N.C.: Duke UP, 1996.

Knoepflmacher, U. C. *Ventures into Childland: Victorians, Fairy Tales, and Femininity*. Chicago: U of Chicago P, 1998.

Koestenbaum, Wayne. "The Shadow on the Bed: Dr. Jekyll, Mr. Hyde, and the Labouchere Amendment." *Critical Matrix* 1 (1988): 31–55.

Kohlke, Marie-Luise. "The Neo-Victorian Sexsation: Literary Excursions into the Nineteenth-Century Erotic." *Probing the Problematics: Sex and Sexuality.* Ed. Marie-Luise Kohlke and Luisa Orza. Oxford: Inter-Disciplinary, 2008. 345–56.

Kohlke, Marie-Luise and Christian Gutleben. "The (Mis)Shapes of Neo-Victorian Gothic: Continuations, Adaptations, Transformations." *Neo-Victorian Gothic: Horror, Violence, and Degeneration in the Re-Imagined Nineteenth Century.* Ed. Marie-Luise Kohlke and Christian Gutleben. Amsterdam: Rodopi, 2012. 1–48.

Kristeva, Julia. *Powers of Horror: An Essay on Abjection.* New York: Columbia UP, 1982.

Kucich, John, and Dianne F. Sadoff. "Introduction: Histories of the Present." *Victorian Afterlife: Postmodern Culture Rewrites the Nineteenth Century.* Ed. John Kucich and Dianne F. Sadoff. Minneapolis: U of Minnesota P, 2000. ix–xxx.

Labbe, Jacqueline. "Illustrating Alice: Gender, Image, Artifice." *Art, Narrative and Childhood.* Ed. Morag Styles and Eve Bearne. Stoke on Trent: Trentham, 2003. 21–36.

Lawrence, D. H. *Pornography and So On.* Amsterdam: Fredonia, 2001.

LeFanu, Sheridan. *Carmilla.* Scotts Valley, Calif.: IAP, 2009.

Lee, Lorelei. "Cum Guzzling Anal Nurse Whore: A Feminist Porn Star Manifesta." *The Feminist Porn Book: The Politics of Producing Pleasure.* Ed. Tristan Taormino, Celine Parrenas Shimizu, Constance Penley, and Mireille Miller-Young. New York: Feminist, 2013. 200–214.

———. "Once You Have Made Pornography." *The Establishment.* May 11, 2017.

Lehman, Peter. "Revelations about Pornography." *Pornography: Film and Culture.* Ed. Peter Lehman. New Brunswick, N.J.: Rutgers UP, 2006.

———. "Twin Cheeks, Twin Peeks, and Twin Freaks: Porn's Transgressive Remake Humor." *Authority and Transgression in Literature and Film.* Ed. Bonnie Braendlin and Hans Braendlin. Gainesville: UP of Florida, 1996.

Ley, David, Nicole Prause, and Peter Finn. "The Emperor Has No Clothes: A Review of the 'Pornography Addiction' Model." *Current Sexual Health Reports* 6.2 (2014): 94–105.

Linehan, Katherine. "Sex, Secrecy, and Self-Alienation in *Strange Case of Dr. Jekyll and Mr. Hyde.*" *Strange Case of Dr. Jekyll and Mr. Hyde.* Ed. Katherine Linehan. New York: Norton, 2003. 204–13.

Litten, Kevin. "Women's Groups, Strip Club Owners Join Forces to Change Stripper Age Bill." *Times-Picayune* May 10, 2017.

lor_. "Porn Dares to Be Different, with Mixed Results." *IMBD.* IMDB.com, Jan. 29, 2015. Web. June 1, 2016.

Lykiard, Alexis. "Introduction: *A Man with a Maid.*" 1981. AlexisLykiard.com.

Maines, Rachel P. *The Technology of Orgasm: "Hysteria," the Vibrator, and Women's Sexual Satisfaction.* Baltimore, Md.: Johns Hopkins UP, 1999.

Marcus, Steven. *The Other Victorians: A Study of Sexuality and Pornography in Mid-Nineteenth-Century England.* New Brunswick, N. J.: Transaction, 2009.

Margold, William, and Joe Rubin. Audio commentary. *Dracula Sucks*. Dir. Phil Marshak. Perf. Jamie Gillis, Annette Haven, and Paul Thomas. Vinegar Syndrome, 2014. DVD.

Marks, Laura U. *The Skin of the Film: Intercultural Cinema, Embodiment, and the Senses*. Durham, N.C.: Duke UP, 2001.

———. *Touch: Sensuous Theory and Multisensory Media*. Minneapolis: Minnesota UP, 2002.

"Mason's New IR Studio: DarkX." *AdultDVDTalk*, Nov. 4, 2015. https://forum.adult dvdtalk.com/masons-new-ir-studio-dark-x.

Mazières, Antoine. "Deep Tags: Toward a Quantitative Analysis of Online Pornography." *Porn Studies* 1.1–2 (2014): 80–95.

McClintock, Anne. *Imperial Leather: Race, Gender, and Sexuality in the Colonial Contest*. New York: Routledge, 1995.

———. "Maid to Order: Commercial Fetishism and Gender Power." *Social Text* 37 (Winter 1993): 87–116.

McNair, Brian. *Porno? Chic! How Pornography Changed the World and Made It a Better Place*. London: Routledge, 2013.

Mercer, John. *Gay Pornography: Representations of Sexuality and Masculinity*. New York: Taurus, 2017.

Michie, Helena. *The Flesh Made Word: Female Figures and Women's Bodies*. New York: Oxford UP, 1987.

Mikkelson, David. "Emotional Rescue." *Snopes* Jan. 13, 1999. Web. June 1, 2016.

Miller-Young, Mireille. *A Taste for Brown Sugar: Black Women in Pornography*. Durham, N.C.: Duke UP, 2014.

Mistress Alice. Phone interview. Dec. 16, 2015.

Moore, Lisa G. *Sperm Counts: Overcome by Man's Most Precious Fluid*. New York: NY UP, 2008.

Nash, Jennifer C. *The Black Body in Ecstasy: Reading Race, Reading Pornography*. Durham, N.C.: Duke UP, 2014.

Nead, Lynda. *Victorian Babylon: People, Streets and Images in Nineteenth-Century London*. New Haven, Conn.: Yale UP, 2000.

"New Pornfidelity Scene a Bit Racist? Bad Taste?" *Adult DVD Talk*. AdultDVDTalk .com, May 24, 2013. Web. June 1, 2016.

Noelle, Nica. Email interview. Apr. 20, 2012.

Oates, Joyce Carol. "*The Picture of Dorian Gray*: Wilde's Parable of the Fall." *Critical Inquiry* 7.2 (1980): 419–28.

Paasonen, Susanna. *Carnal Resonance: Affect and Online Pornography*. Cambridge, Mass.: MIT P, 2011.

———. "Epilogue: Porn Futures." *Pornification: Sex and Sexuality in Media Culture*. Ed. Susanna Paasonen, Kaarina Nikunen, and Laura Saarenmaa. Oxford: Bera, 2007. 161–70.

Patton, Cindy. *Fatal Advice: How Safe-Sex Education Went Wrong*. Durham, N.C.: Duke UP, 1997.

Pearce, Joseph. *The Unmasking of Oscar Wilde*. San Francisco: Ignatius, 2004.

Pearsall, Ronald. *The Worm in the Bud: The World of Victorian Sexuality*. New York: Penguin, 1983.

Penley, Constance. "Crackers and Whackers: The White Trashing of Porn." *Pornography: Film and Culture*. Ed. Peter Lehman. New Brunswick, N.J.: Rutgers UP, 2006. 99–117.

Pfragner, Julius. *The Motion Picture: From Magic Lantern to Sound Film*. London: Bailey and Swinfen, 1974.

Pheterson, Gail. "The Category 'Prostitute' in Scientific Inquiry." *Journal of Sex Research* 27.3 (Aug. 1990): 397–407.

picman. "Family Secrets: Tales of Victorian Lust." *Adult DVD Talk*. AdultDVDTalk .com, Dec. 6, 2010. Web. June 1, 2016.

Pikula, Tanya. "Bram Stoker's *Dracula* and Late-Victorian Advertising Tactics: Earnest Men, Virtuous Ladies, and Porn." *ELT* 55.3 (2012): 283–302.

Pilinovsky, Helen. "Body as Wonderland: Alice's Graphic Iteration in *Lost Girls*." *Alice beyond Wonderland: Essays for the Twenty-First Century*. Ed. Cristopher Hollingsworth. Iowa City: U of Iowa P, 2009. 175–98.

Pinedo, Isabel Cristina. *Recreational Terror: Women and the Pleasures of Horror Film Viewing*. Albany: State U of NY P, 1997.

Rackley, Erika, and Clare McGlynn. "Criminalising Extreme Pornography: Five Years On—McGlynn and Rackley on The Extreme Pornography Provisions: A Misunderstood and Misused Law." *Inherently Human: Critical Perspectives on Law, Gender, and Sexuality*. May 21, 2013. https://inherentlyhuman.wordpress.com.

Rimmer, Robert. *The X-Rated Videotape Guide I*. New York: Prometheus, 1993.

Rodríguez, Juana María. "Pornographic Encounters and Interpretative Interventions: Vanessa del Rio; Fifty Years of Slightly Slutty Behavior." *Women and Performance: A Journal of Feminist Theory* 25.3 (2015): 315–35.

Ronson, Jon. *The Butterfly Effect*. Audible Originals, 2017.

Rosenman, Ellen Bayuk. *Unauthorized Pleasures: Accounts of Victorian Erotic Experience*. Ithaca, N.Y.: Cornell UP, 2003.

Roth, Phyllis A. "Suddenly Sexual Women in Bram Stoker's *Dracula*." *Dracula*. Ed. Nina Auerbach and David J. Skal. New York: Norton, 1997. 411–21.

"Routledge Pro Porn Studies Bias." *iPetitions*. n.d.

Royal, Mickey. *The Pimp Game: An Instructional Guide*. Self-published. 1998.

Rubin, Joe. Phone interview. Dec. 6, 2015.

Sadoff, Diane F. *Victorian Vogue: British Novels on Screen*. Minneapolis: U of Minnesota P, 2010.

Sanders, Julie. *Adaptation and Appropriation*. London: Routledge, 2006.

Sarracino, Carmine, and Kevin M. Scott. *The Porning of America: The Rise of Porn Culture, What It Means, and Where We Go from Here*. Boston: Beacon, 2008.

Sceats, Sarah. "Oral Sex: Vampiric Transgression and the Writing of Angela Carter." *Tulsa Studies in Women's Literature* 20.1 (Spring, 2011): 107–121. JStor. Web. June 1, 2016.

Schaefer, Eric. "Gauging a Revolution: 16mm Film and the Rise of the Pornographic Feature." *Porn Studies*. Ed. Linda Williams. Durham, N.C.: Duke UP, 2004. 370–400.

———. "Sexploitation after Hardcore: Strategies of Soft-Core Sex Films in the 1970s." Society for Cinema and Media Studies Conference, March 30–April 2, 106, Atlanta, GA.

Schaschek, Sarah. *Pornography and Seriality: The Culture of Producing Pleasure*. New York: Palgrave, 2014.

Sedgwick, Eve Kosofsky. *Epistemology of the Closet*. Berkeley: U of California P, 1990.

Seubert, David. "Adult Novels of Men in a Womanless World—Gay Pulp Fiction of the 1950s and 1960s." *Babaluma*. Feb. 1, 1999.

Shelton, Emily. "A Star Is Porn: Corpulence, Comedy, and the Homosocial Cult of Adult Film Star Ron Jeremy." *Camera Obscura* 51 (2002): 114–47.

Shimizu, Celine Parreñas. *The Hypersexuality of Race: Performing Asian/American Women on Screen and Scene*. Durham, N.C.: Duke UP, 2007.

Showalter, Elaine. *Sexual Anarchy: Gender and Culture at the Fin de Siècle*. London: Virago, 1990.

Sigel, Lisa Z. *Governing Pleasures: Pornography and Social Change in England, 1815–1914*. New Brunswick, N.J.: Rutgers UP, 2002.

———. "The Rise of the Overly Affectionate Family: Incestuous Pornography and Displaced Desire among the Edwardian Middle Class." *International Exposure: Perspectives on Modern European Pornography 1800–2000*. Ed. Lisa Z. Sigel. New Brunswick, N.J.: Rutgers UP, 2005. 100–124.

Slade, Joseph W. "Eroticism and Technological Regression: The Stag Film." *History and Technology* 22.1 (2006): 27–52.

Smith, Clarissa, and Feona Attwood. "Anti/Pro/Critical Porn Studies." *Porn Studies* 1.1–2 (2014): 7–23.

———. "Emotional Truths and Thrilling Slide Shows: The Resurgence of Antiporn Feminism." In *The Feminist Porn Book: The Politics of Producing Pleasure*, edited by Tristan Taormino, Celine Parreñas Shimizu, Constance Penley, and Mireille Miller-Young, 41–57. New York: Feminist, 2013.

Smith, Mike Deri. "Porn Filters Block Sex Education Websites." *BBC*. Dec. 18, 2013.

Soderlund, Gretchen. *Sex Trafficking, Scandal, and the Transformation of Journalism, 1885–1917*. Chicago: U of Chicago P, 2013.

Stearns, Peter N. "The Power of Desire and the Danger of Pleasure: Victorian Sexuality Reconsidered." *Journal of Social History* 24.1 (1990): 47–67.

Stevenson, Robert Louis. *The Strange Case of Dr. Jekyll and Mr. Hyde*. Ed. Katherine Linehan. New York: Norton, 2003.

Stoker, Bram. *Dracula*. New York: Norton, 1997.

Talairach-Vielmas, Laurence. *Moulding the Female Body in Victorian Fairy Tales and Sensation Novels*. 2007.

Taormino, Tristan, Celine Parreñas Shimizu, Constance Penley, and Mireille Miller-Young, eds. *The Feminist Porn Book: The Politics of Producing Pleasure*. New York: Feminist, 2013.

Tarrant, Shira. "Pornography and Pedagogy: Teaching Media Literacy." *New Views on Pornography: Sexuality, Politics, and the Law*. Ed. Lynn Comella and Shira Tarrant. Santa Barbara, Calif.: Praeger, 2015. 417–30.

Touchstone, Raven. Email interview. Jun. 5, 2010.

———. *Jekyll and Hyde: The Rest of the Story*. Screenplay. 1999.

Thompson, Dave. *Black, White, and Blue: Adult Cinema from the Victorian Age to the VCR*. Toronto: ECW, 2007.

Trueman, Patrick A. "Porn Creates Demand for Sex Trafficking." *Miami Herald* July 23, 2014.

Utah, Legislature. *Concurrent Resolution on the Public Health Crisis*. 2016. https://le.utah.gov/~2016/bills/static/scr009.html.

Veeder, William. "Children of the Night: Stevenson and Patriarchy." *Dr. Jekyll and Mr. Hyde: After One Hundred Years*. Ed. William Veeder and Gordon Hirsch. Chicago: U of Chicago P, 1988. 107–60.

Voss, Georgina. *Stigma and the Shaping of the Pornography Industry*. New York: Routledge, 2015.

Wallen, John. "The Cannibal Club and the Origins of 19th Century Racism and Pornography." *The Victorian* 1.1 (2013): 1–13.

Walkowitz, Judith R. *City of Dreadful Delight: Narratives of Sexual Danger in Late-Victorian London*. Chicago: U of Chicago P, 1992.

Waugh, Thomas. *Hard to Imagine: Gay Male Eroticism in Photography and Film from Their Beginnings to Stonewall*. New York: Columbia UP, 1996.

———. "Men's Pornography: Gay vs. Straight." *Jump Cut* 30 (Mar. 1985): 30–35.

West, Wash. Email interview. Mar. 9, 2013.

Whisnant, Rebecca. "From Jekyll to Hyde: The Grooming of Male Pornography Consumers." *Everyday Pornography*. Ed. Karen Boyle. Oxon: Routledge, 2010. 114–33.

Whitney, Sarah E. *Splattered Ink: Postfeminist Gothic Fiction and Gendered Violence*. Urbana: U of Illinois P, 2016.

Wilde, Oscar. *The Picture of Dorian Gray*. Ed. Michael Patrick Gillespie. New York: Norton, 2007.

Williams, Linda. "Corporealized Observers: Visual Pornographies and the 'Carnal Density of Vision.'" *Fugitive Images: From Photography to Video*. Ed. Patrice Petro. Bloomington: Indiana UP, 1995. 3–41.

———. "Film Bodies: Gender, Genre and Excess." *Feminist Film Theory: A Reader*. Ed. Sue Thornham. New York: NY UP, 1999: 267–281.

———. *Hard Core: Power, Pleasure, and the "Frenzy of the Visible."* Berkeley: U of California P, 1999.

———. "Skinflicks on the Racial Border: Pornography, Exploitation, and Interracial Lust." *Porn Studies*. Ed. Linda Williams. Durham, N.C.: Duke UP, 2004. 271–308.

———. "When the Woman Looks." *The Dread of Difference: Gender and the Horror Film*. Ed. Barry Keith Grant. Austin: U of Texas P, 1996. 15–43.

Wood, Robin. "Burying the Undead: The Use and Obsolescence of Count Dracula." *The Dread of Difference: Gender and the Horror Film*. Ed. Barry Keith Grant. Austin: U of Texas P, 1996. 364–78.

Yates, Louisa. "'But It's Only a Novel, Dorian': Neo-Victorian Fiction and the Process of Re-Vision." *Neo-Victorian Studies* 2.2 (Winter 2009/2010): n.p.

Zieger, Susan. *Inventing the Addict: Drugs, Race, and Sexuality in Nineteenth-Century British and American Literature.* Amherst: U of Massachusetts P, 2008.

Audiovisual Materials

Alice in Wonderland. Dir. Bud Townsend. Perf. Kristine De Bell. Arrow, 2003. DVD.

Autobiography of a Flea. Dir. Sharon McNight. Prod. The Mitchell Brothers. Perf. Jean Jennings, Paul Thomas, Joanna Hilden, John Leslie, Dale Meador. Cinema 7, 2004. DVD.

Bedtime Tales. Dir. Henri Pachard. Perf. Ginger Lynn, Colleen Brennan, and Honey Wilder. Gourmet Video, 2006. DVD.

Bride's Initiation, The. Dir. Duncan Stewart. Perf. Carol Connors. TVX, 2013. DVD.

Dark Angels 2: Bloodline. Dir. Nic Andrews. Perf. Sunny Lane, Barrett Blade. New Sensations, 2005. DVD.

Dracula Exotica. Dir. Shaun Costello. Perf. Jamie Gillis, Samantha Fox, Vanessa Del Rio. TVX, 2006. DVD.

Dracula Sucks. Dir. Philip Marshak. Perf. Jamie Gillis, Annette Haven, Paul Thomas. Vinegar Syndrome, 2014. DVD.

Dr. Jerkoff and Mr. Hard. Dir. Wash West. Perf. Jim Buck. AMR, 1996. DVD.

Fetish Fairy Tails Volume 3: Alice in Summerland. Dir. Summer Cummings. Perf. Summer Cummings. Starr Productions, 2005. DVD.

Gluttony. Dir. Wash West. Perf. Eric Hanson, Tanner Hayes. All Worlds Video, 2001. DVD.

Heavy Equipment. Dir. Tom DeSimone. Perf. Jack Wrangler, Al Parker. Vidco, 2000. DVD.

Jekyll & Hyde. Dir. Paul Thomas. Scr. Raven Touchstone. Perf. Taylor Hayes. Vivid, 1999. DVD.

Lesbian Adventures: Victorian Love Letters. Dir. Nica Noelle. Sweetheart Video, 2009. DVD.

Memoirs of a Chambermaid. Dir. Eric Edwards. Perf. Krista Lane, Shanna Mc-Cullough, Ona Zee, Brandon. Arrow, 2004. DVD.

Naughty Victorians, The. Dir. Robert Sickinger. Perf. Beerbohn Tree, Jennifer Jordan, Susan Sloan. TVX, 2005. DVD.

Take Off. Dir. Armand Weston. Perf. Wade Nichols, Leslie Bovee, Annette Haven. Video X Pix, 2003. DVD.

Voracious Season One. Dir. John Stagliano. Perf. Brooklyn Lee, Lea Lexis, Manuel Ferrara. Evil Angel, 2012. DVD.

Voracious Season Two: Blood and Cum. Dir. John Stagliano. Perf. Stoya, James Deen, Lea Lexis, Rocco Siffredi. Evil Angel, 2015. DVD.

INDEX

LAURA HELEN MARKS is a professor of practice in the Department of English at Tulane University.

FEMINIST MEDIA STUDIES

The University of Illinois Press
is a founding member of the
Association of American University Presses.

Composed in 10.5/13 Minion Pro
with Trade Gothic LT Std display
by Lisa Connery
at the University of Illinois Press
Cover designed by Jennifer S. Fisher
Cover illustration: Adapted from a promotional poster
for the film *Alice in Wonderland: An X-Rated Musical Comedy*,
1976 (director, Bud Townsend; producer, William Osco)

University of Illinois Press
1325 South Oak Street
Champaign, IL 61820-6903
www.press.uillinois.edu